THE SWAN DETECTIVE

THE SWAN SYNDICATE - BOOK TWO

KIM ALLRED

STORM COAST PUBLISHING, LLC

The Swan Detective
BookTwo
KIM ALLRED

Published by Storm Coast Publishing, LLC

Copyright © 2025 by Kim Allred
Cover Design by Dar Albert / Wicked Smart Designs
Print Edition September 2025 978-1-953832-50-4

"Three things cannot long stay hidden: the sun, the moon, and the truth."

Buddha

AUTHOR'S NOTE

Hello Readers!

This message is specifically for the Historical Romance readers who have found their way to the world of *Mórdha Stone Chronicles*, and specifically to this series and Stella and Beckworth's love story.

Some of you already know I tend to take some liberties with the historical pieces in my books. I don't change history, as far as I know, but I do stray from societal norms of the period.

This particular story is primarily set in London during the Season, when aristocrats come to play while Parliament is in session.

I have no doubt that those of you who have a firm grasp of how society worked in 1806 will mostly gasp at some of the tweaks I've made in my story along those lines. I hope you forgive me for my transgressions and settle into this fantasy adventure for the escapism it was meant to be.

Enjoy the ride!

Kim

PROLOGUE

Note: This prologue is only required if you haven't recently read the *Mórdha Stone Chronicles* series or *The Swan Syndicate*. If you're comfortable with how the time travel works and who the major players are in both time periods, then jump ahead to chapter one. Otherwise, enjoy a quick recap of previous events.

I t all began when AJ Moore climbed a cliff along her home shores of Oregon. Only a small group of people, either in this time or two hundred years before, knew the story. A tale no one would believe if they hadn't been a part of it.

AJ had watched a nineteenth-century sailing ship appear and disappear into the fog. A couple of days later, two men came into her life. Mysterious men who spoke little of themselves yet found ways to gather information from those around them. Unbeknownst to her at the time, the two men, Finn Murphy, a fiery, roguish Irishman, and Ethan Hughes, a reserved, handsome Englishman, had spent eighteen months traveling through time in search of an ancient stone necklace.

As it turned out, AJ had found that necklace at an estate sale a few months before the men came into her life. She was a reporter by trade, so it didn't take her long to decide the old ship and the enigmatic ship's captain would make a good story, but it was never written. Instead, she fell hard and fast for Finn.

Finn, who tried to ignore AJ's appeal, was unable to douse the spark she ignited whenever she was close. Once Finn held the necklace in his hand, his mission complete, he couldn't think of a life without AJ. So, he did the unthinkable. He called upon the fog, and they disappeared from this time and fell into the past—ship and all.

What came next was months of betrayal, heartache, loss, and eventually, a reunion that reignited the passion between AJ and Finn. Then, she learned the secrets of the ancient stone necklace.

Over two millennia before, during an eclipse, a sect of Druids performed a ritual. Lightning interrupted the rite and turned a silver chalice holding colorful beads into six stones that allowed a person to travel through time. The largest stone, referred to as the Heart Stone, had been lost in time, eventually turning up at an estate sale. The other five stones were smaller yet held a strong connection to the Heart Stone.

The Druids believed if the stones were kept closely together, the ability to time travel would be more powerful and predictable. They mounted the stones in a silver torc. Through trial and error, they discovered the mysteries of how the stones worked and wrote their findings in The Book of Stones, otherwise known as the Mórdha Stone Chronicles. While speaking the proper incantation as one held the stone or wore the torc, a dense fog appeared and transported the person to another time.

But the timing and location were far from accurate—in the beginning.

The Druids were a suspicious lot, and while they wrote their secrets in Breton Celtic, they also encrypted the critical pieces of how the stones and incantations worked. Finn's sister, Maire Murphy, being Irish, was able to read Breton Celtic, though the text took time to translate. She acquired the assistance of Sebastian, a member of the Brotherhood of Monks, who lived in a monastery on the northern coast of France. The monks were responsible for protecting rare and treasured artifacts and hid The Book of Stones and the accompanying six stones from the men who raided churches and monasteries during the Reign of Terror.

When the Duke of Dunsmore escaped to France to hide from the King of England's wrath, he heard stories about the stones. And so began the long journey Finn and Ethan traveled in search of the Heart Stone. The power-hungry duke and, eventually, his son, Reginald, were killed, and everyone felt the stones were safe.

Until one fateful day when a man from the past found his way to the future, arriving at the inn along the Oregon Coast that AJ and Finn called home. The couple happened to be on vacation, and Stella Caldway, AJ's best friend, who stopped by to water the plants, found a strange man standing in the kitchen. The man, who worked for their new enemy, Gemini, a woman in search of the stones, mistook Stella for AJ and stole her away through the fog.

Beckworth, a nineteenth-century viscount who had a long and complicated history with AJ, Finn, and the Duke of Dunsmore, was on a mission to locate the mysterious Gemini. When he caught up with her, he convinced Stella to escape with him. They were on the run for two weeks, evading Gemini's men while trying to find safe haven. During that period, they became friends, and eventually much more. After a long and tiring journey, Stella and Beckworth reunited with AJ, Finn, and the rest of the team. The group decided to change the stakes, and Gemini became the prey.

The mission hadn't been easy, and men had been lost, but once Gemini was dead, the stones and The Book of Stones were safe once more. Everything was hidden within the secret passages of the monastery, with a few exceptions. The Heart Stone would return to the future with AJ and Finn. One of the small stones was retained by Ethan and Maire, who returned to the future along with Sebastian, the monk, who was always up for an adventure. The Book of Stones was also sent to the future, keeping it out of the hands of anyone else seeking too much power.

Before leaving for the future, Sebastian gifted Stella and Beckworth with a stone of their own and an updated incantation.

Stella returned home to Oregon, leaving Beckworth behind. Each believed neither could be happy living in a time period not their own. But the heart wants what the heart wants, and Beckworth used his stone to travel to the future, where the two live happily together.

Everyone agreed the stones were only to be used for emergencies.

Beckworth had a different idea. And so begins the story of Stella and Beckworth. What they weren't aware of, because no one could foresee the future, even with the stones, was that their first use of the stones would be the beginning of the Swan Syndicate.

And no one could have been prepared for what happened next.

1

Stella Caldway burst into the kitchen and rushed to set the bags on the dining room table, brushing past a dazed-looking AJ Murphy, who fell back against the sink to give her room. After blowing out a long sigh, her arms now burden-free, she spun around.

"I thought for sure I was going to drop everything in the hallway. I should know better than to bring everything in one trip, but I didn't account for weight." Stella tilted her head and stared at her best friend. "What?" She grinned. "Did Beckworth forget to call?"

AJ pulled out of her dazed response. "Why would Beckworth call?" She hesitated before shuffling to the table to peer into the first bag. A brow lifted.

"I was running late, and he was supposed to let you know I was dropping by." Stella stepped back, waiting for the explosion to come. She wasn't disappointed.

"What's up?"

"What do you mean?"

"You know damn well what I mean. The last time you brought me one of Donna's pies was when you confessed you were going back to Waverly." She stared into the second bag, then slowly glanced up at Stella. "No. The wine isn't going to help, either."

"It's no big deal." She bit her lower lip, trying not to smile, knowing she shouldn't, but AJ was so predictable.

"We agreed we wouldn't use the Mórdha stones like round-trip tickets to Europe."

She managed to hold in a chuckle. It was difficult with AJ's brows scrunched over her eyes, squinting so hard, tiny lines appeared above her nose.

"I agree, the travel through the fog is not pleasant. In fact," She rubbed her backside, remembering the last landing from three months ago. "It seems to be getting rougher."

"That seems a good enough reason not to go." She unpacked the pie and placed it on the counter, shoving the box under a cabinet in a vain attempt to get it out of their line of sight. AJ was very protective of her marionberry pies. "You were at Waverly just three months ago."

"But we didn't get an opportunity to go to London for the season. I hadn't even considered it, but Elizabeth, Eleanor, and Mary cornered me and insisted we come back."

AJ turned a bit green with the mention of the dowager, Dame Elizabeth Ellingsworth, then her expression lightened and a small smile crossed her lips. Was she thinking of her time in London? "We never went to a ball." She laughed. "At least not one that wasn't part of a mission."

Stella was never one to pass on an opening, and she pounced on this one. "Wouldn't it be fun to hang out in London and do nothing but go to parties and balls. Just think about the fashion."

"It was like playing dress-up." AJ stared dreamily into space before shrugging her shoulders. "You seem to have survived the last trip without any issues."

Stella opened one of the bottles of wine and grabbed two wineglasses from the kitchen cabinet. They had survived, but it hadn't been without bloodshed. And she'd been the one to spill it. The thought of Cheval and the crossbow sent shivers down her spine, but her nightmares had diminished, thanks to Beckworth.

Whenever she woke from one, he was always there to hold her. He never gave her the typical responses of "it will get better soon" or "you didn't have a choice." Rather, he comforted her with soft words of "it's alright" or "I'm right here with you" until she fell back to sleep.

It hadn't been her fault. She had to save Beckworth. Cheval had kidnapped her and forced her to watch him torture someone. There was no doubt in her mind that he'd committed countless other atrocities as a smuggler. England was better off without him. If it hadn't been her, it would eventually have been someone else. Besides, most of her memories of their trip were filled with shared stories and laughter among good friends.

She was excited about going back. If she could only get AJ to understand. Pushing thoughts of Cheval aside, she squared her shoulders and handed AJ a glass of wine before strolling out to the back deck. The sun was out and the temperature mild. With no coastal breeze, it was warm enough to spend time enjoying the view.

"I know everyone thinks it would be better for Beckworth to close that chapter of his life and concentrate on his life here. And he is trying."

AJ leaned back in her chair and propped her feet on another, resting her wineglass on her belly in between sips. "He needs a purpose. I get it. I think we've all felt that way at some point in our lives. He had it all in his timeline. A grand estate, a title, and an occasional mission for Hensley."

"He worked hard to climb his way out of the poorest part of

London, eventually rising from nothing to the aristocracy. Though he does admit some of that path wasn't performed with the cleanest of hands."

AJ lifted her face to the sun. "I'm not sure he could have done it any other way. Not in those times. And he was the son of a duke, bastard or not. I know he didn't make Maire's life easy. When I first met her, I'd made a comment that at least she was being held in comfort. She'd called it a gilded cage, and she was right. But after Reginald locked her in a horrid, dark cell for months like some common thief, she looks at Beckworth differently. He had her best interest in mind, keeping her safe and well-cared for while he walked a line with the duke and Dugan." She turned her gaze from the ocean to Stella. "Where is he, anyway? You two are still joined at the hips most days."

Stella grinned. "He's taken an interest in our city and various businesses. He spends a lot of time at the community center. He's actually joined a couple of groups."

"Don't tell me. One of the groups is the old guys who play chess on the waterfront."

Stella laughed. "He loves their stories, and who knows the town better than those who've spent their whole lives here. And they talk about every subject under the sun. Then there's a book club, though he only goes to a few of the gatherings. He's more interested in knowing what books they're reading. And he begged me to let him be my representative on the business council."

AJ snorted. "Did you really make him beg? You hated having to show up for those. And if I remember correctly, you missed half of them."

She grinned at her knowing friend. "If he went to all the trouble of creating the perfect romantic day, who am I to spoil his fun?"

They laughed then fell silent, each in their own thoughts as they enjoyed the sun and the crisp, salty scent of the sea.

"I'm okay if you want to go back. I doubt this will be the last time." AJ placed her empty wineglass on the patio table. "I think we should set some ground rules."

"Should I get a notepad to get them all down?"

"Funny." AJ sat up and turned toward her. "The scariest thing is not being able to pick up a phone and check to make sure you're okay. I know we don't have to worry about the stones or the chronicles anymore, but there's a war going on, and with it being very different times, no pun intended, it can be dangerous."

"I can't argue that." She'd certainly experienced that well enough. "We need to define a period of time for when you're right to start worrying."

"Exactly. What about two weeks? That's several months in that time period."

"And then what?" Stella asked.

"It's best if we send either Ethan or Finn to Hensley's estate in Bristol. If anyone knows what's going on, it would be him."

"What if he's in London for the season or some other reason?"

"Waverly is close. Barrington would be the next best person to check in with."

Stella nodded. Her inclination would be to go straight to Waverly, but Hensley made better sense. "Beckworth wants to leave this weekend. How about a dinner the night before, and we'll nail down the rules." She glanced at AJ, who had turned back to the sea. "You know Finn and Ethan would both want to go."

AJ nodded. "I suppose it makes sense for them to both go. Then, depending on what the problem is, they can either handle it together or one can come back if they need help."

Stella reached across the table and held out her hand, and AJ gripped it. "It's like umbrellas."

AJ snorted. "If you have one, it probably won't rain."

"And backup plans are the same. It brings comfort." Stella had come here without Beckworth specifically so she could have alone time with her friend. Her task was to reassure AJ about their trip in case it did become a regular quarterly event. She thought she'd succeeded, but it was confirmed with AJ's next words.

"Well, let's not let that pie go to waste."

V iscount Theodore Beckworth rose early, leaving Stella to sleep in. They'd leave in a couple of hours to meet the group at the inn's dock for their trip to Waverly. They could leave from any location, but the dock had become the single gathering point from the first time Finn Murphy had stolen AJ away to the past. It had become a ritual that no one was comfortable changing, and with the Heart Stone and the earrings that had been chipped from the stone securely stored at the inn, it simply made sense.

While he had his own reason for getting up early, there was no reason to wake Stella. She wasn't a morning person, and she'd be irritable enough when it was time to lure her out of bed.

He tiptoed down the dark hall to the guest room where he'd set up his office. A bed filled a portion of the room, but there was enough space for a desk near the window. They'd replaced two dressers with bookshelves, leaving one dresser for guests. Though a guest had never used the room, it made sense to make the room dual-purpose, just in case.

He shut the door behind him and turned on the antique

table lamp and his laptop. AJ, a private antique broker, had seen the lamp during one of her shopping trips and mentioned it to him. He'd gone down the next day, knowing what a good eye she had, and bought it on the spot. He rubbed his hands together and flexed his fingers as he considered what he was about to do. It was only a small step, but he hadn't discussed it with Stella.

Without giving it any further thought, he found the document template bearing the name of Stella's brokerage business. He spent thirty minutes writing his letter of intent to run for an open position on the Baywood Business Association Board of Directors.

Stella had given him the titles of financial officer and business manager so he could build a resume. Ethan Hughes, a fellow time traveler from England, had also given him permission to add two years as a security consultant for his private security company. He fudged the dates so it appeared he left Ethan's firm to work for Stella. Work history before that was limited to his estate business in England and his membership in Corsham's Chamber of Commerce. He didn't provide a reference and didn't think the association would ask for one.

He'd spoken with various council members during his short time as a member, and they appeared more concerned about a member's current participation within the community, with only a minor interest in the resume. It was a long shot at best, but it was a start. Something to build on.

Once the email was sent, he sat back and considered when he'd tell Stella what he was about. She'd be supportive, yet something held him back. He wasn't ready to think too deeply about why that might be. Perhaps he wasn't quite ready to become more attached to this timeline. Maybe it was the idea of failing her. If he looked too close, he might discover it was his fear of not being enough.

He shut down the laptop and shoved it aside. It was time to finish packing and focus on the trip at hand.

His first stop was the kitchen, where he started the coffee then prepared one bagel and one banana. They would share the simple meal. There were still a couple of hours before they called for the fog, but Stella had a sensitive stomach.

He carried two mugs of coffee into the bedroom and set them by the bedside table before turning on a lamp near their reading chairs, though he doubted Stella would notice if all the lights were lit. He sat on the bed and watched her. She slept like the dead most nights, her nightmares coming farther and farther apart. She never specifically mentioned what her chaotic dreams were about, but he knew they were about Cheval. He also knew there was nothing he could do about it but be there for her.

She never mentioned that moment on the beach when Cheval would have drowned him without her aid. Since they hadn't told anyone in this time period about Hensley's mission with the smugglers and the trouble they'd run into, there wasn't anyone else she could confide in. Well, there was one person. Sebastian, the French monk, was reliable for not sharing secrets or confessions.

He was one person Stella might seek out to confess the smuggler's death by her hands. Sebastian would be understanding, especially after all the trouble he'd lived through with the Mórdha stones. Beckworth wouldn't ask her. Over time, he'd learned it was best for Stella to think things through on her own. If the nightmares had been getting worse, he would have intervened. But they weren't, so it was best to leave things be.

He shook her. "Stella, darling. It's time to get up." He grinned when her only response was to turn away from him. He shoved her over and slipped in next to her, putting an arm around her. "The coffee's ready. If the stones work correctly, we'll arrive in time for lunch. Perhaps we can convince Nellie to make those strawberry tarts you like so well. Or perhaps a meat pie. They might be Fitz's favorite, but I've seen you put two away in one sitting." He ran a hand over her hip and down her leg before trailing his fingers back up. She moaned, and he judged she was on the verge of opening an eye. So, he went for the final words that were sure to hit a soft spot.

"In order to let you sleep in, I've taken the liberty of packing the rest of your duffel, and I've loaded it into the car."

He was rewarded with both eyes shooting open.

"What about my first aid kit?"

"Ah. So you've been awake all this time?"

She rolled over and reached out for him, her gaze flashing up to meet his eyes. "You're dressed already." This time her moan was of sheer disappointment. She rubbed her eyes and looked around the room. "What time is it?"

"You have less than an hour to get ready, and that includes a quick bite to eat." He picked up her mug of coffee while she pushed herself into a sitting position.

She grabbed the mug from him and sipped the hot brew. Her body immediately seemed to come alive, and she rolled her head from side to side, getting the kinks out. "I barely remember going to bed." After two more sips, she handed him the cup and pushed him off the bed so she could get up. Then she took the mug back and said, "Give me thirty minutes."

He gave her twenty before bringing in a fresh mug and taking the empty one. He was halfway out the bathroom door before she tugged him over and gave him a thorough kiss.

"I love you, Teddy." She ran a thumb over his lips, then gave him one sweet kiss before returning to her morning routine.

"I love you, too." He patted her backside and picked up his duffel, which he placed at the front door.

It was another fifteen minutes before she shuffled down the

hall, and he heard her duffel hitting the floor next to his. She washed out the empty coffee cup and grabbed the immense travel-sized mug, already filled and waiting, and took a long swallow. She glared at the half of bagel with a light spread of cream cheese and the half of banana before rubbing her stomach.

"I don't think that's a good idea. You know I'll just throw it all up on the other side."

"Nibble it on the drive over. There's still time."

She wrapped them in a paper towel. "Everything locked up and furnace turned down?"

"Yes. All the doors and windows have been checked, and you know AJ will be over every two days to check the garden and plants."

"Perfect." She picked up her mug, but when she reached the front door, she stared down at her duffel.

He opened the door and shooed her out. "I'll get the bags."

She was livelier by the time they arrived at the inn. "Maire, Ethan, and Sebastian are already here." She pouted. "Probably having a glorious breakfast without us."

"Now, now. It won't be long before you're eating a nice meal at Waverly."

"There'd better be meat pies and strawberry tarts like you promised." She got out of the car and pulled out her duffel.

He hurried around the car to take the duffel from her and kissed her cheek. "I knew you were listening."

She grinned and led him up the stairs, knocking twice before opening the door. "All hands on deck. The time travelers have arrived."

Finn met them in the hallway where Beckworth dropped the duffels. "You're right on time. I don't know how Beckworth manages it so early in the morning." He gave Stella a kiss on the cheek.

"Funny," she growled. "If he always used the same method, it would be easier for me to ignore it. But you know how sly he is."

Finn chuckled. "Yes." He winked at Beckworth. "We all do."

The group discussed general activities and plans for a birthday bash for Helen, AJ's mom, until it was time to leave for the dock. Once they reached it, Maire gave Beckworth a slip of paper.

"Sebastian and I have been reworking the incantation to see if there was a way to make the trip less..." She groped for the right word and finally said, "jarring."

"It's possible we might have to tweak it some more," Sebastian added. "But we don't want to take any chances with you arriving in the right place and time."

Stella paled. "Maybe it's worth the bruises if it gets us where we need to be."

Maire's eyes twinkled. "Where's the adventure in that?"

Stella, still a bit irritable from the early morning, responded with her normal sass. "You're just irritated that I'll be in London for the season, attending balls and tea parties."

"And perhaps I'm just trying to find the best incantation for when I ask Ethan to take me back for a season."

"Well, you should have just said so. Nothing quite like being someone's guinea pig." She fussed with her jacket. She'd dressed in the pants and shirt she preferred to wear for time traveling. AJ had found a plain jacket that wouldn't draw too much attention in the early nineteenth century and was sufficient for the cool morning air.

Beckworth placed the duffels on the dock and turned to the group. "We all know the backup plan, correct?"

"We wait a month or so," Ethan replied. "And when we eventually notice you've been gone a bit too long, we'll send the women to track you down."

Stella snorted. "Well, if you need something done right, it only makes sense to send the women in first."

The group laughed, and Beckworth tugged Stella to him once they'd slung the duffels over their shoulders. "Take care, mates. We'll be back before you know it."

"Oh, wait." AJ ran up to Stella and shoved a large envelope in her duffel. "I almost forgot the letters and shopping list."

Stella's brow lifted. "A shopping list?" She glanced at Sebastian, who winked at her. "I'll be sure Beckworth takes care of it."

Beckworth reviewed the new incantation and spoke the strange Celtic words as if he'd spoken the language his whole life. Then he gripped Stella's hand as they watched their friends disappear in the fog.

2

———

When the fog came, Stella gripped Beckworth's hand so tightly, she felt him flinch. She would have wrapped her arms around him if it weren't for the duffel bags. The trip through the fog didn't scare her. Not really. Though learning two minutes before the jump that Maire and Sebastian had fiddled with the incantation didn't leave her with a lot of confidence.

Whisps of fog circled her. They appeared almost corporeal, and her stomach twisted in knots, as if her insides wanted to be on the outside. It wasn't until she hit the ground, rolled, and ended face-first in the dirt with the weight of her duffel holding her down that she huffed out a sigh of relief.

The first thing she spotted was her hand and the stone ring that allowed them to time travel. The rest of her worries dissipated. Not because she knew they'd landed in the right place and time, but the knowledge she still had her ring. With the correct incantation that Stella had practiced a hundred times so she'd never forget it, she could always get back home.

Even if Finn came after them with the Heart Stone, the one item the smaller stones were mystically connected with, there were two small pieces of the Heart Stone that had been chipped off and made into earrings. Those tiny bits were connected to all the stones with enough power to bring the travelers back to the dock in Baywood.

She groaned as she rolled over onto the duffel, feeling a bit like a turtle who'd been rolled onto its back. The sky was blue, the sun out, but there was a nip of chill in the air. She turned her head, searching for Beckworth, and noticed the tall trees sprouting young leaves. Spring. The time of year seemed correct, and now, the only question was what year it was, and where they were?

She startled when fingers gripped her leg.

"It's just me," Beckworth said. "Are you alright?"

She shoved the duffel strap off her shoulder and pushed herself up to find Beckworth doing the same thing. "That felt different."

He scanned the landscape, and a smile lit his incredible lips. "At least, we're in the right spot."

Stella followed his gaze, and her own smile surfaced. Barrington strode toward them, and he didn't look surprised to see them.

"Lady Stella, it's good to see you again." Barrington held out his hand, and though he wore his stoic butler expression, she didn't miss the humor in his gaze.

Once she was on her feet, she gave him a long perusal. "I'm surprised you haven't spread chairs around the area, selling tickets for our arrival."

"A wonderful idea, but you're a day late. There have been some speculations on whether you'd arrive at all."

"If you don't mind." Beckworth turned to Stella, and she just waved him off.

"You've been thinking about that colt for the last few days. Go see him. I'll put on my big girl panties and play lady of the manor."

Both men grinned, and though Barrington's cheeks might have reddened at talk of panties, he was astute enough to ignore her.

"You'll be pleased by how the colt has grown." Barrington picked up both duffels and waited for Stella to lead the way.

She gave Beckworth a quick peck on the cheek. "I'll see about food. Don't be long. You can come back and play after you eat."

"Yes, Mother." Beckworth kissed her cheek in return and didn't waste time heading for the stables.

"He seems well." Barrington followed a step behind as they walked out of the trees and through the immense English garden before reaching the back of the manor. "Let's go through the solarium. Nellie is busy with preparations for lunch."

Douglas, one of the footmen, waited for them just inside the French doors, and he immediately took the bags. "Shall I call for Libby? She's helping Mrs. Walker with the spring cleaning."

Stella considered the question. She didn't need Libby's help at the moment, though she was excited to see her. Libby would appreciate getting out of the cleaning, but Stella didn't want to end up on Mrs. Walker's bad side.

She ended up shaking her head. "It can wait. Where can I find her?"

"They're in the west wing in one of the drawing rooms."

"Close enough. Thank you, Douglas."

Barrington left them at the stairs as she followed Douglas up to the master bedroom. She went directly to the windows and opened the drapes wider while Douglas dropped the bags on two chairs.

"Is there anything else I can get you, Lady Stella?"

"How long until lunch?"

"Another hour."

"Could you have a coffee service brought up, if it's not inconvenient?"

"Of course, my lady." His grin was infectious, and she returned one of her own.

"It's good to be home."

He nodded, still holding that grin, and as soon as he closed the door, she raced to the bed and threw herself face down on it. It was lumpier than the one at home, but it still felt good. Flashes of moments with Beckworth in this very bed gave her a warm, tingly sensation, and she closed her eyes, realizing how tired she still was. She hated getting up early. Her stomach growled. Maybe Nellie would send something to nibble on with the coffee.

The sound of a tray hitting a hard surface, followed by the rattling of plates, woke Stella. She rolled over and stared at an angry Libby, her fists on her hips.

"You've been back for twenty minutes and haven't called for me?"

Stella chuckled. "It's good to see you, too." She sat up and wiped her eyes. "I was just stretching for a few minutes. I hadn't planned on falling asleep." She held up her hand before Libby could continue chastising her.

Libby wasn't a normal lady's maid. She could play the part when necessary, but she hadn't been born to service. She grew up in the crews, Beckworth's name for gangs, in London's East End. She could turn from a proper English lady's maid to a street hustler in a span of two seconds. Beckworth gave his staff some leeway when there weren't guests in the manor since several had come from the streets of London rather than service. He made it all work, and Stella was pleased the household wasn't so stuffy.

Mrs. Walker was a different story. She never relaxed, but she also wasn't overly stern. And she'd become an excellent guide in shaping Stella into the proper lady of the manor that was occasionally required.

Stella threw her legs over the side of the bed and scratched her head. Her hair was a rat's nest again. "I considered calling for you, but I didn't want to step on Mrs. Walker's toes the minute I arrived. I was going to have a cup of coffee, then call for you."

She stood and marched straight for the mug Libby held out for her. Nellie had quickly learned how much coffee the new lady of the manor drank, and without asking, began serving it with a mug better suited for ale. The woman was heaven-sent.

Libby couldn't hold in her pout when Stella took the mug, set it down, then pulled her reluctant lady's maid in for a hug. It took a moment before Libby hugged her in return.

"It's good to have you home, Lady Stella."

Stella pulled back and gave Libby a longer perusal. "Mrs. Walker must have been working everyone overtime. You look like you could use a day-long nap."

Libby returned the mug of coffee to Stella, then opened one of the duffels, removing the contents and placing them in separate piles. "It started three days before you were set to arrive. We thought we were done until you didn't appear on the day we expected, so she decided to use the time to go through all the more heavily used rooms again."

Stella apologized and explained the unexpected change in the incantation while mulling over the food offerings Nellie had included with the coffee service. Libby finished removing everything from Stella's bag and stored the items away. When she picked up a pile of Beckworth's clothes and strode toward the dressing room, Stella picked up the tray and strode out to the balcony that overlooked the garden.

It took her breath away, and she grabbed her mug and leaned on the stone railing as she took it all in. Beckworth was a masterful gardener and took his efforts with planning the manor's garden quite seriously. She'd seen the garden at Waverly before. Once in the fall, after most of the blooms had faded, and again in the winter when it was mostly brown. To see it full of color now, she could understand how difficult it was for him to leave Waverly behind and why he continued their visits here. He'd worked so hard for this achievement.

"There you are. I should have known you'd find your way out here." Libby stood next to her. "It's really lovely, but I prefer the summer blooms."

Stella eyed Libby. "I've been here less than an hour. You're not trying to convince me on another trip already, are you?"

Libby batted her eyes and placed a hand on her chest. The only thing missing was a colorfully decorated fan. "That would be completely improper."

They both laughed, and Stella took a seat, patting the chair next to her. "Come have coffee with me and help me with these tarts."

Libby bit her lip as she stared at the treats. "I really should get back to cleaning."

Stella snorted. "Let's not start my time here as if we don't know each other. Sit your backside down and relax. Just tell Mrs. Walker I had a couple of items I needed pressed right away, or something that makes sense. Use that silver tongue."

"Fine, but you should know that Barrington advised me to be a bit more formal with you. He doesn't seem to understand how difficult that is."

"He should know me better than that."

"I don't think it bothers him. He knows me from my days in the East End. He worries that I might slip up with Beckworth's guests."

Stella tilted her head. "I don't remember seeing you anything but professional with the guests."

She blushed. "I think he remembers the little girl rather than who I am now."

"Well, he'll have to get used to it when we're all in London together."

"London? Me?"

Stella gave her a long look. "Barrington didn't tell you." She squinted, trying to remember what they'd agreed on before returning to Baywood after their last visit.

The timing between the future and the past wasn't consistent in both periods. For every week, give or take, they spent in this time period, only a day passed in Baywood. Now that the incantations used with the stones had been fine-tuned, they could predict a time and location for their travel back in time. However, with the recent update in the incantation to reduce the body-jarring arrivals, it seemed the incantation was off a day.

"Maybe we didn't talk about the specifics. I just assumed I'd need my lady's maid with me."

Libby shrugged. "I thought Beckworth would arrange for one at Lord Templeton's manor."

"Doesn't Mary take her personal lady's maid?"

Libby nodded. "Most do."

"Then it's only appropriate for you to go with me." She paused and glanced at Libby, who was staring straight ahead, making it difficult to read her features. "I know we'll be here a couple of days before leaving, but if it's not enough notice and you have other plans, I understand. I'm sure, as you say, Beckworth will find someone. He always does."

Libby sat up, her expression fierce. "I'm your servant. You tell me what to do and I do it." She bit her lip again. "Maybe Barrington was right."

"Oh no, you don't. I'm not a part of this aristocracy and actually prefer to spend time with Eleanor and Bart. And while I love my time with Mary and Elizabeth, I don't fit in with the rest of them. I can't help but think of you as an equal. It's how we do things in the future. Just because Beckworth has money and you work for him doesn't mean you don't have a life and your own commitments."

"I wish you lived here all the time."

Stella barked out a laugh. "And I wish I could take you back with us."

"What's all this?"

The women turned to find Beckworth leaning against the doorframe, his arms folded across his chest.

"I was just ensuring Libby was prepared to travel to London with us."

"I see. I suppose we should have discussed that when we arranged the London dates with Barrington. I'll have him notify Mrs. Walker."

"How's the pony?" Stella asked, smiling at Libby.

"He's not a pony. He's a fine colt from an impeccable blood..." he trailed off and stood straight, a wicked grin on his handsome face. "You're in a mood."

"I am. How long until lunch, Libby?"

"Will an hour do?" Libby grinned as she stood, stealing a strawberry tart from the plate.

"It will have to."

Once Libby sashayed out the door with a grin on her face, Stella offered one of the tarts to Beckworth, who licked his lips after he swallowed it in two bites.

"You're still in your traveling clothes." He took her hand and led her inside.

"We were catching up."

"Hmm. Then let's see if I can help." He stood her next to the bed, then pushed her backward onto it.

She fell back but rose onto her elbows as she watched him remove her boots before he unbuttoned her pants and stripped them off. He left her in just her shirt while he removed his clothes, more hurried than usual, but they only had an hour.

She waited patiently for him to finally grab her shirt and pull it over her head. When she was free, she turned and crawled toward the pillows but didn't make it very far before he rolled her over and positioned himself between her legs.

His kiss was long and full of heat, and she returned it with equal measure. They'd missed their opportunity to stay in bed that morning to smooch, drink coffee, and talk about meaningless topics. Now that they were at Waverly, he'd be busy catching up on manor business, spending time with the colt, and taking his early morning rides. She'd have to take her moments with him when she could.

She wrapped her arms around him, and when his kisses moved down her neck, she reached down to encourage him. They might have an hour, but it would take almost half that time to make themselves presentable to the staff.

He seemed to read her mind because it didn't take long before he was inside her, and she relished the moment. They were at Waverly. Soon, they'd be in London with good friends, enjoying their vacation. No worries about the Mórdha stones or missions from Hensley, the Crown's spymaster.

What a glorious time they would have.

***

Beckworth parked the wagon with his two passengers once it drew up to the steps of Waverly and swore as he jumped down. Bart, otherwise known as Doc, who'd been a surgeon in London for decades until he got tired of what he called the "establishment" and disappeared to live in a cabin in the woods five miles northwest of Waverly, had complained the entire way.

Bart was getting too old to live alone, though he refused to see it. Lincoln, the young lad Bart had all but adopted, would soon be attending the Royal College of Surgeons in London. He had grown into a fine man who did all the heavy lifting at Bart's cabin. Once he left for London, Beckworth would have to find a replacement who wouldn't be seen as a nursemaid to care for the old man.

"Are you going to help me get down, or do I need to yell for someone?" Bart griped as he searched for something to hold onto as if he'd find his own way off the wagon. The irritating old man would kill himself before Beckworth had time to find someone willing to put up with his cranky ways.

"I'm here." Lincoln took Bart's cane, then held out a hand for the old man to take. "You're getting more impatient by the day."

"I can't wait for you to leave for London so I don't have to listen to your constant bickering."

Beckworth grinned, knowing a good portion of Bart's increased complaining had to do with the fact that once Lincoln was gone, Bart would miss him. Not as much for his help around the cabin, but for the loss of companionship. He'd have to discuss the situation with Barrington and find another caretaker soon.

"Bart!" Stella raced down the steps of the manor, remembering to hold her skirts up before she did a face plant at the bottom. Beckworth wasn't surprised by Stella's quick acclimation to life in this century. Though she hadn't spent much time at the manor, the staff had been equally nimble in learning her quirks and seemed to love her all the more for them.

She grabbed the old man and hugged him tightly before he knew what hit him.

"Enough of that." Bart held on a little longer than necessary, though he blustered about it. "I'm old. You want to break my bones?"

She managed to plant a kiss on his cheek, which made him blush as he waved her off. "Enough, woman."

Bart continued to grin while she turned to give Lincoln the same treatment, a trait not too dissimilar from Hensley's wife, Mary. The young lad knew better than to fight against Stella's attention. It was faster to just give in.

"I can't believe you're willing to go to London with us."

"No choice," Bart muttered. "Might as well tag along so I can introduce the boy to some contacts."

"Well, come in. Nellie has a lovely lunch arranged before we start our adventure."

"Is Eleanor here?"

Beckworth hooked an arm around Bart's shoulder and turned him toward the steps. "Yes. But I had to bribe her to go with us once she heard you were coming."

The old man laughed. "Nice try. That woman thinks the world of me."

Beckworth glanced at Stella with a pleading gaze, hoping she'd take pity on him and assist Bart into the manor.

She rolled her eyes and took Bart's arm. "Why don't you escort me to the dining room. You should have come last night so you'd have a good rest before our trip."

Beckworth watched the two move slowly up the steps. Bart's mobility had gotten worse since their last visit, but it had been a cold winter. The warmer spring weather should help.

Lincoln stepped next to him. "I'm worried about leaving for London."

He knew Lincoln wasn't talking about this trip. "I'm considering options." He patted the lad's shoulder. "We'll find a solution. Now, how about going to see that colt?"

An hour after lunch, Bart was loaded into a carriage with Eleanor, Stella, and Libby. Barrington and Lincoln took the bench to drive the carriage while Beckworth mounted his horse.

It was good to be back on a horse. In Baywood, he occasionally went horseback riding with Finn to help exercise AJ's horse. But to ride all the way to London on his beloved stallion, there simply weren't enough words. He rode ahead of the coach, giving the horse its head, then walked him around until the coach caught up.

They overnighted once before reaching London. Stella mentioned privately that, so far, Bart had been on his best behavior, seeming to enjoy getting out and catching up with stories and the local gossip. However, his griping started as soon as the first signs of London could be seen out the window. Bart wasn't fond of London, but he would put that all aside to ensure Lincoln got the best start when it was time for his schooling.

By the time they reached Lord Templeton's manor, which Beckworth had free rein to borrow when the earl was overseas, everyone was ready to stretch their legs. He helped the women and Bart out of the carriage while Barrington went to ensure the staff were ready for them.

"You really need to see about better padding on those benches," Stella grumbled while rubbing her backside. "I was ready to ask you to buy a horse halfway here."

"You would still be sitting on your backside," Beckworth mused.

"Different muscles, and I could ride ahead like you did then walk around until the coach caught up."

"I suppose we should have hitched Smudge to the back of the carriage."

Stella took his arm as he guided her up the steps to the manor. "Next time. I miss that horse."

Beckworth shook his head then glanced up in surprise when he heard Fitz's voice.

"I'll drive the carriage to the coach house before I make a run back to the ship."

"Fitz!" Stella hurried over to give the sailor a hug.

Fitz took it in good stride. "It's good to see you, Lady Stella." Then the first mate scowled. "But you're a day late."

Stella laughed. "And you lost the bet."

"Aye. And Lando's a bit too chipper about it."

"Is he here?"

"Him and Jamie both, but they're back at the ship taking care of some business." Fitz eyed Beckworth. "Hensley wanted to know when you arrived."

Beckworth gave Stella a quick look before nodding. "I'll have a message sent. Are you all staying here?"

Fitz shook his head. "We decided to stay on the ship, but I expect Jamie and Lando will be seeing you at Hensley's."

"Well, that didn't take long." Stella didn't appear happy about the news. She liked Hensley, but she wasn't keen on him wanting to bring Beckworth in for a meeting the minute they'd arrived.

"Let's get you upstairs," Libby said. "We could all use a short rest before dressing for dinner."

Thank heavens for Libby, Beckworth thought. He knew she'd be good for Stella, and he hadn't been wrong. Although when he saw the two women grin at each other before heading for the stairs, he sometimes questioned his wisdom. The two of them together weren't much different than Stella with AJ. Alone, they were smart, fearless, independent women. Together—and with a bit of wine—they seemed to lose common sense, and their fearlessness had been known to get them in trouble.

He wouldn't have to worry for long. Once Mary and Elizabeth heard they were in town, they'd keep Stella busy and out of trouble.

"Did you want to change, sir?" Barrington asked.

Beckworth snorted. "Not a minute in London and it's already sir?"

"I thought it best to get back in practice."

He shook his head. "How about a drink in the study? I need to write a few letters." There were always the bankers, the solicitor, and other business associates he needed to meet with while he was in town. If he was quick about it, he might receive some updates before his meeting with Hensley. Better to be forewarned before walking into the spymaster's web.

3

Stella lingered in the second-floor hallway, staring at the door of the bedroom that Beckworth used when he stayed in Templeton's London manor. The last time she'd been there was when they'd searched for Beckworth after he'd given himself up to Gemini in order to save her. He'd been tortured before they'd been able to rescue him. This was the room where he'd healed. She peeked into the room across the hall where she'd stayed and rubbed her arms to discourage the shivers that ran through her.

When she closed the door and turned around, she noticed Libby's strange look as she stood in the open doorway to Beckworth's bedroom. Now, their bedroom. She took a few steps in and glanced around. The memories they'd shared had been a mix of both good and bad, though they'd ended well enough. They would make new memories here.

"Is everything alright?" Libby asked.

It took a moment for her to register the question, and she gave Libby a small smile. "Just trying to banish some ghosts."

Libby nodded. "I heard the stories. But you know, that wasn't the first time Beckworth faced death. And it wasn't the last." She shook herself as Stella had, trying to erase the memory.

Stella didn't need to be reminded that Libby had been injured during the battle at Waverly. When Stella had shot Gaines to save Beckworth. The night Gemini had died.

"It was a dangerous business he was in," Libby continued. "But every day in London is a dangerous time for those without money."

"You're right." Stella let the silence grow for another moment before she clapped her hands. "Let's start this trip on a more positive note." A knock on the open door made them both turn to find two footmen carrying a trunk. Two more followed with a second trunk, and they all nodded to her as they walked out. Behind them came a young house-maid carrying a tray with an urn, mugs, and a small plate of treats.

"Let's get these trunks emptied, then we can sit on the balcony and eat like the rich."

Libby laughed. "You're part of the rich."

Stella shrugged as she opened one trunk and Libby the other. "It just looks like it because of Beckworth's title, and of course, his money. But at home in Baywood, I'd be considered part of the merchant class."

"When did this get added to your trunk?" Libby held the crossbow Stella had used to kill Cheval and, for a reason she still couldn't explain, held an attachment to.

Stella only gave her a side glance before picking up a pile of Beckworth's clothes. "It was a last-minute thought before Douglas came for the trunk."

"And when do you plan on using it?"

Stella shrugged. "No plans. It's just nice to know it's close."

"Most ladies would keep a dagger close."

Stella chuckled. "I brought one of those, and a pistol as well. You just haven't dug deep enough." She straightened and touched the pocket of her day dress. "Actually, I'm carrying the dagger. The pistol should be in the trunk somewhere, along with a belt of cartridges."

Libby eyed Stella but didn't say a word as she laid the crossbow aside. She pulled out dresses and two pairs of pants, shirts, and a jacket that Stella liked to keep close—just in case.

Once the unpacking was completed, they sat on the balcony, sipping coffee and eating freshly made biscuits. A knock at the door brought back the same housemaid, who carried a message that had just been delivered.

"It's probably from Lady Mary," Libby said as she handed Stella the note.

Stella opened it and gave it a quick read. "Yes. Elizabeth will be arriving soon, and she wants to make sure Eleanor, Bart, and Lincoln come for dinner."

"Lady Mary is a special one. Not many would invite all of Beckworth's friends."

"I imagine you have friends you want to visit while you're here." Stella refreshed Libby's coffee and then her own.

"I might like to take an hour or two to visit."

"Not an hour or two. How about an evening here and there? Maybe a whole day or two to visit, or spend a night over with friends."

Libby stared at her. "I'm your lady's maid. I need to be here." She sounded like the proper Libby, but Stella saw a bit of hopefulness in her gaze.

"I'm sure someone on the staff can play backup lady's maid when you're not here."

She appeared doubtful. "Beckworth might approve one evening..."

Before she could finish, Stella jumped in. "Beckworth has no say in this. You're my lady's maid, and if I want to give you time off, no matter how often, to visit friends and family, then that's what will happen."

When Libby's expression became a mixture of a proper servant and the East Ender she was at heart, Stella laughed. "Don't worry. Beckworth might raise a brow, but he won't get involved."

"Get involved in what?"

The women glanced over their shoulders to see Beckworth giving them both a worried look.

"You have a knack for impeccable timing at the worst moments." Stella turned back to stare at the trees that shielded the neighbor's garden from view. "If you want to speak with us, come sit. Otherwise, I'll fill you in later."

"It's like that, is it?" Beckworth sat in a chair across from them.

"I'm sorry, sir." Jeffries, Beckworth's valet while in London, stood just inside the door. "Did you want to wear the blue or the green for dinner?"

Beckworth gave Stella a glance, and she, in turn, looked to Libby.

"Did you have anything planned for this evening?"

"I thought the royal-blue dress." Libby leaned over and picked up a biscuit, took a bite, and closed her eyes, relishing the taste. When she noticed Beckworth staring at her, she said, "If that's alright with you, ma'am."

"Fine with me."

Beckworth stared at the two women and, with a deep sigh, told Jeffries, "Blue it is."

"Very good, sir."

Once he disappeared, Beckworth scratched his jaw. "So, what's up between you two?"

"Nothing." Stella gripped her mug of coffee and spoke with an air of entitlement. "I'm giving Libby whatever time she wants to visit friends while we're in London. I suggested a few evenings or days, perhaps a sleepover. I'll use one of the other maids while Libby is out."

Beckworth had that look that told her he was considering what he wanted to say and whether it was worth the effort. When he simply nodded and said, "Sounds fine to me," Stella knew he had his own news to share that she probably wasn't going to like. As if she hadn't been expecting it.

When he didn't say anything more, she ran a hand over her dress, brushing away crumbs from the biscuit. "Dressing rather early for dinner, aren't you?"

She sensed Libby go still and was sorry she had to be in the middle of what could be the start of an argument, but it couldn't be helped.

Beckworth shifted in his chair and ran a hand through his hair. He was adorable when she unsettled him. She could have eased his burden, but not this time.

"Hensley requested a meeting." He raised his hands in a preemptive attempt to calm her. "Thomas is in town, and since Jamie and the crew are as well, he thought it would be good to have a quick review of their missions. I'm only there as an observer and to provide any words of wisdom I might have."

"That's fine. I'll be meeting with the staff. I'm sure Eleanor is already running around the manor checking on everyone."

He appeared speechless for a moment, and she held back a grin when he glanced at Libby in search of a clue to whether she was upset or simply playing the role of lady of the manor. He decided to play it safe.

"Very good. I'll be sure to have Barrington bring the coach around an hour before dinner." He stood, rubbed his hands together, and gave Stella a quick kiss on the cheek. "I'll see you for drinks before dinner."

She smiled up at him. "Of course. Say hello to Hensley and the boys for me."

Once he left to change, the two women exchanged grins.

Libby leaned over and whispered, "I don't think I've ever seen him so unsure of what to say. Is he like this in Baywood?"

"No. Not even when he's up to something. But he knows my thoughts about Hensley getting him involved with a mission."

"You think that's what he's up to?"

Stella sipped her coffee and stared out at the colorful garden and beyond. "I have no doubt at all."

4

———

Beckworth stepped out of the coach and stared up at Hensley's London manor. He'd known before they'd ever left Baywood that Hensley would dangle a mission in front of him in the hopes of luring him in. Beckworth was ready this time. When he and Stella had come back the first time for a holiday hunting party, he'd been unprepared for Hensley to be waiting for him. It had proved easy for the spymaster to manipulate him into pursuing a dangerous smuggler.

After his years of working for the crews, he'd fallen into league with the duke, his despicable father, who'd been as corrupt as they came. Beckworth had been naive and foolish to believe he could garner his father's favor. The old man treated him no better than one of his henchmen, giving him assignments that Beckworth continued to atone for long after the man's death. Even with Stella's relentless soothing words that he wasn't that man—had never been that man—he couldn't be thoroughly convinced.

The one good thing he'd been given during his time with the duke was his title. Everyone assumed he'd also received Waverly Manor from the duke, but the only role his father had played was in the money he'd paid Beckworth for his services. Not that it was enough to purchase a manor. But the duke had introduced him to parts of society he'd never thought to mingle with.

His work with the crews taught Beckworth how to build contacts, identify weaknesses, and negotiate. It was these skills that led to the appropriate connections, which assisted in selecting the proper investments. Not only did the investments provide the funds to purchase Waverly, but they also helped him establish a network of opportunities that continued to pay off.

With each visit back to Waverly, Beckworth cashed in on part of that legacy to support a good living in Baywood, though they didn't need much to thrive. Their life in Baywood was simpler than in this era.

The problem was that Hensley understood Beckworth's need for intrigue. The danger just happened to come with the territory, though not all of Hensley's missions were life-threatening. He could have walked away from the last one. Let Jamie and his crew set sail on the *Daphne Marie* without him. It had only been a seek-and-find mission.

Hensley and Jamie knew Beckworth too well and counted on his inability to say no. Stella had also known he couldn't turn down a mission. Yet, he'd danced around the topic, worried—more like terrified—of telling her that she would need to play lady of the manor and work with Barrington to prepare for the party and their guests.

He snorted.

What the hell had he been thinking? In the end, she'd manipulated her way into the mission behind his back. The thought of that adventure sent a sliver of thrill through him. It had been an erotic as well as a dangerous journey that had almost gotten them killed. Hell, she still traveled with that damn crossbow. He'd seen it in her trunk before they'd left Waverly, but he'd said nothing. He picked his battles with

Stella, and she was still working through her part in Cheval's death.

The sound of the coach driving away pulled him out of his reverie, and he jogged up the steps, eager to see his old friends. The butler waved him down the hall, used to Beckworth showing up on their doorstep. He hadn't reached the study when Fitz's boisterous laughter echoed into the hall.

He knocked once, then entered. "I hope you weren't telling stories about me."

"Beckworth!" The group was almost in sync with their enthusiastic greeting.

Jamie was the first to jump up to shake his hand, his eyes lit with amusement and a touch of melancholy. The two had been enemies, as he had been with Finn and Ethan, and pretty much everyone else in the room. But once they'd begun to trust him, he and Jamie developed something more profound, and Beckworth missed his friend.

The rest of the team were as he expected to find them. Hensley was entrenched behind his desk, a quill in his hand as he jotted down his latest thought. Lando leaned against a wall, his arms folded across his broad chest, while Fitz sat on a stool, a glass of whiskey nearby, and devoured what looked like a meat pie.

Thomas, somewhat new to the team, rested in a chair by a low-burning fire. Known for being a serious man, the ex-Sergeant of Arms for the late Earl of Hereford had relaxed and become more jovial since working for Hensley.

"How was the trip?" Jamie poured Beckworth a glass of whiskey.

"After Maire and Sebastian modified the incantation, the jump was less bumpy, but we seem to be off a day." Beckworth leaned back and sipped the Jameson whiskey, a plentiful contraband in the *Daphne*'s cargo.

"And I'm grateful for that." Lando grinned at Fitz. "It earned me some extra coin."

Fitz growled but couldn't respond with his mouth full of meat pie.

Beckworth shared tales about their friends now living in Baywood. Fitz recounted their voyages and missions, with occasional corrections from Jamie and Lando when the stories became more fairytale than truth.

Hensley refilled his drink, and when he resettled behind the desk, he got right to the point of the meeting. "I know this might appear suspicious, considering the last time Beckworth visited us on the cusp of a new mission." He paused and lifted his eyes from his notes to read the room.

Beckworth remained expressionless, as did everyone except Fitz, who snorted. No one had been fooled by Hensley when he'd surprised the group with a mission to locate the smuggler, McDuff. It had been clear as day to all of them that Hensley had waited until Beckworth returned to Waverly, with hopes of enticing him to join.

Hensley cleared his throat and returned to his notes. "Our time in London was to be a social visit with Beckworth, and for the most part, I think it still will be. The *Daphne* moored at a dock near East End three days ago. As you can surmise, the crew has been on liberty since then. A day ago, Michelson and Lane came to Jamie with information they'd picked up from the crew."

Michelson and Lane were shipmates on the *Daphne Marie* and had been helpful with the last mission. They were excellent with surveillance, and if they'd heard something from the crews, they would have checked it out themselves before going to Jamie.

"It appears," Jamie took up the report, "there have been whispers of smugglers in port. It was interesting, but who isn't smuggling these days?" Everyone gave a small chuckle at that. It was wartime, and supplies were difficult to obtain through normal routes. "It was when the name McDuff was heard that the crew took note."

"It was only two or three times," Fitz added. "But when Michelson and Lane visited the pubs late in the evening when the ale hit the sailors hard, they were able to confirm there's something going on with McDuff."

"Pretty foolhardy to show up in London," Thomas said. "The man is still wanted for previous crimes and should be waiting a hangman's noose."

"McDuff might not be in London." Lando moved away from the wall and picked at the leftover remains on the silver platter. "Maybe it's someone working for McDuff and they'll meet up with him later. McDuff could be in Ireland for all we know."

"And if that's true," Beckworth chimed in, "he would have sent someone he trusted to watch over their task. Do you know which ship they're from?"

"We believe they're from the *Nighthawk*." Jamie sipped whiskey before adding, "It's docked on the far side of Wapping."

Beckworth nodded as he considered their dilemma. "Do we know who the captain is?"

"That is why you're all here." Hensley took back the reins. "We need to confirm if any of McDuff's men are on board. We also need more information on what they're doing here. It would be foolish to pick up or unload contraband here, but not impossible. But why take the risk? Something else must be going on."

"We need to know the hierarchy on the ship." Beckworth sat up, a plan already forming. "Confirm who the captain and first mate are, and which men are the closest to them."

"It would be easier if we could just nab one." Thomas chuckled. "It's not too surprising to lose a sailor in the East End, but with our luck, we'd take one who didn't know anything."

Beckworth responded with a laugh. "You're bloody right, mate. There always seems to be a twist we never see coming." He rubbed his jaw. "There's only a handful of us who've seen any of McDuff's men. If we monitor the sailors leaving the ship, we can tail anyone who looks familiar."

"The sailors could be going anywhere." Jamie leaned back, his hands behind his head as he considered the idea. "But if they're meeting up with anyone, chances are they're keeping to one or two pubs."

"We need to keep this quiet," Hensley said. "From everyone." His stern gaze landed on Beckworth.

He meant Stella. Beckworth didn't like keeping secrets from her. It never ended well. But if she knew about this mission, regardless of how small it was, she'd want to get involved. He gave Hensley a slight nod. It shouldn't be too difficult to keep Stella preoccupied in London.

Hensley returned the nod. "Thomas will work with Jamie to organize schedules and gathering of information." He looked at Thomas. "Keep in mind that some of us will be expected at social functions and plan accordingly. I'll determine a meeting schedule to report on activities. Now, if there's nothing else, I have a surprise waiting for you in the stables." He stood and rubbed his hands together, his eyes lit with excitement.

Beckworth stood, his concern over keeping Stella busy pushed aside for a moment. Hensley must have a new horse. If anything could distract him from his worries, it was horses.

"Oh, my dear, you're here! We were so worried when you didn't arrive yesterday. Thankfully, we received Beckworth's message this morning." Mary waddled into the foyer to welcome Stella, Eleanor, Bart, and Lincoln.

Stella met her with a wide grin that faltered for a moment under Mary's suffocating hug. It took a moment to catch her breath. "Sorry. Maire and Sebastian fiddled with the incantation. I'm just glad we arrived at Waverly."

"Are they still happy living in the future?" Mary fanned herself. "I still find that so strange to say."

"You and me both." Stella stepped aside to let the rest of her party receive their fair share of Mary's robust greeting. She turned around for Barrington, but he wasn't there. He must have taken the coach to the carriage house.

She'd expected Beckworth to greet her until Mary answered her unspoken question.

"The men returned to the study after Hensley showed off his new horse. Elizabeth is waiting for us in the sitting room. There's no reason why we can't serve drinks a little early."

"I imagine the men started a while ago," Stella quipped. She itched to interrupt the boys' club, but she'd spent enough time in this era to understand it would be considered rude. If they'd been in Baywood, she wouldn't have hesitated to waltz in without a second thought. Well, she'd at least knock once, though probably wouldn't wait for a response.

When they reached the sitting room, Stella's grin returned.

The dowager Dame Elizabeth Ellingsworth perched on what Stella had learned from AJ was a Chippendale chair. If she wore a crown, she'd be as regal as whoever the current queen was. Stella paused a moment, wondering if that was something she should know before attending the parties. The nobles might ridicule her as one of those "colonists" from America, but she wasn't a heathen. She glanced at the others in the room. Maybe it was best to ask Beckworth.

Stella strode to her, and Elizabeth's gaze brightened as she stood to give Stella a hug.

"My dear, it's so good to see you." She returned to her seat after greeting the others and waved for them to sit.

Two footmen served wine for the ladies and something a bit stronger for Bart and Lincoln. She wasn't sure Lincoln was old enough, then she considered the time period. With the ongoing war, he was old enough to be impressed into service if he were at the wrong place at the wrong time. Though his acceptance into their medical school should save him from that fate.

The group spent twenty minutes catching up before the men joined them. They'd barely greeted each other before they were called to dinner.

Beckworth slipped her arm through his as he guided her to the dining room. He bent low and whispered, "Stop giving Hensley the evil eye. We were just catching up, then got side-tracked looking at Hensley's new stallion." He kissed her cheek.

She wanted to believe him. He wouldn't lie to her. It wasn't until after they were seated and the footman was ladling soup into her dish that alarm bells clanged in her head. He wouldn't purposely mislead her unless he'd gotten involved in a mission he considered dangerous.

He always put her safety first, and that meant the world to her, but now that they were in his time period, he tended to smother with his need to protect. When Mary laughed at something Lando said, she glanced around. She'd been too busy woolgathering, creating issues she had no proof existed, that she'd missed the discussion. She smiled along with the others and pushed her misgivings aside.

They mingled longer than usual over dinner and dessert, and she was thankful when Mary called their time in the drawing room short. She was hosting a garden party the following afternoon and wanted to get an early start on last-minute preparations. The event was in Stella's honor to introduce her to the women who would attend some of the same social venues. It was meant to ease Stella's entry into society. Just call her Eliza.

Even with the shortened time in the drawing room, they returned to Templeton's manor later than usual. Before Stella could climb the stairs, Eleanor pulled her aside to discuss a backup lady's maid for when Libby wasn't available. Mrs. Evans, the housekeeper, had two different maids in mind, and Stella, too tired to care, let Eleanor decide.

When she reached the bedroom, she was surprised by the number of lit candles in the room. Besides the fire in the hearth, they were the only light. She kicked off her shoes, wanting desperately to get out of the gown, and was disappointed when Libby wasn't waiting for her.

She took a few more steps into the room and scanned the bed, but other than being turned down, it was empty. Yet, she sensed someone. Her gaze roamed the room and stopped at the hearth. She almost groaned with pleasure when she stepped closer.

Beckworth had taken a chapter out of her own book of seduction.

He lay naked on a fur rug, leaning on his elbow. His face was shadowed by the fire behind him.

Her mouth salivated. She knew every detailed inch of his contoured body that was hidden by the flames. And though she couldn't see it, she knew there would be a salacious grin on his handsome face.

And here she was, fully dressed and unable to remove her gown without assistance.

When he slowly stood, she understood. He wanted to be the

one to undress her. More of his body came into clarity as he stepped closer.

She inhaled a deep breath. If he didn't hurry, she'd rip the dress off herself, uncaring whether anything could be salvaged.

He didn't speak a word as he drew close, his eyes locked with hers until he moved behind her. Buttons were slowly released, and she closed her eyes as the press of his fingers along the fabric of her dress made her shiver.

He slowly brushed the gown off her shoulders, trailing his fingers down her arms as the dress fell to the floor. His hands gripped her hips as she stepped out of the gown. Goose bumps erupted over her sensitive skin as he continued to unwrap the rest of her.

She almost tipped over when he knelt to remove her stockings. Her legs shook when he kissed each of her upper thighs before standing to take her hand and lead her to the rug. He'd been so gentle through all of it, and she ached to touch him. Not that she hadn't tried while he'd been undressing her, but he kept pushing her hands away.

Once they stepped onto the rug, his desire washed away any gentleness. He tugged her to him, his arms wrapping around her, his kiss almost brutal with passion. Her blood sizzled as his hands roamed over her. Her legs buckled when his hand dipped between them, and she would have fallen if he hadn't gripped her tighter.

He pulled her down to the floor. No time for more foreplay. They were way past that.

Between their late arrival and busy schedule, they hadn't made time for themselves since their first day at Waverly. After that, they'd been too tired to do anything more than snuggle under the covers before passing out from exhaustion. The same went for their travel to London.

She wanted to make new memories here, and she couldn't

think of a better way to begin. He rolled her over until she was on top, and she rode him slowly and deeply, his hands gently massaging her breasts until he pulled himself up, hugging her to him as he pulled her under him.

The tender lovemaking evolved into something more heated, needy, and demanding. Her head rolled back, and she closed her eyes, remembering the stars in the night sky when they made love in their Baywood garden. Then her eyes popped open to the sight of flames. And though she knew they were confined to the hearth, the fire seemed to consume the entire room.

Sparks flew, and she didn't know if they were from a log falling into the embers or the passion rocking through her, ready to explode until it filled the entire manor.

He fell back on his knees, tugging her with him as she rocked to match his rhythm. She bent her head to his chest as the first wave hit, and she gripped him tightly as he nuzzled her neck until the overwhelming sensation subsided. Somehow, she'd held in her scream.

She never let go as he continued until his breathing hitched, and his low growl reverberated against her throat as his own release took him. The last thing she remembered was them falling sideways onto the fur rug, their arms wrapped around each other as sleep took them both.

5

———

The next morning, Stella rolled over, felt the warm empty spot next to her, and opened her eyes. She lifted her head, surprised to find herself in bed. At some point, after their intense lovemaking, she hadn't remembered Beckworth carrying her to bed.

She laughed. He'd put her in a temporary coma. Perhaps there was something to the rumors that abstinence made the sex hotter.

"It's about time you woke." Libby walked by holding a day dress the color of lilacs. "You have twenty minutes until breakfast. I don't think Eleanor will mind if you're a bit late, but no more than ten minutes."

Stella stretched and took in a deep breath. Her head popped up. "Is that coffee I smell?"

Libby chortled. "And you'll have to come get it. I won't pamper you like Beckworth."

"So much for a lady's maid."

"Yes. A lady's maid, not a nanny."

"Funny." She swept the covers aside and rolled to a sitting position, her feet dangling off the side of the bed. She scratched her head. Her hair was its usual rat's nest. It would take Libby the full twenty minutes to make her decent enough to be seen in public.

She grabbed her robe, didn't bother tying it, and shuffled to the table where the coffee service sat. After pouring a cup, she took a long sip, closed her eyes, and waited for the brew to shake the cobwebs loose. It took three sips before they were gone and she could remember what the day held in store.

"Come sit. It will take me forever to get that bird's nest under control."

Stella grinned at Libby's similar thoughts. She stared at herself in the mirror and braced for Libby's brushing.

"You mentioned I might have some time to visit friends while we're here."

"And it's still true." Her eyes lit up. "You're not thinking of a man by any chance."

Libby held back a grin and pointed a brush at her reflection in the mirror. "There will be none of that."

"Oh, I don't think so." Stella tilted her head until Libby's brushing forced it back the other way. "In all seriousness, is there someone back at Waverly?"

Libby bit her lip as she twisted Stella's hair before pinning it up. "There might be one or two gentlemen in Corsham that I see on occasion."

"That's my girl." Stella took a long drink of the cooled coffee, her gaze watching Libby's expression.

"You're a bad influence."

"That's not the insult you might think it is."

Libby stared at her, and they both burst out in laughter.

"There was someone here in London. It was casual, but we lived together." She snorted. "Well, a few of the crew lived together to afford a decent place, but we shared a bed."

"Why did you leave London for Waverly?"

"Would you give up an opportunity for better money and a

grander place to live for a man who was unwilling to commit and had no promising future?"

"If I loved him, I might have encouraged him to come with me. Chances are, Beckworth would have given him a better life."

"I'm not so sure about that. Johnny was a nice enough bloke, but he wasn't very high up in the crew for a reason."

"Then what interested you in the first place?"

"His broad shoulders."

They laughed again until Libby got the hiccups. She was still hiccupping as she dressed Stella.

"Do you mind if I take some time today to go to the East End?" Libby asked as Stella fussed with her shoes.

"Not at all. I think I'll be at Mary's most of the day. They want to go over their stack of recent invitations."

"Oh, that reminds me. Several invitations arrived yesterday. Barrington has them. You should take them with you and see if they're for the same parties."

Stella gave Libby a curious look as she strode to the door. "Where is Beckworth anyway?"

"He said Hensley wanted to take his new stallion out for a ride. Barrington will take you to Mary's after breakfast."

Stella arrived five minutes late and received a disappointed stare from Eleanor. Bart and Lincoln didn't seem to care, and the food was still warm. She did a double-take when she noticed their tailored waistcoats and jackets.

"What's up with the fancy dress?"

Bart growled, and Lincoln grinned.

"Bart's taking me to the Royal College of Surgeons to introduce me to some old colleagues. And I wouldn't mind getting familiar with the place."

"I thought it would be easier to make several short trips since we'll be in London for a while." Bart pushed his food around before cutting into a sausage. "I need to see who's still around who might know me. Flush out friends from enemies. That sort of thing."

Stella held her grin. "Surveillance gathering."

Bart pointed a fork at her. "Exactly."

"Is Barrington going with you?"

"After he drops you off at Hensley's. We'll be fine."

Stella glanced at Eleanor, who focused on her meal, seemingly uninterested in the conversation. She'd selected a sage-green day dress that was much nicer than the plain dresses she typically wore. To be fair, she spent most of her time cleaning or following the staff around, and she preferred to fit in. Besides, part of Eleanor's charm was not caring what anyone else thought.

"Are you coming to Mary's with me?" She pushed her eggs around and nibbled the herb-roasted turnips.

Eleanor took a moment before realizing Stella was speaking to her. "Sorry. I was lost in my own thoughts. Mary asked me, and she's a difficult woman to say no to."

"It would be rather boring to stay here all day alone."

"Perhaps, but I'm not sure I'm ready to be around all those ladies."

Stella blanched. "How many ladies did Mary invite?"

"I don't know exactly, but her housekeeper mentioned setting up six tables in the garden."

Stella did the math. The table sat four to six people, depending on how they arranged the settings. She gulped, not sure she was any more ready than Eleanor to meet that many in a private setting.

Eleanor seemed to notice her discomfort. "It will be a long day, but it's better to meet these women in a more intimate setting before running into them at a ball. Beckworth will guide you away from the nosy ones who are more interested in meeting an American for entertainment value. As Mary said, it will help with the smaller garden and tea parties. You don't seem to have a problem joining a conversation. You'll be fine."

Stella mulled over the last part of Eleanor's statement, unsure if it was meant as a compliment. "I'm not worried about making conversation. I'm worried about saying the wrong thing or not using the proper fork."

Eleanor waved off her concerns. "You're from an upstart country, so they'll expect a certain lack of etiquette." She chewed her food as she considered Stella's concern. "You're also the consort of the Viscount of Waverly and a friend of Dame Elizabeth. No one would dare risk condemnation from Elizabeth."

Stella brightened. "You're right. That makes me feel better."

The words sounded inspiring until the carriage pulled up in front of Hensley's manor, and Stella glanced out the window as two impeccably dressed women climbed the steps. She fingered the invitations Beckworth had received. She'd stuffed them into her left pocket, preferring to keep her dagger in the right one. With a deep breath, she followed Eleanor out of the coach.

She was surprised when they were ushered into one of the sitting rooms where a long table had been set up. It reminded her of the way Mary had organized tables for Hensley's mission meetings when they'd battled Gemini. This time, flower arrangements were centered on the table rather than hand-drawn tactical maps. Two coffee and tea services were placed on either side of the fresh blooms that scented the room, and eight place settings had been prepared—three on each side of the table and one on each end.

Three women were already seated at the table, and her nerves settled when Elizabeth glanced up at her entrance and smiled. Lady Agatha, who sat next to her, lifted her head, and when she spotted Stella, grinned with a slight challenge in her gaze.

"Lady Stella." Agatha pointed to a seat directly across from her. "We saved a seat in the middle. I understand this is your first time in London for the season. You won't want to miss anything."

If it had been AJ who'd been directed where to sit, she would have been immediately suspicious that Agatha was up to something. Stella had to agree the possibility was still on the table. But as conniving as Agatha could be, her manner among friends was simply one of someone who enjoyed control over others. Stella still had much to learn when dealing with the aristocracy, so she'd play Agatha's games.

Before she could take a seat, Mary bustled in.

"There you are, my dear. So good to have you and Eleanor join us. Today's events should properly prepare you for the next few weeks of social activities. But first, you must meet Lady Melbourne."

The woman behind Mary was statuesque. She was a few years younger than Elizabeth, and although she didn't possess Agatha's beauty, her naturally regal air was friendly and would make anyone take a second glance.

"Call me Flora. Edgar and I are good friends of Beckworth's." Flora took a chair next to one of the women already seated. And this is Mabel Ashby. Her husband is also friends with Beckworth."

Stella sat and nodded at Mabel. "I remember you. I think you were at one of Mary's dinner parties the last time I was in London."

Mabel, who Stella guessed was a few years older than her, held a dreamy expression. "I still remember that amazing dress. Periwinkle, if memory serves."

"And the opals." Agatha poured a cup of tea and placed a biscuit on her plate.

"Like the one you're wearing now," Mabel said.

Stella fingered the opal necklace, which, along with the

matching opal bracelet, was one of the most expensive gifts Beckworth had bought her. The leaf-shaped hairpin had been his first gift, and she still treasured it. But she couldn't forget Beckworth's lust-filled expression when he'd found her waiting for him wearing nothing but the opal necklace. Her cheeks flushed, and she searched for a change of subject.

"Eleanor said tables were being set up in the garden."

"Oh, yes." Mary sat at the head of the table and glanced around. "That's for the garden party later today. We're still missing Beth."

"She's always late." Elizabeth placed a large stack of notes in front of her. Invitations.

Now, Stella understood. This was the group of close friends who would collaborate over the party invitations. When she noticed the others setting their invites on the table, she pulled out her own short stack.

"Look at that." Agatha pointed to Stella's invitations. "We weren't sure if you'd received any. Didn't you just arrive yesterday?"

"They're addressed to Beckworth. He sent letters out as soon as we arrived to let his friends know he was in town."

"Well, of course," Agatha said. "But my guess is they're more interested in seeing you."

"And you'll receive many more after Beckworth shows you off at the first party." Elizabeth took her stack and separated it into three smaller ones. "We might have to do this again in a week."

"Oh, yes," Mary said as she stacked her own invites in front of her, also separating them into three piles. "We can have a private garden party."

When Stella glanced around the room, the others had also separated their piles. Eleanor, who'd sat next to Stella, took her pile and spread them out like a dealer at a blackjack table.

Before Stella could ask her what she was doing, a footman entered with a young woman trailing behind him.

She was younger than Stella and seemed a bit timid. Her dress was elegant and probably cost a small fortune, yet she clearly seemed out of her element. The footman led her to the open seat next to Stella.

"I'm so sorry I'm late." Her voice was light and barely audible. When Agatha frowned, she cleared her throat. "I can't seem to get enough sleep these days."

The women glanced at each other and smiles broke out.

"Seems that old fool your father married you off to finally got a seed in you." Elizabeth nodded with acceptance. "Now, he should leave you alone. Hopefully, it will be a boy, then you can find a nice young man to keep your bed warm."

Stella wasn't sure whether to laugh or be appalled, but after glancing at the others, she decided to keep her mouth shut when everyone nodded. Even Beth grinned.

Elizabeth brought Stella up to speed. "Beth's father is a duke with strong connections at court. He thought it would be advantageous to marry his only daughter to a wealthy and powerful man who has one foot in the grave."

"So typical," Agatha replied. "I'm surprised he was able to get a child on her. But, soon enough, he'll be gone, and Beth will be able to choose another suitor. This time without as much influence from her father."

Good grief. Nothing like being prized as a brood mare.

Mary, catching Beth squirming under the attention, turned the conversation to the reason they were there. "We'll go through the invitations, starting with our declines. Might as well weed those out first. Stella, since this is your first time, take a look at the ones Beckworth received and pull the ones that match the names we call out."

Once that round was completed, they went through the ones

that were deemed required attendance. The stack of maybes, which fell into that category either because they conflicted with another party or the women wanted to know what the others thought before making a decision, was discussed last. Mary then reminded everyone to be discreet should any of the declined invitations be from someone who attended the garden party later.

It didn't take long for the conversation and occasional laughter to fill the room as they worked their way through the invitations. Stella, unable to help herself, made origami swans out of the declined invitations and set them around the floral arrangement. Mary and Eleanor were aware of her skill at crafting them, and the others begged to take one home with them. Stella was happy to let them go and told Mary she could have the remaining ones to share with the staff. She was thankful when the conversation returned to the parties.

"Well, I think we can all agree that we can't pass up Spencer's ball." Elizabeth looked at Stella. "He's a duke and hosts one of the largest balls. Though the timing isn't the best." Elizabeth reviewed the invitations that were still in her maybe stack. "It's interesting that Beckworth received an invitation so quickly."

"The ball is in two days," Mary said. "Any later and they couldn't expect Beckworth to accept."

"True." Agatha tapped on the pot of tea, and one of the footmen took it away. Not a minute later, another pot was set in its place once her cup was refilled. "But I see the problem. It's not the best one for Stella's first foray into society."

"What about Lady Percy's party tomorrow night?" Beth spoke up. "I know it's short notice, but I think she'd be pleased if we all accepted. It seems the right size to give Stella an idea of what to expect."

The women looked around the table, a couple of them reviewing their maybe stacks.

"She makes a good point," Mary said. "And I don't see any other that would provide the same experience."

Elizabeth sighed. "She'll probably expect us to attend every year after this."

"Nonsense," Agatha answered. "We've always declined with the reason of conflicting invitations. We'll simply state that we have an opening this year. That way, it doesn't suggest any further commitment."

When everyone nodded, Mary called the gathering to a close. Eleanor made a quick escape, claiming to check with the housekeeper for final preparations for the garden party.

The rest of the day was a blur as Stella met the rest of Mary's friends, names she remembered from their review of invitations, while others were new names to store away. Through it all, she couldn't help thinking of Beckworth and what he was doing with his day.

L ight mist was still burning off under the mid-morning sun along the Thames. A light breeze ruffled Beckworth's hair as he strolled along the docks. Though the horse ride with Hensley had been exhilarating, this walk brought back memories of his youth and early days in the crews. He breathed deeply, and with the combined scents of salt and fish, he could almost hear his mother calling for him.

Once upon a time, those thoughts would have brought him shame and heartbreak. Shame that he hadn't done enough for his mother. Heartbreak, that in the end, he hadn't been able to save her. He no longer had those feelings. His mother would be proud of who he'd become. Perhaps not in the way he'd made it happen, though it had been her idea to seek out the crews rather than stealing on his own. She'd always believed in safety in numbers and having someone at your back.

They both knew stealing was wrong, but survival had a way of twisting one's morals. Eat or starve. Find warm shelter or freeze. Stealing from the rich seemed to be the only solution. When Beckworth discovered he was a bastard son of a duke, living along the shanties on the Thames while the duke ate from a banquet table...Well, it had warped him further.

Beckworth trained to become a specialist. His mentor, an old crew leader who had survived a stint in Newgate, had taught him how to spy, how to read a mark, how to pick locks, and the best ways to kill a man. Once he'd seen his half-brother, who could have been his twin, Beckworth had seen an opportunity and sought out the duke.

He didn't like what he'd become, but he'd gotten in so deep he hadn't seen an expedient way out. Not until AJ Moore came along. If he were honest with himself, it was earlier than that. The moment he read the duke's letter from France, and Beckworth felt the weight of the Mórdha stone in his hand, he knew his life was about to change.

He snorted. If he'd only known the half of it. All those years, he'd hardened his heart, put his head down, and done what was required to open doors. When AJ had given him the chance to become a better man, a man his mother would have approved of, he took it. And in doing so, he built trust with those he'd once considered enemies.

He'd always been a generous man to those less fortunate. He understood them—their struggles, their heartaches, their lost dreams. And he'd found friends in the aristocracy who accepted the newcomer. Yet, his heart remained locked down until he came face to face with a spirited red-haired spitfire.

Stella had seen past all his facades and peered into his dark soul, overlooking all his misdeeds. She'd saved him more times than he could count, and not just his life. She'd ripped down the barriers he'd built around his heart. She loved him. He didn't know what he'd do without her.

It didn't escape his notice that while he was walking the docks, she would spend her day with the women of the aristocracy, planning which soirees and balls they would attend while he was on another of Hensley's missions. A mission he couldn't tell her about.

His first major lie. It tasted bitter.

A soft whistle broke him out of his introspection, and he turned toward the sound. It took a few more steps before he spotted Jamie behind a stack of crates.

Jamie blew warm air into his hands and then rubbed them. "I forgot my gloves. I'm not sure the sun is going to break through the mist."

"Give it another hour, though I doubt it will do much to warm our backsides." Beckworth sat next to him and squirmed to get comfortable. "Here, this should warm your hands and your belly." He handed him a meat pie.

"Mrs. Brubaker's?"

Beckworth laughed. "Where else?"

Jamie eagerly bit into it and closed his eyes. Once he'd swallowed, he moaned with delight. "Eleanor makes an excellent meat pie, but there's something about huddling on a dock with a fresh pie from Mrs. Brubaker."

"I remember cleaning out fish buckets to earn enough coin for a pie."

"It was mutton stew in southern Ireland. I mucked out the pig stalls for a warm bowl."

"Stella calls the meat pies comfort food. The same would be true with your mutton stew."

"Comfort food. Aye. That's a good name for it. The memory is enough to bring on that emotion."

They finished their pies in silence, occasionally glancing around the crates at the ship docked two berths over.

When the last bite was gone, Beckworth brushed off his hands and pulled out a flask. He shared the whiskey with Jamie.

"Anything of interest this morning?" Beckworth asked.

"Fitz saw a few sailors return from the pubs, but he didn't see anyone he recognized. I'm adding Michelson and Lane to Fitz's shift. He wants to follow some of the blokes and get a sense of whether they go to the same pubs or move around."

"Good plan. We might learn just as much from the sailors as the captain or his first mate. How many men have you put on watch duty?"

"Several. Some have family close by, so I'm using those who are staying on the ship while at port. Fitz, Lando, Michelson, and Lane will take the most watches since they can identify the major players. That leaves just one or two shifts for the rest of them."

"Sooner or later, the captain and his mates will leave the ship. It shouldn't take more than a handful of days to get what we need. Then we can spread out our surveillance."

They watched sailors come and go into the afternoon, though most stayed on the ship performing maintenance. Beckworth thought he recognized one man, but after further study, he shook his head. The build was right, and the movements were similar, as was the hair color, but when the sailor turned and he got a full view of his face, he had been wrong.

When Jamie noticed the next shift find a spot not far from them, Jamie nudged Beckworth. "Time to go. Same time tomorrow?"

"Sure. You have plans tonight?"

Jamie grinned. "There might be a lass in my future."

"Be careful, or you'll end up with a lass you'll trade the *Daphne* for."

"I won't be falling into the same trap as Finn."

"Or me?"

Jamie held his grin. "Don't jinx me, mate. It's not time to think about settling down."

Beckworth glanced up to where the sun discouraged the last of the clouds. "To be young and free. But, I guarantee, someday you'll be blindsided, then nothing else will matter."

Jamie chuckled. "We'll see. How are you keeping this secret from Stella? Seems to me you're walking a fine line."

Beckworth ran a hand through his hair, his focus on the ship they'd been watching. "Mary and Elizabeth will have her too busy with luncheons and garden parties to worry about me. She'll assume I'm catching up with old friends."

"That's one way not to feel guilty about the lying."

Beckworth didn't respond. How could he? Jamie wasn't wrong.

Jamie gripped his shoulder. "Sorry. I shouldn't have said that."

He shook his head. "No. You're right. It's the first time I've outright lied to her." He ran a hand through his hair again. "Even though she hasn't asked what I do during the day, I know in my heart I'm lying."

"With any luck, she'll never find out. Once we identify the ones in charge, the *Daphne*'s crew can follow them and see what we can learn. That will give you more time to spend with her. But be careful. She's a smart one."

"You have no idea."

6

___

Beckworth entered the manor and stood in the foyer. He expected voices, if not from Stella, then certainly from Bart or even from Eleanor chasing after the staff. Maybe Stella hadn't returned from Mary's yet.

Neither Templeton's butler nor Barrington had answered the door. He stalked to the study, poured two fingers of whiskey, and dropped into the leather chair behind the desk. He took a sip, laid his head back, and stared at the ceiling.

Barrington was driving Bart and Lincoln to their appointments at the Royal College of Surgeons before visiting the crews in the East End. Beckworth had been certain they'd be back by now. He drank the last of the whiskey in one swallow and got up to pour another.

He paced around the room. Something he rarely did. He thought better when he was stationary, but his head was a jumble of worry. He dreaded hearing Stella's voice as she searched for him upon her arrival from Hensley's. She'd want to know what he did with his day, and he had nothing to tell her. If he told her his cover story of going to the East End, she'd want specifics. Until Barrington returned, he wouldn't have that information.

He could say he'd visited with old friends in Hensley's network. No. If he told her that, she'd be suspicious that he might be involved in one of Hensley's missions. Of course, she'd be right, but not in the way she'd assume.

His bankers. That would be a better answer. He would have to spend several days meeting with all of them, so it wouldn't seem odd. Stella was a sharp businesswoman in her time period, but she ignored his business holdings in this era, so he doubted she'd give it much thought.

He dropped back in his seat. Lies. Building lies and breaking trust all to keep her in the dark about a simple mission. It didn't sit well, and he didn't know what to do about it. He could have said no and not involved himself in Hensley's machinations. But there were only a small handful of men who'd gotten close enough to McDuff and his smugglers to recognize them.

Jamie would need to run around-the-clock surveillance, which would be a burden on the men. If he wanted to remain part of the mission and assist with the assigned watches, he had to follow Hensley's orders. This was an opportunity to discover someone close to McDuff, and he couldn't simply sit around when he could be of help.

He'd just poured his third drink when someone knocked, and Barrington stuck his head in.

"It's bloody well time. Where have you been?" Beckworth pushed the barely touched third glass of whiskey aside.

Barrington, perceptive to Beckworth's various moods, stepped inside and closed the door behind him. He glanced at Beckworth's drink and poured one of his own before sitting in the chair in front of the desk. His slow perusal made Beckworth squirm.

"I just brought Libby back."

Beckworth stared at him and considered whether that was a good thing, then determined it likely wasn't. "Bringing her back from where?"

"The East End."

"You were there together?" Beckworth's voice rose. And while he didn't sound completely hysterical, it was higher pitched than he'd expected.

Barrington's lips quirked, but he managed to remain as stoic as ever. "Stella requested I take Libby to the East End after dropping off Bart and Lincoln at their appointment."

"Damn. Libby and Stella have become thick as thieves. Now, she'll tell Stella you were in the East End visiting the crews rather than me."

"Not necessarily. I dropped her off and gave her a specific spot where I would pick her up. I met with Davies, someone Libby stays away from."

"With good reason," Beckworth growled. "It's only been a day, and I'm at my wits' end."

"It should only take a day or two to identify McDuff's associates. After that, Jamie can have his sailors follow them. Davies is willing to provide a few of his watchers, if needed."

Beckworth finished the rest of his drink and relaxed into the chair. "That's something."

"Stella will return with a host of daytime invitations. Mary and Elizabeth will keep her so busy she won't have time to worry about what you're doing. Give her your full attention with the evening events, and before you know it, you'll be off the hook with Hensley."

He nodded. Libby wouldn't be able to confirm his whereabouts, and if he managed to convince Stella he was simply visiting old friends and dealing with estate business, he should soon see his way clear. He didn't like it, but he couldn't see any other choice. If McDuff was up to something in London, it was imperative that they discover what it was. He lived in America now, but his heart was still with England. How could he walk away from such a simple task? He sighed and wished they'd stayed at Waverly.

"So, tell me what the crews are up to."

After getting a rundown on the crews, which Beckworth would have done without being involved in Hensley's mission, he climbed the stairs to the second floor. He might as well prepare for an evening out. There was a high probability that Mary or Elizabeth had selected an engagement they'd talked Stella into. He stopped short, surprised to find Eleanor at the top of the stairs.

"When did you get back?" Beckworth asked. If Eleanor was home, then Stella should be as well. Why hadn't she come looking for him?

"A couple of hours now."

"I've been here for half that time and haven't seen or heard you."

She wiped a hand across her forehead. "You wouldn't have unless you went down to the kitchen. The staff hasn't performed a proper inventory for some time, and since I'll be here for a couple of weeks, Mrs. Evans asked if I could assist her. We have the entire staff put to the task. I would have had Libby help if Stella hadn't released her from service for the day."

While listening to Eleanor carry on, Beckworth focused on Stella and where she'd been while he'd been drowning his guilt in the study. A nap was the likely explanation. He couldn't fault her. A day entertaining noble women while trying to assimilate would be exhausting for anyone.

"Everything go alright today?" He might as well prepare for any grievances Stella might have bottled up.

She gave him a curious look, then crossed her arms over her chest, a slight smile curving her lips. "Did you expect the ladies to run screaming to their carriages once they got a whiff of Stella's boldness?"

He sighed. Of course, he worried. He wanted them to accept Stella, boldness and all. "Just tell me."

"Well, aren't we in a snit. Everything went smoothly. They're all fascinated by the viscount's new paramour. The fact that Elizabeth has taken her under her wing makes her rather untouchable." Her brows furrowed. "And you're perfectly aware of that."

He wasn't surprised that the troops had fully surrounded Stella. For now, she could do no wrong in their eyes. He was grateful, yet somehow, Eleanor's tone made him feel like the villain.

Maybe he could use a nap. "I'm sorry if I'm coming across as a doting husband. I just want her to be happy."

Eleanor relaxed and placed a hand on his arm. "Stella might seem like a handful at times, but she only wants the same for you."

"I know." He gave her a rueful grin. "Thank you for helping me tread my way through. These are new waters for me."

She chuckled as she descended the stairs. Her amusement grew more robust as she gave her laughter full rein. "I'll do my best, but I'm afraid the waves have reached higher than you know."

He stared after her. What the bloody hell did that mean? She'd given him a moment of peace before ripping it away.

Damn woman.

He stared at the door to the bedroom for a moment, then remembered it was his domain as much as it was Stella's and burst in.

Stella and Libby were standing next to the bed. Dozens of dresses covered it to the point he couldn't see the bedcover beneath.

"What's all this?" Beckworth asked when the women turned to him.

"We're deciding which dresses I should wear to which events." Stella laid down the one she'd been holding and waved toward the writing desk. Dozens of invitations were spread across it. "I have to admit, it's somewhat daunting at the number of them, and from what Mary says, I should expect even more after I've attended a couple of the parties. I want to make sure I have enough to select from so the women don't start gossiping about seeing me in the same dress all the time."

"I think she has enough for the first two weeks." Libby picked up two of the dresses. "If we're here any longer, she'll need a handful more."

He leaned against a dresser and crossed his arms over his chest. This was one of his favorite pastimes—ensuring Stella wore only the finest dresses. In some ways, he was flaunting his money, and perhaps to women in Stella's era, it might seem misogynistic, as if he were dressing her like a doll. But none of that mattered to him.

He wanted Stella to fit in. A properly fitted dress would make her feel confident among the aristocracy, which was filled with snobbish women. A single wrong statement could spread like wildfire, with an attempt to blackball her from further parties. Her friendship with Elizabeth would go a long way in preventing that from happening, but Stella was bold, and with being an American in this century, some of the nobles would consider her primitive, if not downright savage. She deserved the best he could afford to ease her moment in the sun. Besides, he loved buying her dresses, mostly because he loved the imagery of being able to personally remove them afterward.

"I have a few more dresses being made." Beckworth reviewed the invitations spread across the writing desk. He tapped the one in the upper corner. "I see we received the duke's invitation for tomorrow night. I wasn't sure it would arrive in time. A new dress, specifically for his ball, will arrive in the morning. The others should be here in the next day or two."

Stella strolled over to him and placed a kiss on his cheek. "What color is it?"

He grinned. "You'll find out soon enough." He glanced at Libby, who was returning the clothing to the dressing room. "I take it you'll discuss the final decisions with my valet?"

"Of course," Libby said. "At least for the next two or three parties. Stella might change her mind on the others once the new dresses arrive. We'd already selected a dress for the ball, but I'll update Jeffries once the new gown arrives."

"So, how was your day?" Stella looked at his jacket and breeches. "You didn't ride all day, did you?"

He was hoping talk of dresses would skirt this topic, but he should have known better. "I visited with one of the crews after my ride."

Libby's brow rose as she stepped out of the dressing room to collect more dresses. "I was in the East End all day. I didn't see you with Chester or his crew."

"That's because I went to see Davies. It's been some time since I've had a good sit-down with him." He gave Stella a cheeky grin. "I thought Stella might want to visit Chester with me."

"I absolutely want to see Chester and Katherine. And the others, as well." Stella dropped into the chair in front of the writing desk and stared at the invitations. "Based on the number of engagements, it doesn't appear I'll be getting much of a break during the days or evenings."

"We're at the peak of the season here. After the duke's ball, the parties will start to slow, but there will still be plenty to keep both of us occupied."

"I was hoping to do some sightseeing while here. You know, Westminster Abbey..." She paused, her head tilting to one side. "Well, I'm not sure what else. Most of the places tourists want to see in London, like Windsor Castle and the Tower of London, aren't available during this time period. Maybe driving by them is enough."

"I'll arrange for something in between your parties." Beckworth removed his cravat and dropped it over the back of a chair. "Libby, why don't you see if Eleanor needs help with the inventory. I'd like to spend some time with Stella before we have to prepare for the evening."

Libby finished putting the last dress away and strode to the door. He didn't miss the wink she gave Stella. "Do you want me to send up some food and wine? You'll want to eat a bit before you leave."

"Yes, thank you."

He waited until the door closed before he pulled Stella up from the chair and hugged her. "I've missed you." His kiss started off as a light nibble, but when she wrapped her arms around him and tickled his ear with her finger, the kiss deepened until he picked her up and tossed her on the bed.

Then it was all giggles and intimate touches until they were both naked. Neither of them heard the knock on the door when Libby returned with a tray that she'd left by the door.

And for an hour or two, his duplicity was washed away.

7

———

The following morning, Stella stirred and swept her hand across the bed, but it was blocked by a hard, warm body. She smiled and rolled over as an arm snaked out and pulled her close. She breathed deeply, absorbing Beckworth's earthy scent as he kissed her temple.

"Good morning, luv." His voice was husky from sleep, which made her wonder what time it was. He was an early riser, even when they spent a portion of the morning in bed. In Baywood, she would wake to find him reading next to her, a carafe of coffee not too far away.

"No horseback riding today," she mumbled. She ran a hand over his hip and stopped, lifting her head.

There was coffee somewhere in this room.

Beckworth chuckled and sat up, the bedcovers falling to his lap as he ran his hands through his ash-blond hair. "Let me get you a cup."

She watched him leave the bed as he padded naked across the carpeted floor to the pot he'd left by the fire.

"When did the coffee arrive? Did Libby leave it?"

He nodded as he filled two mugs to carry back to bed.

She groaned as she fluffed their pillows, giving them a soft backrest. He handed her both mugs before slipping back into bed. They savored the coffee as it cleared their sleep-muddled heads. After several minutes, Beckworth broke their companionable silence.

"What did you think of your first party at Lord Percy's?"

She gave it some consideration before shrugging. "It wasn't too different than the large dinner party Mary had when I was last in London."

"I was hoping your first official event would have been more similar to what you might expect at tonight's grand affair. The crowd at the duke's ball will be much larger. But Lord Percy is a man of influence, so when you get an invite, even to his dinner party, which is an accurate description, it's rare for someone to decline. He'll remember who was missing. I think the invite list was smaller since his young bride is new at hosting parties. I believe Mary told you that his first wife, who died a couple of years ago, was masterful with a manor full of guests."

"His new wife is rather young. Weren't there children from his first wife?"

He snorted. "Three, if memory serves. One boy and two girls. They're all adults now. I think he wants more. Before you know it, the parties will be larger again."

"That's because his new bride is barely an adult. I can't imagine her having enough experience with anything larger than a dinner party. What is it with old men and young brides?" She gave him a quirky smile. "Before I know it, you'll be searching for someone a bit younger."

He took her mug and set both on the nearby nightstand before turning to her. "Some old men have vanity issues. More than women, I think."

She glanced at her hands, thinking about his words. "I think it comes down to love."

"How so?"

"Well, I never met the Earl of Hereford, but from what Maire says, he'd lost his wife decades earlier, before the earl adopted Ethan off the streets of London. From what Ethan shared, the earl never considered remarrying, despite having no children. How much more prestige can one get than being an earl or duke? Lord Percy married barely a year after his wife's death, then no doubt, finagled a handsome dowry for his new bride. Yet, the earl lived a long time, never able to replace his first wife when he could easily have gotten a new one." She shrugged. "I think the common denominator is love."

Beckworth eyed her, and she felt her cheeks flush. He was the only man she'd ever been with who could make her blush after the months they'd been together.

"Maybe Percy married his first wife for a business arrangement, and his second chance was because of love."

Stella choked out a laugh. "A young girl, barely of voting age in my time, falling in love with what? A sixty-year-old man, when there are plenty of young, wealthy bachelors out there. I suppose it can happen, but..."

She didn't have a chance to finish when Beckworth pulled her down and threw the covers over them.

"Let's not talk about old men and their sensitivities over their eventual demise. You'll need your energy for this evening, and I have no doubt Mary and Eleanor have plans for you today. Let's not waste the morning."

Stella sighed, wishing they could have the whole day together. Other than riding, what else did he have to do? Before she could consider the question further, Beckworth gave her breast a gentle squeeze before running his hand down her side, over her hip, and then between her legs. Then she didn't think about anything at all.

Stella tugged at the bodice of her dark sage-colored gown, then ran her hands over the lace-accented skirt before reaching for her opal necklace as she glanced around the ballroom. Her eyes bulged at the sight, having never seen anything so opulent.

"You're not nervous, are you?" Beckworth's warm breath caressed her neck as he leaned closer, a wicked smile on his handsome face.

"What are you up to?"

He chuckled. "Nothing. It's rare to find an astonished expression on your beautiful face."

She tapped his shoulder with her lace fan, then glanced at the fancy accessory and laughed. "I can't believe I just did that. All I need are smelling salts, and I'll fit right in with all the paraphernalia any proper lady should carry with her." She straightened her shoulders. "For tonight, it appears the fan will be all I need."

He put her arm through his and guided her down the steps. "I think you're perfect, but I understand how overwhelming a ball of this size can be for the first time. The fashion alone could make one marvel all evening."

"I should have known fashion would be the first thing on your mind. So, where do we start? I don't see Elizabeth or Mary."

"I thought I saw Hensley in the crowd when we first walked in, but I don't see him now. Mary is most likely with her circle of friends from the Cotswolds. She's known to circulate more widely at the various parties and balls, but for this particular one, she usually hovers with her local friends from Bristol. Elizabeth, considering her stature as Dame Ellingsworth, will be with Agatha and Lord Osborne. I think I caught sight of the Melvilles, too, but let's steer our own course for now."

Stella wouldn't argue. She shouldn't have disregarded Beckworth's and Mary's excitement for this particular ball, believing them to be too enamored by it all. She'd been dead wrong. AJ never mentioned a party so lavish, but she might not have attended anything of this scale.

From what Mary said, the duke's ball was one of the most anticipated of the season, and anyone who was anyone expected an invitation. Elizabeth had seen to theirs, which probably explained why Beckworth had received one so promptly. Though Stella had a feeling all Beckworth had to do was send a letter, and an invitation would have been on its way. She might be wrong, but she didn't think so. Beckworth had friends in the most unexpected of places.

They greeted a half-dozen couples, constantly dragged into conversations about the war, fashion, and sometimes a little gossip. Stella held onto those tidbits to share with Mary and Elizabeth at their luncheon the following day. It wasn't often she had rumors to share. Not that she didn't have a rowdy tale or two to share from Libby regarding these events. One could always count on the staff to have the juiciest stories that always ended with Mary quickly fanning herself while Elizabeth howled with laughter.

"Let's see if we can find someone in one of the less crowded rooms." Beckworth snagged two glasses of champagne from a passing server and handed one to Stella. "If I see anyone I know along the way, I'll keep the introductions short."

"Gee, I thought you knew everyone."

He nudged her shoulder. "As you often say—funny."

She grinned. "I have no problem meeting people, but you need to tell me if they're important before greeting them. As hard as it is to believe, there's only so much information I can store in my head in one evening. I'd prefer to keep the important stuff in there."

"Fair enough." He chuckled as he glanced around, sliding his arm around her waist. "How about every time I squeeze your waist, it indicates you're about to meet an important person."

She leaned in, her lips gently brushing his ear. "You just want to keep touching me."

"Keep that up, and I'll have to lock us in an empty drawing room."

Her laugh was lusty. "Now you're talking." She nudged him back. "Thank you for erasing the nerves."

He gave her a long look. "Anything for you, luv."

She shook her head, and then her face brightened as she steered Beckworth toward the approaching couple. "Lord and Lady Melville. How good to see you again."

"You look lovely, my dear." Lord Edgar Melville kissed her hand, then shook Beckworth's. "I'm glad you made it. Hensley found himself a competent opponent at chess. They're currently tied at one game each and are now battling to the end."

"Really," Beckworth responded after kissing Flora's hand. "Perhaps we should go cheer him on."

"I was thinking the same thing."

"Why don't you both go?" Flora said. "Stella and I have other interests."

Beckworth glanced at Stella, who nodded. She wouldn't have minded watching the chess match, but she promised Beckworth she'd behave like the lady of his manor, and that's what she'd do. "I'll be in good hands with Flora." She took the woman's arm, and as they strolled away, she gave Beckworth one last look over her shoulder. His worried expression made her lift a brow. How much trouble could she get into at a ball?

Once the men had melted into the crowd, Flora steered Stella back toward the crowd in the ballroom.

"Elizabeth is holding court across the room from the musicians." Flora nodded at a couple of women and stopped long enough for quick introductions before moving on again. "She doesn't like shouting over them, but then who does?"

"Wouldn't a drawing room be quieter?" Stella nodded to a younger couple Beckworth had introduced her to earlier. They didn't seem high on his list of friends, but they'd seemed nice enough.

"Yes, but then she wouldn't be seen by enough people. It's not that she needs to be sought out by so many, but one must keep up appearances and their reputation."

Stella never had the impression Elizabeth cared for such things, but she'd yet to spend much time with her in London. She supposed what one said and did at their country estates stayed at their country estates.

"There you are, my dear." Elizabeth moved away from two women, who Stella guessed were a mother and daughter. "Sorry, Eloise, but you have all the information I know about Lord Hutton. I still think you'd be better off with Lord Fillmore, but that's a decision you'll need to make."

Elizabeth took Stella's arm and moved her and Flora toward the front of the ballroom. "I think I've had enough socializing for the moment. That woman can talk until it's time for the carriages. And I don't know why she bothered asking my opinion on the best match for her daughter when she's never listened to a thing I've said before."

"Well, she might have to this time," Flora said as they worked their way through the crowd. She stopped long enough to unfold her fan and cover her mouth. She leaned over so only Elizabeth and Stella could hear. "I have it on good authority that Lord Hutton has already made a proposal to Lord Dorsey for his oldest daughter's hand."

"Dorsey, really?" Elizabeth seemed surprised, then she shook her head. "Hutton must want that country estate."

"That's what Edgar said." Flora stopped long enough to grab a glass of champagne, and Stella gave the server her empty glass.

She was tempted to grab another one, but it would be a long night, and she needed to pace herself.

The threesome made it to the hallway, where it wasn't quite as crowded, and Stella sucked in the cooler air. They were almost to one of the drawing rooms when there was a commotion behind them.

She turned as a large group surged toward them. Flora's arm was bumped, forcing champagne to splash from her glass. Stella attempted to step out of the way, but droplets sprayed over her dress. Then she heard Elizabeth gasp.

When Stella turned to her, Elizabeth was holding a hand over her neck.

"Someone took my necklace." Her face was pale. "Someone shoved me, and now it's gone." Her voice was becoming shrill.

"Are you sure it didn't fall on the floor?" Stella pushed the women back and scanned the area, which was difficult with the crush of the crowd.

Elizabeth shook her head. "I felt fingers on the back of my neck." She dramatically shivered. "I must have frozen because the next thing I knew, I was jostled, and now my precious necklace is gone. It was a priceless heirloom."

Her friend's devastation was plain to see, but she wasn't sure what to do about it.

"I saw it."

The women turned to find a middle-aged gentleman with overly long sideburns wiping what looked like champagne from his shirt. It might have been from Flora's glass, but several people had been bumped, so it could have been from anyone. "The man was quick, but his hand gripped a silver and jeweled item before he stuffed it in his pocket. It happened in a flash, but I saw what I saw."

"Which way did he go?" Stella asked as she began searching the crowd.

"Down the hallway toward the back of the manor."

"Stay here," Stella shouted to the women and stormed briskly down the hall.

She shoved people out of the way, shouting "Sorry, sorry, sorry," as she stopped every so often to stand on tiptoes in an attempt to catch sight of the man in question. She'd been watching Flora and her glass of champagne, trying to dodge out of the way, and hadn't seen the man at all.

The crowd was thinning as she traveled farther away from the ballroom. She knew she was on the right track when flustered guests peered down the hall in the direction she was headed. Was it the thief?

Then she saw him, or someone who might be the thief. He wasn't moving very fast, but he kept his head down as he maintained an even pace. She quickened her steps as she followed. Would one of the London crews be daring enough to steal jewelry from around someone's neck during a ball? Had there been more than one thief? Chester, who ran one of the larger crews, would never do anything so risky. At least, she didn't think so.

She ignored the stares of the men and women she passed, ready to break out into a run. When he turned for what Stella thought might be the solarium, and the foot traffic became scarce, she decided it was time to call for help, knowing she should have done it sooner. But what if he had a weapon? People could get hurt, or maybe he wasn't the thief. Either way, now was the time to stop him and confirm it one way or another. She was close enough that if she called out, he shouldn't be able to get away.

Four men entered the hallway, headed in their direction.

The possible thief slowed and stuffed his hands in his pockets. His head was still down.

"Stop that man!" Stella broke into a run, swearing at her shoes, which started to pinch. "He's a thief!"

The four men glanced around, and Stella rolled her eyes as she gained on the man. Before she could reach him, the four men suddenly understood the warning. It was too late. The man bent low as he picked up speed and, leading with his shoulder, plowed into them like they were bowling pins.

While the four men weren't able to stop the thief, they had managed to slow him down. Stella grabbed for his coat, but as her fingers brushed an edge, she tripped over one of the men. She landed on all fours and, after two attempts, managed to lift her skirts high enough to get back on her feet. She raced after the thief, no longer caring who was watching or that she wasn't acting like a proper English lady of the manor.

The thief ran through the solarium and out the door to the back patio. He flew down the steps with Stella hot on his trail. When he reached the dew-laden grass of a classic English garden, he stopped and turned.

Stella zeroed in on his face, somewhat shocked by what she saw. Though she didn't know the man, she understood the leer.

She reached into her pocket with one hand while pulling up her dress with the other so she didn't trip down the stairs. The man waited for her, but his eyes bulged when she yanked out her dagger.

He turned to run. With a last burst of speed, Stella leaped. She snagged a leg and held on. The unexpected attack threw the man off balance, and they tumbled onto the lawn.

He had size and weight on his side, but she swung out with her dagger and heard a quick intake of breath. A fist slammed into the side of her head, and it sent her reeling. She reached out one last time, but once again, his coat slipped through her fingers.

Her head hurt like a mother, and when her breath returned, she could only watch the man flee into the darkness. Three other men raced past her as they chased after him. While they disappeared into the night, Stella struggled to get her feet underneath her before she was suddenly lifted up and spun around. She grabbed her head.

"Don't do that."

The dagger was stripped from her hand.

"What the bloody hell were you thinking? You could have gotten yourself killed or stabbed."

She heaved, gasping for breath, her head pounding, but managed to glance up into Beckworth's angry and worried face.

Concern overruled his irritation as he shoved the knife into an inside pocket before he held her face in his hands. They were gentle as he took in every inch of her. When his hand moved over the right side of her head, she winced and pulled back.

"Ouch."

"Alright. Alright. Let's get you back inside, or at least to the patio so you can sit and catch your breath."

She was pulled tight against him in a bear hug she couldn't possibly escape from. His cheek rested on the top of her head, and she wrapped her arms around his waist, turning her head to lean her left cheek against the security of his chest.

"If I'd lost you to a pickpocket, I'd hunt down every crew member until I found the one who did it. I might do that anyway. I know the necklace that was stolen and how important it was to Elizabeth, but you should never have taken it upon yourself to run recklessly into danger."

"No," she managed to spit out before his grip tightened.

"I love you, Stella, but you scare me every time you do something so foolhardy."

She pulled back from him. "I don't think he belonged to a crew."

Beckworth pushed her to arm's length and read her face. His anger over her actions might be returning, but he knew her well enough to listen to her. He might not believe what she had to say, but he'd give her the chance to speak.

"Go on. What do you mean he's not crew? How could you possibly know that?"

She shook her head, then thought better of it as she held a hand to the sore spot.

"I don't know, and I know you're going to find it hard to believe. After being on the *Daphne Marie*, living among sailors, and watching for smugglers in all those pubs and inns while searching for McDuff—well, I can't put my finger on any one thing. Not at the moment. Something might come to me later. Assuming I don't have a concussion or a brain aneurysm. Maybe it's just a headache, but I feel like my head might explode."

"Stella. Just for this one moment, can you please say it without all the preamble?"

She stared at him. Dim light leaked from the outside torches, and it darkened his cornflower-blue eyes to a midnight blue. Deep lines marred his forehead in worry. She sucked in a breath and straightened, though it made her head pound more.

"There was something about him that seemed different yet familiar, and I can't explain it any better right now. But the minute he ran, my first thought was 'sailor'."

8

———

Stella couldn't stop the shivers. She'd been in this predicament before after Cheval's death. Shock was setting in after chasing the thief and their brief struggle. The chilled night air wasn't helping, and she didn't have a wrap. The constant throb in her head was getting worse, and she was irritated with herself for losing the man. The whole combination made for an uncomfortable stew.

"You're freezing." Beckworth never failed to look out for her comfort. He helped her from the chair and pushed her toward the French doors that led to the solarium.

The warmth embraced her, and she instinctively turned toward the roaring flames in the hearth. Flora and Mary, huddled close to the fire, offered comfort to Elizabeth, who held a hand to her neck, her fingers in constant motion as if searching for the missing necklace.

A footman brought a tea service, but Elizabeth, as forlorn as she might have been over the stolen necklace, shooed him away. "I need something stronger. Bring me gin."

The footman looked around, as if someone had to approve giving a distraught woman alcohol, when a tall man with gray hair, a long face, and ire in his gaze, nodded to the footman. The young man all but ran to the bar trolley on the other side of the room to do the older man's bidding.

Stella assumed the older gentleman must be the duke, whose beautiful ball had been diminished by the theft. Yet, music still played, and dozens of muffled voices could be heard in the hallway. Perhaps the ball was still in progress. Many of the guests witnessed her pushing her way through the crowd, but only a handful would have seen her running and then jumping on the thief.

She snorted. Who was she kidding? The gossip would have burned through the party like a short grass wildfire, stoking the macabre need to stay and blather on about it.

No doubt, the talk would turn to how the thief was allowed in, why didn't anyone notice he was a thief, and what was the world coming to? Nothing that wouldn't have been repeatedly discussed in her own timeline, though it always seemed more of a scandal when the rich were affected.

The duke greeted several men who'd made their way to the solarium. She recognized Hensley and Lord Melville, but not the other three men. They found chairs on the opposite side of the room, except for the duke, who took a moment to sit next to Elizabeth. Stella couldn't hear the soft murmurs but assumed the duke was offering sympathy and reassurances.

Beckworth pushed her toward the group and brought a chair over, placing it next to Mary.

"Oh, my dear. Are you alright?" Mary asked, turning away from Elizabeth. She gave Stella a thorough perusal and shook her head. "You don't look alright. Your gown has a few stains, but I don't see any rips or tears." Then she narrowed in on Stella's face. "You've injured yourself. I can tell. Is it a leg or foot injury? No, I didn't see you limp. What happened?"

Stella reached for the side of her face. She'd probably have a huge bruise by morning. "The thief might have gotten a solid hit in, but I'm fine. Just a bit of a headache."

The duke turned to her. The ire still lit his gaze, but it softened as he gave her a thorough appraisal. The intensity of his gaze made her squirm. When Beckworth handed her a whiskey, she downed it in a single swallow, then held up the glass for another.

The duke's brow went up. "I must say, I've only heard about the resolve of the Americans, but I can't say I've ever seen it. Not until this evening. If I might ask, what made you run after the thief?"

Beckworth handed her the refilled glass, and she sipped the whiskey as she considered the duke's question. It would be awkward to ask why none of the men standing around in their finely tailored clothing did anything to chase down the thief. Then she remembered her promise to Beckworth to be the proper lady. It wasn't difficult with him hovering over her.

She finally shrugged a shoulder and gave him as much truth as she could. "A gentleman standing next to us saw the whole thing. He mentioned the man's description..." she paused at the slight fib, knowing that wasn't sufficient reason to chase someone. She glanced at Elizabeth and steered back to the truth. "Elizabeth was so upset about the loss of her irreplaceable necklace. She's been such a good friend to me since I arrived in England, and I hated seeing her so distressed. I didn't think twice about it. I thought if I could find him and point him out to the men, but everything happened so fast."

She ended her story there. Men were particularly good at creating answers to their own questions, especially if led down the right path. Not that women couldn't do the same thing, but men had a tendency, especially in this era, to underestimate a woman's resolve—American or otherwise.

She doubted anyone other than the three men who'd chased

the thief into the night had seen her leap on the man, though it could be passed off as her simply stumbling on the stairs. It was even less plausible that they noticed the dagger, and if they had seen a flash of the silver blade, they'd more likely assume it belonged to the thief.

She'd nicked the man. There was no doubt blood had been on the dagger, and she was thankful Beckworth had the common sense she'd lacked in hiding it. She gave Beckworth a side glance and caught the slight nod of approval of her accounting.

The duke also looked to Beckworth before turning back to her. "Well, I shouldn't be surprised that Beckworth would have a woman by his side as daring as himself. I owe you a debt of gratitude."

"For what? I didn't catch the thief."

"No. But three of my security are on the hunt and wouldn't have been if you hadn't slowed the thief down."

"Have they caught the man?" she asked.

He shook his head. "They haven't returned yet. But either way, Elizabeth is an old and fond friend, and I can't thank you enough for looking out for her interests. If there's anything I can ever do to repay the favor, you only need to ask."

"It seems the party is still going on." She felt Beckworth flinch through the hand he rested on her shoulder, but she ignored him.

She didn't expect the warm smile the duke gave her. "Of course. The gossip will get out whether I shut the ball down or not. And though a few did leave, most have chosen to remain to make the best of the evening."

"Part of the English stoicism," she mused.

"That's exactly right. Now, again, if there's anything I can do for you, either this evening or in the future, don't hesitate to call upon me."

She nodded her head and tried not to wince, but must have failed.

"Were you injured?" The duke waited, and when all he received was a slight shrug in response, he looked to Beckworth.

"A slight wallop to the side of the head." Beckworth gave her shoulder a slight squeeze. "Nothing a headache tonic won't help."

The duke snapped his fingers, and a footman appeared out of thin air.

"Yes, sir."

"Have Mrs. Alders bring a headache tonic immediately."

"Yes, sir, straight away."

When the footman rushed away, the duke turned back to Stella. "I'm sorry your first time to one of my balls turned out to be such a dreadful experience. I hope you won't think too harshly of me."

Stella could play the game as well as the rest of them. "Not at all. Beckworth and I were thrilled to be invited to such a lovely event. I would never blame you for something like this." She rubbed her head more for theatrics than to soothe the dull ache. "The war is making life difficult for so many, but I have no doubt England shall prevail." Nothing like having advanced knowledge of the eventual outcome.

"I appreciate your understanding. Now, I must speak with Hensley." He murmured a few words to Elizabeth, who gripped his hand before releasing it. He strode over to the men and accepted a drink as they grouped close for their discussions.

"I'll be with the men," Beckworth whispered in her ear. "I want to hear what they have to say."

Once he'd moved away, Elizabeth gave her a stern look. "You didn't have to do that for me."

"Of course, I did." Stella paused when a dark-haired woman

with light streaks of gray stepped next to her. She must be Mrs. Alders.

"Are you the one who needs the headache tonic?" she asked.

Stella wasn't sure how the woman knew she was the one who needed it unless she noticed the grass stains on her dress. Or maybe it was her twitching eye. *When had that started?* The footman probably just said the red-haired woman. Either way, the woman appeared sharp.

"Yes." Stella took the glass, swallowed it down all at once, then placed it on the tray Mrs.Alders was still holding. She wiped her mouth, remembering to pull out her handkerchief first, and grinned at the other women. "Sorry. I wasn't sure if it was going to taste bad, so I decided it was best not to stop."

The women chuckled, and Stella glanced up at Mrs. Alders. "I suppose that wasn't proper, but I didn't see any reason for you to make another trip just to retrieve the glass."

Mrs. Alders seemed taken aback but recovered well. "Well, yes, thank you, my lady." She bent lower and whispered, "It does have a bitter aftertaste." She stood straight, nodded with a slight bow, and returned to wherever she'd come from.

"She's right." Stella rolled her tongue around, but the bitter taste was still there. "I think I need a drink."

She glanced around, not seeing the footman, then stood and marched to the bar trolley. She was probably bending societal rules, but Beckworth usually fetched his own drink, and she wasn't in the mood to wait. Let the men talk. Beckworth could handle the flak. She glanced over the bottles, lifting the stoppers to sniff before she found a scotch worth trying. While she poured two fingers, she ignored the women's chatter and focused on the men.

"Littlefield isn't doing enough about this, I tell you."

Stella didn't recognize the voice, so it must have been one of the men who'd followed Hensley into the room.

"I suppose you're right," the duke said. "But the constables don't have the resources, even with the watchmen, to cover the number of parties that occur this time of year."

"Have the thefts only been at night?" Beckworth asked.

"Yes. And, fortunately, there's only been one other." It was the first man who'd spoken. "It might appear that I'm overreacting, but two thefts in three days and both enacted in the same manner...I mean, it seems too coincidental to ignore."

"Alfred is right," Hensley chimed in. "Unfortunately, I don't have any resources to assist, though I can send a few letters and see if anyone has returned to London."

Stella picked up her glass and returned to the women without sneaking a single glance at the men. She felt Beckworth's steely gaze on her, most likely wondering what she was up to. As if she were up to something all the time.

She hadn't been seated for more than a few minutes when a footman stopped by Elizabeth. "Your carriage is here, Dame Ellingsworth."

"Oh, thank you." She got up, and once she'd straightened her gown, her hand went to her neck before she dropped it, her face masked in sorrow.

Stella's heart went out to her friend. The necklace had been important to her. Someone special must have given it to her. Maybe her husband. Or perhaps it had been an heirloom from her mother. Would the thief sell it right away, or would he wait until the constables or watchmen gave up the hunt? Maybe he'd jump on a ship, since she was positive the man had been a sailor. If he wasn't one now, he'd been one at some point in his life. And she'd guess, he'd been a sailor for a long time. He could try selling the necklace in France or Spain. Maybe he only had to go as far as the west coast of England, where no one would be wiser. Or Ireland. She'd be interested in Beckworth's thoughts.

"Stella? Did you hear me, my dear?"

Stella glanced up to see Elizabeth standing over her.

"I'm sorry. I guess that tonic hasn't started working yet."

Elizabeth gave her a long look before placing a hand on her shoulder. "Thank you for trying to help. It means a great deal to me."

Stella placed her hand over Elizabeth's. "That's what friends are for."

Mary and Flora stood, and Stella noticed the men walking toward them. Their meeting was over. Mary slipped an arm through Elizabeth's. "Our plans were to attend Eloise's tea party tomorrow, but if you'd rather, we can have a quiet lunch and tea at the manor. I'm happy to make our apologies."

"I'd prefer that. I doubt I'll be ready for much company tomorrow. And with no parties to attend in the evening, a day with close friends would suit me."

"Then I'll arrange something for the afternoon," Mary suggested. "That way, you can have a long lie-in."

The two women continued to murmur on their way to the front door, and Stella's thoughts went back to the thief. She'd seen his face. If she only knew a sketch artist. Did the police use them during this time period? Another question for Beckworth.

———

Beckworth helped Stella into the carriage and sat next to her on the bench. She was in a pensive mood, her eyes unfocused, with little lines forming across her forehead. When she laid her head on his shoulder, he took her hand and stroked it with his thumb.

He considered conversation but sensed her headache was keeping her quiet. Although that wouldn't be enough to stop her from replaying the events of the evening over and over, wondering if she could have done more. Whenever she overcame a dangerous altercation, she tended to go quiet. She preferred to internalize her emotions rather than discuss them with someone—even with him.

Talk would be useless until she was ready, so he did the only thing he could do. He would comfort her through physical contact, letting her know he was there for her whenever she required it.

It was a short ride home, and she didn't move until Barrington opened the carriage door. She placed a kiss on Beckworth's cheek and exited the coach.

When she reached the front door, she waited patiently for Barrington to open it, and then she thanked him as she entered. Beckworth caught up with her as she approached the stairs to the second floor.

"I need a few minutes with Barrington, and then I'll be up."

She nodded, and as soon as she disappeared, Libby rushed into the foyer.

"You're back early. I was just finishing dinner."

"There was an incident at the ball." Beckworth gave Barrington and Libby a brief overview of the events before Libby raced up the stairs.

Barrington followed Beckworth to the study and closed the door behind him. After pouring them both drinks, he asked, "What can I do to assist?"

"I'll need you to watch over Stella while I go to the East End."

Barrington sat back with a frown. "You think one of the crews did this? That's rather daring, even for Chester's crew."

"I wouldn't have thought it possible, but I've been away from the crews for too long." He considered mentioning that Stella thought it was a sailor, but he had a hard time believing it. Best to check things out first. "I'll meet with the crew leaders. This was the second theft from a society party in three days. An investigator has been assigned."

Barrington snorted. "Only after two thefts? I assume it's getting more attention since it's aristocrats being targeted."

"The duke is quite upset, so yes, the crews will be under more surveillance. They need to be told."

"Will you tell Stella what you're doing?"

"There's no reason not to. She'll want to know if the crews were involved, and if I don't provide an answer, she'll go looking for one. Mary is planning a late lunch for Elizabeth. Stella will want to attend."

"I'll make sure she gets there."

The two men let silence fill the room as they finished their whiskey. Fifteen minutes later, the two parted ways in the foyer. Barrington disappeared down a hall that would take him down to the kitchen while Beckworth climbed the stairs.

Libby was brushing Stella's hair, and their conversation stopped when he entered. Neither appeared guilty, though they were quite capable of schooling their emotions when necessary. However, this time, he assumed they were simply discussing the night in more detail.

Stella was already wrapped in her robe, and what little makeup she'd applied for the evening had been washed clean.

"Shall I call for your valet?" Libby asked.

He shook his head. "Not tonight. And I have an early day tomorrow."

Libby nodded, squeezed Stella's arm, then closed the door behind her.

"How's the headache?" he asked.

"The tonic helped a bit, but I took an ibuprofen, so it should be gone in another hour." She stood and helped him with his jacket.

"I can call for Jeffries."

"Nonsense. The poor man is probably asleep already."

"That poor man is probably happy to have someone to serve."

"He can have you all to himself tomorrow."

Beckworth sat in a chair to remove his boots. "A constable will want to interview you tomorrow."

Stella tugged on one of the boots. "Why didn't they ask me questions while we were at the duke's?"

"They're more sensitive when dealing with the aristocrats, and with you being a woman, they didn't want to upset you."

She barked out a laugh. "How demure am I supposed to be for this interview?" She lost her balance when the boot slipped off his foot but recovered before he could catch her. "Do I meet them at their office or station?" She waved a hand. "Whatever they call it."

"The inspector will want to meet you here at ten."

She set the boot aside and tugged on the second one.

"Isn't that making your headache worse?"

She dropped the second boot next to the first. "A little. Let's get those pants off you. I need to cuddle."

He grinned as he unbuttoned his pants while she worked on removing his waistcoat and cravat. They worked in symmetry until he was naked and they were both in bed, snuggling under the covers.

"How's Elizabeth? I didn't get a chance to speak with her." Beckworth couldn't imagine the sorrow of her husband's tragic death that the dowager was reliving.

"Not well. Mary is canceling the luncheon we were supposed to attend tomorrow. She'll host a small gathering with close friends, so Elizabeth won't spend the whole day alone."

"I did hear that part. Barrington will be available to take you."

"What will this inspector want to know?"

"Just tell him the events from your perspective." He gave her a quick squeeze and kissed her ear. "I imagine there will be a great deal of frowning when you tell him you chased the thief."

She tensed for a moment. "What about my dagger?"

"I gave the dagger to Barrington after you were safely in the coach. There was blood on it."

"I thought I grazed him when he flinched."

"I'm going to ask you to modify your answer to the inspector on that point."

"You don't want them to know I attacked first."

He felt the giggle she held in, but all he could do was close his eyes, wishing he'd never taught her the proper use of daggers. The fact she'd had no problem making the first move worried him. "It would be more believable if you reached for it when the thief stopped and you were concerned he might attack you. It's probably best if you don't mention the blood."

She went quiet as she considered it and was probably revising her story. After a couple of minutes, she nodded. "I can do that."

He kissed her temple. "Of course, you can." He hesitated, then said, "I'll be going to the East End tomorrow." He braced himself, expecting her to want to go with him.

"You're going to talk to the crews?"

"Yes. I expect whoever did this is either new to one of the crews and is trying to make a name for himself, or there's a new crew in town." He waited for Stella to repeat her assertion that the thief was a sailor. She didn't.

"Let me know what they say."

"Of course."

She went silent as sleep took her. Beckworth stared into the dimly lit room as the fire faded to embers. He couldn't shake the sliver of foreboding that touched him. He'd need to keep a close eye on her.

9

———————

The following morning, Stella woke briefly for Beckworth's tantalizing kiss. Before he left for his morning ride, he'd brushed her hair back and told her, "I'll arrange a time for us to see Chester and Katherine. Be gentle with the inspector." She mumbled some response, rolled over, and fell back to sleep until Libby pounced in.

"Get up. You need a decent breakfast before the inspector arrives." She laid the cleaned and mended ball gown from the previous night on the back of a chair and dropped the rest of the bundle she'd tucked under her arm on the chair seat. "Come on, now. Bart is already complaining, and Lincoln is irritable. I swear it's not good for him to spend so much time with that old man. And poor Eleanor is caught in the middle. She could use some help." She marched to the windows and pulled all the drapes open.

Sunshine filled the room, and Stella threw back the covers, groaning as she sat up.

"Is it your headache?" Libby, who was too spunky for that early of an hour, softly lifted Stella's chin. "Well, that's going to be quite the bruise."

Stella moaned again and swatted Libby's hand away. "My head feels fine." She touched the spot where the thief had clocked her. "Ouch. Well, maybe not completely fine. The headache's gone, but it hurts if I touch it."

"Well, then you know what not to do." There was a knock at the door. "Let's get you up. That should be the coffee." Libby tossed Stella's robe to her before opening the door. "Oh, Maggie, thank you for helping out."

Stella slipped on the robe and tied the sash before glancing up. "Morning, Maggie. You're a godsend." She zeroed in on the coffee like a bloodhound tracking a scent. Her eyelids were at half mast, her throat scratchy, and she forced herself to wait patiently while the young housemaid filled her mug.

Maggie watched as Stella closed her eyes after taking her first sip. She gulped the hot liquid twice before opening her eyes.

Stella sighed with contentment and gave them a wide smile, her gaze bright. "The two of you take such good care of me. Now, let's get me dressed."

Maggie's eyes had widened with Stella's miraculous change in mood, and Libby elbowed her.

"I told you it was critical to have coffee ready for her when she first wakes."

Stella plopped down at the dressing table and cringed when she glanced at the side of her face. The blue and purple coloration was indeed the first sign of a good bruise. She could either have Libby try to hide it or use it to her advantage with the inspector. She'd have to mull that over.

Libby picked up the brush and began taming Stella's rat nest. "Maggie is being trained as a lady's maid for when I'm not at the manor." Her gaze dropped. "I was hoping to stay overnight with some friends tonight. I know Maggie has never held this position before, but she's a quick learner. She might make a few mistakes, but she understands the basics."

Stella held up a hand. "Don't oversell it." When Libby gave her an odd look, she said, "It just means don't make her abilities sound more than they are. You might need that for..." Stella paused and then snorted. "I almost said Lady Agatha, but I wouldn't wish her on any lady's maid, let alone a new one."

Libby laughed, and Maggie's cheeks turned a bright red on her porcelain skin. The young maid was quite a beauty. Something that could get her in trouble with the wrong lord of the manor. "Who do you work for, Maggie? Beckworth or Lord Templeton?"

Libby began to answer but stopped when Stella shook her head.

It took Maggie a moment before clearing her throat. "I've been temporarily hired by Barrington to assist Libby and Mrs. Evans while you're in London."

"Well, I'm sure Libby told you that as an American, I sometimes need help with proper English decorum. I imagine we'll both make mistakes along the way. As long as I have plenty of coffee first thing in the morning, you can do no wrong." She pushed Libby and her brush away and turned to face her two lady's maids. "So, what do you think I should wear to meet the inspector?"

Thirty minutes later, Stella entered the dining room in a powder-blue day dress that made her appear demure and was immediately sorry she hadn't taken another ibuprofen. Her headache was gone, but she felt another one brewing when she was confronted with a full-blown argument.

Bart, his face blotched red with anger and spittle flying, shouted out a comment that Stella didn't understand. Lincoln had apparently been expecting the old doc's opinion. His face contorted into exasperation and a touch of his own ire. Eleanor had moved to the banquet table to get out of the line of fire and was filling a plate with more food than Stella had ever seen her eat.

Stella snorted when Eleanor shoved the plate in front of Bart.

"Eat this, and don't say another word. We're not alone anymore."

Bart stopped in mid-sentence and stared down at his plate before glancing up and spotting Stella, who took a seat next to Lincoln. He picked up his fork and waved it at her. "She doesn't count."

"Hey," Stella sounded wounded, but she couldn't hold back her grin. She took Bart's statement as a compliment that he considered her one of this odd collection of friends.

"You know what I mean." He bent his head to focus on his food but couldn't hide his own small grin.

"You don't need to wait for me before eating." Stella waited while Matthew, one of the footmen, placed a plate filled with fried eggs, sausage, and diced turnips in front of her. He'd been extremely helpful on her first morning at the manor, and it seemed she could do no wrong in his eyes. He'd since become her favorite footman.

Barrington entered the room and glanced at Bart with irritation, but his expression softened when the old man appeared focused on his plate of food. He turned to Stella. "The inspector should be here in half an hour. Which room would you like to greet him in?"

She swallowed her bite of food and considered the question. What would Mary do? "Perhaps one of the sitting rooms. What do you think?"

"The sitting room would be sufficient." Barrington seemed pleased she'd guessed the right room. She didn't have the heart to say she'd almost said a drawing room, not that she really knew the difference. "It would also be proper for you to offer him tea, which I'll make sure is ready regardless of his answer. You should pour a cup for yourself. You're the lady of the manor and have full control. You are a victim, not the perpetrator, regardless of how the inspector will frame it."

"What does that mean?" Stella asked. She hadn't been worried about the inspector until now.

Eleanor took a sip of coffee and stared at her over the rim of her cup. "He means that the inspector will consider your actions of chasing down the thief to be improper, and that it impacted the duke's security from doing their job."

Stella couldn't tell for sure, but Eleanor seemed to find the entire ordeal humorous.

"You mean I was in the way because I'm a woman. Had I been a man, then everyone would have been shaking my hand instead of wringing theirs. Everyone is more concerned about my improprieties than a thief getting away because none of the gentlemen seemed inclined to go after him." She used air quotes with the word gentlemen, even though no one would understand the gesture.

"Exactly," Barrington responded. "I'd advise not to let him intimidate you, but I'm currently feeling sorry for the chap."

Everyone tittered at that, even Stella. Her anxiety washed away with the solidarity she felt from the group. Besides, it wasn't like this was the first time she'd been in a situation like this—in this time or her own.

At a few minutes to ten, her itchy nerves returned when a knock echoed through the foyer. She peeked around a corner to watch Barrington open the door for the inspector.

The man was of average height, slightly stooped, and carried a bit of a belly. He kept pushing back the few strands of hair left on top of his balding head. His suit was clean but of modest quality, which reflected his station in life. She didn't know much about the economics of the time, other than her awareness of the large gap between the rich and poor. She imagined the inspector's salary ranked below most merchants of the time. What did he think of the aristocrats? Did he find their concern over a couple of bits of jewelry to be worthy of his time, or was he here simply to keep the duke happy?

She jumped back when Barrington escorted him to the sitting room. A deep breath shook some of the nerves away as she waited patiently for Barrington.

What seemed like forever but wasn't more than a couple of minutes, Barrington strode down the hall.

He gave her a stern look. "You shouldn't have been eavesdropping."

"Do you think he saw me?"

"No." He continued down the hall, but said over his shoulder. "I'll have the tea service brought out."

Stella waited several minutes, not wanting the inspector to think she was anxious about the meeting. When she'd stalled long enough, she straightened her shoulders, brushed at her dress in case there were leftover crumbs from breakfast, and strode into the sitting room with her wide, realtor smile in place.

"Inspector. I'm so sorry to keep you waiting. We had a slight emergency in the kitchen that couldn't wait." She had no idea what she was talking about, but she'd heard Mary make the comment once or twice and decided to follow her mentor's lead.

The inspector stood when she entered, and he bowed his head. The act should have calmed her nerves, but when he lifted his head, his gaze was sharp and penetrating. Not a fool, this one. Just stick to her story, and if possible, lure him into answering her own questions.

"I'm sure caring for a house of this size has its daily dramas." His tone wasn't exactly condescending, but it carried the ring of a practiced speech.

If she were a betting person, she'd say he didn't have much time for the wealthy. But his boss probably took the rich quite seriously.

The inspector had taken a chair across from the sofa, so Stella sat across from him, purposely sitting in the middle of the couch. Thankfully, the ones made in this era weren't plush, so she didn't have to worry about sinking down into a less dominant position. Before the inspector could say anything, a footman came in with the tea service, which he placed on the small table between them.

"How do you take your tea, inspector?" Stella poured two cups, not bothering to ask him if he wanted one.

He glanced down, somewhat taken aback. Perhaps she should have asked, but if it put him off his game, that was okay by her.

"Just a touch of milk."

Once the tea preparations were complete, she sipped hers and gave him a pleasant smile. "The viscount said you might have some questions for me." She didn't think it hurt to remind the inspector that the viscount would most likely want to know how the meeting went. Nothing like throwing around a title.

"Yes, well, I would have spoken with you last night, but I understand you were recovering from an injury and thought it best to let you rest."

Her anger instantly spiked, but she shoved it down and remained cool. She had to remember what year this was, and whether she liked it or not, she was the weaker sex in his mind.

The inspector sipped his tea, more out of propriety than anything else. "Are you feeling better today?"

"Yes, I am. Thank you for asking."

He gave her a long look. "You're not English."

Well, that took him a while. "I'm American."

"I see." He said it as if that explained everything, and this was all nothing but a waste of his time. "Can you tell me what you remember of the events?"

Stella replayed the evening—the push of the crowd, the confusion, her fussing over spilled champagne, and the gentleman who saw the whole thing. "Dame Ellingsworth was quite upset over the loss of a precious heirloom. I didn't see anyone else concerned about stopping the thief, and my instincts just took over. I thought if I could follow him, I could find the duke's security men and help point the way. It wasn't until I ran through the solarium that others took notice."

"And what happened after the other men noticed the thief?"

"The thief ran right through the group. He seemed to have caught the men off guard." She placed a hand at the base of her throat, sorry that she hadn't thought to carry her fan. She held back her smirk. "I suppose I got so caught up that I chased the man down the steps. That's when he stopped and turned toward me. I tripped on my own skirts and fell, hitting the side of my head on the ground." She touched the spot that was still sensitive, and the inspector leaned over, his eyes widening when he noted the newly forming bruise."

"That was quite dangerous. What possessed you to do such a foolish thing?"

Here we go. She sipped her tea as she considered his question. "I haven't been in England very long, and Dame Ellingsworth has been like a mother to me. I knew how important the necklace was to her, and I just reacted." It required every ounce of patience to lower her gaze in a submissive manner. "I know how foolish it was, but I felt like I had to do something."

"An act that most likely interfered with the duke's own security men."

She decided to go with the old adage that if you didn't have anything nice to say, then keep your mouth shut. So, she nodded and forcibly relaxed her lips that were staging their own rebellion by forming a thin line of anger.

The inspector sipped his tea and said, "I understand you got a good look at the thief."

"Yes. His attire suggested he was a nobleman. He was a bit tall and of average build. His face was clean-shaven. Not much to really say, other than I would recognize him if I saw him again."

"You were on the back lawn, where there was very little lighting. How can you be so sure?"

"There was some light from the back of the manor, and I was close enough to see him quite plainly."

"Yes. I see." He glanced down and scratched his jaw as if he were thinking. "You're sure he didn't have a mustache or beard?"

"Quite sure."

When the inspector seemed to be out of questions and looked like he was ready to leave, she added, "I think he was a sailor."

The inspector's head popped up. "Why would you say that?"

"It was the way he walked."

He stared at her as if she'd suddenly spoken a different language.

"I've spent some months on a ship coming over from America." Good grief. It was as if she were having dinner with the smuggler, McDuff, again, creating stories to keep him interested. "You get to notice a sailor from others by the way they walk. Like they're still on a ship."

He continued to stare at her, his eyes a bit glazed. It was easy to tell he had stopped listening at some point, or maybe he was thinking of the best way to extricate himself from this crazy woman. He finally came out with another, "I see."

He suddenly stood. "I think I have everything I need."

Stella rose and stepped from around the table to escort him

out. "Perhaps I could provide enough details for someone to sketch his face."

He hesitated as if he were considering it. "I don't think we're at that stage yet."

He didn't believe she'd seen the thief. "So what are your next steps to finding the thief and Dame Ellingsworth's necklace?"

"It will be quite difficult the find the thief with so little to go on, and the necklace will most likely have already been sold off."

"I heard there was another theft similar to this one before the duke's ball."

They were in the foyer now, and Stella glimpsed Barrington walking to the front door, no doubt having been listening.

"Yes. I'm afraid so, but while the robberies appear similar, we can't assume one had anything to do with the other."

"You don't think it will happen again?"

"Oh, quite doubtful. Now that the police have been engaged, it's quite unlikely anyone will attempt such a thing again."

When they reached the door, Barrington opened it for the inspector. Before the man made it through the door, Stella touched his elbow, making him turn back.

"The viscount will be very interested in hearing your progress on the matter."

The inspector looked surprised for an instant, but he forced a smile. "Of course. Good day to you, my lady."

Stella stood behind Barrington as they watched the inspector walk down the steps and enter his coach without a backward glance.

Barrington shooed Stella back and shut the door. "That went well enough." Barrington watched for her reaction, knowing quite well she could go off at any moment.

"He's not going to do anything about it."

"No. Not unless there are more thefts."

"There will be. That's a given."

10

———

That morning, Beckworth had kissed Stella, who'd only stirred long enough to roll over, and grabbed a quick breakfast in the kitchen with Eleanor. She confirmed she would attend Mary's luncheon with Stella, which would keep them both busy for the day. He was due at the docks by midday to run surveillance with Jamie, which gave him time to check in with the crews regarding the theft.

After breakfast, he saddled his horse and rode to Chester's. The air was crisp, but the sun was out, and he felt a deep sense of homecoming as he entered the Whitechapel district. The housing was shabby, the clothing threadbare, and many times, food was hard to come by. Each time he returned to the East End, he understood Bart's rage at the disparity between the rich and the poor.

Guilt had once ridden Beckworth as he clawed his way into the aristocracy. With his rise into the nobleman class, he found a way to pay respect to his mother by donating a portion of his wealth to charity. He also contributed money to the crews. His way of upsetting the natural order of London society.

He understood he was playing both sides, but walking away from everything he'd built to live in the East End would have diminished his own dreams. Yet, he would never turn his back on those who gave him his sense of purpose, so he did what he could.

Smoke drifted above the narrow house where Chester and Katherine lived. Chester was an early riser, even though most nights his crew ran one or two jobs. He compensated with naps in the afternoon. Another reason why it was always best to catch Chester early in the day.

He tied his horse to a post and knocked on the door.

When Katherine opened it and found him on her doorstep, her smile lit up an already bright morning. She pulled him in and gave him a tight hug before stepping back to give him a once-over.

"Well, you don't look like the lord of a manor." She grabbed his chin and turned his head to the left and then right. "But you're still the handsome charmer. Come in. You're just in time for breakfast."

Beckworth chuckled as he stared down at his attire—the plain pants, shirt, and jacket of a commoner. "I'm on assignment later today, and Eleanor has already fed me."

"An assignment? Ah, yes. Chester said something about watching a ship down at the docks. Something about smugglers, isn't it?"

He should have known word would have spread quickly. "Did Barrington say something?"

"It was Fitz." Chester walked in, and the two men shook hands. "Good to see you. We weren't sure if you'd make it to London this time."

Beckworth grinned. "This trip was all about London. We'll be here for a few weeks."

Chester glanced behind him. "Where's Stella?"

"You know this hour is too early for her, but I'll bring her around once we're more settled. She's still getting acquainted with the balls and parties."

Chester gave him a long, assessing look. They'd known each other for decades, and he would correctly assume this wasn't a visit to catch up on old times.

They sat at the kitchen table, and while Katherine plied Beckworth with coffee and sweet rolls, Chester ate his breakfast. They spoke of mutual friends and the unfortunate passing of one of the old timers from consumption.

Once the plates were cleared, Katherine refilled the coffee before taking a seat. Chester never kept anything from Katherine, something Beckworth tried not to think about, considering his current job with Hensley. Besides, Katherine had worked in the crews and, in a way, still did by keeping an open ear to the happenings in the neighborhood.

"Will you be meeting with the other crews?" Chester asked as he filled a pipe. "I hear Barrington was around yesterday."

"He'll be back tomorrow to visit with the rest of the crews. I have some time this morning to visit with the others before I head to the docks."

"I heard there was some trouble at the duke's ball last night." Chester puffed his pipe, and soft swirls of aromatic smoke filled the room.

"Someone took a necklace right off Dame Ellingsworth's neck." Beckworth focused on his coffee rather than look at Chester.

"In the middle of the ball?" Katherine asked as she glanced at her husband. "That's rather bold, even for the crews."

Chester didn't say anything as he watched Beckworth. He was aware of Beckworth's long friendship with the dowager, understanding he had friends in many places. Chester puffed a couple more times as he considered the information, then a slow smile appeared.

"I heard someone chased the thief and almost caught them."

Beckworth sighed, not surprised by the amount of information Chester had gained from the night before. "Stella chased the man through the manor and out to the back gardens. Nicked him before he got away."

"She cut him?" Katherine didn't bother to hide her admiration.

"With her own dagger." Beckworth cringed as the words came out.

Chester threw his head back with a loud guffaw. He laughed so hard, he began to choke. Beckworth thought he'd have to thump the man on his back before Chester caught his breath. The cackles continued with Katherine joining in, and all Beckworth could do was smile and shake his head.

While he'd been irritated to discover Stella had chased the man down, he'd also been proud of her. And there he was again, walking the line between ensuring the aristocracy accepted her as an equal and cheering her tenacity for what she believed in. She'd gone after the thief because it was Elizabeth's necklace, but at the same time, he found it difficult to approve of her actions.

He snorted as the couple attempted to curtail their joviality. It didn't matter what he thought. He could no more control Stella's actions than he could calm a storm at sea. The most he could do was softly influence her to a different way of thinking or, when necessary, barter.

"If Katherine hadn't already snared my heart," Chester mused, "I'd be chasing after that woman."

Katherine gave his arm a nudge. "I think she's more than either of you can handle. I knew she had gumption the first time we met." She turned on Beckworth and shook a finger at him. "You mind how you treat that woman."

"I wouldn't worry about that, dear heart. He knows what he has. Besides, he's finally opened his heart to someone, and he couldn't have picked a better match."

Beckworth squirmed. He should have known they'd be on Stella's side, but then he grinned when he agreed that what Chester said was true. He'd found a woman who understood his two natures and accepted them without question or judgment. How had he gotten so lucky?

"If you've had enough fun at my expense," Beckworth steered the conversation back on topic. "I'm curious if any of the crews might have done this. I'm willing to exchange good coin to get that necklace back."

Chester's brows rose, and his eyes narrowed. "Do you think a crew would be daft enough to do something like that? It's too risky and puts the entire crew in jeopardy if anyone were caught. You should know better."

Beckworth lifted his hands in supplication. "Of course. But I had to ask. I'm becoming more out of touch with the crews." He ran a hand through his hair, and Katherine placed a hand on his arm.

"We understand. And we don't take offense." She glared at her husband. "We'd know if it was any of the crews. And this was the second time, right?"

Beckworth sighed. "I had a feeling you would have heard about it." He shifted in his seat, uncomfortable with showing his emotions, even with friends. "I'd been quite upset, worried she'd been hurt. The thief gave her a solid hit to the head, and I raged that I'd track the thief down. I might have said something about chasing down whatever crew had been responsible." He glanced sheepishly at the two of them. "Then Stella said something that surprised me, and it still sounds unbelievable. When I mentioned a crew, she said it wasn't crew. She swears the man was a sailor."

Chester looked to Katherine, but she shook her head. "We haven't heard anything about a sailor. Someone like that would be better suited for working the docks. My guess is that it's a single man, or at most, one or two others." He covered the pipe to smother the smoke then laid it gently on the table. "I doubt the duke's ball was the last one."

"I agree." Beckworth finished his cup and put a hand over it when Katherine tried to refill it. He stood. "I'll see myself out."

Chester pointed to the pot of coffee, and Katherine refilled his cup. "If we hear anything, we'll pass it along."

"We should have a party," Katherine said. "How about tomorrow night? Or do you have one of your fancy balls?" She said it with a bit of sass and a wink.

"I think we have the evening free. I can bring Eleanor and Libby along."

"And don't forget Barrington. It wouldn't be the same without him."

Beckworth was almost out the door when Chester called out, "I wouldn't worry about the thief. Stella will catch him." Then laughter erupted, and Beckworth grimaced at the thought, but he was smiling as he mounted his horse.

After meeting with four other crews, all with the same response to the thefts as Chester's, he made his way to the docks, putting the matter aside while turning his attention to Hensley's assignment. They'd been monitoring the docks for two days with no sign of McDuff's accomplices. How long would they stay on the ship? According to Lando and Jamie, most of the crew had already left the ship, and they'd furled the sails. They appeared to be in port for a while.

When he slipped through the small gap that opened up to an area behind a stack of crates, he was surprised to find Fitz.

"I was expecting Jamie again." Beckworth sat on the ground, positioning himself so he had a clear view of the dock and the *Nighthawk*.

"He decided to have one of the yard arms replaced and wanted to help since most of the men have been given leave." Fitz sucked on his pipe, though it wasn't lit. Not while on surveillance. His focus never left the dock.

"He's turning out to be a fine captain."

"Finn taught him well." Fitz grinned as he took another smokeless puff. "And just like Finn, he gets fidgety when he's stuck in his cabin for too long."

They sat in companionable silence, leaning against barrels as they watched a string of sailors from multiple ships wander back and forth between the docks and town. After an hour, Beckworth sat up, forcing Fitz to follow.

"What is it?" Fitz whispered.

"That bloke looks familiar."

Fitz leaned toward Beckworth as he searched the string of men leaving the ship. "The one behind the big bruiser?"

"Yes."

Fitz squinted. "Wasn't he on one of the ships in the cove where Cheval was loading cargo from the jolly boat? Maybe the first mate?"

Beckworth thought back to when he, Fitz, and Lando had watched two ships in the cove from a high point on the surrounding cliffs. The men had been loading long crates onto *The Horseman* that were the perfect size for rifles. "The *Tidewater*. We never saw her after that."

"Maybe the captain decided to fill a gap now that Cheval is out of the way."

"Either way, I think we should have someone follow him."

"I'll go. Let's leave Lane in place in case someone else comes along."

Lane and another sailor watched from another spot farther up the dock. There were times when the docks were deathly quiet, with only the creak of a ship as it knocked against its mooring. Then, before you knew it, the docks were filled with so many sailors milling about that it was impossible to track anyone.

Fitz moved swiftly, stuffing his pipe in his pocket. A few minutes later, he fell in behind the suspected first mate of the *Tidewater*, now either a passenger or a new crewmate on the *Nighthawk*. Fitz made a hand signal as he passed the spot where Lane was holed up, then stuck his hand in his pocket and focused on the ground. He might look like he was just another sailor heading for the pubs, but Fitz would have a steady eye on the first mate.

Ten minutes later, another sailor from the *Daphne* slipped in beside Beckworth.

"Lane sent me in case you spot someone else."

Beckworth nodded. "Did everyone get a look at the first mate?"

"Lane thinks he's the captain."

"Well, that's interesting. I wonder what happened to *The Horseman* and the *Tidewater*."

"Probably still plying their trade on the west coast."

If that were the case, this bloke, who just got off the ship, either decided to get out of the smuggling business after Cheval's untimely death, or Hensley's team had only scratched the surface of McDuff's network. McDuff had told Stella that he'd amassed a group of ships. Was the *Nighthawk* part of that network? And if so, what were they doing in London?

Barrington opened the carriage door and helped Stella and Eleanor step down. "I'll return in a few hours to retrieve you. I have a few errands to run."

"Take your time. Mary will want to spend time in the drawing room after lunch." Stella took a few steps but stopped when she heard Barrington chuckle behind her. She turned and lifted a brow. "You couldn't wait until we were inside to laugh?"

Barrington didn't appear chastised, and his grin only widened.

"She really is getting better." Eleanor's attempt to show solidarity with Stella would have gone over better if she hadn't been hiding a smile.

"I don't know what the fuss is about being able to embroider," Stella mumbled. "I need to introduce lawn darts as an acceptable pastime."

Neither Barrington nor Eleanor knew what lawn darts were, but they chortled as Stella picked up her skirts, turned her back on them, and, lifting her head high, marched up the steps like a queen. She might appear regal on the outside, but the thought of stabbing her fingers with those damn needles made her shiver. She should have brought her first aid kit.

Hensley's butler waited at the door, and though she'd accepted that none of Hensley's butlers would ever smile, she gave him a bright one of her own. He didn't disappoint when he responded with a simple nod and a placid expression.

A housemaid waited in the foyer and led Stella and Eleanor to the solarium, where a table for six had been decorated as if they were joining one of Mary's garden parties. Four women were already seated and in full conversation.

Lady Agatha saw them enter and lifted her glass of wine. "There you are. We were wondering when you'd show."

"I didn't realize we were late." Stella was certain they were fifteen minutes early.

Flora Melville, who sat next to her, smiled at Stella and patted the open spot next to her. "You're not. Agatha was eager to check on Elizabeth."

Before Agatha could respond, Stella jumped in, her focus on the dowager. "And how are you today?"

Elizabeth waved a hand in dismissal and took a long drink of what looked like a gin and tonic. The woman drank it like soda, but Stella couldn't blame her. Not after a night like last night.

"I wish everyone would stop asking. It just makes me relive the entire event. I'd rather put it behind me."

"Don't you want to get your necklace back?" Stella took the seat next to Flora and leaned back when a footman placed a glass of wine in front of her.

Elizabeth waved her hand again and turned to look out the window, a faraway look in her gaze. Was she reliving the event again, or a memory about the necklace? "It's gone. They'll never find it. The wicked thief has already sold it, and probably for a farthing of what it was worth."

"That necklace was one of only a handful made by Louis Pierre Deschanel." Agatha fiddled with her necklace as she glanced at Elizabeth. "Surely, the inspector will find it."

Stella couldn't help rolling her eyes, and Eleanor must have caught it because she smirked.

"What's wrong, Stella?" Mary asked. "Do you know something?"

She hadn't expected to be put on the spot. Someday, she'd learn how to be more demure in this century. Who was she kidding? Demure just wasn't in her wheelhouse. She wasn't sure where to start. While everyone waited for her, their gazes hopeful, she drank a long swallow of wine. She hated to disappoint them, but neither would she hold anything back.

"I keep wrapping my head around a few things. First, was he alone?" When the women's expressions turned skeptical, Stella pressed on. "Well, think about it. We were standing in the hall-way, and then this huge surge of people came at us, knocking us around. Seconds later, the necklace was gone."

"Someone created a distraction." Flora was so matter-of-fact the women turned their gazes on her. "What else would explain so many people stumbling forward unless someone pushed them? If it was the thief, how would he have gotten to Elizabeth so quickly?"

Mary held a hand to her mouth. "What if they were after Elizabeth's necklace?"

The women gasped, but it was Eleanor who spoke. "You're saying they knew about the necklace and, for some unknown reason, arranged the theft on the off chance she'd be wearing it? It would be easier to break into her manor and steal it."

Stella's thoughts whirled. She hadn't considered the thief might want that specific necklace. "She always wears it."

Her words had been mumbled, but Elizabeth asked, "What did you say?"

Stella glanced up, her thoughts so chaotic she had to replay what she'd said. "I remember you mentioning you wore it almost all the time."

She shrugged. "I might have. It was the last present my husband gave me before he died. This particular piece meant even more since he'd commissioned it from the jeweler."

"That's why they're so rare." Agatha picked up the story. "The order would have been placed months in advance. The communication between London and Paris takes a month in itself."

"It was made in France?" Stella asked. Surely, the fact the necklace was from France, which was currently at war with England, was simply a far-fetched coincidence. When the women nodded, it posed another question. "Does anyone know what was stolen from a party three nights ago?"

"There was another theft?" Elizabeth's eyes, partially glazed from the gin, widened in shock. "I hadn't heard that."

Mary and Flora shook their heads, also surprised.

"I heard about it, but everyone thought it was taken from an aristocrat in debt." Agatha sipped her wine, then relaxed back in her chair, an impish grin on her face, seemingly pleased to be the only one with the gossip. "It was at Eloise's party."

When the other women nodded in understanding, Stella racked her brain, vaguely remembering the name. She snapped her fingers when the memory of them reviewing their stack of invitations came roaring back. "Didn't I hear that name regarding a garden party?"

Mary nodded. "Yes. Eloise holds a small ball and a garden party each season. In fact, I believe the garden party is in a couple of days."

"It's tomorrow, actually," Elizabeth said. "But that explains why I didn't hear anything. She stopped inviting me to anything years ago."

When the others nodded in agreement, Stella became confused. "Well, someone must have been invited if we had an invitation for it."

This time, Eleanor piped up. "I believe Beckworth received the invitation."

Stella looked at Agatha. "Did you hear what was stolen?"

Agatha shook her head. "I didn't pay that much attention. If I'd thought it would happen again, I would have." She glanced at the ceiling, her finger tapping her cheek. "A broach. Maybe a bracelet. It might have been a necklace. Oh, I can't remember."

"Did we respond to the invitation?" Stella asked.

"Well, no dear," Mary said. "Not unless you did. The invitation wasn't for us to respond to."

"If I sent a note accepting the invitation today, would that be rude?"

The women laughed, but Agatha of all people gave her an out.

"You've only been in town a few days. If you tell her you were overwhelmed by the number of invitations and just realized you'd overlooked hers or something to that effect, I'm sure she'd understand. Besides, I have no doubt they want to get a chance to meet the viscount's consort." She winked at Stella.

"So, who wants to go with me?" Stella glanced around the room, her eyes on Eleanor, who refused to look up from her plate, where she pushed food around like a six-year-old attempting to hide the vegetables.

"I don't have anything planned." Flora's face was pinched, but she gave Stella a weak smile. "I don't receive invitations from her either, but she still speaks with me at social gatherings. Her husband has a few business dealings with Edgar, so if I arrive as your guest, she can't say anything." Her eyes twinkled with amusement. "If you show up with me, don't expect an invitation from her next year."

"What do you hope to accomplish?" Elizabeth asked.

"I want to know if there's anything in common with that theft and the one from last night."

"Isn't there an inspector working on the theft?" Mary asked.

Elizabeth's interest seemed to have waned as a new gin and tonic was placed in front of her. Stella couldn't blame her. She reached for her opal necklace. If someone ever stole it, she'd be drowning her sorrows, too, until her anger turned her into that woman who kept dragging a crossbow around with her. She didn't mind carrying Elizabeth's burden for another day or so. Once the woman got past her grief, the anger would come. Then she'd help Stella in any way she could.

"The inspector interviewed me this morning. I hate to say this, but I don't think he's taking either theft seriously. Besides, isn't this what all the parties are for—gossip? It can't hurt to know what happened and what was taken."

For the first time since Stella arrived, Elizabeth's eyes cleared, and a conspiratorial smile appeared.

When Mary changed the topic, Stella glanced at Eleanor and was surprised to see the woman nod with a sly grin.

The game was afoot.

11

———————

Stella tapped her foot while Maggie latched the last button. She'd opted for one of her nicer day dresses for dinner. Even in the company of close friends, dinner at the manor should maintain some etiquette. If for no other reason, it made the staff happy to be doing something more than polishing the same serving trays over and over.

"I'm sorry, Lady Stella." Maggie waved her hands, her face scrunched. "My fingers can't seem to grip the buttons fast enough."

Stella's foot stopped, and she realized her mistake. "I'm sorry, Maggie. It's not you. You're doing fine. I'm just a bit anxious. This is my first time hosting a dinner without any real support. I don't know this staff well, and Mary was always around to help with the little details." She glanced at Maggie, and a slow grin started. "There is Eleanor."

"Then that's your answer." Maggie patted the chair. "Let me just brush your hair and put some clips in to pull it back. You'll look quite stately."

Stella sat, her body sagging as the stress leaked out of her.

"I'd bet five pence Eleanor is already in the kitchen watching over everyone's tasks." Maggie sorted the hair clips, pushing them around until she found the ones she wanted. "The footmen were excited to hear about the dinner, so you don't have to worry about them." Maggie pulled Stella's hair back to just beyond her ears and placed three jeweled clips on each side.

Stella looked back and forth in the mirror, and pleased, she stood and gave Maggie a quick hug. "It's perfect." She picked up her wrap. "Quickly do whatever you need to do this evening with my clothes, then you're done for the night. We'll be sleeping in late, so you can leave the coffee service at the door and just knock." She winked at Maggie, and when the young girl blushed, Stella wondered if she'd ever been that innocent. It would have been a long time ago.

She strode into an already filled drawing room. Jamie, Fitz, and Lando, whom she'd barely spent any time with since arriving in London, had cleaned up without the waistcoats and cravats. Stella found it refreshing, and it matched the equally less formal attire of Bart, Lincoln, Eleanor, and Barrington, who rounded out the guests. Beckworth met her with a glass of wine and steered her toward the center of the group.

It was fun to play a noblewoman in London, but these people were who she truly was. She enjoyed listening to the men spin tales, and the more they drank, the taller and grander they became. The last of her tension drained away. These were her peeps. And even Bart was at his best, sharing stories of his earlier days spent in London. But when dinner was called, the group paid her deference. Jamie was the first one by her side to walk her into the dining room, and she suspected this might be one of her best nights in London.

The evening was exactly as Stella had expected, with the group going through a replay of her various exploits and heroics of chasing down the thief at the duke's ball. Other stories followed before Beckworth invited everyone to Chester and Katherine's party the following evening in the East End.

Then came a moment, fortunate, or not, depending on how one might interpret the possible fallout, Stella had her head down as she tried to remove capers from the boiled lamb. The lamb was perfect, but she despised the little green balls. It was by sheer accident, a mere slip of the tongue, and something Stella would most likely not have heard since Fitz was sitting at the other end of the table, but the timing of his words came during the split second all other conversation had ceased.

She'd been so focused on her task that she'd barely listened to the discussion. Beckworth had just invited everyone to the East End when she heard Fitz mumble, "Hensley won't be happy with no one at the docks."

Then, like someone had just cleared the wax out of her ears, several conversations started, drowning out any response Fitz's statement might have produced. She'd stopped her task for only a second, but something made her examine Fitz's words. Would Beckworth have noticed the slight interruption in her battle with the capers, and if so, why should she be worried about that?

Then it hit her. Hensley. She pushed the last caper away, ate a piece of lamb, then lifted her head and glanced around the table as if trying to decide which conversation to join. She purposely didn't look at Beckworth until after she'd first glanced at Bart and Eleanor. She met his gaze for only a moment, not surprised to have found him watching her. She smiled at him before searching for the first person who could deflect his studied gaze.

"Lincoln, tell us about your tours at the Royal College of Surgeons."

While she listened to Lincoln's excited recital of events, the first kernel of doubt settled in. What was Hensley up to at the docks? It might be nothing, but then again, nothing was simple where the spymaster was concerned. She dearly loved Hensley. And while he was a good friend, he was single-minded in his pursuit of protecting England. But until she heard some other tidbit of information, she needed to let the statement pass.

She didn't have long to think about it when Beckworth changed topics.

"Stella, is there anything you can share about the inspector's visit?"

She didn't miss a beat. "Well, he's no Sherlock Holmes." She grinned, and Beckworth's eyes sparkled. He'd become obsessed with the complete collection of Sherlock Holmes's books that AJ had found at an estate sale. They read them together in the evenings while cuddled next to each other.

When Jamie cleared his throat, she cursed the heat that had quickly risen up between them and shifted her gaze to the group.

"Sorry." Stella sipped wine as her cheeks cooled. "Sherlock Holmes is a fictional character written by an author who hasn't been born yet. The character is an exceptionally bright inspector at Scotland Yard in London, which doesn't exist yet. He had unique instincts for uncovering a mystery and always caught his man." She sighed and leaned back against the chair. "Inspector Littlefield's visit seemed more an exercise in satisfying the duke's request than solving anything. He spent most of his time chastising me for interfering with the duke's men."

Fitz snorted. "I bet he left with his tail tucked."

Everyone laughed, as did Stella, but then she turned sad. "He's not going to do much about it, and that necklace was precious to Elizabeth."

There wasn't much to say after that. Once dessert was concluded, instead of the men going off to the study and the two women to the drawing room, they all moved to the library. Two chess sets had been prepared in addition to tables for whist, and they enjoyed another couple of hours until Jamie, Lando, and Fitz left for the ship.

Stella went upstairs shortly after and was finishing her nighttime routine when Beckworth joined her. She sniffed the jar of lotion, then rubbed the soft lavender scent over her arms. "I forgot to tell you. I decided to go to a garden party with Flora tomorrow."

Beckworth stepped behind her and rubbed her shoulders. He leaned in and kissed her collarbone. "I thought we might spend the day together before Chester and Katherine's party."

She closed the lid and stood, slowly turning toward Beckworth. The belt on her robe had fallen away, and she let her robe slip open to provide an enticing sight. His gaze lowered, and her skin grew hot.

She placed a hand on his shirt. "Why don't we have a sleep-in tomorrow? I'm sure you can find something to occupy your time while I'm at the garden party."

His eyes shifted for a second. She probably imagined it because his smile was blinding. "I haven't had a chance to visit the gentleman's club. Barrington normally checks for mail once a month or so, but I might as well go and see if any old friends are about."

She matched his smile and held it as she brushed a few locks from his face, though she couldn't forget Fitz's slip at dinner. It probably meant nothing, even though she was certain she was missing something. But she had her own agenda, and unless there was more evidence than shifty gazes, she trusted Beckworth to tell her if there was anything important to share.

The last thing she wanted was to create an argument while Beckworth removed his clothing. Though she considered helping, tonight she preferred to watch. She climbed onto the bed, leveraging the robe to reveal just enough skin to keep his eyes rooted on her as he removed the cravat and the waistcoat. After removing his boots, he strode to the stand in front of the fire to remove his pants and shirt. His sly art of seduction, using the firelight behind him to conceal his finer details, worked its magic, though she knew his body well enough that her imagination had no problem keeping up.

He stalked to the bed as she backed away. A strong shiver of anticipation washed over her when he stepped close enough for her to melt into the heated desire in his eyes. He crawled onto the bed and tugged her robe to pull her closer.

His lips crushed hers, and she wrapped her arms around his shoulders, feeling the flex of his muscles as he lifted her up to sit on his lap. They kissed for what seemed like hours. Deep, lustful kisses that gentled to a simple touch of lips on lips before teasing tongues swept them back to passion-filled kisses. The moment was as intense as it was gentle, and soon they fell back, legs entangled, as their hands roamed, seeking tactile contact.

The fire blazed in the hearth, the firelight casting fanciful shadows on the ceiling. It reminded her of those first nights when they were running from Gemini. They hadn't been intimate, their relationship too new, while questionable trust lay between them. But with each passing night, they'd lain closer and closer for warmth. She found it strange that somehow, her body knew Beckworth was safe before her mind caught up.

When their fervor was sated, he pulled her close enough that she could feel his rapid heartbeat. The weight she'd been carrying for a distressed Elizabeth had melted away, leaving only the two of them.

The following morning, Beckworth stared at the ceiling. Stella's head rested on his shoulder as she slept. He was looking forward to an evening in the East End with old friends. The event would be a welcome reprieve from the stuffiness of the balls. Everyone could be themselves, and Stella was as excited as he was.

The question was what to do with his day while she was at the garden party. He didn't know why she decided to go with Flora, but she knew her mind, and they would have other days for just the two of them. The gentlemen's club was a good idea, even if it had come to him on a whim.

He could say he was off to see *Daphne*'s crew, but the idea would have come up at dinner. Now that Jamie's crew had their eyes on the bloke from the *Nightwawk*, his part of the mission was over. But what if they ended up with more questions than answers? Was it possible the man hadn't been the first mate on the *Tidewater*? He might not have been part of the crew at all. It was possible that McDuff or Cheval had placed him on the *Tidewater* for some other reason. According to Stella's unfortunate stay with Cheval, she'd learned that both smugglers used spies, which shouldn't have been surprising. He should stay out of it. And as much as he wanted to walk away, he had to know what was going on, if only to stay updated on the mission.

It was time to see Hensley. Before he could organize his thoughts for an impromptu meeting, a light tap on the door signaled someone leaving a tray. He slowly extricated himself from Stella and grabbed his robe before opening the door to retrieve the coffee service.

After placing it on a table, he poured a cup and wandered to the window, pulling back the heavy drapes and squinting at the sun breaking over the horizon. He loved watching the sunrise, and today it reminded him of all the times he'd witnessed it growing up on the Thames. Early mornings, when the docks were quiet before the hustle and bustle began, he and a few of his friends would race through the vendors who'd been setting up their carts. They would steal a fish or two so their mothers could make a watery stew that would last a couple of days.

When he began earning decent money, he wanted to help everyone. It was a hard lesson to learn that not everyone could be saved. He hadn't been able to save his mother. Then, when he'd received his title, he discovered the aristocrats didn't think about the poor at all. Once he became one and was no longer the duke's henchman, he was in the position to make a difference. It seemed he'd always walked a line between good and evil. Always standing between the haves and the have-nots.

He'd understood the motive behind Finn's willingness to smuggle when he'd been the captain of the *Daphne Marie*. He'd only take the risk when he was positive he could get away with it, and it was for a good cause. Beckworth had thought him a fool when they'd first met. And through everything that had been thrown in Finn's way, his only thought was for what was right.

They'd gone through some harrowing times before Beckworth realized they were cut from the same cloth; they simply approached solutions differently. Stella had recognized it right away. He'd tried to hide his East End beginnings from her, but she'd called bull shit—her words—on the whole thing. She loved him all the more after discovering his roots and meeting the crews. People he still called friends and would lay down his life for, just as he would for Hensley and the Crown.

When he'd found Stella, he'd found someone who wanted to partner with him in all things—even the dangerous ones. It rankled that he was following Hensley's orders to hide his activities from Stella. It wouldn't have bothered him a year ago, but he hadn't known the ginger-haired beauty then.

He sighed. He'd meant to have a discussion with Finn and

Ethan after their first trip back to Waverly on how to deal with old paradigms once he arrived back in this century. He'd never found the right time.

"Come tell me what has you worried."

Stella's voice startled him, and a few drops of coffee tumbled from the cup. He forced a smile as he turned to her.

"What makes you think I'm worried?" He strode to the table and refilled his cup before pouring one for her. Without Libby around, the kitchen staff always forgot to send mugs instead of cups. He'd have to speak with Mrs. Evans again. He handed Stella her cup, then brought over the pot so he wouldn't have to get up multiple times.

Once he'd settled back on the pillows she'd rearranged for him, she nestled close and sipped half her cup before answering his question.

"Your morning ritual, when I'm awake for it, is to open the drapes to watch the sunrise. But when you hover there for an extended period, it's usually because you're working through something." She paused to sip, then said, "I'm not saying you're worried over anything bad. For all I know, you're worried you don't have enough fancy clothes for all the invites we've accepted. Or, you might be worried whether Bart will be a help or a hindrance to Lincoln at the Royal College of Surgeons. Or, you're wondering what Hensley's up to."

The last statement bothered him. Not that she hadn't been correct on all her points. He did have to stop at the tailor to order more clothing for both of them. He'd planned on accompanying Lincoln to the college to give Bart a day off, but mostly to ensure the old doc wasn't creating friction for the lad. But her comment on Hensley rang a minor warning bell.

"And if I told you it was all those things?" He might as well play it safe.

She leaned over and kissed his temple before handing him

her cup for a refill. "Then I'd say everything was alright." She took the refreshed cup and sipped it immediately, her nose wrinkling. "The coffee doesn't taste the same this morning. I'll ask Eleanor to check it out."

He laughed. "Why don't you speak with Nellie directly? She's the cook."

"Because Eleanor has a rapport with Mrs. Evans and Nellie. At this point, if I were to go to them directly, I'd hurt Eleanor's feelings."

"What a complicated life we live, Lady Caldway."

"Indeed, Lord Beckworth."

They nudged each other's shoulders and leaned against each other as they drank their coffee.

After several quiet moments, Stella returned to the topic that made his skin itch. "I'm serious about Hensley. It's been a couple of days since you've had a decent talk. Maybe you should see what he's up to after you visit the gentlemen's club. But, I want to get to Katherine's early so I can help, so you can't stay long."

He hesitated, wondering why she would bring up Hensley. Did she know something, or was it his guilt making him paranoid? She was right. Neither of them had seen much of Hensley other than at parties. There wasn't anything suspicious about going to see the man to play a game of chess and catch up.

"I admit, I was thinking of doing that." He might as well stick with the truth when he could.

"Excellent." She handed him her cup and ran her fingers under his robe. "Now that we both have our day planned, let's focus on each other."

He barely had time to set both cups down before her hand strolled lower. And he forgot all about the coming day as he elicited screaming giggles from her until he smothered them with kisses.

12

———

Libby arrived at the manor in time to help Stella prepare for the garden party and retrieve a change of clothes, having heard about Chester and Katherine's party.

"Do you mind letting Maggie help you this evening?" Libby put the last clip in Stella's hair, then selected a thin lace wrap for her.

"That's fine. I want to wear one of my simplest gowns. I'll just need help getting out of this one since I don't know when Beckworth will be back."

"You know you don't have to dress down for the East End."

Stella chuckled. "I'd decided to do that the first time Beckworth took me there. I wanted to fit in." She gave Libby a conspiratorial smile. "Now, it's for my comfort and a reprieve from the ball gowns."

Libby shook her head. "I'm afraid you're a bad influence on Maggie."

"But not on you?"

Laughter bubbled up as Libby dropped into a chair while Stella put on her shoes. "What's that phrase you use?" She snapped her fingers. "I'm afraid that ship has sailed."

Stella grinned. "I won't argue with that."

"What do you hope to discover at the garden party?"

"What makes you think I'm going just to uncover something?"

"You're going with Flora and not Elizabeth, Agatha, or Mary. From what the staff tells me, Eloise is a horrible busybody who looks down on anyone not born into wealth. I'm surprised Beckworth even got an invitation. And it sounds like you're only going to be there for as long as necessary."

Stella picked up the wrap and pulled it around her shoulders. "You're too smart for service. In my time, you'd probably be running your own business."

"Sounds like too much work to me."

"I forgot. You weren't here when I found out that Elizabeth's necklace was a one-of-a-kind piece made by a jeweler who only made a small number of items each year."

"That's why she's so upset?"

"Her husband had it commissioned shortly before his death."

Libby clucked her tongue. "I suppose that would upset me as well."

"And here's the other thing. The jeweler was French."

Libby's eyes widened, but then they narrowed. "What does his being French have to do with it?"

"I'm not sure that it does. But no one in my circle of friends knows what the first stolen item was." She shrugged her shoulders and stuffed her dagger in a pocket. "I'm just curious."

"Well, now I want to be here when you return."

"I'll leave that up to you." She took one last look in the mirror and grabbed her fan, which barely fit in her tiny purse. Libby would put everything away before she left. "We leave at four for the East End if you decide to stay and need a ride."

She strode out the door, through the house, and down the

stairs to the waiting coach that belonged to the Melvilles. Flora was inside, staring out the window at the manors across the street. The woman turned and smiled at Stella as she positioned herself on the bench across from her.

"Are we ready?" Stella asked, tugging at her gloves.

"Promise me we won't stay long. Edgar made a last-minute decision to have dinner with some friends." Flora glanced outside again. "I really don't want to have to talk to that woman."

"We'll find a table far away from her. Maybe we'll get the information we need from the other party goers. Certainly, some of them must have been at the party when the theft happened."

"True. I can ask around while you visit with Eloise." Flora visibly shivered.

Stella found the whole matter of who likes whom and who can be at whose party both amusing and irritating. She didn't mind not being invited somewhere, and she also didn't mind showing up to support someone she considered a friend. But the aristocrats took it too far. And while she enjoyed attending one or two balls to have something to share with AJ and Maire when she returned to Baywood, she couldn't see herself doing this for months. They'd only been in London a handful of days, and she was already exhausted by it all. Hard to believe she didn't have the stamina for a few parties.

Eloise's manor home was beautiful, but nothing special compared to the others she'd seen. She preferred Mary's homes most of all. After joining the group of women on the back lawn, it was immediately apparent by the hushed whispers behind fans and the obvious stares that Beckworth had received an invitation merely so they could get a close-up look at the American he'd become infatuated with.

Stella heard two women discussing him when she hid behind a thick conifer to rest from the constant smiling.

"Well, I have to say this for Beckworth, he certainly does find the gorgeous women," Lady A said. Stella couldn't remember who was who, so she gave them code names.

"But how long can it possibly last? I mean, she's American. An American shouldn't be allowed to be a viscountess. Weren't we just at war with them?" Lady B hiccupped, and Stella wondered if it had anything to do with the amount of punch the ladies had drunk. Stella had stayed away from it because she hated the taste of gin, regardless of what it was added to.

"And to think Lady Melville is willing to be seen with her," Lady A mused.

Stella had only been at the party for an hour. Most of the women were still eating, though a few had gotten up to walk around, which had been her cue for a bit of solitude. She would have stayed with Flora, but the woman seemed to have found one of her friends and thought it would be easier to ask questions without Stella with her.

Stella understood and readily agreed. That gave her time to speak with a few women she'd singled out during her brief introductions. All she needed was a quick five minutes of solitude, but listening to the women talk about her made her angry and then sad.

Was she a liability for Beckworth? Was this the reason he never brought up marriage? Not that she was in a hurry to get married. Their relationship was new. It was hot, it was heavy, and they hated being apart for too long. For the most part, their thoughts were one. But was English propriety holding him back? Was his title not worthy of her?

She wallowed for another five minutes after the two women had wandered off before she shook herself. She would have kicked her own backside if she could have reached it. Why was she letting these women dictate and question her relationship with Beckworth? Yes, most Englishmen would have perhaps brought up marriage, but Beckworth wasn't most Englishmen.

His relationship with her didn't cause any grief with Hensley and Mary. Nor with Elizabeth, who was above reproach in most circles. The hell with these women, and now that her dander was up, she rubbed her hands together as she peeked out from her hiding spot, deciding which group to seek out first.

She was formulating how to steer a conversation to the first theft, but, as it turned out, she needn't have worried. She'd barely reached the first group of women before they peppered her with questions. She took a step back as they moved closer, each vying for her attention.

"Ladies. Ladies." A loud voice rose above the others. "Decorum, please. Let the young woman have some air." A surprisingly short and robust woman parted the women as she stepped close and looked up at Stella, who had at least five or six inches on her. "Lady Caldway, it's so good to finally meet you."

One of the women toward the back snorted before covering her face with a fan. She whispered, "She's no lady. Just an American trollop looking for easy money."

The woman next to her twittered and covered her own mouth. The others, who had moved their heads slightly to hear the remark, managed to keep most of their focus on said trollop. Stella wasn't sure whether to be irritated or laugh out loud.

"I'm Lady Howard. It's not often we have a guest visiting from America." If the woman had heard the snide comment, she didn't give any sign of it. But Stella guessed the woman was well-versed in the art of diplomacy.

"It's nice to meet you. You've all been so wonderfully attentive to a stranger in your midst." She glanced at the woman in the back, who at least had enough decency to blush.

"Yes. Yes." Lady Howard took Stella's arm and walked with her toward the far side of the tables. The bevy of women followed.

Stella was directed to one of the chairs. They all gathered

around her as if she were going to read them a bedtime story. Oh, the tales she could share.

Once everyone was seated, Lady Howard wasted no time. "We hate to gossip, but we heard you were at the duke's ball and saw the thief take a necklace straight from Dowager Ellingsworth's neck."

"Then, when the duke's men almost had the thief red-handed," another voice spoke out, "you got in the way, and the thief ran off."

"I heard the necklace was stolen in the ballroom," a third voice rang out. "When Lady Caldway chased the thief, she knocked one of the duke's friends to the floor."

"That's not what I heard," yet one more raised her voice to be heard over the others. "Several people had already seen her in the solarium, and she hadn't been anywhere near the dowager. She happened to see a man walking quickly and raced after him and attacked him without provocation."

Stella studied the women, and though she kept a smile plastered on her face, she was too angry to care what they said. Those who declared they hated gossip were usually at the center of it. The question was, would the information Stella got from these women be the truth or just more gossip? She wasn't sure if it was worth telling them the truth, but it was up to them whether to believe it or not. If it helped get her the answers she was seeking, it would save her from having wasted a perfectly good afternoon she could have spent with Beckworth.

"I was standing with Elizabeth in the hallway, but I was looking elsewhere when the necklace was taken. A gentleman next to us saw the thief. I knew how precious the necklace was to Elizabeth, and the gentleman pointed which way the thief had gone. It happened so quickly, my instinct was to follow the man. I expected the duke's men to do something, but by the time I reached the solarium, I'd spotted the thief." She pulled out her fan and waved it a few times as she scanned the women. They were salivating for new information to spin to their liking. "He was acting suspicious, you know? His head was down, hands in his pockets, not looking at anyone. He just seemed the perfect candidate, so I called out. Unfortunately, the men standing around weren't able to stop him, so I kept following." She fanned herself faster. It was the closest she could get to appearing upset over the ordeal. She was too irritated with the group to pretend. "As you can imagine, it was a difficult situation, but the duke's men didn't show up until the thief was running off into the bushes. I'm not sure how I could have been in the way."

The women had gathered closer, not caring one iota whether she'd been in the way or not. It had simply been their way to get the conversation started. The questions came, one after another, for several minutes before Stella turned the conversation around.

She placed a hand on her chest and leaned into the group. "Did I hear there had been another theft before the duke's ball?"

Lady Howard hushed the women, who'd all spoken at once. "Our poor Eloise was standing in the dining room, choosing between the canapés, when she felt something brush against her shoulder. She assumed it was someone passing by, but when she glanced down, she noticed her brooch was gone." Lady Howard glanced around as if one of the women would call her out on her story. "Well, Eloise was beside herself. She immediately called out that someone had stolen her brooch. The staff looked everywhere in case it had come undone and fallen off, but they later discovered that someone had been seen running through the halls and out toward the solarium, just like at the duke's ball."

The other women nodded up and down, seeming to agree with the story.

"This was a brooch that was stolen." Stella focused on Lady Howard. "I assume this was an expensive piece, or was it more sentimental?"

"It was one of a kind," someone on her right exclaimed.

"Eloise had commissioned it from a jeweler." Lady Howard hushed the other women. "I'm told the man only made a handful of items each year."

"Do you remember the jeweler's name?" Stella asked.

The other women glanced at each other, probably surprised that her question was about the jeweler rather than the thief.

"He was quite popular a couple of years ago." Lady Howard lifted her gaze to the sky as if trying to remember the name.

"Louis Pierre Deschanel." This came from the woman who'd quietly insulted Stella earlier in the conversation. The other women chattered for a bit before nodding in agreement.

"Was there a reason for your question?" Lady Howard asked.

"Not really. I was just wondering. I suppose we all need to be careful what we wear to the next party." Stella touched her opal, then reopened her fan and waved it as if fighting off the vapors or for whatever else the fan was good for other than hiding behind for idle gossip. She lowered her head and frowned, her eyes blinking rapidly as if she might tear up. "It's all so dreadful."

That started the conversations again, giving Stella time to glance around, looking for an easy way to extricate herself from the group now that she had her answer. Fortunately, Flora strode up and nodded at the women.

"I'm so sorry. I was hoping to borrow Lady Caldway for a moment."

Stella stood without preamble, more than grateful for Flora's arrival. Once away from the vultures, Flora guided her to Eloise and begged their early departure, claiming she had another appointment with her husband.

Once they were in the coach driving away, Flora grinned. "I

was told Eloise was in the ballroom. She was swaying, listening to the music with her eyes closed, when she felt someone snatch the brooch right off her dress." Flora sat back, rather proud of what she'd gathered.

Stella clucked. "I heard Eloise had been in the dining room, deciding which canapé looked the best. At least the version I heard was also a brooch."

Flora shook her head as she leaned back and glanced out the window. "I shouldn't be surprised that the stories differed."

"It wasn't much different than the gossip about me at the duke's ball."

Flora looked horrified. "I heard them as well. Are you alright?"

Stella had been watching the landscape go by and was surprised by the question. "I don't care what people think of me. Perhaps if I lived here, I'd be more upset, but one thing I learned rather early in life. People are going to think what they think. The only thing that matters is what I think about myself." She pushed the hurtful words away, more irritated by what they thought of Beckworth than her. She would take the next invitations more seriously. She refused to feed the gossipmongers more fodder against Beckworth.

Flora slapped Stella's knee with her fan. "Aren't you going to ask if I discovered anything remarkable about the brooch?"

Stella pulled herself out of her thoughts, forgetting all about the jewelry now that she had her answer. "Maybe the comments affected me more than I thought." She sat straighter. "From what I was told, Eloise commissioned a jeweler to make it."

Flora's eyes glittered. "A jeweler by the name of Louis Pierre Deschanel. Apparently, not a coincidence after all."

Stella grinned. "I think we have a mystery to solve."

13

———

Beckworth weaved his horse through the crowds of carriages and carts as he made his way to the gentlemen's club. He should have been focused on his meeting with Hensley and whether anyone had discovered the name of the man whom Lane thought was the captain of the *Nighthawk*. The next logical step would be to determine whether this captain was associated with McDuff, and if so, what role he played. But, rather than focus on the issues those answers might produce, his thoughts drifted to Stella.

All he could think about was the two hours of snuggling, making love, and planning their day. Mornings that were more akin to her time period. He rubbed his steed's neck and grinned. What made the difference in this time period was his horses. He loved morning rides when the sun had barely risen and the air was cool and fresh. It wasn't just a time to appreciate the beauty around him but to organize his thoughts.

He didn't have that opportunity in Baywood, though Finn had offered him one outlet. He'd bought horses for himself and AJ and made it a point to ride once or twice a week. Beckworth had been surprised when, a month after their first jump to

Waverly, Finn had taken him to the stables. AJ looked at horses the same way Stella did. If they had to ride, they would, but it wasn't their first instinct.

He understood. They hadn't grown up in an era where you didn't get very far without a horse, whether on its back or in a wagon or coach. Finn's concern was that AJ's horse, Seraphina, wasn't getting enough exercise. When AJ was too busy to go, Finn often asked Ethan, but Ethan's security business was growing, and his time became limited. That was when Finn turned to Beckworth, and he never turned down an offer to ride.

In fact, just before leaving for this trip, he'd chatted with Finn about owning his own horse, and Finn agreed to talk to the ranch owner to see what she could find. Ethan hadn't made a commitment to buy one, but if Beckworth had one, that would allow all three men to go riding without arranging a rental with the ranch owner. Not that finding a horse to ride was a problem for her. She was happy to have the horses exercised, and Finn had proven to her that if he said someone could handle a horse, she took his word for it.

If he'd only taken the time on that last ride to ask Finn how he'd controlled his innate nature to protect AJ while in this century.

When he arrived at the club, he found a few letters waiting, and he tucked them in his jacket pocket before heading to the lounge to see if any of his friends were about. He lucked out and found three merchants with whom he'd done business in the past having a midday discussion. They'd always been reliable for tidbits of information, and he spent an hour discussing current events with them.

The men had always been opposed to smugglers, who sometimes undercut their own businesses, but it seemed their positions had shifted since the war. Commodities were becoming difficult to come by, so he wasn't surprised when they asked if Beckworth had any connections. After gathering a short list of items they were looking for, Beckworth promised to see if he could help them out. He'd pass the information on to Jamie since he was still running cargo through the smuggling operations Sebastian had started at the French monastery.

To most, French monks turned smugglers might seem odd, but the monastery sat on the edge of a private cove that was ignored by most French patrols. The Brotherhood of Monks, committed to helping the local community and other French citizens buy supplies difficult to obtain during the war, took only a small profit in the exchange. Sebastian had used the money to purchase sacred and historical items that had been stolen during the Reign of Terror. One of the monks' missions had been the protection of these items, so they believed it was their responsibility to find the items and have them returned.

With Beckworth's mind on the monks, he remembered Sebastian's list, and he stopped to purchase the monk's requested items on his way to Hensley's. He should have sent a note to Hensley to advise of his arrival to ensure the man would be home. When he reached the manor, he was surprised to find not only the spymaster at home, but that Jamie and Lando had arrived moments before him.

Since it was close to lunch, Mary had food served in Hensley's study along with ale.

"Where's Fitz?" Beckworth, happy to find his favorite leather chair available, sat back with a plate of roast beef and other delectables.

"He's keeping an eye on John Leclair and was out all night. He needed sleep before going back to keep an eye on the *Nighthawk*." Jamie had settled at the corner of Hensley's desk and focused on his food.

"Who's John Leclair?" Beckworth asked.

Lando answered while the others had their mouth full. "That's the bloke we'd seen on the *Tidewater*."

"He's French?" The name certainly suggested it. "How did you discover this so quickly?"

Hensley wiped the corner of his mouth and took a sip of ale. "He's a French spy, or that's what we believe, and someone my network has spent a great deal of time tracking down. He also goes by the name Le Renard and has been spotted several times with known smugglers."

"It was a fluke, really." Jamie wiped his hands and sat back to take up the tale. "Lewelyn, one of Hensley's men who spends time on the docks, met up with Fitz to help keep an eye on Leclair. The man had been seen going into a private establishment, and they decided to wait outside. When Leclair left the building, Fitz confirmed he'd been on the *Tidewater*, but it was Lewelyn who gave us the name."

"That was bloody lucky." Beckworth remembered Lewelyn from their joint mission in Ipswich. A job that ended with Beckworth trading himself to Gemini in exchange for Stella's safe release. Lewelyn was a good man and one who could be trusted.

Lando shrugged. "Maybe not as lucky as you'd think. Apparently, Leclair isn't a stranger to London, and he's been on the watch list for smugglers for a while now. This particular building is a suspected safe house for French citizens working under the noses of the constables."

"That will be difficult to infiltrate." Beckworth got an itch that he might have a solution, but whatever it was, he didn't see it yet. "Give me a day or two. I might have an option. I need to think it through."

They all agreed it was better than any idea they currently had. They could have the man picked up and taken to Newgate for interrogation, but the chances of getting anything worthwhile were slim. It was better to wait, watch, and gather more intelligence, especially if it could get them closer to McDuff.

With a bit more luck, Beckworth might remember why he thought he could help.

Stella exited the carriage and gave Flora a wave and a big smile before climbing the steps to the manor, forcing herself not to take the stairs two at a time. First, she wouldn't look like the lady she was supposed to be, and second, she'd probably step on her hem and do a face-plant on the stairs.

Barrington greeted her at the door.

"How do you always know when someone is arriving?"

"It's a butler's secret we take to the grave."

She snorted and stormed through the foyer toward the stairs, then stopped. "I need stationery, quill, and ink. Is the study the only place to find that?"

He gave her a long look, and she could tell he was holding back a grin. A few months ago, she'd think he was just being a stubborn butler, who looked down on Americans—or women. But after being around him and working missions with him, she now understood that he wanted to smile, but it conflicted with his role as butler. So, the long stares were most likely the time he required to reconcile the clash of emotions. Though with his wickedly dry sense of humor, he was probably doing it on purpose to force her to reconsider whether her actions were those of a lady. Considering the whiplash of differing etiquette between the centuries, she was doing her best.

She stood quietly, except for one foot that refused to stop tapping.

"Since you're not staying in Templeton's master suite, your office is in the library rather than your room."

Before he could say anything else, she turned and marched toward the library. Then, as an afterthought and without turning around, she raised her hand in a wave and shouted back, "Thank you, Barrington."

When she reached the library, she stood in the doorway and glanced around. Fortunately, Bart and Lincoln, who spent most of their free time in this room, weren't home, so she had the place to herself. It took a moment to spot the writing desk, and she sat down to search through the cubby holes and two small drawers, pulling out linen stationery, an inkpot, a quill, and pounce.

She ran the feathered end of the quill under her chin as she considered what to say that wouldn't reveal too much. Not that she thought anyone else would read the note, but just in case. When she was satisfied with what to write, she dipped the quill in the ink, tapped the tip three times as she'd seen Beckworth do, and with calm patience, wrote the note. Once she'd dusted the letter with pounce, she waited several moments to ensure the ink was dry, then folded the note and addressed it to Elizabeth.

The letter was simple.

Dear Elizabeth,

I hope this note finds you doing well. What a marvelous time I had with Flora at Eloise's garden party. I couldn't believe all the beautiful jewelry on display. You wouldn't, by any chance, know anyone who owns a piece of jewelry from Louis Pierre Deschanel? I would love to see more examples of his designs. Can't wait to see you again.

All my best,

Lady Stella Caldway

She stared at the note. No mistakes with the ink. She really was getting better with a quill. Elizabeth was a smart woman and should read between the lines. If nothing else, it should pique her interest. She stored the writing supplies away and went in search of Barrington. She probably should have told him to wait for her.

That would have been a waste of breath because the consummate butler entered the foyer at the same time she did. Had he been hiding behind a corner waiting for her? She had mentioned stationery, so he might have assumed she'd be sending a note.

"Barrington, could you have this message sent to Elizabeth right away?"

He gave her that long, cool stare again, but eventually his lips quirked into a slim grin.

She put a fist on her hip and stared back. "What's so funny?"

"Not funny. I just realized this is the first time you've actually asked me to perform a task as lady of the manor."

That couldn't be right. But when she thought about it, she couldn't remember doing anything more than ask questions of where something was or how to do something that didn't make her look like an idiot. Not an easy task for anyone.

She refused to look pleased with herself. She'd have to wait for the sky to turn green before he'd actually compliment her on anything, so she went with her usual flippant tone since it suited her best.

She handed him the note and said, "Don't get used to it."

When he turned the note over and glanced at the way she addressed it, he nodded. "Nicely done. I'll have it delivered immediately."

She stared after him as he wandered off. A compliment after all. The poor man was going soft.

She was halfway up the stairs when the front door burst open and Beckworth strode in. It took him a moment of glancing around before he noticed her.

"Did you just get home?" He glanced around again. "Where's Barrington?"

"He just left to send a message for me."

Beckworth was climbing the stairs when he stopped. "You sent a message?"

She rolled her eyes and continued up the stairs. "Yes, believe it or not, I can write with a quill now. Call me crazy."

He sighed deeply and followed her. "You know that's not what I meant." When she didn't respond as she strode down the hall, he asked. "Who did you send a message to?"

"Elizabeth. I wanted to know how she was doing."

Once they were in their room, and Beckworth closed the door, she turned to him but wasn't expecting him to grab her and plant an intoxicating kiss on her lips. She released her building worry that he'd dig further into what she might be up to and wrapped her arms around him.

When he finally lifted his head, leaving her more than breathless, he grinned. "I love how independent you are."

Her brows dropped as she considered him, forgetting that she hadn't wanted to discuss her investigation into the thefts, and asked, "What are you up to?"

He laughed. "Nothing. Just thinking about your day. A garden party with the elite in the afternoon and an evening of drinking ale and dancing in the East End."

"And I have no doubt I'll have a better time tonight than with that stuffy lot at Eloise's." She removed his cravat. "I'd ask how you spent your day, but right now I don't care." She tossed the cravat on the floor and unbuttoned his waistcoat. That went on the floor as well.

"What are you about, Lady Caldway?" He grinned as his hands reached behind her to undo the buttons of her dress.

"Just finding something to do while I wait for one of my lady's maids." She unbuttoned his pants and slid them down to his thighs, then shuffled him backward until he fell, laughing, into a chair.

He had most of her dress undone, and she pushed it off her shoulders and let it fall around her. She stepped out of it and kicked it out of the way so she could pull off his boots. It didn't take long after that before they were both naked, and he chased her around the room. They were both laughing and out of breath by the time he picked her up and dumped her on the bed, crawling over her, which made her squeal with delight.

He pulled the covers over them until they were completely hidden from view, on the off chance either Libby or Maggie came looking for her. If they did, all that would greet them would be shifting covers and lots of giggles.

For Stella, that was an afternoon well spent.

14

———

Beckworth leaned against the door to the dressing room and folded his arms across his chest. Stella stared at two dresses, apparently still undecided on which one to wear. Libby had left several minutes earlier after finishing Stella's hair so she could change for the party.

He still questioned his decision for Libby to be Stella's lady's maid. They were alike in many ways—bold, too curious for their own good, loyal to a fault, and always seemed to find their way out of trouble. Which was why, when they'd become more than lady and lady's maid and developed a strong friendship, he knew he had trouble on his hands.

When they'd traveled back for the holiday hunting party, Stella was always around. It wasn't that she was clingy—they spent most of their time in Baywood together. From his perspective, once in this time period, her reason for staying close was twofold. They'd spent a good portion of their time on a ship that provided little privacy. He believed the rest of her time was spent gaining her footing in this time period. Without AJ and Maire available for counsel, she had to carve her own path.

Stella had been a very different woman on this trip. They

146

were spending more of their days apart and only finding time together in the evenings, with little time to share the details of their day. Of course, being in London meant she would need to attend parties both during the day and some evenings, and neither of them cared much for gossip.

After they'd roused themselves from an afternoon lounging in bed, Stella called for a bath, and he went downstairs to write a message to Hensley. He'd given further instructions to Barrington, who would personally deliver the message and be back in time to take them to the East End.

When he arrived back in the bedroom, he thought it odd to find Libby and Stella huddled at a table whispering. He'd cleared his throat when he entered, and though they'd jumped, they wore sincere expressions.

"Well, there he is." Libby stood and pointed to the half bath near the hearth. "There's fresh water for your bath. I'll be back to finish Lady Stella's hair."

Doubt still itched at him, until Libby winked.

"I'll trust the two of you to mind the fact we have to leave in an hour."

Then she was out the door before he could think to reprimand her. Instead, he growled. "That woman is becoming a bit too familiar."

Stella laughed. "Well, aren't we the stuffy one this evening, Lord Beckworth. You know you'll be drinking ale and telling bawdy jokes in a couple of hours." She pulled him to her, and all thoughts of Libby slipped away as she kissed him before undressing him for his bath.

He was tempted to pull her in with him. The hell with Libby's orders. But Stella must have suspected his intentions because she remained stubbornly out of reach.

She sat on a chair and ran her fingers over the edge of her robe. That small gesture was a tell. There was something she wanted to talk about but wasn't sure what his reaction would be. He'd learned it was best not to ask and wait for her to bring up the topic.

"I forgot to mention something I learned at the garden party." She glanced at him, then dropped her gaze. Then, without warning, she straightened and lifted her chin. There she was. Demure wasn't a natural state for Stella. The only time he'd seen it was after she faced a traumatic experience or if she felt guilty about something.

He soaped his hair and leaned over to pour water over it. "There's bound to be gossip with all those women."

Stella snorted. "It only takes two to gossip." She stood and handed him a towel, waiting for him to dry off before taking it from him once he was done. "I know the inspector is handling the jewelry theft but..." she sighed. "Did you know everyone is talking about me chasing the thief?"

He grinned. "Did you expect them not to?"

"I suppose not."

She dropped the towel in a basket and watched him dress in what she called his good East End clothes. Not to be confused with what she considered his crew clothes—simple pants, shirt, and jacket. The only difference between the two was that his good clothes were newer and cleaner.

She disappeared into the dressing room and came out with an older pair of boots and placed them by the chair where his polished boots sat. "My escapades weren't the only topic. The first theft was at the ball hosted by Eloise Stanton."

The name sounded familiar, but he couldn't place the woman or her husband. "That's right. I remember the inspector mentioning it."

"She's also the one who hosted the garden party."

He pulled on his pants and then his shirt. "Is that why you went with Flora?"

Her cheeks flushed a lovely shade of pink that highlighted her auburn hair. "I was curious."

Of course, she was. He would probably have figured it out on his own if he weren't so busy with the smugglers. Another example of them drifting farther apart.

"Anyway, it appears the two thefts have something in common."

"You mean besides the fact that both items were jewelry?"

"Jewelry made by the same designer."

He shrugged as he sat in the chair and pulled on the first boot. "That's not uncommon among the aristocrats. Word spreads quickly whenever someone finds a good tailor, cobbler, or dressmaker. The same holds true for jewelers." He pulled the second boot on and gave her a side glance. She picked up his jacket and waited for him to stand so she could help him with it. There was something more.

"The interesting thing was that this particular jeweler only commissioned a small handful of pieces each year. Don't you find that odd?"

He tugged the jacket into place, then poured two fingers of whiskey. "I would have to agree, it seems more than coincidental."

"Would a crew be that particular?"

"No. Not unless they were being paid by someone." He considered the thefts. The inspector hadn't appeared happy to be involved, and Beckworth hadn't given it another thought. He was sorry that Elizabeth had lost something so precious to her, but he didn't see how they could find the thief with such random thefts. "It doesn't appear to be the crews. Chester believes the thief is working on his own, possibly with a partner."

There was a brief knock on the door before Libby entered, holding a tray with an urn of coffee and two cups. "Let's get your hair done." She waved Stella over and began brushing her hair. "Barrington had to run an errand, but he'll be back soon. Bart is in the library, complaining about something, and Lincoln is trying to calm him. Eleanor is avoiding the library."

Stella laughed. "Sounds like we're off to a fun evening."

Beckworth finished the whiskey and poured two cups of coffee, carrying one over to Stella. He sat where he could watch Libby prepare Stella's hair. They wouldn't do anything fancy, but Libby had a way of making the simplest style appear elegant.

His gaze roamed to the base of Stella's neck, her hair pulled back with clips. He followed the elegant line of her neck to the delicate structure of her jaw and chin. Then he locked on her lips and had an incredible urge to push Libby out of the room. He grinned. Would he ever tire of the heat and passion she lit in him just by her mere presence? He couldn't imagine such a day.

When Libby finished, she scurried from the room, and Beckworth rose, setting his cup on the service tray. He followed Stella when she disappeared into the dressing room, where he now stood watching her.

"I like the dove gray." He slipped off her robe. "It might not be colorful, but it's stately, and no one will think you purposely dressed down for the night."

When she didn't argue, he helped her into it, then followed her back into the bedroom. She picked up her wrap from the back of a chair and slipped on her shoes. "Shall we wait downstairs?"

He met her at the door, and she put her arm through his as they strode down the hall. Then their earlier conversation came back to him. "What was the name of the jeweler?"

She didn't hesitate. "Louis Pierre Deschanel. Interesting that he's French."

"It's not odd for French fashion to be seen all over London. That includes the jewelers."

"I suppose." Her voice was light, and he might have noted her quick appeasement if he hadn't been lost in his own thoughts.

The jeweler's name didn't mean anything to him, but the fact that he was French and the stolen jewelry had been his designs made the hair on the back of his neck rise. Could the thieves be French? Before he could give it more thought, Bart's angry voice drifted through the foyer.

Stella gave him a mischievous smile. "I'll look for Eleanor. You can deal with Bart."

B arrington pulled the coach into an alley behind Chester's house, and Lincoln jumped off the bench to open the door. He could have squeezed in with the five of them, but after listening to Bart's loud arguments before they'd left, Stella figured Lincoln needed time away from the old doc.

Beckworth climbed out first and helped Eleanor, Libby, and Stella down before Bart, who had cooled his temper during the ride. He seemed genuinely happy to be included.

Stella glanced around to get her bearings, never having seen the back of Chester's house. Several wood piles had been created that she assumed would be lit once the sun had set. It would be the only light besides oil lanterns and what little came from the nearby buildings.

Beckworth, still beside her, dragged her away to a quiet corner and slipped an arm around her.

"I think tonight is going to be one of my best nights in London." His kiss was light and lingering.

"Only *one* of the best?" she teased.

His grin widened, and her heart skipped a beat. "Time will

tell, but the first night we made love is a difficult evening to beat, though others come to mind."

She never understood how one's knees could go weak by mere words, but she might be experiencing the real deal. Her skin prickled, and she tugged him close. "There's no doubt that tonight will beat any of those fancy balls."

"If we don't stop, I'll have to drag you back into the coach."

Her brow lifted. That location had never occurred to her before, and when Beckworth caught her expression, he pushed her away. "God's blood, woman. Stop seducing me."

She laughed as she found a path to the house. "You're such a tease, Lord Beckworth."

"Back at you, Lady Caldway."

She'd visited Chester and Katherine a couple of times, but on this evening, with dozens of people milling about, it didn't seem the same place. Although the evening was cool, outside tables had been hobbled together to provide the guests a place to sit and eat. The crew, along with Beckworth, had chipped in for the food, and Beckworth had bought the barrel of ale Chester had set up in the alley where most of the men were congregating until it was time to eat.

She found Eleanor in the kitchen, which was no surprise. The woman had already pushed up her sleeves and was following behind the women who were cooking, cleaning as she went. Libby had disappeared, but she found Bart in the living room sitting with three other men about his age, all of them in deep conversation. Stella hoped he'd remain on his best behavior.

She ventured out the front door, where more tables had been set up and several groups of men loitered with their mugs and flasks. That's where she found Lincoln, chatting with a group of young men and women. She didn't see Barrington or

Beckworth, and knowing they'd eventually show up, she returned to the house to see how she could help.

Suddenly, Libby was behind her, her arms loaded with makeshift tablecloths and second-hand dishware. "Can you help me prepare the tables?"

Without a word, Stella took the dishes and followed Libby out the back, where they worked in harmony. Once completed, they repeated their activities with the tables in the front of the house. By the time they finished, the crowd had grown to the size of a huge block party.

"Aren't you worried about the constables?" Stella asked.

Libby placed the last of the plates and utensils. "They don't bother us when we get together. If we're too busy celebrating something, they don't have to worry about us getting into trouble." She took Stella's arm and led her toward the alley. "They should have the fires going by now. Let's warm up and get some ale."

All the small fires had been lit in addition to a larger bonfire and appeared to be well-contained. People congregated around them, laughing and drinking. Libby handed her a mug of ale as the music started.

"Where's that coming from?" Stella asked.

Libby glanced around and pointed to the other side of the alley. "It's a local group of musicians that play in the pubs. Let's go, I have some people I'd like you to meet."

A couple of hours later, after the meal was done and the cleanup completed, the party got started. The men tore down the tables to make room for dancing. Beckworth had shown up to eat with Stella and share a dance, which was more freestyle compared to the formal dance steps at the balls.

When Stella became overheated, she begged off from one of the crew she was dancing with, and he led her to a table where men were filling their mugs from a barrel of ale. When she asked whether he'd seen Beckworth, he told her he'd left with Lando and a couple of his shipmates to get another barrel. The crowd was so thick, she'd only seen a glimpse of the men from the *Daphne.*

The man tipped his head as if he wore a hat, then left her to find another dance partner. She took her mug and strolled toward the back of the house to find a place to cool down. A stack of crates, one of which was low enough for her to sit on, had been moved far away from the dancing. Before she had a chance to sit, she noticed Chester on the far side of the crates, and he waved her over.

"Having a good time?" he asked, his hand wrapped around a mug of his own. He patted the bench he was sitting on. His smile was warm as always, and while he wasn't drunk, his eyes had a slight glaze to them, probably not much different than her own. She was definitely feeling a buzz.

"This is amazing. How often do you have parties?"

"Of this size, maybe once or twice a year."

"It took a lot of work to prepare in such a short time. Beckworth and I were just hoping to see a few friends."

"Beckworth means a great deal to the crews in the East End. Someone who not only found a better life but hasn't forgotten where he came from."

She considered his statement, something she'd already known about Beckworth. She'd seen firsthand how Chester and other crew leaders had come together to rescue him from Gemini.

"Hear, hear." She lifted her mug, and Chester met it with his own hard enough to splash them both.

They laughed, and neither of them cared about the droplets that dotted their clothing. In between watching the dancers, which made them laugh more, they exchanged quips until Chester brought up the topic she'd been uneasy to ask.

"Libby said you've become somewhat obsessed with this stolen necklace."

Stella leaned back against a row of crates and crossed her arms. There was a hint of humor in Chester's gaze, but it could have been the firelight. "I think obsessed is a rather strong word. I'd call it an interest in helping a friend recover a precious sentimental gift from her dead husband."

Chester barked out a laugh, and Stella did her best to hold her own in. "So, do you have any idea who stole the necklace?"

"Not a one. But I have a plan."

He'd been taking a swallow of his ale when she said it, and he choked as he tried to catch a breath. "Damn, woman." He was still smiling. "I don't know how Beckworth keeps up with you."

"He seems capable."

He barked another laugh and wiped his eyes. "Fair enough."

Stella took a sip of ale and swayed to the sound of the music.

"I also heard you think it was a sailor and not crew."

"Did you hear that from Beckworth or Libby?"

"Beckworth. The day after it happened, when he came to see if I knew of anyone crazy enough to cop anything at a ball."

"He didn't think it was crew, either, but I'm not sure he believed me when I said sailor."

"I haven't heard a peep on the streets. That kind of thing typically slips out."

Stella considered that. "I can understand why Beckworth wouldn't consider a sailor attempting something so risky, but maybe the thief isn't a sailor anymore. I can't get the way he walked out of my mind. He spent a lot of time at sea at some point in his life."

"Does Beckworth know you're poking around?"

"He seems to be busy with his own business." It wasn't the first time she'd noticed he'd been spending a great deal of time on business affairs. He hadn't been that involved on their first trip. Maybe it was because he was in London, and it had been some time since he'd been in town. He must have dozens of contacts to catch up with, and he would prefer face-to-face meetings.

"Has the ale gotten to you?"

She'd been caught woolgathering. In response, she drained the last of her mug. "I think it's time for another." She hesitated when he continued to watch her. "Did Libby tell you about our plan? We're still working out the kinks."

"I was wondering how long it would take you to ask, or if you would."

"It sounds silly for a necklace."

"Yet, simple enough to lend a hand if you ask."

She glanced around but didn't see Beckworth or anyone from the *Daphne.*

"Beckworth hasn't returned with the new barrel yet."

Stella played at the edge of her wrap, picking at a loose strand of yarn. "Are you willing to keep this from him?"

He sighed. "You put me in a touchy position. But this is what I'm willing to do. I'll let you borrow a few of the urchins. They like you, and you always bring treats."

She grinned. "I think I can pay them for their time with more than just treats. I appreciate your help."

His eyes narrowed, and he pointed a finger at her. "Once you have your answer, I trust you'll tell Beckworth before you get Libby in trouble."

"No one will be getting me in trouble."

Chester sighed when Libby stepped out of the shadows. "Christ, woman. How long have you been there?"

"Long enough." She grinned at Stella. "Seems I still have it. Are we on for tomorrow night?"

Stella bit her lip. The musicians picked up their tempo, and she tapped her foot to the music. "I have two problems. I'm not sure which party we'll try first." She hadn't even discussed the plan with the women. To be honest, they weren't even aware there was a plan. "And I haven't figured out how to keep Beckworth distracted."

After a minute of silence, Chester shook his head. "I can deal with Beckworth. There's been something I've been meaning to take care of, and I'm fairly certain he and Barrington will be willing to help. But you need to be quick about your plan."

Stella wasn't sure why she did it, and it surprised the hell out of Chester, but she threw her arms around him and gave him a quick hug. "You won't be sorry."

"Of course, I will." His voice was gruff as he straightened his jacket, but Stella didn't miss his quick grin.

"Then let's go." Libby strung an arm around Stella's. "I feel like dancing."

15

Stella, dressed in one of her simpler day dresses, sat in the middle of the bed, legs crossed, and folded the paper into a swan. A tray sat on one corner of the bed with a small coffee urn and a mug of cooling coffee. Crumbs from one of Nellie's pastries littered a plate.

When someone knocked, she pushed a loose lock of hair out of her eyes and yelled, "Come in." She finished the last fold and set the swan next to the others in the growing flock.

Eleanor peeked in, glanced around, then slipped in, closing the door behind her. "Bart's been looking for you."

She sighed. "I know. He wants to play another round of chess, but I need some time alone."

"You mean Bart is in a mood, and you don't want to listen to his complaining." Eleanor sat in the closest chair facing the bed.

Stella quirked a grin. "I think that's what I just said."

Eleanor laughed. "I know he can be a cranky old man, but he's not wrong in his thinking."

Stella couldn't argue. It had been Beckworth's idea to get Bart and Lincoln out of the manor the night before, and based on their chatter on the way home, they had a great time at the

East End party. But the morning brought the stark reminder of the vastly different worlds Bart and Lincoln experienced at the manor versus the conditions in the East End. And Bart had no qualms about repeating his never-ending outrage at the gap between the classes, made more apparent during the war. Bart should have become a politician.

She gave Eleanor a sly look. "Wasn't it you and Bart I saw dancing in the firelight?" The musicians had started the evening with sweet Irish melodies, but as the drinking began in earnest, the tempo picked up, and the lyrics grew more bawdy.

"I don't know what you're talking about." Eleanor glanced around the room as she ran a hand over her hair and tightly woven bun. "You drank quite a bit of ale, so it's no doubt you were seeing things."

"Uh-huh. You're still going to Mary's for lunch with me, right?"

"I don't know…"

"Stop, right there. You spend too much time in the manor."

"I went out last night."

Stella finished the last swan, set it in the pile, then gently moved off the bed so she wouldn't disturb the tray. "Yes, but it's not the same as having lunch with the women. Besides, I have some news from yesterday's garden party, and after sending a message to Elizabeth, I think we might have a lead."

Eleanor picked up the tray without a word, but her silence told Stella she was considering her options. After setting the tray on a table near the door, she watched Stella place the swans in a box. "I have to admit, I'm curious about that. What are you doing with all those swans?"

Stella wiped her forehead and replaced a hairpin to keep her long bangs in place. "I heard the staff talking about a party they're holding downstairs for their children in a couple of weeks."

"Yes. With Lord Templeton on one of his long trips, the staff gets bored, as you can imagine. There's only so much cleaning they can do with no one but themselves living here. Anyway, it was a tradition the lord's mother started long ago. One day a year, the staff is allowed to bring their children to the manor and have a proper English lunch served to them by the footmen. Then afterward, the children are taken to the music room where they can play games, and the staff are released from their duties to join them."

"That's a marvelous idea. Why doesn't Beckworth do that at Waverly?"

"He does, but not in the same way. You haven't spent enough time there to see Waverly in all its seasons."

Stella put the last swan in the box and closed the lid. "That's true enough. It's difficult. I love living in both worlds, but is it a good idea to go through the jump so frequently?"

"I heard Beckworth mention something about once every three months in your timeline."

Stella nodded. "That's the plan. AJ and Finn have expressed their concern, but Sebastian and Maire don't see a problem."

"Well, there you have it. I would think Sebastian and Maire would be the experts on that topic."

Stella nodded and moved the box to a table. "Beckworth agrees."

Eleanor stood next to her and stared at the box. "So, the swans are for the children?"

"Exactly. I wanted to make sure they were done before we leave for Waverly, and while there's still plenty of time." She shrugged. "I didn't want to forget."

Eleanor placed a hand on her arm. "You're a good woman, Stella. Beckworth was lucky to find you." When the silence grew too long, she clapped her hands. "Now, I suppose I should go change for lunch. I don't want to be confused with one of Mary's staff."

***

Stella and Eleanor descended from the coach as Agatha and Flora arrived with Elizabeth. Mary was already at the front door, her hands clasped together as she waited for her guests to enter.

When Stella met Elizabeth at the steps, relief swept through her. This was the first time since the night of the ball that she caught a flicker of something other than deep sadness in the dowager's sharp gaze.

That spark of determination told Stella all she needed to know about Elizabeth's response to her letter. Dame Ellingsworth was ready to fight back, and that could only mean one thing. Elizabeth brought them a lead.

The group, minus Mary, who'd wandered off after greeting them, followed a footman to a drawing room Stella had never been in before. She'd hoped to be outside, but she'd known better. White puffy clouds slowly drifted across deep azure skies, but the air was cooler than on previous days, and a light wind had picked up. Though why they were in this room rather than in the solarium, she couldn't guess, but Mary had her own mind about such things.

The drawing room was decorated with Mary's typical, cozy yet elegant charm and was furnished in various shades of blue. A table had been set in preparation with a sweet-smelling collection of garden flowers arranged in the middle. They took their seats, everyone chatting about this and that, from the weather to the latest gossip.

Mary arrived ten minutes later and took the open seat. "Lunch is on its way. I know this is rather unusual to have a meal in the drawing room rather than the solarium or dining room." She waved an arm around to encompass the room. "This is my needlework room while in London." She winked at the group. "And Hensley never comes in here."

That explained it. Mary was a smart woman who portrayed herself as whimsical and ambivalent to the politics surrounding her. But she was always in lockstep with her husband, understanding his work, his needs, and orchestrating the household around that. The two were never intimate around other people, but something told Stella that Mary carried influence with Hensley once they were behind closed doors.

When lunch was over and the plates removed, the group moved to a more comfortable seating area by the hearth. After a housemaid brought the tea service and everyone had doctored their first cup, all eyes turned to Stella.

She didn't notice at first, adding a touch more milk to her cup after tasting the strong English blend. She'd taken a sip and placed the cup on its saucer when she glanced up and noticed the eager group.

"What?" Her gaze traveled back and forth over the group.

"Well, you're the leader in this merry band of junior inspectors." Agatha gave her a shark smile, which Stella understood was also her let's get down to business smile, which made more sense in this situation.

When the others nodded that it was their opinion as well, Stella brushed her hands over her skirt. It had been some time since her palms turned clammy. The first image that came to mind was of kneeling in front of Gemini when Beckworth had given himself over in exchange for her. A more recent moment flashed of Cheval grinning after he'd shot a crossbow bolt in his own sailor's leg. Her hands had turned to ice when he released the final bolt into the man's chest. She blinked away the troubling sight. That vision still invaded her dreams. Not as often, but it was still there.

She cleared her throat as she refocused on the harmless women. The only mission in front of her was identifying a thief. No crossbow required. She swallowed a hysterical giggle and launched into their discovery at the garden party that Eloise's brooch, made by Deschanel, had been stolen right off her dress.

"When I got back to the manor," Stella concluded, "I sent a message to Elizabeth, asking if she knew of other women who had jewelry made by Deschanel."

"If it were any other designer, the list would have been much longer." Elizabeth pulled a folded sheet of paper out of her pocket. "I could only remember a few."

Stella noticed three names on the paper.

"Let me see." Agatha wriggled her fingers impatiently, and Mary passed her the sheet. "Hmm. Yes, I can add two more." She passed the list to Flora.

"I only know of two, and they're already on the list."

Mary studied the list, then her eyes shifted upward in thought before closing as she began to sway. After a brief moment, her eyes flashed open, and she blinked several times. "I'm sorry. I had an image of his work, but I couldn't remember where. A melody came to me, and I realized I'd seen it at a ball." She turned to Agatha. "It was a lovely diadem belonging to Lady Dorsey. Was that one you were thinking of?"

Agatha's brows rose and her eyes widened as she sat back, her teacup leaning precariously on her lap. "I forgot all about the tiara. I'm not sure how, considering all the frenzy over it the first time she wore it."

Unable to help herself, Stella's broker persona took over with the urge to organize, something she excelled at. It might not be apparent to people in this century when she made rash, dangerous decisions under what she would consider duress, but, dammit, she was always organized about it.

"We need to write down what's already been stolen, when and where it was taken, and who owned the item. Then we'll add the additional names and the items they own. Let's see if we can discern a pattern. It might not be obvious with only two stolen pieces, but I think it's the best place to start."

She glanced around, worried she'd gone overboard, but everyone was nodding at her, filled with excitement. They were having fun. She'd use whatever it took to keep them engaged.

Mary called for a footman, who immediately appeared. She must keep one or two nearby in case they were needed. Stella stored the information away for the next time she had guests. "We could use a warm-up on the tea, a few sheets of paper, an inkpot, and a quill."

Eleanor agreed to scribe, and Stella breathed a sigh of relief. She'd improved her use of a quill, but she wasn't fast and didn't need five sets of eyes watching her.

While the women helped Eleanor with the list, Mary excused herself and returned with a journal, which she held on her lap. Once everything was written down, they passed the paper around, giving everyone time to review it.

Mary opened the journal. "I keep my list of events in here. A couple of the women on the list probably won't accept the same invitations we did."

"We should try to match up which women might be attending the same parties as us," Flora suggested.

"I would think the diadem would be the most difficult to steal during a ball," Agatha said. "One needs to be extremely careful removing a tiara so it doesn't get stuck in your hair. I can't imagine a thief getting away when that happens."

Something had nagged Stella since the party in the East End. "Why aren't they stealing the jewelry from the manors?

Why wait for someone to wear the item in a room filled with people?"

"Because they're not natural thieves." Eleanor closed the ink pot and sat back. "I've only worked with a crew from the outside, helping with clothing and makeup. But one thing I've learned, other than a natty boy, most prefer to steal when there are fewer chances of witnesses, unless they have several crew working the job. And manors can be tricky when trying to avoid the staff." She grinned. "Unless they are part of the staff."

When she received blank, and somewhat concerned stares, Stella added, "A natty boy is a pickpocket. Someone who mainly steals from people in crowded streets." She snapped her fingers. "Don't they usually work in pairs? Someone creates a distraction either before or after the theft, so the one with the goods gets away?"

Eleanor nodded. "Most times."

Elizabeth perked up. "You think there was an accomplice."

"Yes," Flora added. "I'd thought that from the beginning. There was a surge of people that quickly crowded the hallway."

Stella nodded. "So, with all those people, how did the thief get from somehow shoving the crowd to reaching us in barely a minute's time?"

"I don't see how finding two thieves is any easier than finding one," Agatha said.

Stella felt dejected because Agatha was right. The thief had been dressed like any other aristocrat. She doubted she'd give him a second glance if she hadn't been looking for him. "For now, let's keep in mind there might be two thieves. And Agatha is right. I think the diadem would be difficult. The next ball is tomorrow, right?"

She waited as the women reviewed the list again and decided who on their list might be there. As they did that, Stella had to question the wisdom of what they were doing. She wasn't worried about interfering with the inspector. Based on his perception, he no doubt considered the case closed. The problem was predicting where and when the thief would show up next.

Eleanor stared at the list. She wouldn't know who might attend which party, but as she'd said earlier, she knew a bit about how a thief worked. "We have two more necklaces, a bracelet, the diadem, a pair of earrings, and another brooch."

"The earrings will be as difficult as the diadem." Elizabeth rubbed her earlobe. "They're easy enough to pull off, but they're worthless if you don't get both."

"Alright, let's put the diadem and earrings at the bottom of our list." Stella wished she could speak to Beckworth about the best way to track down the thief without him thinking she might be in the middle of it all. She didn't want to personally catch the thief—just track him down. See where he lived or who he was working for. Or, as she initially suspected, what ship he was on and whether it would be in port long enough for the thief to steal the entire Deschanel collection. She couldn't let Beckworth shut them down before they got started.

"That leaves two women who should be at the party tomorrow night." Mary's eyes were huge. "What do we do?"

"Rather than looking for the thief, we should keep our eyes on the women." Elizabeth finished her tea and reached for her neckline, where a new necklace rested.

Stella didn't think Elizabeth was thinking about this necklace. Her thoughts were still on the one she considered lost forever. Stella's resolve, which had been slowly seeping away, was hardened once again by sympathy for her friend.

"Yes." She nodded her head up and down. "Elizabeth is right. We should split our forces and follow these two women around."

"That's something I can work out with Elizabeth." Agatha

glanced around the room, her eyes falling on Eleanor. "Will you be attending?"

Eleanor shook her head. "It's not a place for the likes of me, but I'm happy to help in some other way."

"So, there are five of us to monitor Mabel and Patrice." Agatha turned to Stella. "And if we catch sight of the thief?"

"I'll know if it's the same thief." Stella perked up as a plan began to formulate. "I just have to make sure that as soon as I hear a scream, I head for the closest doors leading toward the solarium. The thief has used that exit twice. He might change tactics since the duke's ball, but I doubt he'll change what's worked for them so far because of one woman."

"And then what?" Flora asked. "How far can you chase him in a ball gown?"

Stella grinned. "It won't be me chasing him."

16

———

Beckworth paid the stablemaster to board his horse for a few hours. He strolled along the dock toward the *Daphne Marie* that was moored nearby. He was early, having enjoyed the ride through London, taking note of anything that had changed since his last visit and stopping to chat with crew members he recognized along the way. Two urchins, a lad and a lass from one of the crews, raced past him but stopped after a few steps and turned around. Their eyes lit up with recognition, and they ran back to him, managing to beg a couple of coins from him—the ruffians. He grinned at their audacity, something that would serve them well for their future.

When he spotted the *Daphne*, he stopped and settled down on a barrel to simply admire her. He'd traveled on her several times before he'd met Stella. Now, whenever he saw the ship, it was Stella who first came to mind. As much as he'd been against it, and how dangerous it ended up being, he'd enjoyed traveling the coast by her side, searching for smugglers.

Similar to AJ, Stella never hesitated to pitch in where she could, happy to perform menial labor if it helped the ship's crew or the cause. He thought about the times they'd made love on that ship, which reminded him of that morning when Stella had woken him. It was a rare time indeed when she woke before him; unfortunately, it was usually associated with her broker business.

That morning, she'd had more intimate thoughts in mind, and he spent a few minutes replaying those moments before someone nudged him off the barrel. He spun around, reaching for his dagger, irritated that he'd let his defenses down. The docks could be a dangerous place, even during the day.

When he found himself face to face with a grinning Fitz, he put his dagger away. "For God's blood, you could have gotten yourself stuck like a roast pig."

Fitz swayed back and forth on his feet as he held in his laughter. "That could have been a knife in your back rather than my boot on the barrel."

"How did you know I was here?"

"Jamie had me run a small errand, and I was surprised to find you sitting here, staring into nothing with a huge grin on your face." He pulled out his pipe and lit it. After a few puffs, he gave Beckworth an appraising look. "You weren't thinking of anyone special, were you?"

Beckworth glanced away. "So, where's this secret lookout you found?"

He caught Fitz's grin, but the first mate let him off the hook and pointed toward the ship. "Let's grab Lando, and we'll show you."

Lando hunched on a crate a few feet from the *Daphne's* gangway. He was carving a piece of wood and only glanced up when the two men stopped in front of him. He blew the wood chips away and rubbed his thumb over the piece before stuffing it in his pocket. Beckworth couldn't be sure, but he thought it might be some type of bird.

"Hello, little man. That was quite the party last night."

Beckworth ignored Lando's nickname for him, which was meant to get a rise out of him, and grinned instead. "If I remember correctly, didn't I see you dancing with several lovely lasses?"

It was difficult to tell with Lando's darker skin, but Beckworth was pretty sure there was a slight blush to his cheeks.

Fitz snorted, but Lando didn't take Beckworth's bait, either. He puffed out his chest. "I can't help my charm with the ladies."

Beckworth shook his head and slapped the big man on the back. "So, Fitz is rubbing off on you."

Lando scowled, but Fitz nodded and puffed on his pipe as they left the docks. "When it comes to the lasses, it only seems right to share my good fortune with my friends."

They laughed and continued to share barbs for several blocks until Fitz stopped next to a warehouse.

Beckworth gave the building a long look before turning to view the other buildings. "This doesn't look like anything special. I expected something smaller and dodgier."

"Wait until you see the rooms upstairs." Fitz led them down an alley that ran alongside the building to a door. A small wooden wedge kept it open.

"Are you the one who unlocked the door?" Beckworth asked.

"Aye. There are a few items stored in here, but it hasn't seen any activity for some time." Fitz entered, and Beckworth shut the door behind them.

The warehouse was smaller than most—long and narrow. Light from the front windows was sufficient to expose the entire interior. Crates and barrels, layered with a fair amount of dust, had been lined up against the far wall, but most of the available space was empty. A set of stairs at the far end led to a landing and a row of rooms that ran the width of the building.

Fitz wasted no time as he climbed the stairs, and as they approached the upper floor, Beckworth counted the number of doors, which were four in all. Fitz opened the second door from the stairs, peered in, then waved for them to follow.

A row of dirt-streaked windows spread across the back of the room, starting at eye level. There was a single desk with a handful of files and papers spread across it, a single lantern, and a thick layer of dust covering everything.

Fitz stood next to the only chair in the room, which had been positioned by the window, and pointed down. Beckworth and Lando stood on either side of him. The street was busier than the one the warehouse faced, and the businesses were open. All except one, which sat between a cobbler and a tobacco store. In one way, it stood out because, like the warehouse, it was narrower than the other shops on the street and had no front windows. It had the feeling of a dark pub, but there was no signage that he could see.

Before Fitz could tell them more, a bruiser of a man who'd been walking closely behind two other men suddenly split from them and slipped inside the building. When several minutes passed and he didn't reappear, Beckworth assumed this must be the private club the men had mentioned at Hensley's.

"Leclair has been seen entering this establishment twice since we've been watching." Fitz took a puff of his pipe. "He stays a couple of hours before returning to his ship."

"How do we know if this is truly an exclusive club?" Beckworth asked.

Lando chuckled. "Lane says he tried going in. The front part of the building, which is only about ten feet deep, has a wall that blocks off the back portion of the building with only a single door for access. Lane picked up some conversation beyond the door, but not loud enough to understand anything. From what he said, a rather unfriendly man, who had a slight French accent, met him at the door, and apparently, knew straight away that Lane shouldn't be there."

"Lane sensed the man was only going to ask him to leave once before using force." Fitz tapped on the window, drawing everyone's attention back to the building.

Another man entered the establishment.

Fitz snuffed out his pipe and tucked it in a pocket. "This appears to be a standard time for some of the members to meet."

Beckworth stared at the door of the club. "How does anyone know to come to this place?"

"We've been monitoring where they go," Fitz said. "Some go to their homes, some to their places of work, but most return to a pub close to the docks."

"The same pub?" Lando asked.

Fitz nodded and grinned. "The same one."

The three continued to watch as two other men, each arriving separately, entered the building. No one came out.

Beckworth was satisfied with what he'd seen. "Now all we need is a Frenchman."

Beckworth followed Fitz and Lando back to the ship in search of Jamie, only to discover he'd left an hour earlier to meet with Hensley.

"That should save us time having to update them separately." Beckworth would need Hensley's support for his plan, but he also wanted Jamie's agreement to help. It might be easier to convince them while the two were together.

Fitz stepped away from them. "You don't need me at Hensley's. My time is better spent at the pub. I need to get a feel for the atmosphere and whatnot." He pulled out his pipe and lit it before strolling up the dock toward town.

Beckworth retrieved his horse from the stables and tossed the stableboy a coin. Lando hitched a ride on a wagon departing for town, whose driver was willing to drop him off close to Hensley's manor. Since Lando would be arriving after him, Beckworth stopped at a store along the way that he hadn't frequented for some time. After fifteen minutes, he stepped out of the shop, tucked a package in his jacket, and rode to Hensley's with a grin.

When he entered Hensley's study, Lando had just arrived, and once again, Mary had the footmen deliver food to the office. While they ate and before getting down to their business, Hensley filled them in on news from Inspector Littlefield regarding the jewelry thefts.

"I'm afraid he's had little evidence to work with and hasn't found a connection between the thefts other than they happened at a nobleman's party." Hensley sat back and picked at his food, a sign he wasn't happy with his own report. "He's spoken with numerous witnesses, but, at this time, with no further leads, he's temporarily closing the investigation. He'll reconsider opening the case again if other thefts are reported."

Beckworth wasn't too surprised. He'd never met the inspector, but he'd heard the gossip. The man was good at his job but seemed to have a chip on his shoulder whenever dealing with the aristocrats. "I find it interesting that the inspector wasn't able to uncover a single connection with the myriad people he'd spoken to, while Stella, on the other hand, found a connection by attending one garden party."

Hensley's eyes narrowed as Jamie and Lando chuckled and shook their heads. No one was overly surprised.

"Tell me more." Hensley pushed his plate aside, leaned back, and placed his hands over his robust stomach, ready for an interesting story, if nothing else.

While Beckworth had opened the door regarding Stella's activities, he wasn't sure why the spymaster was suddenly so interested in the theft of jewelry he'd shown little interest in before.

"The first theft was at Eloise Stanton's party, where a brooch was taken. The second, as you know, was a necklace from the duke's ball. What ties them together is that both items were one-of-a-kind pieces designed by a jeweler in France by the name of Louis Pierre Deschanel. He's only made a small number of pieces, which are all commissioned and require months to create."

"And Stella uncovered this?" Hensley asked.

"You shouldn't be surprised," Jamie said. He wiped his hands on a napkin and took a sip of ale. "Even I know how upset Dame Ellingsworth was about the loss. I can't imagine Stella not getting involved."

Beckworth should have known that as well. With this business with the smugglers and his guilt in keeping it from Stella, he'd lost focus. She'd become more independent during this time jump, and with her array of friends, he'd assumed they would stay busy enough with the number of parties they had to juggle.

He'd been a fool.

Stella, no matter how richly she was dressed or how many parties she went to, was the same woman underneath. Curious and loyal to a fault. She'd mentioned what she'd discovered, but he'd given it no more thought. What else was she up to?

"Is she going to stir up trouble?" Hensley asked. The question was barely out of his mouth before Lando and Jamie laughed.

Beckworth had to smile. "She doesn't consider searching for the truth to be trouble, but I'll keep an eye on her."

Jamie gave him a look that said good luck with that, and Beckworth had no doubt there would be a new betting pool on the *Daphne*, because there wasn't a chance in hell that Fitz wouldn't hear about this conversation. Fitz was always up for a good bet, though as Beckworth thought it through, he doubted it would have much of a return. There wasn't a sailor on the *Daphne* who'd met Stella who wouldn't bet on her.

"Why don't we return to the matter at hand?" Hensley took a bite of a pastry and shuffled papers around until he found his journal. "You say Fitz is at this pub now?"

"And he'll be there for a while." Lando updated Hensley and Jamie on their morning at the warehouse and the handful of men who'd entered the club. "They must be hearing about the meetings from somewhere."

"The pub is convenient enough." Beckworth set his plate on a side table and leaned toward the group. This next part was going to require some convincing. "Being close to the docks, even Frenchmen can blend with a crowd, especially if it's filled with other Frenchmen and sympathizers. But it's also an opportunity."

Lando nodded. "But as you said earlier, we need a Frenchman."

"And I know of one who might be willing to help us out." Beckworth waited until the others quieted, wanting their full attention when he dropped the name. Stella wasn't the only one who could stir things up.

"Alright. Enough with the suspense." Jamie sat close enough to prod his knee.

"André Belato."

Lando and Jamie required a moment to recognize the name, but Hensley was already shaking his head. Beckworth wasn't worried, but he would let Hensley have his say first.

"I see no reason to help anyone in league to steal the Mórdha Stones and the chronicles." Hensley huffed. "I'd be a laughing-stock for even asking for a temporary release."

"Not a temporary release." Beckworth stood and poured four glasses of Jameson. He handed the first one to Hensley. "A permanent release and a transfer back to France."

He handed out the other glasses while he waited for Hensley to bluster.

"There's only one way out of Portchester Castle. The end of the war or a peaceful transfer of prisoners." Hensley drank half the whiskey.

"There is another way," Jamie offered.

"In a box," Lando answered.

"He's actually in Norman Cross." Beckworth ignored Lando's remark and refilled the glasses.

Hensley sucked down more of the whiskey. "I see you've put some thought into this, but my answer is the same."

"Come now." Beckworth leaned against his chair rather than sit and stared down at the amber liquid, trying to remember a name that wouldn't come. It didn't really matter. Hensley would remember the details. "Let's not be naive. It wasn't long ago that the Crown gave a Frenchman a pardon and sent him on his way for providing critical information."

Hensley huffed, still working through the reason why Beckworth had made the suggestion. He was getting close.

It took months of working with Hensley and many games of chess before he learned to read the spymaster's expressions, particularly his blank ones. And while his face didn't change much between the first mention of André's name and now, there was a slight lift to his left brow. The opportunity was showing itself, and Hensley took another moment before he looked up at Beckworth. He was on board.

"What would I tell Lord Langdon?"

Lord Langdon was one of the war ministers and father to Elizabeth Ratliff, the first Keeper of the Heart Stone. He'd been privy to the troubles with the Mórdha Stones and the chronicles and generally helped when he could. Beckworth was certain he'd also see the opportunity.

"Nothing more than the truth," Beckworth answered. "The

only reason André came to England was his uncle's death and the fact that he was destitute. He chased the lies he'd been told since childhood and hoped to cash in on Gemini's plans." He took a long sip of whiskey and turned his gaze to Hensley. "I've met the man, spoken with him. He simply wants to go home. He's no more a spy for France than you or I." Beckworth sat and looked at the other two men, hoping to gain their support. "He can be our spy. Or at least, get inside the club and find out what Leclair is planning."

"You think he'll agree to be a spy?" Jamie asked. "The offer to return home is a powerful one, but it comes at great risk."

Beckworth couldn't argue the point. He'd only met the man once in a tiny, dank cell in Newgate. At that time, the man would have given his left arm to be released. He'd been nothing more than a dupe for his beloved sister.

Something about André had given Beckworth pause in that cell. He was a man who'd hit bottom. He'd finally realized that his life to that point had been a waste. What he would be asked to do might go against his loyalty to France, but it was still an offer for freedom. Beckworth was a betting man, a risk taker, and he'd seen the look of a man who needed a rope.

The only real problem that Beckworth could see was his increased participation in the mission. His one task had been over. He could spend the rest of his time in London handling business affairs and catering to Stella's every whim. He grinned. There would still be time for him to gladly cater to her requests.

Beckworth pushed away his wandering thoughts and his lingering guilt to answer Jamie's question. "I think André wants to prove himself to be better than his past actions have demonstrated. We only need Langdon's signature."

17

Stella leaned against the pillows and sipped her morning coffee. Beckworth lay next to her, reading a newspaper. It was strange that a simple morning ritual practiced back home in Baywood seemed more intimate in this timeline.

She didn't interrupt his reading, not when she was focused on figuring out how she could follow women around at a ball while watching for a thief. After the first couple of balls, Beckworth became more relaxed about her wandering off with her friends while he visited with his. He still enjoyed showing her off, which she'd become used to, and they even danced on occasion. But he was as unpredictable as she was, and if he thought for one second that she might be up to something, he'd never leave her side.

The ball the evening before had been a bust. She'd taught the women a few of the crew's hand signals she'd learned from Beckworth. With the crowded events, verbal communication was all but impossible and made switching who would follow which swan easier. Rather than using the term target, Mary suggested using the word swan since they were regal creatures and it fit Stella's persona. The women enjoyed their games.

Stella watched her friends for the first hour, amazed at their expertise in following someone without being noticeable. No doubt a skill they'd developed after attending dozens or, more likely, hundreds of these gatherings. If a thief had been out there, she didn't see how they would have been scared off by anything their group of amateur sleuths was doing.

Once she'd been assured the women were working the room as they'd planned, she stayed close to the hallways in case she had to hurry to the solarium, but it was awkward being alone, and if Beckworth had been with her, he would have wanted to move around. It was only their first ball, so it made sense the plan would require some tweaks. There was another ball that evening, and two of their swans should be there.

"Am I remembering correctly that we have a party each of the next three nights?" Beckworth continued reviewing the paper.

"Yes. Then a bit of a reprieve for two evenings." Stella finished her mug of coffee and swung it in his direction.

He laid down the paper and refilled it from the urn on the bedside table. When he returned the mug to her, he picked up his paper again.

She sipped and ignored him as she continued reviewing the women's plan. Once Chester had agreed to let them use the urchins, Libby worked out the fewest number they would need to watch all the exits from the manor. Stella didn't want to irritate Chester by overextending his charity while maintaining the coverage they required.

Libby had reviewed the plan with Chester, who'd quickly agreed. While Inspector Littlefield seemed to have given up on the thefts, Elizabeth had learned that the duke was still applying pressure on the constables, and all crews were feeling it. Chester had spoken with the other crew leaders, and they doubled Libby's request for four urchins. Chester had wanted to do more, but after Libby explained the women's position on the topic, he agreed that a smaller surveillance team would have a better chance for success. However, he insisted that once the thief was identified, they would bring in more crew members to help with surveillance.

Stella's legs twitched. She was eager to get out of bed and discuss the weak points of their strategy with Eleanor and Libby.

"Stella?" Beckworth nudged her.

"What?" She startled, and a drop of coffee landed on the bed cover. She blotted it with the edge of her robe.

"You seem to be in another place."

She snorted. "When aren't I?"

He chuckled as he shifted and fussed with the pillows. "I was mentioning Jamie's idea of spending a couple of days or so at the riding club."

She blinked several times. The club sounded familiar, but she couldn't remember from when. Then it hit her. After Beckworth had been nursed back to health from his ordeal with Gemini, Finn had suggested a couple of days at the riding club to assist Beckworth in regaining his strength for horseback riding.

"That's the club just west of town."

"Yes." He laid the paper down and turned toward her. "I know this is short notice and poor timing with the upcoming balls. I'd completely understand if you'd prefer I not go."

"When is Jamie leaving?"

"Daybreak tomorrow. I'll attend the ball with you this evening, but then I won't be back until after the other two balls."

She should have questioned the timing. She should have asked who was going, but assumed it would be men from the *Daphne*. But the timing of their male bonding trip couldn't have been more perfect. This would give her the freedom to work two of the balls without his interference.

She did have the presence of mind to appear somewhat upset by his abandonment. However, he deserved the time to spend with his friends while in London, and she was a grown woman who had plenty of friends to keep her occupied.

She picked at the bedcover, then finished her coffee and handed the mug to him for another refill. "I'll miss going to the balls without you, but there are plenty more for us to attend together. I'm sure Jamie and the men need a break from their confinement on a ship."

"You'll still go to the balls?"

She took the mug from him and drank most of the lukewarm liquid down. "Why not? I can't imagine spending multiple evenings in a row with Bart."

He chuckled and ran a hand through his hair. She wasn't sure what he'd been expecting, but if he had an issue with it, he didn't bring it up. Instead, he suggested something she'd been dying to do since they'd arrived in London.

"If you don't have anything special planned for the day, how about a sightseeing tour of the city?"

And that's exactly what they did.

Beckworth watched Barrington, who sat on the other side of the desk and assimilated his request.

"You want me to watch Stella while you're gone in addition to caring for Bart, Lincoln, Eleanor, and Libby?"

Beckworth was going to argue that he hadn't meant Barrington to watch everyone, but he couldn't say that with all honesty. As the presiding lord of the manor, it was his responsibility to ensure his guests were comfortable, not Barrington's. But he'd been too busy getting drawn into Hensley's mission, though his upcoming travel to Norman Cross had been his idea.

They needed a Frenchman, and he hadn't seen any other solution to the problem.

Hensley's missions had become an addiction.

"Well, do the best that you can. This is the first time I've left Stella alone for this long."

"Except for the moments when either you or she had been kidnapped."

Beckworth eyed his butler and friend, and as irritated as Barrington was making him, he couldn't fault him. "What's your point?"

"Stella is going to do what she wants to do, whether I'm watching after her or not. Besides, she'll be with Elizabeth and Mary most days and evenings. Then there's Eleanor and Libby, both of whom are perfectly capable of watching out for her."

Beckworth leaned back in his chair and grumbled. "That's what I'm worried about."

Barrington had the audacity to laugh. "Do what you need to do, and I'll do the best I can. That's all I can promise."

An hour later, as he rode to meet Jamie for their ride north, he stewed over whether he'd made the right decision. The last time he and Stella had been in this time period, he'd planned on leaving her at Waverly for a week while he went with the crew of the *Daphne* to hunt for a smuggler. Why was he more worried this time? She had two evenings of balls and two luncheons to keep her busy.

She'd be fine.

"I assume Hensley was able to get the letter from Lord Langdon?" Jamie reined in his horse next to a pub at the northern edge of London, where Beckworth had been waiting. "I see you brought an extra horse with you."

Beckworth, woken from mulling over his worries about Stella, patted his chest where the sealed letter rested in an inside pocket. "It was easier than Hensley had anticipated."

They kicked their horses into a trot, and after the first mile, Jamie glanced over his shoulder.

When they moved their horses to a faster pace, and Jamie continued watching their back, Beckworth had to ask, "Did someone follow you from the ship?"

Jamie grinned. "I was just checking to see if Stella was following."

Beckworth grumbled a few unintelligible words, and Jamie's laughter increased as he gave his steed more rein. Once Jamie had pulled ahead, he couldn't help but snort. His friend wasn't wrong.

A nagging feeling came over him, and, at first, he wasn't sure why. Then he remembered waking Stella to give her a kiss good-bye. She'd mumbled a few words before she rolled over and returned to sleep.

"Have fun and take as much time as you need. I have plenty to do."

At the time, he'd been pleased with her words. Now, doubt replaced his ease. She hadn't questioned him once about the hunting party. He replayed her last words to him over and over and came away with only one thought. He wasn't sure what she'd meant by them at all.

18

———

Stella found a chair in one of the sitting rooms and dropped into it. Her feet were killing her. She knew the shoes hadn't fit properly, but they were the only ones that went with her new dress. One that Beckworth had delivered the day before and never got to see her wear.

Well, she'd wear the dress again the following week as long as her new shoes arrived in time. She'd been following Lady Ashby around for the last hour, and not a hint of a thief or a distraction. She glanced up when someone plopped down next to her.

"I thought this would be the perfect party for a thief." Elizabeth waved a fan over her pale face.

"Are you alright?" Stella asked.

"Not really." When Stella looked around for a footman, Elizabeth patted her hand. "I just need some food."

When a footman passed by, Stella called him over. "Can you please have someone bring a plate of food for Dame Ellingsworth?" Once he'd scurried off, she admonished Elizabeth. "You need to keep up your strength. Maybe you should take tomorrow night off."

"Perhaps. But if there's something I can do to help catch the thief, even if I never see my necklace again, I have to do it."

Stella considered her friend. There was fire in her eyes, but it didn't change the pallor of her skin. They watched the guests, and Stella remained by her side until Elizabeth had eaten every item on her plate, though she helped when Elizabeth insisted it was too much food.

Before they went back to the ballroom, Stella had an idea.

"Look, we have one more ball and another luncheon over the next couple of days. Why don't we have a sleepover at Templeton's manor? We have plenty of rooms, and you can bring your lady's maid. I'll ask the other women to join us."

When Elizabeth didn't appear interested, Stella pushed on. "It would be like coming to Waverly for a few days. Just because we're all in London doesn't mean we can't do the same thing here. We can send letters in the morning and see if the thief showed up at a different ball. If we missed him, we'll have more time to consider our plans. You know, like what items are still left on our list, whether we should change our tactics, that sort of thing. It would have been a miracle for us to find the thief on our first two attempts."

At some point during her rambling, the dowager's expression changed from disinterest to thoughtfulness. Stella held her breath as Elizabeth slowly nodded her head.

The dowager suddenly stood, startling Stella. "Let's go find Mary and Flora and see what they think. Agatha's mother is in town now, so we'll only see her at the balls and luncheons." She marched out of the sitting room, and Stella had to increase her pace to keep up with her, wincing each time the shoes pinched. "Will Eleanor agree to this? It seems it might tax an already light staff."

"To be honest, I think the staff would be thrilled to have more to do. Barrington hired a few temporary staff when we arrived, but from what Eleanor tells me, they get excited whenever they have an opportunity to serve dinner parties."

When they found Flora and Mary, who were still watching Lady Taylor, Elizabeth announced the plans to overnight at Templeton's manor as if she'd thought of it. Stella didn't correct her. If that's what it took to make sure the dowager was surrounded by friends while they tracked down the thief, she didn't care who got credit for it. Mary was excited for an adventure, and Flora was on board as long as her husband didn't have other plans.

Stella hoped Barrington and Eleanor would be alright with the unexpected guests. It wasn't until she was in the carriage and on her way back to the manor that Bart came to mind. She sighed. She could ask Lincoln and Eleanor to keep an eye on the old man so he didn't offend anyone, but this had been her idea. It was up to her to ensure the old doc remained on his best behavior.

S tella woke in a good mood and earlier than usual. It was the first night she'd slept without Beckworth in a long time, and while she knew she was being silly, she already missed him.

Libby must have picked up on it because the woman would not stop talking. Stella let her ramble because it kept her mind off Beckworth and what the men were doing. The good news was that Barrington had already received messages from Elizabeth, Mary, and Flora of their pending arrivals in time for lunch.

At first, Barrington seemed put out with the extra guests, but once she'd explained her concern for Elizabeth, he'd agreed it was a sound decision. Now, as she looked at herself in the mirror while Libby brushed her hair, his change of heart seemed a little too quick.

"What's going on in that head of yours?" Libby asked.

Stella wasn't sure if she should ask the question that had abruptly come to mind. She hated pitting Libby between herself and Beckworth, but she had to know. "Did Beckworth ask you to watch me while he was away?"

Libby laughed and nudged Stella's shoulder. "He knows we're too close." She brushed a few more strands, then pointed the brush at her through the mirror. "But I bet he asked Barrington."

Of course, he would have done that. She should have known, but like everything else, her attention was solely on the thief. If only she had surveillance equipment. Did any of Ethan's security equipment work off solar energy? She chuckled to herself, picturing Beckworth holding duffels filled with security equipment for their next time jump.

Libby laid down the brush, added a couple of clips to pull her hair back, then tapped her shoulder. "Let's get you dressed. You'll want to check with Eleanor and Mrs. Evans after breakfast to make sure the rooms are prepared and lunch is on time."

Stella sighed. "Do you know what Bart is up to today?"

Libby picked up Stella's robe and returned it to the dressing room with one of the day dresses Stella had decided against wearing. "You're safe for today. Lincoln has a couple of interviews, so he and Bart won't be back until dinner. A late afternoon tea with plenty of food is being planned in the garden, so you have little to worry about for one day."

"Thank heavens for small favors. I hope the staff is alright with this."

"The staff is thrilled to have something different to do. Don't worry. Everything will be perfect."

———

Several hours later, Stella watched the women as they gossiped over their afternoon tea in the sunny backyard. Eleanor had been particularly pleased to have the women in the manor, which had been a surprise to Stella. The woman must have grown tired of Bart and Lincoln as her only companions, which was most likely the reason she spent so much time with Mrs. Evans.

Mary was in the middle of juicy gossip when Libby hustled out of the solarium doors, performed a quick curtsy to the ladies, then whispered in Stella's ear.

"We have a problem." Libby glanced toward the manor and bobbed her head to the side, evidently wanting to speak with Stella privately.

"Excuse me, ladies. I have something I need to attend to."

The women barely gave her a glance, too interested in Mary's story.

Once they were inside the solarium, Libby led her to a far corner. Her gaze flitted toward the door they'd come through and then to the door leading to the inner hallway.

"What's wrong?" Stella asked.

"A kitchen maid from next door came over with fresh eggs and told Nellie about a theft at Lady Dorsey's."

"What?" That was the woman who owned the diadem. One of the few items they didn't believe could be stolen at a party. "How is that possible? Was it done right in front of everyone? And how did the kitchen maid from next door hear about it?" She was surprised one of Mary's maids hadn't heard about it, or maybe they had, but Mary was here.

Libby shook her head. "The kitchen maid is friends with a housemaid at Lady Dorsey's. She'd been sent over to trade some baked goods. Lady Dorsey hadn't been feeling well, so she didn't attend a party last night." Her voice lowered. "Someone broke into the manor during the night and took the diadem from a locked box in her bedroom."

"While Lady Dorsey was sleeping? What about her husband?"

Libby shrugged. "Apparently, Lady Dorsey was given something to help her sleep, and from what I hear, the lord of the manor takes one too many nips from the bottle each evening. He was most likely passed out asleep."

Stella moved to the closest chair and sat. "The timing seems somewhat suspect. How would the thief know she wouldn't be at the party?" That didn't make sense. She still believed the diadem would have been problematic to take from a party. "Maybe the thief always planned to take it from the manor. He'd probably been watching it, but when the couple never left, he had to wait until everyone was asleep. When did they discover it missing?"

Libby glanced at the doorways again. "They discovered it sometime before lunch. Her lady's maid was preparing her attire for tonight's ball."

"Was Inspector Littlefield notified? Did she know to call for him?"

"That part wasn't mentioned. I imagine they would have called a constable, but I doubt they'd connect it to the other thefts." She lifted her chin like a noblewoman. "They're not that bright."

Stella hid a grin. "Well, that puts a new twist on things." She tapped her chin. "I wonder if the thief is monitoring all of their targets to ensure they leave for the ball? Or was it because they'd already planned on stealing the diadem from the manor?"

"I think they follow them from their manor. It's not always easy to find someone in a crowded ballroom. If they see them leave, they'd know exactly what the lady was wearing, her hairstyle, and possibly get a glimpse of the jewelry."

Stella took a deep breath and stood. "I'll inform the women, but I don't think it changes our plans. Other than we have one less item to keep an eye on."

Libby squeezed Stella's arm before scurrying out of the room. "Let me know if I need to update Chester."

Stella returned to the table as Mary was winding up her story. She must have missed a good one because the other women were dabbing at their eyes to clear their tears of laughter.

Elizabeth was the first to notice Stella's return. "What's wrong?"

Once Stella explained what Libby told her, the women didn't doubt the story from the kitchen maid. And, as much as she wanted to share her opinion, she let the women work it out for themselves.

"It's terrifying to think we're being watched," Mary said, her hand resting on her chest as she glanced around the garden as if someone might be spying on them.

Flora laid a hand on her arm. "That's why we're being proactive. But, I have to say, how can we possibly guess where the thief will attack next?"

"That's why we stick with our plan." Eleanor cleaned crumbs off the table onto her empty plate. "We didn't know where he'd strike next, but it's clear our list appears to be accurate in regard to who he's targeting."

"Eleanor is right." Elizabeth took a sip of her tea, and Stella was pleased to see she wasn't drowning her sorrows. "We have one more ball this week. At least those we responded to. We have to remain diligent in our investigations."

The women turned to Stella, apparently waiting for her opinion, and she was pleased she wouldn't have to encourage anyone to stay the course. "I agree this latest theft has validated two things. We know what the thief is after, and based on the previous two thefts, he waits about two days before striking again. If that's true, the chance of another theft tonight isn't very likely, but he might be getting greedy. Are there other balls tonight?"

"There are two, I believe." Flora nodded as she fussed with her napkin. "Although I think one is more of a large dinner party. We should see if Lady Dorsey contacted a constable or Inspector Littlefield."

Elizabeth snorted. "If the diadem was taken from the manor and not a party, will Littlefield make the connection with the other two thefts?"

"I doubt Lady Dorsey would mention the name of the jeweler." Mary appeared calmer once she remembered the thief was focused on specific jewelry. "If it were me, and I wasn't aware of the background of the other stolen items, I might suggest how rare or special the piece was. No one, other than another woman interested in pursuing a piece of her own, would think to ask who the jeweler was."

"We know the brooch, the bracelet, and the two necklaces can be stolen from a party." Stella steered the women into a new plan that was formulating as she spoke. It had been something Libby said about updating Chester. "We knew the diadem and earrings would be a problem to steal in a room full of people. We can't be certain why the thief was at the Dorsey's manor. However, Libby and I believe he's watching each of his targets to ensure they're wearing the item he's seeking, then he follows them to the ball. We don't know if the thief hoped to steal the diadem while Lady Dorsey was at the ball or if he'd already decided to steal it later in the evening once the household was sleeping." She stopped, considered everything she'd said, and once satisfied, glanced at the women. They were focused intently on her and didn't appear to have any questions. She had quite a few but was determined to convince the women of her new plan.

"If we want to be sure to catch the thief, it might be wise to have the rest of the women on our list monitored at their homes over the next couple of evenings while we continue our surveillance at the parties."

"You're talking about using more of the gangs?" Flora asked.

"The crews want this thief caught as much as we do. They've given us the use of the children." She lifted a hand. "I know you think it's dangerous for them, but this is their life every day in the East End. No one sees a street urchin. They're perfect for this, and the money they earn helps to feed their families."

"It disturbs me that you're right." Elizabeth laid a hand at the base of her neck, which, this afternoon, was bare of any necklace. "The children are invisible, and I can't say I'm proud of that." She sipped her tea, and when she turned her gaze on Stella, the fierceness she'd come to expect from the dowager was lit in her stormy eyes. "We use whatever means necessary to stop these thefts."

"Perhaps it's time for me to talk with Hensley and see what, if anything, he's heard about the thefts." Mary stared at a spot on the table, her head bobbing as if she were talking herself into it. When she finally looked up, her eyes were a bit glazed. "I never speak to him about the matters of men, but it's becoming more and more apparent that this might be the one time we have more information than he does."

Stella grinned at the women. She couldn't be more proud of her friends. They might just be noblewomen helping their friend, but to Stella, they had the hearts of true warriors.

19

———

The ride to Norman Cross Prison had been quick. Beckworth and Jamie stopped for a few short hours of sleep under the stars and made time for quick meals while giving the horses a rest. Once in town, they left their horses at the stables and wandered toward the walls of what appeared to be a fort. From Beckworth's understanding, it had been designed based on the plans of an artillery fort, but rather than keep intruders out, this one focused on keeping the enemy within. This site had been developed for prisoners of war.

Beckworth glanced at Jamie, hating to admit his concern now that they were almost at the prison gates. "I'm not sure André will be happy to see us."

"I think it was pretty obvious that André might not be willing to work with the people who killed his sister. There wasn't any possibility of you finessing your way around that." Jamie looked up at the imposing main entrance and the guards manning the door. He shuddered. "You probably should have brought Lando. I doubt they take kindly to Irishmen in here."

"I considered asking Lando and Fitz, but it wouldn't be wise to bring too many men. It makes André appear more dangerous than he is. If it's just us two blokes, they won't question orders from the Crown. My understanding is that the War Office has plucked a handful of our spies from various French camps. The idea is that André is another one of ours, and we're his comrade in arms."

"A reminder of why Hensley finds value in your skills. I'm not sure I've ever heard such a silver tongue as yours."

They chuckled as they approached the main door. Beckworth eyed the pudgy guard, his hair sticking up at various angles, his jacket riding above his dark pants on one side. He looked like he'd just woken from a nap. He wouldn't be a problem. The man next to him was a sergeant, and he wore a deep frown. His hand rested on the flintlock pistol riding on his right hip.

Beckworth spoke low without turning his head. "I would suggest you let me do all the talking."

"Aye. He looks like a tough old ram." Jamie slowed, so he was a step behind Beckworth.

When they reached the gate, Beckworth kept his eyes on the gruff old soldier as he pulled a folded letter out of his pocket. "Good afternoon, Sergeant. I have a letter for Captain Pressland on behalf of the Crown. Time is of the essence."

The sergeant stared at Beckworth for a long moment, only giving Jamie a passing glance. "Let me see the letter."

Beckworth held it up so the man could first read the captain's name on the front and then the wax with the Crown's moniker on the back. There was a brief widening of the eyes before his formidable expression returned, complete with his eyes now squinting as if peering into harsh daylight, though the clouds hung low in the sky.

"Open the gate," the sergeant yelled as he turned toward it.

Beckworth walked through first, and once Jamie was through, they both turned and waited. After a brief moment, the sergeant realized someone would need to lead them to the captain's office.

He huffed at the private. "Don't let anyone in or out until I return." He gave Beckworth a frown. "This way."

Beyond the gate, a long, wide courtyard ran between fenced yards. In the distance, what Beckworth guessed to be the middle of the yard was a tower that housed the on-duty guards. He could just make out the gaping holes of cannons, encouraging the prisoners to remain on their best behavior. The sergeant turned right, leading them past fencing that prohibited a view of the yards, but he could see the upper halves of the prisoner's quarters.

They didn't walk far before the sergeant led them into a two-story brick building and down a hall to a room with an open door. A young corporal sat at a desk and glanced up. When he noted the visitors, he straightened.

The sergeant stopped at the edge of the desk. "These men claim they're delivering a message from the Crown."

Beckworth scanned the plain room that housed two book-cases and a couple portraits of military men Beckworth didn't recognize. A single closed door stood off to the right. Jamie remained one step behind him, his expression blank as he stared at the wall in front of him.

The young corporal held out his hand. "I'll need to see the message."

Beckworth retrieved it from his pocket and, sidestepping the sergeant, handed it directly to the corporal without a word.

He quickly read the front, but spent more time reviewing the back of the note, turning it back and forth, searching for flaws or breaks in the wax seal. He stood, apparently satisfied, and walked around his desk to the single door that had no identi-fying moniker.

He knocked and entered, closing the door behind him.

The sergeant shuffled his feet as they waited. It was only moments before the young man returned and held the door open. "Captain Pressland will see you." Then he glanced at the guard. "That will be all, Sergeant."

The older man didn't seem to know what to do as he looked between Beckworth and the corporal. When the younger man simply stared at the sergeant, it was another few seconds before he shrugged and left the office.

Beckworth, with Jamie in tow, entered the office and took several steps in, stopping ten feet short of the desk. The door closed behind them, and Captain Pressland, a man a few years older than Beckworth with dark hair graying at the temples, read the open letter. He was of average height and seemed fit enough for an army man, but he probably hadn't seen much of the fighting. This was undoubtedly a political posting, which should be in their favor.

"Sit." He gave a slight wave toward the two wooden chairs in front of his desk. He continued to read as Beckworth and Jamie took a seat.

They sat for a while. The captain was either a slow reader, or he was rereading it. He finally set the letter down, rubbed his chin, then shook his head.

"André Belato. That's a surprise."

"Why is that?" Beckworth asked. The man didn't ask his name, and Beckworth assumed the letter explained everything. Since he hadn't been able to read the message, and Hensley didn't say what was in it before giving it to him, he could only hope it explained enough that he wouldn't have to answer too many questions before getting André out of the prison.

The man shrugged but didn't look away from Beckworth's steady stare. He sat back and relaxed into this chair. "We had a French spy in here a few months ago who'd been working for England. He wasn't rebellious, per se, but you could tell he stayed aware of everything going on around him. But Belato? He does everything he can to avoid others. He keeps to himself, does his work, and rarely speaks.

Beckworth smiled. "You mean the perfect spy who blends in unnoticed?"

The captain gave him a long look before his lips twitched, and Beckworth let his pent-up tension slip away. "I'll have Belato collected. If you could wait by the front gate, I'll have him delivered within the next half hour. He doesn't have much in the way of belongings."

Beckworth nodded. "I appreciate your promptness to the Crown's request." He paused. "The sergeant at the gate won't be a problem, will he?"

"Yes, but I'll send someone with Belato who the sergeant won't question." He handed the letter to Beckworth. "There's no need for me to keep this. It might help you, should you be stopped on your return to London."

Beckworth returned it to his pocket. Without another word, he stood, nodded to the captain, and left the room with Jamie in tow.

The sergeant waited outside the building, giving them a sneer before turning and leading them back to the main gate. The two men remained several feet behind the sergeant, and Jamie nudged Beckworth's elbow.

"I feel like an anchor without a ship."

"Let's just get André and put this place behind us."

"No argument there."

Beckworth continued walking until they were several yards from the gate, not wanting to engage with the sergeant until necessary. He turned his back on him, as did Jamie, and while they waited for André, Beckworth started a conversation on one of his favorite topics—the three-month-old colt from his prize stallion. Jamie had been at Waverly a couple of days after its birth and had taken a personal interest in the foal. They were so involved with their discussion that Beckworth almost missed the three men walking toward them. Two were in uniform, and the one between them wore clean but tattered clothing.

André Belato.

He was leaner than the last time Beckworth had seen him, but prison would do that to a man. André had turned his face to the sky as if seeing it for the first time in months, though the prisoners had an exercise yard. Beckworth understood, after being held captive himself. It wasn't that André was looking specifically at the sky. He was smelling his first day of freedom, and he had a smile on his face until they were a few yards away, and he recognized Beckworth.

André didn't scowl, nor did he pull back, but his eyes narrowed, and he gave the two soldiers a quick glance.

"I think our prisoner smells a trap," Jamie whispered.

"Let's hope he waits until we're clear of this place before it becomes ugly."

When the trio reached them, a man about Beckworth's age, with a clean shave and impressively sharp uniform, gave them both an appraising look.

"I'm Lieutenant Forster. I understand this prisoner, André Belato, is to be released to you on behalf of the Crown."

For a split second, André's eyes widened before he stood a bit straighter. He might not have a clue what was happening, but he understood the importance of his release being approved by the king's court.

"Yes, and the Crown appreciates your promptness in this matter."

"I'll see you through the main gate." The lieutenant nodded to the other guard, and the three moved forward, with Beckworth and Jamie following.

The sergeant looked like he wanted to say something when

the lieutenant ordered him to open the gate, and though Beckworth couldn't see the lieutenant's face, he did see the sergeant's. It had turned a blotchy red, but he lowered his gaze and nudged the guard next to him to open the gate.

Once they were outside, the lieutenant gave André a push toward Beckworth.

"It's good to see you again, André." Beckworth held his breath. Would the man play along?

André glanced up at the sky again then cleared his throat before meeting Beckworth's gaze. "I thought I'd rot in there."

"Apologies. It took some time to find you." Beckworth nodded at the lieutenant and then turned, touching André's elbow to guide him away as Jamie took a position on his other side.

None of them looked back as they walked toward the village. Once they reached it, they went directly to the stables, where they collected their horses.

Before André approached the horse, he asked, "Why did you get me out?"

"We'll talk about that once we're away from here. For now, this is Jamie, captain of the *Daphne Marie*, and one of your saviors." Beckworth dug into his saddle bag and brought out a pair of pants, a shirt, and a jacket that he handed to André. "I'm afraid I didn't bring any boots, but we'll get you squared away once we're back in London."

"London?"

"Yes, and we're on a short timetable. Get changed, and once we stop for a good meal, we'll explain your early release."

Within fifteen minutes, the three of them were on their mounts, racing for London.

———

"**G**ive me a moment." André rubbed his forehead and took a drink of his ale.

Beckworth didn't push him and refilled everyone's mug from a pitcher the barmaid had left behind.

They'd traveled a couple of hours before stopping at a roadside inn. He would have stopped earlier, but Jamie had taken the lead, and André rode between them. André appeared to be enjoying the ride, and Beckworth could only imagine how the young man was feeling. He'd wanted to give him more time to enjoy this bit of freedom before they immersed him in their problems.

They sat at a quiet corner table, the farthest from the door. Once they finished their meal, along with a couple pints of ale, Beckworth told André the reason he'd been released, with Jamie providing more specifics about the smugglers and their operations. The more they spoke, the more André withdrew into himself, though he kept his fist tightly gripped around the mug of ale.

After several long minutes, André picked at the remnants of his second serving of boiled pork. "You want me to spy on other Frenchmen?"

Beckworth hadn't expected André to get right to the point. It shouldn't have surprised him, but he'd been expecting a question or two. He glanced at Jamie, who decided to field the question.

"Aye. I suppose you can look at it like that. All we really want is information on what they're talking about. Anything you might hear that involves McDuff."

"He leads these smugglers?"

"In a way. He runs a network of smugglers, though we don't know how many. Smuggling can be a rather lucrative business, but it's also cutthroat, and there has been some trouble within their ranks."

"And you want me to get involved with them?" André's voice rose an octave, and he cringed. He wasn't the bravest of souls, but it wasn't his fault he'd been born into the wrong family.

"We want to keep this as simple as possible," Beckworth interjected. "You signed on to a smuggling ship in France, never having sailed before. Your family lost everything after the Revolution, and you wanted to get away from Paris. While crossing the Channel, you discovered opportunities in smuggling. Most of it isn't a lie. And since you're new to sailing and smuggling, they'll understand if you don't know the lingo."

André nodded along. He relaxed and drank a good portion of ale. He looked at Jamie. "Why aren't I on that ship anymore?"

Beckworth answered first, wanting to ensure the right tone for his role. "You worked for your travel, but the captain wasn't interested in adding any new hands with limited skills, so they left you here. You either need to find a new ship or find another way to earn money."

André glanced away. At first, he scanned the room. Beckworth couldn't guess what he might be searching for, and he doubted the man would find his answer here. André was a lost soul. Beckworth wasn't sure what, if anything, the man had spent his days thinking about. Was he ready for another chance, even if it meant working against French smugglers?

"Look, we're not asking you to sign up for anything," Jamie said, trying a different approach when André went silent. "Not with us and not with the smugglers. You simply want to connect with other Frenchmen. If you feel uncomfortable, just leave. We can try again another night. In fact, it would be more believable if you didn't stay long on the first couple of visits."

André's glance seemed focused on a young man and woman a few tables over. The woman was blonde, and though she didn't look anything like Gemini, Beckworth didn't miss the longing in

André's gaze. Did he miss Gemini, the sister he never had a chance to know?

André broke his stare and finished off his ale. He leaned toward them and lowered his voice. "What if what they're selling sounds better than what you're offering?"

Jamie sat back and turned to Beckworth. He understood. While this was Jamie's mission with Hensley, it had been Beckworth's idea to bring André in.

Beckworth sighed and gave André the straight truth. "Once upon a time, I worked for a dangerous man. A wealthy man who wielded great power. I sought to win this man's favor. But after a handful of years, I discovered that it didn't matter how many egregious actions I performed on his behalf, he would never see me as the man I was. I eventually walked away, but I didn't do it alone." He glanced at Jamie, who simply nodded, before he continued.

"This is your chance to walk away a free man. Free from prison but also free from your past. We know you have no love for the English, but all we want is some information." Beckworth leaned toward André, and he pushed the plates aside. He tapped a finger on the table to keep André focused. "We want information without fabrications. Just the truth of what they talk about. These blokes are going to leave soon, and we're not going to stop them. They're not the ones we're after. Provide us with solid information, and with any luck, we'll be able to validate it. Either way, once they leave, if you want to jump on one of their ships, so be it. We only ask that you don't tell them what you've told us."

André studied Beckworth for a long moment before blowing out a sigh. "I'm not convinced I'm the best person for the job, but I'm willing to try."

"Why?" Jamie asked. "I mean, it's the answer we want to hear, but you haven't pushed back that much."

André shoved his mug toward Beckworth, who refilled it. With a fresh mug in hand, he leaned his arms on the table, his brows lowered, and anger flashed in his steady gaze. He gave the room a quick glance, but Beckworth didn't see anyone interested in their conversation, and apparently, neither did André. His tone was harsh when he answered Jamie's question.

"I have no love for France at the moment. My grandfather was the last respectable Belato. My father and uncles were nothing but drunks who lost our entire family estate with their foolishness. My sister, whom I'm aware died at your hands, left me for the gendarmes as she made her escape. Once she'd been sold to the English, she'd become as much a stranger to me as I to her. Some would say I have reason to plot revenge against you, but it was that same greed and vengeance that killed my entire family."

He sat back and picked at the edge of the table before pinning Beckworth with a fierce gaze. "You were the only one who visited me at Newgate. I know it was for your own benefit, but you made a promise to me that day. A promise that you would find better accommodations where I could wait out the war before going home. You were true to your word." He took a breath and spit out, "An Englishman showed me better hospitality than my own sister." His focus shifted to Jamie as he straightened. "So, I'll repay that debt to get my life back on track. If that means spying on some French smugglers, then so be it. It certainly won't be difficult to play dumb."

Jamie slammed a fist on the table and grinned. "We have a plan."

20

Stella woke early, but not so early that Libby hadn't left a coffee service. Thank the heavens for that woman. She poured a cup and stumbled out to the balcony to let the caffeine do its magic while she enjoyed the view of the garden. She missed their garden at Waverly, strolling through the flower beds with Beckworth, deadheading blooms along the way. She pictured them digging their fingers in the rich soil as they moved plants around. That was something they'd planned on doing before leaving for London.

Last night had been the second night in a row without Beckworth, and she missed him terribly. But she had plans today, and her tasks would be better accomplished without him snooping around. Although she hadn't missed Barrington's attentiveness to her activities.

Between Eleanor and Libby, most of his efforts had been thwarted. Other than the careful planning the women did in the privacy of the outdoor garden where Stella could keep an eye out for snoops, they never spoke a word of the thefts or their plans. Barrington knew something was going on. She could see it in the narrowing of his eyes whenever he watched her, and the slight frown he gave her whenever she greeted him with her bright, realtor smile.

She grinned at her recollections before returning her thoughts to her current dilemma. The information they'd received about the stolen diadem had been discovered too late to speak with Chester before last night's ball. Nothing had appeared to have happened, as she'd expected, but she was curious if the thief had changed his pattern of stealing every couple of days.

Today, they would reorganize. Elizabeth, Mary, and Flora had a garden party to attend, and their job was to confirm whether the thief had taken the previous night off. Stella was supposed to go, but she asked them to make apologies to the hostess.

Lincoln had been eager to borrow one of the coaches to take her, Eleanor, and Libby to the East End, though as far as Barrington knew, they were simply going shopping. He'd wanted to be the one to take them, but Elizabeth, being the high-ranking woman of the group, demanded that Barrington see them to the garden party and was unwilling to take no for an answer.

He couldn't refuse, and it wasn't lost on Stella that he'd been irritated by it. She'd been surprised that Elizabeth was able to suppress her laughter through it all. It wasn't that Barrington minded taking the women to their parties. No, he was annoyed that he couldn't keep an eye on her and Libby. She didn't blame him. He was likely following Beckworth's orders. The meant one of two things: Beckworth was simply ensuring her safety, or, at worst, suspected she was up to something. But if he'd been truly worried about the latter, he wouldn't have gone off on his male bonding trip.

She finished her second mug of coffee and pushed thoughts of Beckworth aside. There was business to attend to. She selected one of her nicer day dresses, brushed her hair, and was placing a couple of clips in it when Libby waltzed in with a breakfast tray.

"You're already up?" Libby walked through the room and out to the balcony, setting the tray on the table.

Stella followed her. "It's either because I don't like sleeping alone anymore, or I'm too anxious about meeting with Chester." She sat and opened a silver lid, pulling out a piece of bacon to nibble. "We're getting close. I can't explain why I think that, but I feel it in my bones."

"I know that feeling. Most of us in the crews do. Right before a job when you know it's going to go well, and you get all jittery that you can't stay seated for even a minute."

"Exactly." She scooped out eggs, more bacon, and a sausage. "Why are we eating out here?"

Libby filled her own plate and poured coffee from a fresh urn. "It's a beautiful morning, and I thought we might want to plan our meeting with Chester."

"Is Eleanor still coming with us?"

"Yes, but she got waylaid by Bart. She'll meet us in the foyer in an hour."

It was more like two hours by the time Eleanor and Stella calmed Bart, sitting him down in the library with several books that caught his interest. They were heavy tomes and should keep him occupied while everyone spent the day outside the manor.

The three women offered their well-wishes to Elizabeth, Mary, and Flora and climbed into the coach. When Lincoln clucked to the horses, Stella glanced out the window to the front steps where Barrington watched them leave. She was tempted to wave but decided that would only convince him they were up to no good, so she relaxed into her seat and people-watched as Libby and Eleanor discussed staff rumors.

The East End was bustling when Lincoln pulled the coach

into the alley behind Chester's house. A couple of the locals who'd met Lincoln at Chester and Katherine's party gathered around the coach to keep him occupied while the women disappeared into the house.

"Oh, it's so good to see you." Katherine waved them into the kitchen, where she had coffee and tea waiting. "Chester had to run a quick errand, but he'll be back soon. Can I get you something to eat?"

Stella rubbed her belly. "If I keep eating like I have been, I'll have to beg Eleanor to loosen the stitches on all my gowns."

"Not even a berry tart?" Katherine gave her a sly grin.

Stella gave Libby and Eleanor a quick glance, their gazes already turned toward the plate Katherine set on the table. She laughed. "I suppose one can't do any more damage."

Chester arrived thirty minutes later to find the women laughing so hard, they were crying.

"I'm not sure this is a meeting I want to be involved in." Chester sat in the open chair at the head of the table and pulled out his pipe.

Katherine pushed the last of the tarts his way, along with a cup of strong coffee. "Don't worry. We've already discussed it, and it sounds like they have a solid plan."

Chester's brow lifted. "Well, it sounds like you didn't need me at all then." He eyed Stella, who was picking crumbs off her plate with a fingertip.

When silence descended, she glanced up to find everyone watching her. "What? It's Libby's plan."

They all laughed at that. Libby might have offered the suggestion on how the crew would handle the situation, but they all knew Stella was the ringleader of their little gang.

She sipped her coffee while she organized her thoughts. "With the recent theft of the diadem from Lady Dorsey's manor, that only leaves one item we believe would be difficult to snatch at a party—the earrings. We don't know if the theft at the manor was his plan all along, or if Lady Dorsey's last-minute decision to stay home was a boon for him."

"Rather bold of him to go in while they were sleeping, but not unheard of." Chester puffed on his pipe, and the aromatic scent of cherry and woodsmoke floated through the kitchen.

"I'd say." Libby picked up empty plates and took them to the sink. "But I doubt there aren't too many in our crew who couldn't pull it off. There are just too many other easy marks to take the risk."

"The other pieces are relatively easy to grab at a party." Stella didn't want to be a burden on Chester. He was being good in helping them out when he didn't have to, and a large part of it was due to his long friendship with Beckworth. "We believe our original plan for using the urchins to watch the manor exits is still the right way to go. And if the thief works within his normal pattern, he should make another play tonight, or tomorrow at the latest."

"And you don't have a ball to attend tomorrow night," Eleanor pointed out.

"So, we'll continue with our plans for the urchins," Stella said. "If there isn't a theft tonight, Libby and I can join the urchins and be the watchers at one of the manors." She feared it wouldn't be enough, and the thief would get away with another piece of jewelry.

Chester shook his head, and Stella's heart sank. "Beckworth will be back by tomorrow. We need to get ahead of this chap. We don't have any big jobs planned for the next couple of nights. Give me the addresses of where the remaining items are located, as well as which manors are holding the parties where the marks will be. I'll put crew at all the locations. Four urchins at each manor—two in front and two in back. We'll do the same for each of the parties. Watching one manor at a time could drag on for days, and we could still miss the thief."

"I can't ask you to do all that." Stella was thrilled with the offer, but she hated asking so much from him, especially behind Beckworth's back.

Chester puffed out another billow of smoke and shook his head. "I ran late this morning because I was meeting with two other crews. The constables and watchmen are putting pressure on us because of these thefts. We want this man caught or scared off as much as you do. If you provide the money for meat pies—" he winked at Stella, "—the urchins can find their hiding spots early. They'll be happy to sit and watch while they eat their supper."

"I can have one of the kitchen lads deliver a message before dinner with the information you need," Eleanor called from the sink where she was washing dishes. Katherine had attempted to stop her while Chester had been talking but gave up quickly rather than make a scene. Eleanor turned to Stella with a grin. "And we'll send enough coin for a meat pie and a sweet tart."

Stella brightened at Chester's idea. "Well, the only thing we have left to do on our outing is to go shopping."

When everyone stared at her, she added, "There's no way in hell I'm going back to the manor and face Barrington without a package or two."

Stella stopped a footman and exchanged her empty champagne glass for a new one. She'd been gripping the previous glass for the last hour as she meandered through the ballroom, keeping an eye on Lady Russell, who flitted from one group to another like a hungry hummingbird, each new group rich with gossip rather than nectar. If the thief was going to attempt removing her brooch, his distraction would have to be a good one. Perhaps a butterfly net.

Mary had paired with Flora to monitor Lady Seymour. It was a perfect match. Lady Seymour was the exact opposite of Lady Russell, preferring to work her way through the guests like a garden slug, striking up a conversation every few feet. Whenever she stopped, Mary instantly started up a conversation with whoever was close by, leaving Flora to keep an eye on Lady Seymour and nudging Mary when it was time to move on. If the thief wanted to take Lady Seymour's necklace, he'd face another difficult challenge—he'd need gunpowder and a good match to interrupt the woman's nonstop chatter.

Stella grinned when Lady Russell circled back toward Agatha's friend, Lady Taylor, who wore the Deschanel bracelet. Agatha had considered advising her friend not to wear the bracelet, but after she discussed it with Elizabeth and Flora, she decided it wasn't worth the risk of gossip. The last thing they needed was everyone hiding their jewelry in a safe.

The women had planned for two swans to monitor at the party, but Lady Taylor's last-minute decision to attend the ball spread the team thin and made it impossible for Stella to remain near the hall to the solarium.

Stella didn't want to use the women as bait, but how else could they attract the thief? It wasn't like anyone was going to get hurt in the middle of a ball with dozens of witnesses. The thief wanted a quick exit without any viable witnesses. Agatha's solution was simple. She'd stick to her friend like a bodyguard.

It was the best decision all the way around.

"I think I'll ask Flora to come give you a break." Elizabeth appeared by Stella's side, waving her fan. "I've taken enough of one, but I prefer Mary and Lady Seymour's pace."

"Are you sure Flora is up to it? I don't know how Lady Russell does it. She even has me questioning my stamina."

Elizabeth chuckled. "Lord Russell's estate is a fair distance north. He only brings his wife to London for a couple of months. It seems he keeps a mistress in town. I don't think Lady Russell particularly cares about that, but she misses her friends and has a limited amount of time to see everyone."

"Well, I'm sure the good lord wouldn't want them to end up at the same garden party together."

Elizabeth stopped waving her fan long enough to hold it over her mouth as she whispered, "I heard she threatened to expose his mistress if he doesn't give her an apartment in London so she can spend more time with her friends."

"Good for her." Stella sipped her champagne and glanced toward the door to the dining room, where a huge banquet table had been set up. She'd eaten a decent lunch after returning from Chester's and shopping, which they'd limited to an hour, and then Eleanor brought the women a tea service an hour before leaving for the party. It hadn't been enough, and her stomach growled.

"Haven't you eaten anything?" Elizabeth asked.

"I've managed to grab a couple of items whenever a footman passed by." She'd been more like a wedding crasher, grabbing two or three items from a tray whenever one was close enough.

"Go get something more substantial. I see Flora making her way over."

Stella didn't argue. She'd made it to the door of the dining room, trying to decide whether to sit for a minute to rest her feet or get a plate of food first, when a woman screamed and the music abruptly stopped.

She spun around, scanning the crowd in the direction of the scream, but it was difficult to tell where it had come from. Not until she noticed faces pointing to the far corner of the room. She searched for Agatha and Mary. Agatha was within sight and was directing Lady Taylor toward a group of men. Good idea. But she couldn't see Mary.

When her gaze stopped on Elizabeth, the dowager was staring at her, and that was when her brain snapped into place. The scream had been the distraction. Without another thought, Stella rushed from the ballroom and pushed her way through the crowd, and once again, like a broken record, she shouted, "Sorry, sorry, excuse me, pardon me," as she struggled to get to the door and into a clear hallway.

She'd made a point when she'd first arrived to learn where the solarium was and the different paths to get there from the ballroom. Before she got two steps out of the ballroom, she heard another woman scream. If the first scream was the distraction, was the second scream the discovery of a missing piece of jewelry? It didn't matter. Better safe than sorry.

There wasn't a chance in hell she'd miss this opportunity. She slowed and slipped into an alcove to catch her breath and think. There were only a few people in the corridor who were heading toward the ballroom, drawn by the macabre like motorists slowing for a deadly accident. No one wanted to miss out on a juicy story.

She didn't want to get ahead of the thief. If he spotted her, he might change directions. While there was crew at the front entrance, what if he went out a window? The alcove was the perfect spot, but this wasn't the only hall that led to the solarium, and the thief would already be on the move.

After a last glance toward the ballroom, she hurried her pace toward the solarium. When there were only a handful of people, she pushed decorum aside and began running, her sprint taking her through the solarium and out into the garden.

Damn.

There he was, racing a hundred yards ahead of her, trampling the garden beds in his rush to escape. She followed, but took a more circuitous route. There was no way she would catch him if she traipsed through the flowers. Not in the shoes she was wearing. But she kept an eye on him as he reached the back of the garden. She stopped behind a tree.

The thief slowed and quietly opened the gate, being equally careful as he shut it behind him. He glanced both ways down the alley before striding left.

Stella crept down the path and followed the thief through the gate. He was nowhere in sight, which she'd expected. He'd been too far ahead to do her any good.

"Don't worry, Lady Stella."

She jumped and spun around. A young boy, no more than eight, stared up at her with a huge grin. "There you are." She returned his grin, hoping their trap worked.

He nodded. "Maddy is following him. He'll never see her."

"She's by herself?" She knew the answer before she'd asked the question. That had been the plan. One would follow while the other remained behind to report.

He nodded. "She'll let Chester know. But now that I've told you everything, I'm going to run and try to catch up. Is that alright?"

She considered it for half a second. "Don't get too close. Be careful, and don't let anyone see you."

He gave her an exasperated look, accompanied by a sigh that almost made her laugh. "It's our job, Lady Stella. We know what we're doing."

And then he was off, racing down the alley. She wasn't sure how he'd catch up with her, then remembered that the nights belonged to the crews. They would have seen the thief and the urchin tailing him.

Then the last few minutes hit home. She stood with her

hands on her hips in the middle of the alley, threw back her head, and laughed. By morning, all the crews would know exactly where the thief had gone.

21

───────────

Stella rolled over. In the deep recesses of her brain, something told her to wake. She didn't want to, and she ignored her intuition. She breathed deeply as sleep returned, but then her senses snapped into place. The strong scent of horse and body odor made her nose wrinkle.

A soft chuckle brought her fully aware as her eyes popped open.

"Teddy! You're home." She began to sit up, then dropped back and waved her hand over her nose. "You stink."

Beckworth sat back and chuckled. He glanced down at the dust on his well-traveled clothing, and when those cornflower eyes sparkled with mischief, she couldn't help it.

She threw her arms around him and gave him a passionate kiss, but when his hand dipped lower, she pushed him back.

"Oh, no. I might be starved enough for your affection to hug you in filthy clothes, but that's as far as I'm willing to take it. I'll have Libby call for a bath."

She scooted around him and crawled out of bed. When he began to say something, she held up a finger. "I haven't had my coffee yet, so be careful where you tread."

He shifted his position so he could watch her as she poured two cups of coffee. She wondered if Barrington had told Libby that Beckworth would arrive in time for morning coffee. Although Libby often brought a second cup if she had time to sit with Stella.

"Fortunately, I can run faster than you in the morning when you haven't had your coffee."

"Funny." She sat at the table and grinned over her cup. "It's good to have you home. Did you have a good time?"

He hesitated. "It was an interesting three days, and I'm glad to be home. And how were your parties? I hear the women have been staying here with you."

"The parties were as expected, and yes, with no one else in the manor but Bart and Lincoln, Eleanor and I wanted more womanly company."

He removed his jacket and then his boots before joining her at the table. His stubble told her he hadn't shaved since he'd left the manor. It must have been some three days. He picked up the mug, sniffed the brew, and sighed. "I've missed Eleanor's coffee." He swallowed two large gulps then turned his gaze on her.

She typically enjoyed when he watched her, but she started to squirm when his stare went on for too long. Then she understood. There was something he had to share, something she wouldn't like, and he was waiting for the right moment.

"What is it?"

He started to speak but paused. She knew that look. He was reconsidering his words. She tried to remain pleasant, but her eyes narrowed just the same.

"With Mary staying here for one more evening, Hensley arranged an evening at the gentlemen's club with some friends." Before she could respond, he held up a hand. "In exchange for leaving you alone for yet another evening, I've made arrangements for a day together."

She considered him and his offer. Hensley, as much as she loved the old man, wasn't to be trusted. Yet, with Beckworth busy at the gentlemen's club, which could run late into the evening, this gave her and Libby the perfect opportunity to put their own plan in play without making up a story.

She gave him an endearing smile. "What did you have in mind?" She followed it with a wink.

There was a slight twitch of his brows and a bit of a squint. He was suspicious, but when he glanced down at her partially open robe, his gaze turned heated. "I wouldn't mind a bit of a romp in a nice clean bed after a hot bath, but I was thinking more of a day at Hyde Park."

"Really?" She didn't care if he was hiding something. She loved Hyde Park. And she'd missed him terribly. She tried to recall what the women's plans were for the day and then remembered Flora mentioning a new shop opening.

She leaned over the table, took his hand, and whispered, "Why don't I go downstairs and entertain the women at breakfast. I'll see if Lincoln is available to drive us while you take a bath." She kissed his hand and squeezed it. "I can't think of a better way to spend a day with you than a drive through Hyde Park followed by a good romp in bed."

Stella tucked a loose curl behind her ear and turned her head, pleased by Libby's latest hairstyle that was simple but highlighted her long neck. Beckworth often mentioned how much he liked her neck, and a blush came over her cheeks as she remembered their dalliance after returning from Hyde Park.

They'd raced through the foyer, grateful to find a quiet manor with the women still out shopping and Bart tucked away in the library. She'd tripped running up the stairs, and Beckworth swooped in and carried her the rest of the way. Her giggles echoed down the hallway. A housemaid, who'd been heading their way, slipped into another room, but not before Stella caught her quick grin.

Beckworth didn't even wait to undress her. He'd tossed her on the bed, then fumbled with his boots, giving Stella time to kick off her own shoes before she scooted up to the pillows. Beckworth stood before her, and she bit her lip, more than eager to watch his seductive moves.

He pulled his shirt up inch by inch, slowly revealing a hard body as it slid up his chest. When his full chest was on display, she couldn't look away. He didn't have the six-pack abs women drooled over, but his flat stomach was enticing enough, especially when she followed the thin trail of hair lower.

She wiggled as he unbuttoned his pants, and she forced herself to remain where she was when all she wanted to do was jump up and yank the damn things off him. When she glanced up, she inwardly swore. He lived to tease. Instead of letting the pants drop with their own weight, he stood in such a way that they glided down his legs. Legs that were carved with lean muscle.

The first time they'd made love, she hadn't considered them runner's legs, but Finn and Ethan had coerced Beckworth into their morning runs. He wasn't an avid runner, but he ran a couple times a week. It was enough to add definition in all the right spots.

She licked her lips as he crawled across the bed, a wicked smile on his beautiful face. He lifted her skirts, and his head disappeared underneath.

He placed hot kisses along her legs, and when he reached her upper thigh, her anticipation building, he stopped. She released a groan, and she heard his soft chuckle as he slowly removed her stockings, more inviting kisses trailing behind.

Once the stockings were gone, he slid up her body, kissing her deeply as he traced his fingers up and down her dress-covered thighs. The soft pressure of those strong fingers through the fabric pricked at her nerves.

"Do you know how much I missed you?"

When all she could do was groan her response, he planted soft kisses on her lips, the base of her ear, and then several down the side of her neck before he rolled her over.

He pushed her hair aside. His heated breath created tingles down the back of her neck, and he gave her feather-light kisses as he released each button. She squirmed. She wanted to roll over and touch him, but her dress and underclothes were removed faster than she expected. Then his body covered her, the weight comforting and arousing.

There was something to be said of abstinence. Not that she wanted to try it that often, but those lonely nights without his warm body next to hers made her appreciate this time all the more.

And when the waves of release came, he pulled her close and hugged her as if the end of the world were coming and this was how he wanted to see it out.

"It's only been three days, but it felt like weeks." She strummed her fingers along his back. The rapid beat of his heart matched her own, and his warm breath brushed against her temple. It didn't matter which century they were in—this was home.

"I don't like being away from you." He kissed her forehead.

She grinned against his chest. "At some point, we need to be adults."

"Never."

"Lady Stella. Did you hear me?"

Libby's words broke the spell that had overtaken her, and she blinked rapidly, a bit irritated at being ripped away from such a pleasurable daydream.

When Stella refocused on her surroundings and managed to hold back a retort, Libby laughed.

"I know that look." Libby strolled to the bed and began stripping off the linen. She stopped halfway through, a dreamy look on her face. "I think I had a similar look just the other night." She sighed and dropped the sheets in a pile by the door.

Stella's thoughts of Beckworth vanished, too curious about Libby's latest dalliance. "And do I know this man?"

Libby tilted her head for a second before gathering Stella's dress. "You might have met him at the party. His hair is a touch lighter than yours."

"An Irishman?"

"A Scot actually."

Stella considered it for a moment. "I remember. Doesn't he have a dimple on his right cheek when he smiles?"

"That's not the only place he has a dimple."

She let that sink in for a moment before laughing. "And he appeared to have broad shoulders."

"Broad enough for a girl to get a good grip."

Stella was still chuckling over the discussion as she made her way downstairs to dinner. The women were already in the drawing room, sharing their shopping trip with Bart and Lincoln. When they moved to the dining room, Stella noticed Barrington hadn't been the one to call them to dinner.

"Where's Barrington?"

She expected Eleanor to answer, but Bart answered first.

"He took Beckworth to Hensley's." He scratched his head and picked up his spoon, stirring it in the soup as if searching for something before giving Stella a side glance. "Or maybe they were going to the gentlemen's club. I don't remember."

Stella didn't believe him for a moment, but before she could ask more, Mary changed the subject. "Elizabeth mentioned you have a lead on the thief."

Stella glanced at Bart, who was head down, slurping the soup. When she hesitated, Eleanor said, "Don't worry about Bart, he has his own mission to worry about."

The scraping of a spoon on the bowl made everyone turn to Bart, who swallowed down the last drop. He wiped his mouth with a napkin, then pushed the bowl aside before the footman could get to it.

"Don't worry about me. I don't get involved in other people's affairs." He winked at Stella. "But that doesn't mean I don't enjoy watching the games. Especially with all the covert activity going on around here."

"What does that mean?" Stella asked. Did he mean the women's activities or something else?

"We're off topic." Elizabeth clanged her soup spoon on the side of the bowl until all conversation stopped. "I understand from Libby that the crew was able to follow the thief to a pub down at the docks."

"That's right." Stella scanned the footmen in the room, hoping Barrington hadn't paid anyone to spy on them. She wouldn't put it past him to be devious on Beckworth's behalf. "And since the theft was last night, we're hoping the thief is taking a night off."

"How is that supposed to help us?" Flora asked.

Stella leaned back as a footman removed the soup bowls. Once the main course had been served, Stella laid out her and Libby's plan to find the thief and see if he led them to others.

"That sounds dangerous." Mary pulled out her handkerchief and blotted her forehead. "Wouldn't it be better to tell Beckworth and Hensley?"

"They never saw the thief. They wouldn't be able to identify him." Eleanor's statement was logical, and the women glanced at each other.

"They could at least go with you for protection." Flora nibbled at her food as lines creased her forehead.

The women were worried for her safety, and she understood, but their plan had always been to find the thief. This was their opportunity. Though it was becoming clear that some of them hadn't thought they'd actually find the thief, let alone track down where he went. They were finally understanding the power of the crews.

"I'll be there to drive them to the pub." Lincoln, who never said anything during meals, appeared confident in his ability to keep them safe. She didn't know what defensive skills he had, but she was thankful for his support.

"There you have it." Elizabeth, who was back to drinking gin and tonics, signaled a footman to take her plate. She'd barely touched her food. "I trust Stella knows what she's doing, and besides Lincoln, she has the crew." She took a long sip of her drink and gave Stella one of her dowager stares. "We should have solid information to share with Beckworth by morning."

"Well, I won't be able to wait until morning." Eleanor buttered a dinner roll. There was nothing wrong with her appetite. "I think I'll forgo the drawing room this evening in favor of a nap. I want to be awake when Stella returns."

Flora giggled. Something Stella had never heard the stately woman do. "This is marvelous. It's all so dark and mysterious. Why don't we all do that? We can have hot cocoa or a brandy in the library while we wait."

The women, alive with the excitement of intrigue, were all smiles as everyone waited for plates to be cleared so dessert could be served.

Stella kept her eye on Bart, who'd kept his head down, focused on his food, during the entire conversation. But he took a moment to lift his head and give her a wink. He was having the time of his life. And if he'd been watching her and the women, what did he know about Beckworth and what he might be up to?

Beckworth stepped down from the coach and glanced around, not looking for anyone in particular but more as habit. His senses didn't give him any warnings, so he nodded up at Barrington, who clucked his tongue and drove the carriage away.

This wasn't the gentleman's club he or Hensley usually frequented, but that was the point, especially for a clandestine meeting. The footman at the door gave a slight bow before opening it to the waiting butler inside.

Beckworth took a moment to look around. This wasn't the most upscale club he'd been in, nor the most aged, but it was sufficient for this evening's meeting. At least he hadn't lied to Stella that he was going to a gentlemen's club.

"Good evening, sir. Are you a member?" The butler gave Beckworth a quick perusal and, finding him to be dressed appropriately, retained a welcoming expression.

"No. I'm here to meet with Mr. Black." Beckworth tugged at his sleeves, an affectation he thought he'd gotten away from, but it seemed to fit the moment. It was followed by a dusting off of his sleeve for a piece of lint that wasn't there.

"Ah, yes, sir. I believe most of your party is already here." He turned and waved for a footman. "Please escort this gentleman to the Gold Room."

Beckworth scanned the rooms as they passed, keeping his head low, but he didn't see any familiar faces. For a city as large as London, finding a meeting location where someone wouldn't be noticed could be challenging, but it would be too dangerous to take André to Hensley's manor.

Muffled voices drifted from the room at the end of the hall. He nodded his thanks to the footman and waited for him to leave before knocking twice and opening the door. Everyone was already there. Hensley, Jamie, Lando, Fitz, and André filled the leather chairs in what was more a drawing room than a meeting room.

He stopped to pour a glass of whiskey before taking a seat on the couch.

"We weren't sure if you were going to make it after being away from Stella for so long." Jamie gave him a wink, and Beckworth resigned himself to the teasing as Fitz and Lando added in their own rubs.

"It would have been better if I hadn't arrived home to discover a household of women staying at the manor."

Hensley huffed. "And they'll be there one more night. I must say the manor is much too quiet without Mary."

Beckworth had a feeling it was more than that. There was no doubt the housekeeper and butler kept everything running smoothly under Mary's tutelage, but a man missed his woman no matter the situation.

Two knocks at the door made everyone turn around to watch Barrington slip in. Rather than take a seat, he leaned against a bookcase, and other than nodding at everyone, he retained his butler air.

Hensley turned his attention to André. "Do you understand your role in this endeavor?"

André shrugged and ran a hand over the back of his neck. "I go in for an ale, complain about my English captain, and hope to make contact with my French compatriots."

"More like your Irish captain," Lando joked, and everyone laughed while André gave them a sheepish grin.

"And your goal?" Beckworth asked.

"To receive an invitation to join them in their secret clubhouse."

"I'll wander into the pub a few minutes behind you." Fitz puffed on his pipe, the scent blending with Hensley's cigar and filling the room with hazy smoke. "You might not recognize me, but I'll be there. If you're lucky enough to get an invite this evening, Lando—" he nodded to the big man who'd taken a seat rather than lean against a wall like he usually did, "—will follow from a safe distance. I'll be behind him. If we think you're in trouble, we'll get you out."

"Don't be too eager." Beckworth had faith in the man, though he couldn't say why. This was a risky opportunity for Hensley, but for André, it was a chance to return home.

André gave Beckworth a long look before speaking, and for the first time, Beckworth worried he might say something that made Hensley question the wisdom of the mission.

"The only thing I owe any of you is for getting me out of that prison. But I have nothing other than your hospitality and a chance to make some money to see me back home to France. I'm no sailor, and I have no desire to be a smuggler. I only want my freedom and money for a new start."

"And if this French captain offers you more money than us?" Hensley asked. Jamie had already asked the question of André, so Beckworth expected the same answer, but it was important for Hensley to hear it straight from the source.

André released a slow grin. "Let's hope your offer is better than theirs."

The men glanced at each other, but Beckworth wasn't worried. It was an honest answer.

André must have guessed the concerned glances were questioning his loyalties, which was only to be expected since he was a Frenchman being asked by the English to spy on his compatriots. So he delivered the additional words Beckworth had anticipated.

"My uncle raised me to have no values, no honor, and no future. My sister left me for the English gendarmes. I'm not a spy by nature. At this point in my life, I have few needs. Prison has taught me that much."

Jamie was the first to speak, and he made no bones about his feelings. "I need an honest man for this job, regardless of your nationality. If you help us determine what this French captain has planned, or give us any information of value, I personally guarantee to see you to France with enough money for a good start." He glanced around the room. "In fact, I know a group of Frenchmen who would be willing to get you back on your feet and provide you with something worthwhile to work for."

Jamie was speaking about the monastery and the small port where the merchants and monks ran their own smuggling operation to bring food and supplies to the people in northern France.

"If all you need is information, that is something I can do. I don't think I have to pretend that I'm down on my luck." André turned to Beckworth, who nodded to him.

"I'll be there as well, mate. This isn't our first mission."

André nodded and stared into his glass of whiskey. He seemed to be internalizing something, and with more vigor, he nodded one more time as he looked at each of the men. "This has been a great deal to take in since yesterday." He finished the whiskey in one gulp and held up his glass. "I could use another."

Beckworth took the liberty of filling everyone's glasses and was blindsided by Hensley's change of topics.

"We've had a fourth jewelry theft since you and Jamie were away."

"When was this? Stella didn't mention it."

Hensley's brow lifted. "Interesting. It was last night, and I took the liberty of checking with Inspector Littlefield. He appears more invested; however, he's hesitant to reopen the case because he still doesn't see a connection between the thefts. Other than adding a guard or two at the more prominent balls, he has no idea how to prevent them or determine where they will happen next."

Beckworth considered the day he'd spent with Stella. Neither of them spoke of the last few days, and now that he thought about it, that was odd. It wasn't that Stella was overly nosy. She was a curious person by nature, and yet, she hadn't asked for details about his time away. At the time, he'd been grateful because he was tired of lying to her. But now, he wasn't sure what to think.

"Has Stella mentioned anything about the thefts?" Hensley asked.

"No. I only returned home this morning, and we spent the day at Hyde Park. The parties never came up."

"Why are the women staying at Templeton's manor?" Lando asked. "Is that normal?"

Beckworth didn't really know. He'd never paid attention to what women did with their day, unless it had been someone he enjoyed spending time with.

"It's not unusual." Hensley's brows scrunched together. "Though not as typical when in London. Mary simply said the women would be attending several gatherings within a handful of days, and they thought it would be fun." He trailed off, and his sharp eyes landed on Beckworth. "What did Stella say about you having an appointment tonight after being away for three days?"

Beckworth squirmed in his seat as the men watched him. The crew from the *Daphne* grinned, already guessing the answer.

"She was fine with it." In fact, from his recollection, she'd switched the topic to something more intimate. He shook his head. Something told him she'd played him while he'd been devious with his own plans.

Fitz broke out with a full-bellied laugh. "I believe the master spy has just been outwitted by a woman."

Even André laughed with the men, and Beckworth had to accept it. What the hell was she and the other women up to? He thought Libby was the problem, but it was the whole lot of them. And he had no one but himself to blame.

He glared at Hensley, whose smile seemed shrewd. He was the real one to blame. Beckworth wouldn't be in this situation with Stella if it hadn't been for him.

Was it possible the spymaster was running his own game?

22

Stella tugged on her waistband, sorry she hadn't worn a dress after all of Libby's nagging.

"What are you doing?" Libby asked. She was tucked behind a stack of crates that barely covered her head.

"Just getting more comfortable," Stella whispered back. She'd curled up next to a barrel, and her right leg had gone to sleep.

"I told you not to wear those pants." Libby's brows lifted, and her lips were twitching. "What's wrong with them? Aren't they the same ones you wore the last time you were here?"

"Yes. And they were a bit snug then. I should have tried them on before leaving Baywood. With all those garden parties and balls, I think I've picked up an extra pound or two."

Libby grinned. "Beckworth doesn't seem to mind."

Her cheeks flushed, and she peeked around the barrel. "I don't think he's come back out." They were lucky to have seen the thief before he entered the pub. The same one he'd run to the night of the ball, but no one had stayed to see where the thief went after the pub. In Stella's experience, and not an unpopular opinion, people are creatures of habit. A sailor might go to another pub if he were meeting a friend or going with a group. But on their own? She'd bet money a sailor stuck to the same pub. A place they grew comfortable with. So, maybe not all luck.

Libby leaned over to look at the pub's door. Her eyes searched the surrounding area before leaning back against a crate. "It hasn't been that long. We just need to wait. Maybe he's meeting a contact or having a leisurely dinner." She peered around the crate, glancing up. "The pub owner might rent out rooms on the second floor." She squirmed into a different position. "I hadn't planned on sitting out here all night, either."

"We should have found a better place for our stakeout." She ignored Libby's questioning stare, not up to explaining what a stakeout was. She rubbed her leg and muffled a whimper when she rolled to her left. Pins and needles ran up her leg, and she squeezed her eyes shut as she rode out the pain.

"Are you sure this is the guy?" Libby sounded as dubious as she had the first time Stella pointed him out.

"Not at first, but once the pub door opened and that guy in a cape stopped him before going in, I got a good look. I'm sure." She'd never forget that sneer. It must be a common expression for him.

Libby giggled. "It wasn't a cape; it was a cloak."

Stella grinned. "If you say so." She rubbed her head where the thief had hit her. The pain was gone, and the bruise had faded to an ugly yellow, but the memory was as real as yesterday.

Libby's smile faded. "We should tell Beckworth or Captain Jamie. The *Daphne*'s not far from here."

"It would take too long, and I don't like the idea of splitting up. We need to know where he's going. I have a feeling he's staying on a ship." That would fit with her first impression that he was a sailor. "It would be better if we knew who he was meeting with. Maybe it's a buyer, or someone who sells the jewelry for him. We should just go inside and get a table."

"That would draw too many eyes." Libby checked the door again, and not seeing anything of importance, glanced back at Sella. "And a proper lady would be spending Beckworth's money in a reputable place and wouldn't be dressed like some natty boy."

Stella snorted. "You do recognize the problem with that statement."

Libby rolled her eyes. "There's nothing special about being a proper lady. Still, what if Beckworth is home when we return and sees you wearing pants?"

"I've already thought of that. I have a day dress and different shoes in the duffel."

Libby grabbed the bag and looked inside. "I thought you might have brought a snack and your crossbow."

Stella sighed. She hated to admit that she'd thought of bringing the crossbow. It wasn't safe for two women to be on their own by the docks. She didn't worry about Libby, who was raised on the streets. Stella was handy with a dagger in close quarters, but her throwing aim needed improvement. A weapon that could be used from a distance seemed safer. She could handle a flintlock, but the crossbow was faster to reload.

Libby tossed a pebble at her and motioned toward the pub.

Two men had exited and scanned the street. They were both dressed for a finer pub, though not fancy enough for a ball, but any doubt she might have had vanished. The guy on the right was the thief. The other man seemed familiar, but she couldn't place him. For now, he wasn't worth the distraction. She'd eventually remember where she'd seen him before.

"Do you think the guy on the left is his partner?" Stella asked. "You know, the one who created the distractions."

"Anything is possible." Libby moved from her seated position into a squat.

Stella did the same, wincing at the numbness still lingering in her legs. She tugged at the backside of her pants, wishing she hadn't eaten dessert. She rubbed her legs while she waited for Libby to make a move. This was her area of expertise.

The sound of the men's receding footsteps had almost disappeared before Libby crawled out of their hiding place and hurried down the street, her shoes silent on the cobblestones. Stella followed several feet behind her, wincing at the sound of her boots that were hushed but not completely silent.

When they reached the end of the building, Libby put a finger to her lips. This was the hard part. Stella wasn't known for keeping her mouth shut, but when she pictured handing Elizabeth's necklace back to her, it suddenly wasn't so hard to stay quiet.

Libby stopped frequently, her head lifting and tilting to one side as she listened. When she moved, it was quick, and Stella held her duffel close as she trailed behind. They traveled down two streets and two alleys before coming to another street with more activity, though that wasn't saying much. A couple scurried by, and sailors stumbled from one pub to the next.

Libby peered around the corner and, seeming satisfied, waved for Stella to stand next to her.

Stella huddled next to Libby in time to see the two men enter a door that had no visible signage. At least, not that she could see. If it were a pub, there should be a sign hanging overhead. Maybe there was one on the door that wasn't easy to see at night.

"I think I saw a man greet them just inside the door," Libby whispered.

They fell back against the brick wall. Libby's breath came fast, but Stella didn't think it was from fear or their on-and-off run through the backstreets of London. If she had to guess, her lady's maid loved the thrill and adventure.

Stella's heavy breathing was more from overindulging during her time in London. When her heart rate lowered, she glanced up and noticed Libby staring up at a building across the alley from them.

"What are you looking at?" She glanced up to see what caught Libby's attention.

"There are two people in that upper warehouse window."

Stella leaned over to get a better view, but only caught a glimpse of shadows as someone, maybe two someones, turned away from the window. "That seems strange. Why would there be someone up there in the dark?"

Libby squinted as she continued to stare at the window. "I think Beckworth might be up to something."

"You think that was Beckworth?"

Libby nodded. "And Lando."

"How could you tell with no light?" Although when she considered it, there had been a light glow. Maybe from a lantern in a different room or on the first floor.

"There was enough shadow, not to see a face, but body movement. I could be wrong, but someone was watching the street. It might be a coincidence."

"Or maybe they're watching that door."

"There are a lot of doors on this street. They might have their own secret meeting, and they were watching the street for anyone following them." Libby rubbed her face. "Maybe I just thought it was Beckworth because I expect him to jump out from a side street at any moment. Where did you say he went this evening?"

"A gentleman's club with Hensley."

Before Libby could respond, her head spun around. "Someone's coming." She grabbed Stella's hand.

Before she took a step, Stella reached into a pocket, pulled out a swan, and dropped it.

Libby watched it float to the ground. "What's that for?"

"If Beckworth is out there, he'll know."

"And if he's not?"

She shrugged. "It's not like there's a limited supply of paper swans." In fact, after she'd made the swans for the staff's children, she'd continued to make more. They were everywhere in the manor.

They giggled like schoolgirls as they ran. Stella tried to pay attention to the streets they turned down, but it didn't take long for Libby to get her lost, and she was grateful she'd thought to stuff several swans in her pockets. There were more in the duffel, though Libby barely slowed down for Stella to drop the swans.

She dropped one at each turn, leaving it on the right side of the street or alley if they turned right, and one on the left side if they went that way. Beckworth, as well as anyone from the *Daphne*, would know what that meant.

Libby's pace increased, and Stella didn't ask why. The footsteps behind them were getting louder. There was no doubt they were being followed.

When Libby turned down an alley filled with dozens of crates and barrels, the nasty scent of the Thames invaded her senses and told her they were close to the docks. She almost rammed into Libby when she came to an abrupt stop.

"Help me move this over." Libby pushed at a barrel.

Her instinct was to ask why, but the sound of boots close to the alley entrance kept her mouth shut as she helped move it. A small door that led to a basement had been hidden behind it. There was an alcove just the right size for the two of them.

Stella jumped down next to Libby.

"Pull that board over." Libby pointed to an old piece of lumber.

Stella dropped the duffel and yanked on the board, cringing at the sound it made. Libby pressed into her as she grabbed part of it, and soon the board covered most of the doorway entrance.

Libby pulled her down to sit in the darkness. The doorway wasn't completely covered, but there was limited light, so they should be well hidden from the men following them. It didn't reduce her anxiety. If the men hadn't heard the screech of the board, they would certainly hear the thumping of her heart that sounded like a bass drum.

Libby gripped her hand, but it wasn't because she was scared. Her breaths were calm and even, and soon, Stella's heartbeat slowed as she leaned her head back against the door. She would need a good bath after this, and she took a moment to sniff her armpits. She was sweating like she was sitting in the Arizona desert at high noon in the middle of summer without a cactus in sight for shade. And she didn't want to know what her hair looked like.

It seemed like forever before the bootsteps slowed as they approached the women's hiding spot. Three men strode by, but rather than continue, they slowed to a stop.

They turned around and stopped with their backs to the women. They must have sensed they'd lost the trail. Or were they privy to the hidey-hole Libby had found?

When one of the men turned in a slow circle, scanning every inch of the alley, Stella sucked in a breath.

Once the meeting with Hensley was over, and the spymaster had left the room, preferring not to be seen with anyone, Beckworth glanced at the others.

"It's still early enough to check the pub," he suggested, looking to Jamie, who was directing this mission. Now that

Stella expected him to be out most of the evening, he might as well make the most of it.

"It's about the right hour that we might catch something." Fitz was always up for surveillance.

Jamie looked to André, whose gaze flitted from one man to the next, not anxious, just waiting to see what the next move might be. "Are you game to give it a go this evening?"

The Frenchman shrugged. "It's a good hour for loose lips. And it would make sense that I might be relieved of my station or watch—whatever you call it."

Fitz grinned. "That's what I like. A man up for a challenge. I know I said I'd follow you in, but I think I'll go in first and find a spot for a quiet drink." He covered the bowl of his pipe to snuff out the fire. "Keep a sharp eye, but once you spot me, don't look my way again."

André nodded, but his smile was melancholy and perhaps a bit defeated.

Beckworth slapped him on the shoulder. "That's exactly what we want." And seeing the light in André's eyes dim, he leaned in. "Pull on that experience while you're playing your part. Stay in that role if that's what you need to do, but your days of being at the bottom are over. This is your first step to something better. But what you do with it is on you. Understand."

André's rare smile flickered. "I understand. But, for now, I feel more comfortable with what I know."

"Then let's be off." Jamie stood. "Let's give it an hour this evening, unless André finds someone to listen to his woes." He glanced down at André, who remained seated. "Do you know where the *Daphne* is moored?"

He shook his head.

Fitz stood. "Not to worry. When you're ready to leave, make a left out of the pub and a right on the main street. It will lead you to the docks. Sit on a crate and wait for me. I'll be right behind you. When you see me, wait for a bit to make sure no one is following me, then come along. I'll wait for you farther down the pier."

André stood on somewhat shaky legs but nodded.

Jamie turned to Beckworth. "And where shall we go?"

"To our lookout. I don't expect André to get an invitation this evening, but we might as well see who comes and goes from the clubhouse."

Twenty minutes later, Beckworth climbed the stairs to the second-floor office in the old warehouse. Jamie and Lando followed once they lit two lanterns on the first floor, which provided enough dim light to guide their way upstairs.

The street wasn't nearly as busy as during the day, but a few couples with their heads down scurried through. Most of the traffic came from single men heading home from a pub or stumbling to the next one. No one slowed for the door to the clubhouse.

A half hour quickly passed as the men traded stories about various missions, but through it all, Beckworth wondered what Stella was up to. He couldn't help but question why he was standing in a cold warehouse watching a door that no one entered, rather than being back at the manor with her.

"Here we go." Lando, who'd been leaning against the window, sharpening his dagger, tucked the blade away. "Two men approaching the door."

"They look better dressed than most of the men that enter," Beckworth observed, waiting to see if they went in.

When the men disappeared inside the clubhouse, Beckworth scratched his jaw. "Do you think they came from the pub?"

"Did you see that?" Jamie straightened as he stepped closer to the window.

"In the alley?" Beckworth had caught the movement, but it had been quick.

"Two people. Too big for the crew urchins," Lando said.

Beckworth focused on the spot, attempting to pick up the nuances of the night shadows. He'd seen two people as well. Their heads had been down. One had been in a dress, the other in pants. There was something familiar about them, though it had only been a flash as they raced down the street in the opposite direction from the door the men had been watching.

"Maybe a young couple," Jamie said.

Beckworth's gut twisted. It couldn't have been. How would they have gotten down here, and why would they be at the docks? Another movement caught his eye. Two burly men marched out of the alley where the other two had come from. After a quick glance both ways, they turned toward the direction the first two had run, and they picked up their pace.

"We need to get down there." Beckworth didn't wait for the others as he ran out of the office and down the stairs. The clomping of boots assured him they were right behind him. He was racing out the door as the lanterns in the warehouse turned dark.

Beckworth made a left out of the building, then turned again when he reached the first alley, cutting over to the street with the clubhouse. He rushed to the alley entrance.

"This isn't the way they went." Jamie glanced around, then peered down the street where the others had run.

"Damn it to hell." Beckworth bent down and picked up the one item he hadn't wanted to find. He held it up for the others to see.

"A swan?" Lando rubbed his face when he realized what that meant.

"Keep your eyes out for more." Beckworth pocketed the

swan and raced down the street in the direction the men had run. They must have been chasing Stella and Libby.

"How could she have gotten down here, and who was with her?" Jamie asked.

"I thought they looked familiar, but I couldn't put it together fast enough. She's with Libby."

No one said another word. They didn't have to. After Hensley's mention of a fourth theft, and Stella not saying a word about it, he had no doubt they were tracking the thief. How the hell had she located someone the constables and watchmen couldn't? It might have been one of her gut instincts, or maybe Libby had gotten her involved with something else entirely. Either way, if men were following them, it wasn't good.

They found three more swans, understanding the directional placements where they'd been dropped, before they came upon the two men at an intersection. They spun around when they heard the hurried footsteps behind them, and Lando fell back to remain in the shadows. Beckworth had a clear view of their faces, even in the dim light, but didn't recognize either of them.

"What do you want?" The man on the left spoke with a deep London accent and was an inch shorter than the other man, although it didn't mean much as they were both husky.

"We're looking for a couple of natty boys who stole a few quid and a crown from us." Beckworth was grateful that while his days of spying were few and far between, his ability to come up with a quick lie hadn't grown rusty.

Jamie glanced at the ground by the corner of the building. Beckworth followed his gaze and spotted the white swan lying on the cobblestone like an injured bird.

"We haven't seen anyone." He nudged the bigger man and gave him a head nod in the direction opposite from where the women had run, if the placement of the swan was to be believed.

The men hustled off quickly, and if it hadn't been for the swans, Beckworth would have thought they'd made a mistake in the men's intentions.

Lando stepped out of the shadows and picked up the swan.

"Did you recognize the men?" Jamie asked.

Lando nodded. "The sailor on the right has been seen on the *Nighthawk*."

Jamie looked at Beckworth. "What are Stella and Libby up to?"

Anger at Stella's rash decisions nipped at Beckworth. "I don't know. But let's see if we can find them."

They continued to follow the swans and were surprised a block later when they didn't find any more of them. They scanned the intersection in all four directions.

"Beckworth. Over here."

He whipped around. "Stella?" He peered into the darkness and walked toward the voice.

Jamie and Lando followed as they kept an eye on their surroundings.

"Yes. Get over here. There are men following us."

"I know. They're gone." Beckworth's anger was tempered by curiosity while he watched a board pushed aside to reveal what looked like a doorway.

There was a shuffle of feet as Stella, followed by Libby, stepped out of the small alcove.

"What are you doing down here?" Beckworth hissed.

Stella and Libby stared at each other but didn't seem eager to share.

"What made you drop the swans?" Jamie asked, seeming to understand that a different tactic was required.

Beckworth would have done the same thing if his anger and fear for Stella's safety hadn't overridden his common sense. He should know that his darkening mood wouldn't sit well with her.

"So you could track us." Stella pulled up the duffel strap that kept sliding down her shoulder.

"What made you think anyone who understood the swans would be down here?" Beckworth asked.

"Because you were watching from the warehouse window."

Beckworth took a step back and ignored the low chuckles coming from Jamie and Lando. "How did you know that?"

Stella rolled her eyes and pointed to Libby. "She saw you moments before the bad guys saw us."

"I should have known." He gave Libby an appraising look. His inner crew member found it difficult to admonish her for her excellent skills. "Good to see you haven't become lazy."

Libby tsked. "Please. I'm not as old as some." She grinned, then elbowed Stella. "We should get going. They might come back this way."

Beckworth grabbed Stella's arm when she moved toward the alley. "Not that way. You're coming with us."

Stella tugged her arm free. "Lincoln is waiting for us."

Beckworth's original irritation returned. "You got Lincoln involved in your scheming? And you still haven't explained why you're here in the first place." He pointed at Libby. "You know how dangerous it is down here." He waved his arm down the street where the two brutes had gone. "Two men were chasing you."

Stella took a step back and planted both fists on her hips. "I'm not sure where to start with you." She ignored another round of chuckles from Jamie and Lando. "First, we were not scheming. We were investigating a theft. Something the police, guards, inspectors, whatever you call them—" she waved an arm in the air as if the universe could provide the answer, "—should be doing. But they don't seem to care that precious items are being stolen." She stood straighter. "I'm going to find Elizabeth's necklace, and now we're one step closer." She stopped, her eyes rolling upward as she thought. "What was I saying? Oh, yeah. We're not scheming.

"Secondly, and I suppose my only other thought, is regarding Lincoln's involvement. How else were we supposed to get down here? It's too far to walk, and I can't drive the coach in these narrow streets." She considered her statement. "Maybe I need to learn to do that. You know. In case we have to escape in a hurry and there's no other conveyance."

Libby attempted to hold back a grin but failed miserably. Lando stared at the dark night sky as if searching for answers to life in the stars, and Jamie, unabashed about his wide smile, looked on in apparent adoration.

Beckworth rubbed his temple. He couldn't remember the last time he had a headache. All he could do was growl out, "We'll walk you back to your carriage."

Libby nudged Stella. "Shouldn't we tell them about the thief and his partner going into that unmarked door?"

"Back where we first saw you?" Jamie asked.

Libby nodded. "Two men, dressed in fine clothing, though not nice enough for a ball. One had a cloak."

The men looked at each other.

"We still need to check on Fitz and André," Lando said.

"They'll be alright for another hour. Let's go back to the warehouse and see if we can catch them leaving, if they haven't already." Jamie waited for Beckworth. "We can catch up with Barrington."

When Beckworth nodded, the men rushed off, leaving him to follow behind Libby, since she was the only one who could lead them to Lincoln.

His anger at Stella diminished slightly as he watched her march alongside Libby. She kept her chin lifted and her stride confident all the way back to the coach. He jumped onto the bench with Lincoln rather than be enclosed with two hostile women for the ride back, and mused, not for the first time, how he could be so upset with her yet proud at the same time.

23

———

When the carriage reached the manor, Beckworth jumped down to let the women out, then returned to the bench. Anger hovered at the edges, and he needed more time to let it wear off. Lincoln didn't say anything. He'd been around enough of Bart's tantrums to know when to stay quiet. When they reached the carriage house, Beckworth squeezed the lad's shoulder to let him know everything was fine before he trudged back to the manor.

He'd barely entered the foyer when Libby darted around a corner and out of sight. His fear and concern for Stella came tumbling back, as did the fact she'd gone behind his back to sneak around the docks in the middle of the night.

That nagging feeling of double standards poked at him as he raced up the stairs to their room, but he pushed it aside when he reached the bedroom door. Who would he face on the other side? The spitfire or the diplomat?

Stella sat at the dressing table, brushing her hair. She didn't glance his way, nor did she say anything. At first, he thought she might be contrite about her actions. It was possible. Then he caught a glimpse of her stubborn expression in the mirror, and his fear-induced anger flared before he could pull it back.

"What the hell were you thinking?"

She brushed her hair for another ten strokes before setting down the hairbrush and opening a jar. The lavender scent wrapped around him as she spread the cream over her arms. Her nightly ritual.

When she turned toward him, her head tilted to one side. "Exactly what are you referring to?" Before he could answer, she stood, tied her robe closed, and planted her fists on her curvaceous hips.

He swallowed and waited for the storm. It hadn't taken him long to learn, back when they were running from Gemini, that it was best to let her get it all out. Then they could speak rationally about her poor decisions.

"Are you angry because two women shouldn't have left the house without a proper escort? Oh, but wait, Lincoln was with us. Or perhaps it's because we were tracking a thief. Well, perhaps we should have waited for the indifferent inspector to figure it all out. Maybe we should let the crews continue to take the heat for some interloper. Or, maybe I should have just told Elizabeth that her precious necklace, a special one-of-a-kind necklace that her dead husband had commissioned for her, was gone forever, and she needs to suck it up." She tapped her foot in rhythm to her heated speech. "Well, which is it?"

He waved his hand in the air to stop her, refusing to be taken in by another one of her lists, as if he were in the wrong for worrying about her. He had every right to worry over her. He loved her. And she had to understand how dangerous her actions had been.

"All of it," he snapped. "First, Lincoln isn't an appropriate escort. He's too young, and you left him at the carriage."

"Too young to escort us, but not too young for the Royal College of Surgeons?"

"He should have been at your side. But then, you shouldn't

have been crawling around the back alleys of the docks. It's too dangerous for women on their own."

"Would it have been too dangerous if Libby were working a job for the crew? Or are you going to tell me that Chester doesn't have young girls and women all over the East End in the middle of the night without proper escorts?"

"You're not one of the crew."

"And I'm not part of the aristocracy, either. I'm simply accepted, or partially accepted, because I'm your consort." Her eyes narrowed. "Or perhaps it's more that I'm an oddity to be examined."

That made him step back. "That's not true."

She shrugged. "Maybe. Maybe not. The point is, there was a theft. More than one. And no one—no one—is doing anything about it." She pointed a finger at him. "But the women got together and we figured it out." Her gaze lifted to the ceiling for a moment. "Well, we almost have it figured out. The thief was tracked to a pub near the docks. We were just trying to see where he goes after that. We got lucky tonight and tracked him to that building without any signs. Doesn't that seem odd on a street full of vendors and pubs?"

"And whose idea was it to track them on your own? Elizabeth? Mary?"

"Don't pick on them just because they're bold enough to help a friend. Besides, they're enjoying their part in finding the thief. And all of our work before tonight has been at the balls, keeping an eye on the women who wore jewelry the thief was after." She hesitated, wanting to say more, but was considering her words carefully, which meant he wasn't going to be like what came next. "We used the crew to follow the thief."

"You got the crew involved with this? I should have known. It's Libby I should be reprimanding."

Her green eyes flashed with a fire he hadn't seen for some

time. "Don't even think about bringing her into this. You know this has nothing to do with her, and being in service to me, she was only doing what I asked."

He opened his mouth, then shut it. There was something he was missing. Libby still held some sway with the crew, but enough to gain resources for their scheming? Would Stella have asked her to do that? Not when she had direct contact with the crew leader.

"You went to Chester." Saying it out loud made it even more unbelievable. Had Chester worked with her behind his back? Had this all occurred during the three days he'd been gone to retrieve André? He'd been so involved in his own mission that he hadn't spoken to Chester since their party. The thought gutted him.

The steam seemed to go out of her until she turned the conversation to his activities.

"Lando mentioned someone by the name of André. I've been racking my brain ever since we left the docks, and I could only think of one André. But then, I must have been mistaken, because last I heard, André Belato, Gemini's brother, was in Newgate prison. That couldn't be the same André that Lando spoke of. I'm just curious, because the name sounds French to me."

Had he really thought she wouldn't discover what he was up to? Over the last week, they'd grown apart. Oh, they had their dalliances, but they had a deeper connection than their intimate moments. They shared everything, until this trip. Until Hensley stepped in between them. Hensley didn't do it on purpose. The man was single-minded, and with the war, his pursuit to protect England only became more dogged.

Beckworth was suddenly quite weary, and he leaned against the dresser. He wanted to sit, but he was feeling too defensive, and it was time to come clean.

"Sometime after the *Daphne* docked, Michelson and Lane heard rumors of smugglers in port who might be working for McDuff." When Stella's face drained of color, most likely thinking of Cheval more than McDuff, he hurried to explain the rest. "Jamie's crew found the ship, the *Nighthawk*, but Hensley needed confirmation of someone on the ship who'd been seen with McDuff."

Stella turned away from him as she paced, not something she typically did, and he wasn't sure if that was a good or bad sign. She had that look that she was mulling over what he'd shared and was trying to connect the dots.

"So those times you told me you were in the East End or taking care of other business, you were running surveillance."

"There are only a few of us who've seen the men in McDuff's circle. Since we don't think McDuff is in London, we suspect someone he trusts is. We've been able to identify the ship's captain as someone we'd seen on the *Tidewater*. That's the ship that was with *The Horseman* when they were loading crates in that cove. We've seen the man go in and out of the same uniden-tified building that your thief entered."

"And no doubt, Hensley told you to leave me out of this." She tapped a finger on her chin. Now she was in thinking mode and didn't expect a response. His assumption proved correct when she strode to the window that looked out over the manor's garden.

There were a dozen things he wanted to say, but she wouldn't hear them. At least not consciously. She was working through the past week, trying to make sense of things.

"For some reason, you need a Frenchman, and you thought André could help, so you got him out of prison. At least, I assume he was still in prison if he's in England." She spun around. "You think McDuff sent someone here to find a source for French guns since Cheval is out of the picture and Lady Swan disappeared?"

That had only taken ten minutes for her to suss out. How had he or Hensley ever expected to hide anything from her?

"They have to pay for the guns, right?" She turned to him, her forehead still scrunched in thought.

He chuckled, even though it was strained. "That's usually how it works."

"What if the one-of-a-kind jewelry created by a Frenchman is more valuable than we think? What if these thefts were a way to pay for the guns?" Her excitement built as she stepped through it. "It's probably not enough to cover the entire payment, but it seems more than a coincidence that the thief went to the same building where you've seen McDuff's allies."

He'd been thinking the same thing on the drive back to the manor. As much as he'd been irritated with Stella's escapades, the fact they'd both followed different men and ended up at the same unmarked building spoke volumes. Had Hensley foreseen this possibility once he'd heard about the provenance of the stolen jewelry? He should have seen it himself.

He didn't move from his spot, somewhat comforted by the hard edge of the dresser that poked into his hip. "I knew what Hensley asked of me was wrong. I wouldn't have before I met you. Or maybe it's more than that. Living in your time period, seeing the enlightenment that comes from decades of science and education has put a rather sharp spotlight on my actions as a nineteenth-century man.

"AJ's brother, Adam, doesn't speak often of his addiction to gambling or the results of it that almost destroyed his family and his career. Yet, it brought AJ, Finn, and Ethan together. I've seen the downfall of many from gambling in this era. My father lost his ship to Finn because of it, after all. I never thought I'd fall prey to something so insidious, but I think I understand Adam better now.

"It seems I have my own addiction, less identifiable but no less powerful. These missions I've been involved with over the last couple of years have become somewhat habit-forming. I don't know if it's the thrill of adventure, the allure of danger, or for love of country. Perhaps it's all those things. I know every time I meet with Hensley, he'll have something to dangle in front of me, and when these little missions tie together to become a larger one, I can't stop myself from getting involved."

He rubbed his face with both hands then dragged them over his head. He refused to look at her, unsure of what he'd see. "All Hensley asked of me was to take a few hours' watch each day to help identify McDuff's man. But, like all of his missions, with each new lead it was like a thread slowly wrapping itself around me until the threads became ropes, and I couldn't do anything to unbind them. The decision to release André was my idea, and it became one more binding."

He glanced at her, but instead of an irritated wildcat, he found the reflective Stella. It didn't reassure him.

***

Stella had fought between irritation and exasperation when Beckworth admitted he was working with Hensley behind her back. When he took full ownership of his actions and spoke as if it were an addiction, she backed off any ill-advised words. He'd been caught in the middle between the woman he loved and the man who'd given him a respectable career that fit his singular skills. Something he'd yet to find in Baywood.

The fault lay at Hensley's feet, but could she blame him? He was a man of this century, and as much as he listened to and included women in his missions, he'd only involved AJ, Maire, and her because they'd been the focus of the mission, whether they'd wanted to be or not. Or, as in the mission to locate McDuff, Stella's manipulations had fed off Hensley's plans to find a way into the smuggler's operations. Not because a woman was as skilled or smart as a man, but because she could play a specific role to get close to McDuff.

Hensley must tell Mary about his work, but after Stella considered it, there would be a great deal he wouldn't share. He would never completely understand the relationship Beckworth and she shared, the one where there were no secrets between them. Not important ones. Beckworth had struggled with Hensley's request, and she'd been too wrapped up in her own mission to notice.

She sat on the bed and patted the spot next to her. "Come, sit." She almost laughed when his brows inched together. He was suspicious. Well, he wasn't going to get out of this completely unscathed.

She waited patiently as he removed his cravat. It was probably feeling like a noose about now. She did her best to keep her expression blank. It wasn't easy, especially when he sat several inches away. Not nearly as close as usual. She let the distance remain. He was feeling guilty and defensive, emotions she was quite familiar with after this evening's events.

How was she supposed to know her activities had been connected to a mission she hadn't known existed? Her brow lifted, and she gave Beckworth a quick glance. He was watching her, and he caught her raised brow because his own lifted. She stared at the dressing table and let her thoughts play out.

If Hensley hadn't prevented Beckworth from telling her about the mission, which she agreed would have irritated her if she hadn't been allowed to help, they might have connected the dots faster. Not because she would have been part of their meetings, but because Beckworth and she would have shared information. Something true partners did.

"Where are you?"

She turned back to Beckworth. He was a few inches closer, this time with a concerned pinch between his eyes. "What do you mean?"

"You seem a hundred miles away." He pulled at one of her locks, a tentative smile flashing across his face before disappearing. He wasn't sure where he stood with her, and it tore at her heart.

She took his hand and turned it palm up. He'd done that with her before, pretending to read her palm as Maire often did with Ethan, which had only confirmed in her mind that Maire was some kind of fairy.

This time, it was her turn to run a light finger along the lines that crisscrossed over his palm. He shivered underneath the soft touch.

"What do you see?" he asked.

"I see a line that forks into two where another line intersects it."

"What does it mean?"

She quirked her lips. "That a devious man forced you to take the wrong road." She felt him tense. "Fortunately…" She traced her finger farther along the crease. "The two lines join into a single one again." She folded his fingers over his palm and brought his hand to her lips, where she placed a small kiss before setting it on his leg.

She smiled at him. "And now all is well."

"I shouldn't have listened to Hensley."

"No. But I understand why you did. I know I can be difficult and manipulative, but I also know how important the missions are to you. I admit I would have been irritated by Hensley's request if you'd told me at the time."

"But you would have given it some thought and stayed out of it. I know."

She snorted. "I'm not sure I would have stayed out of it completely. I'd want to know everything you were discovering, but I didn't see many of McDuff's sailors and wouldn't have been of much help. And with the thefts, I've been too busy to pay attention to what you've been up to."

"Apparently, we're too alike, Lady Caldway."

"So true, Lord Beckworth."

Silence fell, but he took her hand and squeezed, which told her everything was alright between them.

"Whatever possessed you to consider André Belato?"

"It was when I went to Newgate to gather information on Gemini." He rubbed a thumb over her hand as he stared at some spot on the wall. "I've seen a lot of bad while living in the East End. But here was a man, living the most bitter of lives, imprisoned for being nothing more than a gullible Frenchman. He was neither a soldier or a spy. He was nothing but a drunk in the wrong place at the wrong time, left for the guards to find by his own sister. A sister who'd been sold into servitude as a child. I've seen men as hapless as him. Yet, it wasn't their faces I've seen in my dreams."

He didn't say another word as his head drooped. His gaze focused on the floor, but his hand still gripped hers.

There wasn't anything she could say. He'd never spoken of André to her, and he'd said little of Gemini since her death. Stella had assumed it was because she'd killed Gaines, and he avoided the topic for her benefit. She'd never killed a man until then. Though it was traumatic, she'd do it again under the same circumstances. Since they'd both put it behind them without a word, she'd never considered how Beckworth might have felt. She understood he had mixed feelings about Gemini's death, but she had never considered he would be haunted by the Frenchman's fate.

She wasn't a psychiatrist, and could be overthinking it, but Beckworth's irrational connection to André's life was tied to his own harsh background. The more she thought about it, the more it made sense.

She nudged his shoulder. "So, what's the plan with André? And what can we do to keep him safe?"

24

Stella stepped down from the carriage and stared up at the manor. A small smile curved her lips as she considered the next hour. Her thoughts that morning had leaned toward giving Hensley a stern lecture, but then she had her first cup of coffee and sanity returned. Although the moment would have been satisfying, it would have accomplished nothing. Hensley lived for the long game.

When boots hit the ground behind her, she didn't bother turning around. She was still irritated with Beckworth. Though their talk had cleared the air, he'd remained distant. He'd cuddled when he'd finally come to bed, but he was up early for his morning ride. And though he'd made sure to hang the pot of coffee by the fire to keep it warm, he'd been aloof when he'd returned just in time to leave for Hensley's.

She had no idea what was bothering him or what to do about it, and it had put her in a foul mood.

"The women will be anxious until you meet us for lunch." Eleanor stepped beside her, jarring Stella out of her dark thoughts.

Barrington had taken Mary, Elizabeth, and Flora, along with

their trunks, to Hensley's earlier that morning. Hensley would see Elizabeth and Flora home after their luncheon. The manor would be quiet without them. Well, except for Bart.

"I doubt they'll have to wait long. I'm sure Hensley will dismiss me as quickly as he deems it proper."

Eleanor snorted. "You know quite well how it feels to be caught doing something wrong."

Stella took Eleanor's arm in hers and grinned as they mounted the steps. "I can't remember the last time anyone caught me doing something wrong. Although one or two might have blamed me for simply helping an unfortunate soul."

Beckworth, who followed them up the stairs, released a long sigh he didn't bother hiding.

The two women glanced at each other and chuckled as they entered the manor. Mary was waiting for them, so Stella didn't hear Beckworth's response, which was probably for the best. She hugged Mary, promised her a thrilling adventure story, then turned toward Beckworth and straightened her dress.

"Let's get this over with."

A brief smile lit his lips before he remembered his irritation, which quickly reappeared along with a creased forehead and squinty eyes. He waved toward the hallway. "After you."

She didn't hesitate as she marched toward the study. He had no reason to be more annoyed than her. The women's investigation into the thefts shouldn't have been a surprise. Not in the beginning, especially when she'd uncovered the connection with the stolen items, but he'd been distracted. She huffed. Now she knew why.

She stopped at the study door and waited for Beckworth, who had lagged behind. When she glanced back, it appeared he was lost in his own thoughts until he finally looked up. His gaze was unfocused, almost as if he'd forgotten where he was, but he recovered with a grim smile before nodding.

Her lips quirked when she considered pounding on the door as if it were a raid, but she gave a dainty knock instead.

"Come," Hensley called out.

Stella strolled in and smiled at the usual group of suspects. Jamie, Lando, and Fitz relaxed in chairs, each with a glass of whiskey in hand. Smoke from Fitz's pipe curled over the group, giving the room a hazy overtone. For a split second, she pictured them around a poker table, the tallest pile of chips sitting in front of Fitz, and the second highest next to Hensley's elbow.

Her grin grew larger at the thought, and Hensley's stern expression softened.

"Excellent timing." Hensley moved a piece of paper to the side and closed the inkpot. "Have a seat and let's discuss the events of the last few days."

Lando stood and waved Stella to his seat. "I've been relaxing far too long."

She squeezed his arm as she sat and noticed Beckworth affixing the stopper on a decanter. He picked up his glass and, rather than find an open seat, leaned against a bookcase.

"It appears we have two investigations that have intersected." Hensley leaned back and set his hands over his well-fed belly. "The question is, what do they have in common, and how does it fit into our primary mission?"

Stella watched Hensley, who returned her stare. She wouldn't have questioned it under these circumstances until she caught the glimmer in his eye. She'd seen it before when they played chess. It usually meant he was planning a surprise move.

"You've been monitoring the progress of the jewelry thefts." She treaded carefully in her inquiry, never knowing where Hensley might have planted a landmine.

"I had a brief discussion with Inspector Littlefield after he interviewed you. I wasn't impressed with his motivation and had planned on giving the case to one of my men. That was before I discovered I already had someone working on the investigation. Someone who had better access to information with a tenacity difficult to replicate."

"You knew Stella was investigating the theft and encouraged it?" Beckworth stood straighter, his temper rising.

"Come now," Hensley said. "You were aware she was gathering information. She was the one who suggested there was a connection between the stolen items and then pulled a team together to investigate."

"You were kept updated by pumping Mary for information." Stella released a breath to calm her growing annoyance.

"Pumping?" He thought about it. "If you mean discussing the status of the operation, then yes." His gaze hardened a fraction. "Elizabeth is my friend, too."

The bluster seeped out of Stella. Of course, he'd try to help.

"Apparently," Hensley continued, "your initial assessment of the thief being a sailor appears closer to the mark, considering his friends."

"If this thief is working for someone in McDuff's network," Jamie interjected, "why would they bother stealing jewelry off the neck of aristocrats when there are easier ways to fund their operations?"

"Didn't I hear someone mention all the pieces were specially designed by a Frenchman?" Lando asked.

"Yes." Stella didn't wait for Hensley. She wasn't going to be pushed into a corner, especially since Hensley had been the one who declared her the lead in the investigation. "Elizabeth mentioned it was one-of-a-kind, and when we learned that the first item had been stolen in a similar manner, it piqued my interest. Once we learned the brooch had been made by the same designer, Louis Pierre Deschanel, the women mentioned other jewelry known to have been created by him. It was a hunch, but it paid off. It would have taken longer to track down the thief if we didn't have the use of Chester's urchins."

"You used Chester's crew?" Fitz puffed a stream of smoke and almost choked on his laughter. He pointed the pipe at Beckworth. "Right under your nose? That has to sting a bit." His grin didn't waver under Beckworth's glare.

A trickle of sympathy ran through Stella, but her team of women was on the verge of either being given a larger role or being shut down. She wasn't willing to risk it by diminishing her efforts. Besides, Beckworth had thick skin and would get over the razzing, which at this point, she felt was rightly deserved.

"Let's remain on track." Hensley pulled another sheet of paper over, and Stella stretched her neck to see writing on it but wasn't close enough to make out any of the words. "We've been able to identify who we believe to be the highest-ranking member of McDuff's network currently in London. John Leclair, also known as Le Renard, was seen on the *Tidewater* during the mission to locate McDuff. We first thought he might be the first mate on the *Tidewater*, but whether he worked his way up the ranks or we were wrong about his role, he's now the captain of the *Nighthawk*, which is the origin of our current investigation." He cleared his throat, took a sip of whiskey, and let his gaze sweep the group. Stella didn't know if he was expecting someone to correct the information or ask a question. When the men remained silent, she did the same as Hensley continued his report.

"We know he's been meeting other Frenchmen at what we assume to be a members-only club. We've also identified the pub from which most of the men leave before going to the club-house. Based on our surveillance, the majority of the men who come and go appear to be regular members, but the team has spotted several new faces."

"Which, for now, we assume to be new recruits," Jamie

added. "I've kept a random group of sailors taking shifts in the pub, which thankfully caters to all sailors, French or otherwise. All the reports have been consistent. There are two to three men, the number varies, who keep a table in the back. A handful of sailors stop by during the course of a day and night, but every once in a while, one of the men will leave with a sailor. They've all been tracked going to the clubhouse."

"Are these all Frenchmen?" Stella asked.

"From what we can tell," Lando responded. "I believe that's why our little man decided to bring in André."

Beckworth ignored the jibe, his expression almost one of boredom. "We needed a Frenchman if we hoped to learn more. And while we could have found one in Hensley's network, I believe McDuff's men to be more cunning than your average smuggler." He glanced at Jamie and said, "Nothing personal, mate."

The men chuckled, and he continued. "I knew André could be a risk, but he's naive, down on his luck, and while previous acts might have reflected otherwise, I believe him to be trustworthy. He's been cautious, still feeling the sting of his family's betrayal. His performance will be truthful."

"I agree." Fitz smothered the fire in his pipe but kept hold of it. "André is the perfect target. Anyone with a keen eye would note a man without hope. Up to now, he's mumbled a few words to a couple of sailors, and though no one has directly approached him, one of the men at the smuggler's table has kept an eye on him. I don't think we'll have to wait long before he's invited over for a drink."

"That's excellent news." Hensley looked down at the paper he was holding and seemed to be reading it. Whether it was the first time or the fifteenth, Stella couldn't tell. The man was an enigma. "Now that we've connected the thief with the private club, we have an opportunity to bring our two investigations together."

"I don't understand." Beckworth's words echoed Stella's thoughts.

This was the moment Hensley had planned all along. She'd thought he'd already played his hand, but she should have known better. Hensley never crowed about his wins. He was always planning the next move and the three beyond that. When he pinned his gaze on her, she straightened but felt more like squirming.

"I believe it's time to bring our long-lost Lady Swan out of hiding."

"Absolutely not." Beckworth hadn't seen this coming, and he'd be damned if they put Stella into another dangerous situation.

He tried not to glance at Stella, but he couldn't help himself and was surprised to see that she appeared more shocked than he was. It wouldn't have surprised him if she'd given Hensley the idea since she'd gone to Chester without his knowledge. She hadn't done it to be devious; she simply feared he'd have told her to leave the crew out of it. As if that ever stopped her before. But he hadn't noticed. And that said more about him than it did her.

His calming demeanor vanished when Stella's startled expression softened, and a grin replaced it. She might not have anticipated it, but she was clearly interested in Hensley's game.

"It makes perfect sense." Jamie shrugged when Beckworth gave him a scathing look. "News would have reached McDuff about Lady Swan jumping from Cheval's ship shortly before his death. No one should have been surprised by her disappearance from the western coast after that. Her arrival in London, three months later, wouldn't be that unusual as she waits for any repercussions from Cheval's death to die down."

"And if she were to arrive with French arms, what better way to get an invite to the clubhouse," Fitz added. "But we should wait until André receives an invite so we have a man inside."

"And where exactly will she get French firearms?" Beckworth asked. "Assuming this Captain Leclair has any knowledge of Lady Swan, he'll want to see the goods before working out a trade." He swallowed the rest of the whiskey and refilled his glass. The clink of the stopper settling onto the decanter rang in his ears, or perhaps the odd ringing was from the vision of Stella leaping off Cheval's ship. Or the memory of salty brine on his lips as Cheval tried to drown him. Or that damn crossbow Stella insisted on traveling with.

"What woman wouldn't be interested in a collection of one-of-a-kind jewelry?" Stella's question irritated him.

The idea was both sublimely naive and almost perfect, assuming the jewelry hadn't already been sold.

Hensley, as usual, had prepared in advance. "The War Ministry has a warehouse filled with French firearms confiscated from smugglers. We should be able to borrow a few crates that would interest any smuggler." He seemed pleased with himself.

The old spymaster had planned to use Stella, or had at least considered it, the minute he'd heard someone from McDuff's network was in town. Hensley knew damn well he and Stella were due in London, and it also explained why he'd wanted Stella kept out of the initial surveillance. If she had been seen on the docks before Hensley's plans were set in motion, it could have jeopardized his mission.

When he met Hensley's eyes, the old man had that grin on his face whenever he said, "Checkmate." Beckworth tossed the rest of the whiskey down and savored the burn. He fought for the right words, unsure what to do. He considered it from a professional angle. The plan required some work—confirm the ability to obtain the firearms and ensure André was in place. It made sense. But as Stella's lover and loyal companion, he had no desire to put her in danger again. Hell, he'd been terrified when he'd spotted her and Libby being followed in a London alley. He was surprised when Stella agreed with him.

"Hensley's plan," Stella gave the spymaster one of those looks that said she saw past his bullshit, "makes sense on several levels. But since I'm the one being put in the middle of this, and the one who's already been kidnapped once by these assholes, I won't commit to anything without hearing a solid plan that includes my personal protection."

Hensley appeared dismayed by her outburst. However, before Beckworth could agree with her, Hensley lifted a parchment he'd been holding and waved it at the group. "I've already taken the liberty to write down the necessary steps to put our plan safely into play."

Of course, he had.

T he meeting ended rather abruptly once Hensley announced the return of Lady Swan. Stella considered her mixed feelings as she wandered down the hall, not really thinking about where she was going. On one level, she was excited to be part of the mission. On another, the memories of her time with Cheval flashed by—his torture of the sailor in a dark cargo hold, her jumping from the ship, barely making it to shore, and then using the crossbow to save Beckworth's life.

Beckworth wasn't happy with the plan. Although it was brilliant, he worried about her. He'd be fully onboard if she weren't part of it, but she didn't know how to reduce his worry. He couldn't stop his natural instincts to protect any more than she could ignore hers.

When she reached the foyer, Beckworth pulled her aside. She hadn't realized he'd been following her.

"I need to speak with Chester and then check on André. Barrington will take me back to the manor so I can get my horse, then he'll return for you and Eleanor. When you're ready, of course."

For the first time since he'd returned from retrieving André, Stella gave him a long assessment. She didn't like the dark circles under his eyes or the dullness of his usually sharp gaze. He hadn't been getting decent sleep. Had he been eating well? He couldn't go on a new mission like this. She would find a way to remedy that.

She didn't argue with him. "Be safe, Lord Beckworth."

Something flitted through his gaze, and she wondered if he'd seen something reflected in her own. A smile appeared with a quick bow. "Always, Lady Caldway."

She watched him as he said a few words to Jamie and Fitz before walking out the door. He was dealing with his own demons, but something in his smile made her believe he'd found a way to banish them. If not, she'd have to do it for him. That was her job as his partner. No one had to teach her that.

"There you are."

Stella plastered a smile on her face as she turned to greet Mary. "Sorry. I didn't expect the meeting to take that long." She let Mary take her arm and lead her to the solarium, where the other women waited.

Elizabeth, a gin and tonic in hand, stared out the window. The fingers on her free hand tapped to a beat only she could hear. After a moment, she wiped at an eye before returning to the tapping.

Stella's heart squeezed. Was her friend thinking of her husband? She'd find that necklace if it was the last thing she did.

Flora and Eleanor were startled out of their deep conversation when she sat down.

"I'm so sorry, my dear." Flora patted Stella's arm. "Eleanor was sharing a story about her time working as a costume seamstress. We should plan an evening at the theater once all this nonsense with the thief is over."

"What news do you have for us?" Elizabeth's sharp gaze caught Stella by surprise. If she'd been melancholy before, she'd moved past it. She wasn't ready to give up.

"We found the thief and followed him to a private club that is apparently Frenchmen only." Stella described in full detail the events of the previous evening, starting with her and Libby hiding behind crates as they kept an eye on the pub. Mary had the most questions, but Flora asked her to repeat a couple of parts twice. They laughed until tears flowed when Stella shared their race through the alleys to escape two men, only to have Beckworth and the men from the *Daphne* find them.

Once the laughter died away, Elizabeth wiped her eye with a handkerchief, this time from amusement rather than grief, and sipped her drink. "So our mission has crossed Hensley's."

Mary clapped her hands. "Isn't that marvelous? We're actually part of a mission for the Crown."

The women nodded and chattered while Stella sat back. She'd never thought about Hensley's missions being for the Crown. She'd known it was his job, but she hadn't considered the importance of it. They were working for their country. And considering the time period they were in, they must feel a sense of empowerment in doing the work of men. Something she took for granted in her own century.

Suddenly, the role of Lady Swan took on a different meaning. With crates filled with French firearms, a team of brave and loyal men, and a Frenchman named André at her back, she had power. Not invincible power. Her kidnapping had proven that. But they also had the crew, and she wondered if that was what Beckworth wanted to speak to Chester about. Or maybe he planned on yelling at him for helping her chase the thief. She had to smile at that.

"So, what part do we play in this?" Eleanor's words didn't mean she wanted a part. She sat with her arms crossed in a "convince me why I should be involved" sort of way.

Stella shrugged because the plans were still being sorted. Now that the men knew what the women had been up to, she suspected Hensley would want to see an end to Mary's involvement. There was still one more thing they could do that was perfectly safe. Something Stella considered crucial now that they knew who the players were.

"It's time to contact the women who own the remaining jewelry and advise them to add heightened security around them. Let's take the rest of the pieces out of play."

25

Beckworth left Hensley's manor with so much information swirling in his head that he barely registered his arrival at Templeton's manor. He worked through the last few days, organizing the data into buckets: the mission, the jewelry theft, Stella's role in all of it, where everything intersected, and the damage it was doing to their relationship.

Perhaps damage was too strong a word, but the intimacy that came easily between them had slipped away. Once he quieted all the other distractions, a spark of inspiration released the tension and urged his race up the steps and through the foyer.

In order to put his plan in place, he needed Libby, who was doing such a marvelous job of staying out of his way that it took fifteen minutes to find anyone willing to tell him where she might be. He marched through the manor on his way to the garden, shutting down his irritation. He'd wanted Libby to be Stella's lady's maid because she had the same innate bold nature as Stella. Then he'd worried—perhaps with a bit of irritation—when she'd become Stella's accomplice and, at times, the instigator.

When another realization hit him, he stopped in the

solarium to sit for a few minutes. Libby had become more than a lady's maid and sidekick. She'd become her protector. And she had enough gumption to use the skills she'd learned as a member of a crew to stand between him and Stella if needed.

Her actions weren't proper in this time period, where men ruled the house, but it wasn't the same in Stella's time period. He'd never had an issue with Libby before Stella came into his life. In fact, he depended on her for many reasons. She was one of the best spies in his service. Libby was who she was because she had to grow up fast and grow up tough to survive in the East End. But as much trouble as the two could get into, he knew Libby would keep her safe.

He found her cutting blooms from a group of wallflowers. There were also sweet peas, daffodils, and roses lying in her basket.

She turned when she heard his footsteps, and though he caught her initial guard go up, she gave him a pleasant smile. "Hello, sir. Stella is still at Hensley's manor." She snipped another stalk of blooms and held it to her nose. "These aren't her favorites, but they have such a lovely scent."

He sat on a nearby bench. "She doesn't have any in her garden in Baywood, so she's not as familiar with them, but she'll appreciate them if not for their color alone. And yes, she'll be at Hensley's for another couple of hours." He was going to apologize for his recent behavior, then decided on a different approach that wouldn't ruffle her feathers. For now, he ignored the tension between them.

"I was wondering if you'd help me with something I'd like to do for Stella." When her brow lifted, he gave her a sheepish grin. "I owe her an apology."

Libby straightened and did her best to hold back a smile. "What did you have in mind?"

The tension between them eased after he discussed his

plans, and his spirits were higher than they'd been in days as he rode his horse to the East End. Though the closer he got to his destination, the more he grumbled at the prospect of dealing with taunts, no matter how well deserved.

He hadn't expected Chester to answer the door, but he had anticipated the wide grin he received.

"Did you enjoy helping Stella behind my back?" He kept his tone light as he handed Chester a bottle of Jameson.

Chester barked a laugh. "Feeling left out? I assume the flowers aren't for me." He gripped the bottle of whiskey and gave his back to Beckworth. "Shut the door behind you."

Beckworth closed the door and followed Chester down the narrow hall to the kitchen, where Katherine was busy making biscuits.

"Hello, stranger." Her grin was as warm as always, and she wiped her hands on a towel when she spotted the flowers. "Such a grand gesture." She sniffed them. "Oh, they're lovely. Did you snip these yourself?" She waved for him to sit.

He pulled out a chair while Chester opened the bottle and grabbed two glasses from a cupboard. "Libby might have helped. She was the one with the snippers, but I pointed out the ones I wanted."

"You've always had a way with flowers." Katherine found a pitcher and poured water into it before arranging the blooms. "I was just getting ready to feed Chester. Do you have time to stay?"

"When have I ever said no to your food?"

Katherine set the pitcher of flowers on a nearby table and patted his hand on her return to the biscuits. "You've found yourself a strong woman in Stella. You'd be unsatisfied with anything less."

"And you played a large part in making Libby the sassy wench she is." Chester pushed the glass of whiskey over, then pulled out his pipe. The soft scent of cherry mixed well with the pot of stew on the stove.

Beckworth held up his hands. "I'm not here to question why you helped Stella. I'll admit I was upset when I first discovered it, but now that I've had time to think, it might have been worse between us had I known at the time."

"Are things not right with you and Stella?" Katherine gave Chester a worried glance.

"It's more that I've been distracted with a new mission of Hensley's."

"And the mission would be more important than a theft of jewelry." Chester nodded as he released another pleasant puff of smoke. "I understand that. Though I would think Stella would understand it as well."

Beckworth took a sip of whiskey, and his words came out in a rush. "Stella didn't know about the mission."

"You didn't tell her?"

"Hensley requested I not mention it."

Chester pulled the pipe from his lips in time for a loud belly laugh to burst out. "Well, that put you in quite the dilemma."

He didn't look at Katherine because he didn't need to see the pity. He downed the rest of the whiskey instead, grimacing as the amber liquid heated him from the inside out. "It was a difficult lesson to learn."

"I don't know what I'd have done in that situation, but I know how Katherine would have responded. As long as you've learned, there's nothing more I can say that Stella hasn't already advised."

Beckworth lifted his empty glass. Chester refilled it then lifted his glass in a toast to Beckworth's growth as a committed man.

Chester caught him up on events since the crew party. "This theft among the nobles has created problems for the crews."

"That should ease up soon. If you haven't heard, your crew's help has led us to the thief's den."

"We knew the urchins would be able to track him, but we didn't know if it would help beyond that."

"Stella and Libby did the rest."

"The urchins thought he was a sailor." Chester scratched his jaw, and rather than give Beckworth a hard time since Stella had claimed that fact from the beginning, he moved on. "Now, why would a sailor be stealing jewelry from the rich? And specific jewelry made by a Frenchman."

"You should be in Parliament. You made the connection faster than most of us."

"Is the jewelry worth the price of rifles or other contraband, or is there a fat Frenchman with a penchant for rare French fashion accessories?"

"Smugglers might believe they're worth it."

Chester sat back and puffed on his pipe as he considered the information. "I take it Hensley has made the connection."

Beckworth snorted. "He already has plans drawn up. He wants to put Lady Swan into play."

Chester's brow lifted.

Katherine squeaked out, "Oh, my. That sounds dangerous."

"I agree." Beckworth still had misgivings, regardless of how sound the plan.

"Are you looking for protection?" Chester asked.

"Maybe for a couple of nights. Only when she's around the docks, the pub where the thief led the urchins, and the private club that appears to be French only."

Chester nodded. "The one a couple doors down from Harrington's tailor shop?"

"You know it?"

"We've been aware of it and the clientele it attracts. Just let us know when and where." Chester put the cork back in the whiskey bottle and gave him a sly smile. "And this time, we'll expect payment."

Beckworth grinned and pulled out a pouch. The coins jingled as they hit the table. "I wouldn't expect anything less." When Chester reached over to take it, Beckworth laid a hand on his arm. "And thank you for helping Stella with the urchins. I know she paid them, but you've been a good friend."

"She's one of us. You only need to ask."

<hr>

Stella was quiet on the carriage ride back to the manor. Eleanor didn't seem to mind as she watched the city go by. The women had been reenergized with hope that the stolen jewelry might be recovered.

She'd also been positive that, if the items hadn't already been sold, there was a chance of retrieving them. Still, she'd only picked at her food, her nerves a jumble about assuming the role of Lady Swan again. In many ways, she'd been excited about being included in the mission. She liked working with Beckworth—discussing the mission, working through various strategies, and getting his opinion on her thoughts.

They worked well together and had since the first day they'd met when she refused to get on his horse. It wasn't as if she'd had a choice. She either did what he asked or be recaptured by Gemini's men. But she'd been stubborn and scared.

He'd seen through her nonsense and had simply walked off, his horse trailing behind him. She didn't think he'd have left without her, but he could have just grabbed her and tossed her over the saddle as Gaines, Gemini's henchman, had done. Beckworth had given her the opportunity to work through her options, knowing she'd get on the horse with him, someone AJ had known and trusted, rather than deal with Gemini's mercenaries.

However, she wasn't stupid. If the thief and the captain of the *Nighthawk* were associated with McDuff, they were dangerous men. Beckworth was right to be upset with Hensley, but in the end, he knew it was a good plan, regardless of how they got there. But if they were going to be successful, she and Beckworth had to work as a team. That meant she'd have to find a way to repair the rift between them.

Eleanor left her in the foyer, storming down the hall toward the library. Stella didn't hear any raised voices, but Eleanor had a sixth sense whenever there was a storm brewing between Bart and Lincoln. Lincoln deserved a medal for putting up with the old man, but Stella knew part of Bart's irritability was being back in London. The other half that he would never admit was that he'd miss Lincoln once he left for school.

She trudged up the stairs, suddenly bone weary, and hoped Beckworth wasn't back from the East End. Number one item on her list was a nap. She rubbed her stomach, sorry she hadn't eaten more. Maybe a snack before the nap.

She expected Libby to have met her on the stairs if not in the foyer. Maybe she was downstairs and hadn't heard the coach pull up. She pushed through the bedroom door, her head down as she fussed with the buttons on her dress while kicking off her shoes. When she lifted her head to see if Libby might be in the dressing room, she stopped dead in her tracks.

The drapes that were normally opened halfway and been completely drawn back, filling the room with sunshine and giving it an entirely different appearance. The door to the balcony had been left open, and a light breeze, while a touch on the cooler side, brought the scent of blooms from the garden. A headier floral scent drifted to her from colorful blossoms displayed on one of the side tables.

Libby had been busy while she was gone. The question was why.

She stepped toward the balcony but stopped when she caught a glimpse of something on the floor near the hearth. She fussed with the buttons on her dress again as she ventured toward it. A blanket was spread across the floor with two pillows piled on top. A basket sat at one end, a bottle of wine and two glasses next to it.

A small gasp escaped her. Beckworth. This could only be his doing.

She startled when warm fingers brushed hers aside and began unbuttoning her dress. The tingle of lips scraping against the small hairs at the base of her neck sent shivers through her, and she would have leaned back against him, but she wanted the dress off.

"I thought we could make time for a picnic." His voice was deep as his lips moved to her ear. "A private one."

No longer caring about the dress, she fell against him with a small moan, but he pushed her forward as his fingers deftly released button after button until the dress fell away. Once it lay puddled at her feet, he pulled her back and placed soft kisses across her shoulders.

"Don't move. Not an inch."

She didn't. Excitement replaced the shivers. This was her Teddy. And when she felt the silky touch of her robe sliding over her, she almost purred with delight. She'd always found his dressing her almost as erotic as when he undressed her.

When her robe was on, covering her undergarments, he took her hand and led her to the blanket. He was dressed in pants and a loose shirt, but his feet were bare.

"I had Nellie make us something light since you just had lunch." Beckworth sat and pulled her down next to him. When her stomach growled at the scent drifting out of the basket, he grinned. "Or maybe I should ask for more food to be sent up."

She slapped his leg. "I didn't eat much at Mary's."

He gave her a speculative look, then poured the wine. "Let's not talk about that. No one else enters this room, not physically or through words. This is our afternoon."

She took the glass and then a sip. "I've missed us."

"Me, too." He leaned over and gave her a soft kiss, but pulled back before she could respond.

She wanted to pout but decided to let him take the lead on the afternoon. This was his plan, and she didn't want to spoil it. When he tugged the basket over, she noticed the stack of paper, an inkpot, and two quills lying on the floor behind it.

"Ah, you've discovered my surprise."

"I thought the picnic was the surprise."

"Just phase one." He leaned over to pull the items closer. "I believe I mentioned wanting to make a few changes to the gardens at Waverly."

"I remember."

"I thought we could make those plans together. I know you haven't spent a lot of time in the gardens or seen everything in full bloom, but I want your opinions in the planning."

Stella stared at the pile of papers, suddenly wanting to grab a piece to fold. Her fingers danced over the sheets instead, getting a chuckle out of him. "Don't worry. I won't make a swan out of them."

"You didn't think we were going to make plans on every sheet, did you? I thought you might want to make some swans while you think."

Rather than the paper, she ran her fingers over his cheek. "You know me too well." When her stomach growled again, they both laughed. "But I think we should feed the beast first. Then we can make plans."

After devouring most of their meal and a good portion of the wine, they lay on their bellies, their heads close together, sheets of paper spread around them. Each sheet was a hand-drawn picture of a flower bed or section of garden, filled with numerous lines, circles, and squiggles along with notes on possible flowers, bushes, and trees.

A few folded swans lay about, and Stella's knees were bent, her legs slowly swaying back and forth as she finished noting the colors of flowers she preferred for the sitting area by the lake.

Beckworth added notes on a new area that would be their secret garden. A place where they could have more intimate outdoor picnics.

"I assume Waverly has a greenhouse I haven't seen?" Stella asked as she closed the inkpot and laid the quill on one of the sheets of paper.

"Yes. I'll need to give you a tour of it when we return home. Gilroy is the head gardener and masterful at propagation." He chuckled. "I can't believe I haven't taken you there yet."

She bumped his shoulder. "It might have something to do with that new foal you prefer to spend your time with."

"That might be an accurate assessment." He pushed the sheets of paper away, along with the inkpot and quills. "But I'd rather not talk anymore."

"What did you have in mind, Lord Beckworth?"

He inched over until their bodies were fully aligned and pulled down the edge of her robe until her shoulder was bare. His kisses were warm and light as he moved the robe down her arm, revealing more skin along the way.

She closed her eyes, relishing the shivers that ran through her. Her anticipation of what would come made her squirm, so when his lips suddenly crushed hers, her surprise quickly gave way to a passionate heat that overtook her. If he'd meant to slowly seduce her, he'd tossed out his playbook. And she was ready for it.

They were like young lovers again, unable to get enough of each other. Clothes, unwanted barriers between them, disappeared as if by magic. Neither were happy until they were skin on skin, hands roaming, fingers caressing, and kisses torching.

All the hidden secrets and misunderstandings floated away like ashes in the wind. The tensions between them evaporated. They were one in mind and spirit. Whatever came next with the mission, they would handle it because they were stronger together. Unstoppable.

Before his ministrations took her fully to the height of pleasure, one odd thought slipped through. Thank the heavens she had the foresight to bring her crossbow.

26

____

Beckworth gripped Stella's hand as they ran down the dark, foggy street. He stopped before he reached the warehouse and tugged the hood of her cloak over her head where it had begun to slip down. She'd dressed in one of her East End day dresses, and no one would suspect her to be Lady Swan as long as she kept her hair and face hidden.

He glanced around and noted the old man who stepped out from an alcove, nodded to him, and stepped back. All was clear. He opened the door and pushed Stella inside, closing the door behind them. Two lanterns glowed bright enough to reveal the staircase to the upper level.

"This is spooky." Stella refused to let go of his hand as he climbed the stairs. "Is this an abandoned warehouse?"

"Just unused for now." He led her to the dark office, but as he entered, the sound of pistols being cocked stopped him. He pulled her behind him, though he didn't stop her from poking her head around his shoulder.

"Welcome, Lady Swan." Jamie bowed his head and put the flintlock away.

Lando simply grinned before shoving his into a leg holster and turning back to the window.

"That was rather theatrical." Beckworth released Stella's hand, and she tugged her hood down.

"I would have checked when the door opened, but we have a lot of activity this evening." Jamie waved Stella over. "Come see."

Beckworth stepped next to Stella and scanned the street. He wasn't too surprised by the number of people, even at this hour. "I've noticed two new ships since yesterday."

"Aye." Jamie brushed off the desk that had been dragged closer to the window to give the watchers a place to sit. Or at least, lean against. "I've had a few men keep an eye on their crews, but they don't seem interested in the *Nighthawk*."

"So, no new smugglers." Beckworth was relieved. After juggling Cheval and McDuff, one smuggler at a time was enough while in London.

"I didn't say they weren't smugglers. I expect one of them is, but they've made no contact with anyone on the *Nighthawk*. We'll keep track of those who meet with Leclair. If anyone goes back to this new ship, we can take a deeper look."

"Fair enough. Any activity at the clubhouse?"

Stella leaned against the desk, her gaze never leaving the street below, but after a few minutes, she straightened. Beckworth shifted his gaze from her in time to see two men exit the clubhouse. The men scanned the street, then pulled their hats low as they hurried away.

"That's the third group of two that have left in the last fifteen minutes," Lando said.

"A meeting that ended?" Beckworth asked.

"Most likely." Jamie put away his spyglass. "It's difficult with the limited lighting, but I haven't seen Leclair leave."

"Did you see him enter?"

Lando nodded with a grunt. "He had two big men with him. Most likely bodyguards."

"Any sign of André?"

Lando and Jamie shook their heads.

"Are we expecting André?" Stella asked.

"Not really," Beckworth answered. "Didn't Fitz say André has spent most of his time talking with the man pouring the drinks?"

"Aye." Jaime peered through the spyglass before setting it down. "We've seen him speaking with the men at the back table. He's been able to confirm they control who's invited to the clubhouse, so he's getting closer."

"Hey, isn't that him?" Stella asked, pointing to two men coming out of an alley.

"It looks like André." Jamie pulled up the spyglass. "I don't recognize the man with him."

"This seems too easy." Beckworth had hoped for a quick result, expecting it to take at least a week for him to earn more attention, not a couple of days.

"Maybe they need the men," Lando suggested.

"André mentioned a couple of men his father worked with who had access to firearms. He didn't know if they were smugglers, but he thought it might be helpful if anyone asked him."

"And there's Fitz." Jamie moved the spyglass from one point to another. "He's staying just inside the alley."

They waited another thirty minutes, but other than a handful of more men leaving, no one else entered.

"I never asked..." Beckworth put an arm around Stella, who leaned against his shoulder but never took her eyes off the street. "We did confirm there's no back door, right?"

"Not one that's obvious." Lando pulled an apple from his pocket and used his dagger to slice off a piece. "There could be a tunnel that exits at some other point."

Beckworth rubbed his chin. "I know of a couple, but not on this street. I'll check with Chester."

"Here we go." When Jamie uttered the words, everyone stood and gathered closer to the window.

Two men exited, one of them André, and a few words were exchanged. André ended the conversation with a nod. He glanced around, not once looking up, stuck his hands in his pockets, and shuffled away, passing the alley and continuing down the street that would take him back to the docks. The other man watched him for a solid minute, then, as André had done, scanned the rest of the street before disappearing back inside.

"That's it for the night." Jamie turned his back on the window and followed Lando out of the office.

Beckworth took Stella's hand, guiding her back to the staircase.

"We're not going to wait for the captain?" Stella asked.

"No need. André will tell us what he's discovered, and we'll determine our next steps from that."

"What about the thief? Have you been keeping an eye on him?" Stella would want to know. She might be willing to continue her role as Lady Swan, but her reason for being here was to retrieve the stolen jewelry.

"We didn't get a good look at the two men you followed to the clubhouse, other than a general size and shape." Jamie gave Beckworth a glance, but he shook his head.

"I didn't see enough of either man's face."

Lando doused the lanterns as the group hovered by the door. "I noticed that one of the men who followed the women that night came from the *Nighthawk*. The question is whether they were originally watching the thief, or did they just happen to come across the women and decide to follow for some other reason."

"Let's see if the thief keeps regular rounds at the pub." Beckworth considered the players. The man they wanted Lady Swan to get close to was Leclair. If André found a way into the clubhouse, he might be able to tell them who the other men in charge were and what Leclair was doing in London. They had assumed the group was raising money or possibly picking up a shipment, but they had no evidence of either. The thief had entered the clubhouse, leaving one to believe he had some connection to Leclair or their business. He didn't like it, but he only knew of two people and a couple of street urchins who could identify the thief. He gave Stella a glance, though it was impossible to see her features in the darkness.

"Let's see if we can put the thief in play."

***

The following evening, Stella picked at her sleeve and tugged at the breastline of her dress as Libby added finishing touches to her hair. When Stella continued to fidget, Libby tapped her hand with the brush before pulling thin tendrils of curls from her updo.

"Stop that. Why are you so nervous? You've walked into dangerous situations before, and Beckworth has plenty of men in place to make sure you're safe. It's not like you're in a port where you don't know all the players. Even Chester has men on the streets."

Stella touched the side of her head where the thief had almost knocked her senseless. "None of that will help me much if the thief decides to throw a punch in the middle of the pub."

Libby winked at her. "He might get one in, but a pub full of drunken sailors won't let that pass, especially with how nicely you're dressed."

Stella grinned. "Do you think the dress is too much?" Beckworth had selected the emerald-green day dress that showed off her auburn hair and green eyes. It was one of her best day dresses, and he'd insisted it reflected a prosperous smuggler. If something similar had impressed McDuff, it should make the thief take notice.

"No, I don't. And I would never bet against Beckworth's suggestion when it comes to fashion."

She snorted. "You're right about that." She released a sigh. "Then I guess it's best we get this over with." She stood and picked up a shawl.

"Do you have your dagger?"

Stella patted her pockets. "Yes." She was grateful that Beckworth had insisted upon an afternoon training session to brush up on her close-contact fighting. She grinned, remembering how the three-hour session had turned into more intimate pursuits.

"What about your pistol?"

"Beckworth said to leave it. My bodyguards would be expected to carry the pistols, and my dagger shouldn't be surprising, considering my role."

Libby shrugged. "I suppose that makes sense." She gave Stella a long perusal. "Do you have your swans?"

Stella snapped her fingers. "I can't believe I forgot them." She rushed over to a side table and pulled open a drawer. Dozens of paper swans had been stuffed inside. She pulled out several and shoved them in both pockets of her dress.

On her way to the door, she squeezed Libby's arm. "What would I do without you?"

"Your life would certainly be more dull."

They laughed their way down the hallway, and though Beckworth would have no idea what they were giggling about, he grinned at them just the same.

Libby gave Beckworth a fierce stare. "You better bring her back the same way I'm leaving her with you."

Beckworth's grin drained away, and his tone turned serious. "I promise."

Libby nodded and picked a piece of lint off Stella's shawl before turning back toward the bedroom to finish her nightly duties.

Beckworth held out a hand and led Stella down the stairs to the waiting carriage. It wasn't the one from the manor or the one from Waverly. This one was a bit more weather-beaten. Barrington was on the bench, but rather than his normal butler's attire, he was dressed more for the merchant class.

They followed side streets and alleys, crossing back and forth to the point Stella had no idea where they were until she smelled the Thames. Barrington stopped a couple blocks from where the *Daphne* was moored.

Beckworth gave her a long, slow kiss. "We'll have many eyes on you this evening. This won't be like a small port village with limited constables."

"I know."

"Chester has men stationed in several places between the pub and the clubhouse."

"I know."

"You've got this."

She grinned at his twentieth century speak. "I know."

He leaned back. "Is that all you have to say?"

She considered his question, then shrugged. "I love you."

He barked out a laugh. "Now, I know you're fine." He gave her a last quick kiss then hopped out of the carriage. He said something to Barrington she couldn't decipher before the coach rolled away. She stuck her head out, but by then, Beckworth had already slipped away into the shadows.

Barrington stopped the coach a couple blocks away from the docks, and the door opened to reveal Michelson. He helped her down, and once they'd stepped back, Barrington drove off. They strolled down the street toward the pub as Stella eyed the people.

It was more crowded than the night she and Libby had spied on the thief. Beckworth had mentioned a couple of new ships had arrived, but at this late hour, the crowd appeared to be mostly sailors, many of them already weaving and stumbling along.

Michelson steered her down a block that she recognized as they drew close to the pub. "Do you remember your lines?"

"I remember what I was told to say, but I'll freeze up if I have to remember lines. I get the gist of the assignment. I'll get us a meeting with the captain or, at least, a look inside the clubhouse."

"Keep in mind that the thief might not show up."

Stella shrugged. "There are only two balls this evening, and the women with the remaining Deschanel jewelry have agreed to either lock up the items or remain home. Chester has placed a couple of men at each of their manors to deter the thief. With any luck, if he'd hoped to steal something tonight, he'll be frustrated enough to want to drown his sorrows."

Michelson lowered his head, seeming to consider his next words, then lifted his gaze to the people around them. "That's a possibility, but there are many other reasons why he might not show. I just want you to be prepared."

"I understand. How long should we stay if he doesn't show?"

"Let's start with an ale and then order food. We'll eat slowly, and if he hasn't arrived before we finish a second ale, then we should call it a night and try again tomorrow."

"Won't that seem suspicious?"

"Sailors do it all the time. We find a good pub and spend a good portion of our free time there."

That confirmed her earlier thoughts that sailors tended to congregate at their favorite watering hole. "But I'm not a sailor, and being a woman, I'll be remembered."

He chuckled. "True enough." He scratched his head and then rubbed an elbow as he glanced around the street, either confirming their watchers were in place or searching for danger. "Lady Swan is a smuggler. You're waiting for a friend or customer, however you want to phrase it, whose ship is due to arrive any day. You have to leave port soon and don't want to miss them."

She patted his arm. "Perfect." She stood straighter and ran a hand over her hair, tugging at a curl. "Let's go."

The pub was dark, smoky, and smelled of ale, overcooked fish, and the abhorrent body odor she'd become accustomed to from this time period. It was busier than she expected, and even with the boisterous voices, she heard murmurs in French.

When they reached an empty table toward the back of the room, they sat next to each other so they could talk without yelling. She'd spotted André the minute they'd walked in. He held a mug of ale while speaking to a burly man whom Stella assumed was a sailor. She made eye contact with him for a mere second. It was enough to elicit a slight nod in return.

While they waited for their first ale, Stella scanned the room, getting a feel for the place as well as the customers. She'd felt everyone's eyes on her as she'd made her way across the pub, and while she wouldn't want to be caught in a dark alley with most of them, she didn't perceive anyone threatening. She also didn't spot the thief.

They didn't have to worry about purposely dragging out their time. The two servers were kept busy, and fifteen minutes passed before their first ale arrived. By the time the meal arrived, they needed a second ale.

"Our French friend has been rather busy." Michelson's voice was low before he stuffed a chunk of bread in his mouth. He kept his eyes downcast with only an occasional glance at the door.

"I've counted five different sailors so far. They all seem to gravitate to him after they've purchased their first ale."

"And they talk for about ten minutes before moving on."

"It's almost as if they're checking in or sharing information." Stella pushed her plate away after only taking a few bites. "And the food is terrible."

Michelson took the last bite from this meal and pulled Stella's plate over. "You've gotten used to all that fancy dining at the balls."

She grimaced when she glanced at the meal. "It's overcooked, and the meat's stringy."

Michelson shrugged. "It's a hot meal, and most sailors can't complain about that."

After living on a ship for over a week, with the occasional port stops, she understood. She rubbed her stomach. She'd been spending too much time sampling the buffet tables at the parties and could use a few less meals.

"I don't think André is gathering information," Michelson said after a few bites. "I think he might be passing information on."

"Really?" She hadn't considered that.

"It's just a guess, but whoever is running the operation only brought him in two days ago. It's too soon to trust him to gather the information. And I doubt the information he's passing on is of much value."

"They're testing him."

"That's part of it. And, unless he's someone of importance, he has to start at the bottom like everyone else."

"I wonder if the visit to the clubhouse was a one-time thing."

The server dropped two mugs on their table, and as she moved off with their empty plates, Stella watched two men make their way to a table. She hadn't seen them come in and must have missed it while the server had been clearing their dishes.

She tapped Michelson on the arm. "That's our thief. The tall one with the sandy blond hair." When she made to get up, he shook his head.

"Not yet. Wait for them to get settled and get an ale. Let's see who else they speak with."

She knew he was right, but it grated. She rubbed the side of her head again, a reflexive action to seeing the thief, but she couldn't seem to stop. He'd almost given her a concussion. No doubt he would remember the prick of the knife once she got in his face, which she was itching to do. Instead, she grabbed her mug of ale and settled back in her chair.

The second man steered toward André while the thief selected a table. André's gaze flickered to Stella for only a moment before he began speaking with the man.

"Have you seen him before?" she asked Michelson.

He continued to stare at the man speaking to André, and he rubbed his jaw, his eyes squinting as if trying to remember a specific moment. "Not here in London, but somewhere." He turned away and focused his attention on the other side of the room.

The thief had settled, and when the server rushed by, he caught her by the arm and pulled her over. She gave him a smile but kept her distance from his wandering hands. By the time she left, the man who'd been speaking with André made his way toward the table. The two men surveyed the room while they waited for their ale.

Stella lowered her head and turned away so he couldn't get a clear view. She needn't have bothered, since a drunk sailor bumped into an empty chair where two sailors were eating. Several loud, harsh words were spoken, and all eyes turned to them.

The drunk apologized over and over before stumbling toward Stella and Michelson. He never lifted his head and never met their gaze. Stella played with her empty mug, hiding a grin. Fitz never failed to amaze her at the timeliness of his actions.

She snapped her fingers and leaned over to whisper to Michelson. "I think the man with the thief was also with him the night we followed them to the clubhouse. I didn't recognize him with his cape." She snorted at her term for his cloak. He was a big man, and the cloak had been too small for him.

Michelson gave her an odd stare, then shook his head, returning to the topic from wherever his mind had wandered. She had that effect on people.

"I can't be sure, but the more I think about it, I might have seen him during our trip to find McDuff. I just don't remember where."

"It will come to you, but it won't stop me from going through with the plan."

"Understood."

She felt safe with Michelson, but having Fitz stroll through when she hadn't expected it gave her more courage. If anyone ever asked her why she trusted Fitz, the only words that came to mind were bold and unrepentant. Her mother had harped on her being both, but then, her mother blamed her for many things.

She fingered the paper swans in her right pocket to be sure they were easily accessible. Satisfied, she slammed her empty mug on the table loud enough for the men at the surrounding tables to notice and stood, shoving her chair aside.

Michelson didn't stop her, and she could tell he was having difficulty working through his mirth while appearing concerned.

Men from the other tables lifted their heads as she passed them. She never looked back, her focus on the thief's table. She swayed as if she'd drunk too much, then stumbled as she knocked into an empty chair before coming to a stop in front of the thief.

"I know who you are." She didn't yell, but she didn't lower her voice, either.

The two men hadn't noticed her until she'd run into the chair, and now they sat with their mouths frozen open as if their words had been snatched from their lips.

She tapped her foot, hands on her hips, as if waiting for a proper response. After several seconds ticked by, she pointed a finger at the thief. "Don't bother denying it."

The men closed their mouths and appeared unsure of what to do. Stella didn't miss the moment the thief recognized her. She didn't give him the chance to speak.

"You know what you took. You're nothing more than a two-bit hustler and thief."

The last word was barely out of her mouth when the other man grabbed her arm, wrenching it in the process, and dragged her down to the empty chair. "I suggest you hold your tongue in here." He had a rough but surprisingly light French accent.

Stella tugged her arm out of his grip and ignored him, her eyes locked with the thief's. She didn't have to look around to know others were watching. She didn't dare look away, but the scuff of chair legs suggested someone might step in, and she depended on Michelson to settle them down.

She kept her voice to a whisper. "I won't call the watchmen." Now, she let her gaze roam as she leaned in, catching sight of Fitz and André both attempting to appear disinterested. "In fact,

I'm willing to make it worth your while to hand over all the items you've stolen." She considered the statement for a second. He might have pinched quite a lot of things, so she further defined her offer. "Specifically, the Deschanel jewelry you've stolen from the noble women. I'll buy them all, but it has to be tonight. Otherwise, I'll have no choice but to use other means."

"I don't know what you're talking about." The thief's accent was pure English, which surprised her.

She made a show of rubbing the side of her head and didn't bother whispering. "I remember the bruise you gave me." Her grin was full of malice. "Did my knife prick leave a scar?"

The other man turned his glare from Stella to the thief. "This is the woman who chased you?"

"And he wouldn't have gotten away if my skirts hadn't hampered me." She sat back, ready to negotiate. "I'll make it a fair deal. I like to call it a blue-light special. But the offer is time-limited."

After a long, tense silence, the thief sat back and laughed. "Assuming I'm the man you think I am, why the rush?" His leer was worse sitting this close to him. He gave her a long, slow perusal, his eyes pausing on her breasts before traveling up to meet her gaze. "We should spend some time getting to know each other."

Stella slowly shook her head. "If you'd rather deal with the watchmen, that's up to you. But that would be a waste of an opportunity for me and will land you in Newgate." When she began to rise, the other man pulled her back down as he glanced at the thief.

"Leclair won't be happy if you create a scene."

"Shut your mouth." The thief didn't seem happy that a name had slipped by, but then he asked, "Why tonight? I don't have the items with me."

Well, at least they'd gotten past that hurdle. The rest should be simple if she didn't oversell it, assuming they were smart enough to keep up.

"My ship leaves with the first tide on the morrow." On the morrow? Had she just fallen into a *Wuthering Heights* novel?

He laughed. "Then find another passenger ship if you're so interested in making a deal."

"It's not a passenger ship, you dolt. It's my ship, and I have cargo to move." She leaned in and whispered, "Cargo that I can't leave in dock any longer than tomorrow."

It took a moment, but then the men's brows lifted at the same time. When they didn't respond, she blew out a long sigh.

"Come now, gentlemen. Do you think a fine noble woman like myself would be in this rathole of a pub by choice?"

The thief grinned and leaned forward. "And what would a fine noble lady be doing owning a smuggling ship?"

She sat back, her eyes wide at the suggestion, but after a long moment, she gave them her realtor smile. "You heard my offer."

"I didn't hear a price."

Gotcha.

"I haven't seen all the items. I've only seen the necklace and heard about the others. I need to see them all, then I'll tell you my price."

Silent communication passed between the two men.

"Who are you?"

She glanced around, noting André and Fitz watching more intently, but everyone else had returned to their own business. She reached into her pocket and almost grinned when the two men visibly tensed.

She placed a swan on the table. "My name is Lady Swan."

27

The thief stared at Stella as if what she said meant nothing to him. "Never heard of you."

Her brows lifted, and she gave him a serious pout. "Really? Well, that's disappointing. I suppose that doesn't surprise me here in London. I do most of my business along the western coast, into Scotland, and soon Ireland." She leaned over and gave him a sly smile. "You must admit it's more dangerous to carry certain..." She paused to consider the appropriate word. "...prohibited supplies while sailing past Parliament, especially now with so many rules against French-made products."

His eyes went blank as he took in the information. While she waited for him to put two and two together, she sat back and surveyed the room. Fitz had moved from the back of the room to a spot closer to the door.

After several minutes, the thief grunted, then nudged the man next to him. "Get the messenger."

The other man waved toward the bar.

Stella's nerves ratcheted up, not understanding who this messenger was. She sighed inwardly when André arrived at the

293

table. So, that was what they'd been using André for. Michelson had been right.

"Can I help you, sir?" André gave a nervous glance to Stella and the thief, as if he didn't understand why he'd been called over. He was either an excellent performer or truly feared these people. She didn't blame him. He was playing a dangerous role.

"I need a message delivered to Captain Leclair," the thief said. "This woman calls herself Lady Swan. She supposedly runs her own cargo and is interested in the Deschanel collection." He laughed, and his buddy joined in.

André, attempting to fit in, smiled and nodded in agreement. "I'll see if he's in." He was gone in a flash.

Stella didn't turn to see where he went, but assumed he was off to the clubhouse. "How long will this take?"

"Not long."

Stella stood, keeping her arms away from any grabby male hands. "Then, if you don't mind, I'll wait with my man. As I stated earlier, you're not my only business, and my time is short."

When the other man began to stand, Michelson stepped next to her. "Your ale just arrived, and we need to complete the final decisions on the return cargo for The Monk."

Hensley and Jamie thought it best if she could mention a contact in France. No one wanted to specifically mention the monastery or give away any names, fictitious or otherwise. Jamie had been the one to come up with The Monk. While not completely spot on, it held a ring of truth. And it wasn't like the bad men didn't have their own aliases—Le Renard and *The Horseman* were perfect examples. More importantly, it created an air of mystery. A well-planted seed that, with the proper germination among the right people, opened up dozens of opportunities within Hensley's network.

She reclaimed her seat with Michelson at their table while

the thief kept his eyes on her. At least, Michelson hadn't lied. There was a fresh mug of ale, and she took a long, slow sip, hoping the drink would calm her nerves.

This one moment would determine whether the plan would move forward or they had to return to the drawing board.

Beckworth stared down at the clubhouse from their warehouse lookout.

"Take a seat and let us keep an eye out, little man." Lando gave him a good-natured thump on his shoulder. "You'll wear yourself out before the action starts."

"At least he stopped pacing." Jamie leaned back in a chair. He'd dragged two others over from another office, but Lando rarely sat.

Beckworth wasn't typically a pacer, and it wasn't lost on him that whenever he did it, Stella was somehow involved. It usually happened as an exasperated result of something she said, did, or was about to do. This time, his pacing was entirely focused on her well-being, and the fact that, once again, he'd been left behind to watch and wait while someone else was responsible for her safety.

He trusted Michelson, but the only thing that made him not race over and sneak into the pub was knowing that Fitz was there too. It wasn't that he trusted Fitz more than Michelson; Fitz had uncanny senses and the ability to get inside the head of a mark. Beckworth possessed the same skill—all good spies did. But there weren't many that delved as deeply as Fitz, whether it was understanding his prey or creating the persona he blanketed himself in.

Of course, Stella kept her dagger handy, and she wasn't afraid to use it—as she'd already proven with the thief. Her skill in hand-to-hand fighting had greatly improved. He remembered a time in Baywood, laughing with glee, when she surprised Finn with a combination martial arts toss followed by her dagger at his throat.

It was all in jest when they'd been working on their defensive skills, something they'd agreed to remain proficient in. If it had been a real match, Finn wouldn't have let the session end there. But the look in his eyes—a mixture of shock and awe—had Beckworth and Ethan doubled over in laughter until tears fell. If he recalled correctly, AJ and Maire had clinked their wineglasses together as if they never had a doubt. Stella had been right. The men hadn't been taking them seriously, and Finn had paid the price.

He grinned at the memory as he stared down at the clubhouse. Only one or two men had entered in the last hour, and none had left. "Are we certain they'll send André if Stella's offer is enticing enough?"

"Can't be a hundred percent," Jamie answered. "But they made him a messenger, so it makes sense he'd be the one sent."

The words were barely out of his mouth when Lando stood straighter. "Here we go."

The street lighting wasn't the best for identifying people. Although everyone felt positive they'd be able to identify André, Beckworth had given him a timepiece on a silver chain to wear so he'd be easier to spot. He didn't want to miss anything where Stella was involved.

His focus returned to the man rushing through the street and entering the clubhouse, agreeing that it was André.

"He seemed to be in a hurry," Jamie observed.

Beckworth's chest tightened at what that might mean and forced a breath. André was simply being prompt in delivering the message. There could be other reasons for his haste, but Beckworth refused to ponder them.

"Get the men in place and give the signal to Chester's man," Jamie ordered.

Lando nodded and turned for the door. Before he left, he nudged Beckworth. "Don't worry, little man. We'll be ready."

Ten minutes later, André left the clubhouse, but instead of returning the way he came, he paused at the entrance to the alley. He appeared to be removing something from the bottom of his boot before turning down the dark lane.

"That's our cue." Jamie rushed out the door with Beckworth a step behind.

They raced down the stairs, stopping to turn out the lantern. Jamie inched the door open with Beckworth peering over his shoulder as they searched for Chester's man. He was across the street, tucked into the alcove of a dress shop. He nodded, giving them the all clear. They burst out of the door and jogged to the end of the block, where the door to the clubhouse was visible.

"If we're going, it's best to do it now." Beckworth pushed Jamie, who didn't protest.

They strolled toward the clubhouse as if they were on their way to the next pub before turning into the alley and returning to their jog. The first of Chester's urchins waited on the next street, and she pointed to the left. At the next corner, an old woman dragging an empty cart behind her nodded to the right, and the men turned again.

Halfway down the block, an old drunk teetered on an oak barrel, a bottle of something gripped in an aged hand. The liquor would be real, and the old drunk, who was more sober than he appeared, would stink of stale whiskey. Beckworth grinned. All these years later, Chester still loved using old Thomas.

Thomas waved his arm toward the right before almost falling off the barrel. A couple of doors down, a young girl stood next to what appeared to be an empty building or perhaps a small warehouse.

Beckworth winked at Thomas as he passed and grinned when the old man winked back. Jamie stopped by the young girl and looked around as if searching for something or someone. The girl tugged on his pants, and when he looked down, she held out her palm. A paper swan, its wings battered by many handlings, was still identifiable.

This was the building for the meet.

Jamie took the swan, and the girl raced off, instantly swallowed up in the shadows.

"That worked better than expected," Beckworth observed.

"It was a fifty percent chance at best that André would be able to pick up the swan and drop it off here." Jamie turned the origami piece over in his hand and tried to entice a wing to stay upright. "If they'd sent anyone back with André, it would have made our task more difficult. We're not even sure Leclair will come."

The team had considered various possibilities when they'd discussed where the meeting would take place. Leclair wouldn't want anyone talking at the pub. Too many ears. And they wouldn't take someone they didn't know to the clubhouse. If André wasn't able to give them a heads-up on the location, Chester had several men in place to follow Stella. It was a risk, but still doable. Whether Leclair would attend the meeting was the critical question.

Beckworth didn't doubt for a minute that Leclair would be too curious not to show up. "We stirred up McDuff's network when Lady Swan lured him into believing she had a continuous supply of French guns. Cheval believed her to be a threat to his partnership with McDuff. It will be widely known by now that Cheval kidnapped Lady Swan and then ended up dead. McDuff would have heard the rumors, and now, three months later, she shows up in London. Barrington and Chester were already spreading rumors of the mysterious woman smuggler when rescuing me from Gemini. It won't take long for word of her return to London to get around." He stopped because Jamie would have the gist of it.

"If Stella gets a meeting with Leclair through someone from the pub, which is known to welcome French sailors, it will confirm the rumors that she has connections to French guns." Jamie laughed. "And with Leclair connected to McDuff, they'll have their entire network looking for her next stop."

"And Hensley would have considered all of this."

Jamie chuckled. "And probably two steps beyond that."

"Are the two of you going to stand out here and personally welcome Stella and the thief to the party?" Lando's whisper was loud enough to stop their laughter, and they straightened as if they'd been caught stealing meat pies from Mrs. Brubaker.

"It's about time you got here." Beckworth decided to play along. "We thought it would be another five minutes before you found us."

Lando growled through their chuckles as he led them to the back door of the building.

Stella tapped her fingers on the table. Her anxiety had eased with the three ales she'd drunk, but as Michelson shared stories from the *Daphne*'s adventures, she considered ordering something stronger. She paid enough attention to laugh at the appropriate times. He knew she was barely listening, but he continued on in a soothing voice as if settling a child.

Michelson soon turned the tables on her as he asked about her first encounter with Beckworth after escaping Gemini. She relaxed as he laughed at her antics that drove Beckworth crazy until the pub door burst open for the ninth or tenth time since André had left.

This time, she was rewarded with the sight of the messenger as he stopped at the door. He surveyed the room as if he hadn't frequented the place in days. After a moment, she realized he did what any other patron would have done the first time they walked into a pub. The same thing she and Michelson had done —check for enemies and friends.

André's gaze barely lit on her and Michelson, but he stopped on Fitz, who was speaking with a sailor, for a fraction longer. Once he seemed satisfied that all was well, he lowered his head and marched to the thief's table. He whispered something then returned to his stool at the bar.

Michelson touched her hand and whispered. "The thief is coming over."

She braced herself, but she wasn't expecting a hand on her arm pulling her up. What was with all the handsy men? Michelson was up in a heartbeat, his chair tipping over with a loud crash, gaining the attention of everyone in the place, which she assumed was his intention.

"Unhand me, sir." She tugged her arm out of his grip.

The thief's face turned red, and based on his exceptional sneer, it wasn't from embarrassment. His buddy stepped up beside him and gave him a nudge. The thief scanned the room and took a step back. The place might be filled with sailors and mercenaries, but they apparently had a code on how to treat a lady.

He swallowed what had to be a huge lump of irritation and managed to spit out, "Apologies, my lady."

He didn't mean it, but Stella ignored it. If all went right, and she hoped to hell it would, the thief wouldn't like the results of the next twenty minutes.

"Well, what is it?" Stella snapped.

The thief leaned in and lowered his voice. "If you want to see the jewelry, you need to watch your tone with me." He glared at Michelson, but Michelson glared back.

"I need to take you to another location." He sneered at the others in the bar, most of whom had returned to their drinking. "It's not safe to discuss business here."

He waved for her to go first. She didn't waste time as she headed for the door, but stopped when she heard, "Not you."

She spun around, hands on her hips. "I'm not going anywhere without my man at my side."

When the thief appeared to question her decision, his buddy nudged him again. "We're making a scene."

The warning must have been enough, because the thief attempted a more accommodating expression that failed at his steady, cold stare. "Fine. Let's be quick about it."

Michelson took Stella's arm, and they walked out of the pub with the thief and his man trailing behind. Once on the street, the thief took the lead while his buddy followed behind them.

After turning down several streets, the thief turned down an even darker alley. She gripped Michelson's arm tightly while her other hand caressed her cache of swans. Memories of the alley where she'd been kidnapped played havoc with her nerves, and she wanted to drop a swan, just in case, but the thug behind her might notice. She'd clutched one in her fist when she noticed the tiny girl backing away into the shadows.

It had been barely a glimpse, but the urchin had been staring right at her, and a quick smile had appeared before she'd disappeared.

Stella's shoulders relaxed, and her breathing calmed. Everything was going as planned. Although that didn't stop her from releasing the swan and grabbing the hilt of her dagger.

The thief stopped at the door of what appeared to be another abandoned building. He opened it and stepped aside for Michelson to go first. Not one of Chester's people was in sight, and her nerves crept back, but as soon as Michelson disappeared into the darkness, the thief pushed Stella through the doorway. She tripped and almost fell, but Michelson caught her before she did a face-plant.

She turned to sneer at the spot where the thief should have followed her in, but no one was there. It took a moment for her eyes to adjust to the low light that hadn't been there moments before, and she noticed the boots and the body they were attached to.

The thief was spread-eagled on the floor. He rubbed his head, either unable to lift it or seeing no reason to bother. His buddy wasn't in any better shape.

Two sailors from the *Daphne* stood over the men, and the knot in her chest dissipated along with the heavy stone that had been lodged in her gut. Beckworth and Lando stared down at the thief, and when the thief focused on them, he simply groaned.

The sailors hefted him up with no concern for his aching head, and two more sailors rushed in to collect his buddy.

"Tie them up nice and tight." Lando returned his flintlock to his thigh holster and gave Stella a wry grin. "That turned out better than expected."

"I wasn't sure that was going to work." Stella was more than pleasantly surprised. Their jobs, while typically successful, never seemed to go as planned. She had to remind herself that the hard part was yet to come.

"Let's get into position." Beckworth stepped next to her and appeared to want to hug her, but he'd keep it professional, no matter how much she could have used one. "I'm sure Leclair will send his men in first."

She glanced around, but most of the building lay in shadows. The others were there, but all she heard was light rustling sounds that could have been rats.

Beckworth touched her cheek, his smile encouraging. "You'll need a weapon."

"Did you bring my pistol?" she asked.

"The little man thought you might prefer this." Lando's grin was eerie in the low light, and when she glanced down at what he was holding, she didn't think she could love these men more.

Her hand shook as she grasped her crossbow with a reverent hand. It was silly and a bit macabre, but she couldn't stop her wide smile. There was no doubt. She was certifiable. Wacko crazy. But she loved this thing.

Beckworth handed her four crossbow bolts and gave her a stern look, which did nothing to erase her grin. "Try to play nice."

<hr>

They left the thief hog-tied and gagged on the ground about twenty feet from the door. His buddy was similarly confined and had been dumped in a corner. The building was about half the size of the warehouse that overlooked the clubhouse. The only windows were those that fronted the dark street, and two lanterns had been positioned near the entrance to keep the rear of the building in shadow.

"You shouldn't be here," Stella said when Jamie came up to confirm the next steps.

He tapped the scarf around his neck. "I'll pull it up once Leclair arrives."

"How many men do you think he'll bring?" Stella had heard the men discuss it at length and knew the answer, but her need to chatter during a tense moment got the better of her.

Jamie rubbed his jaw. "It's hard to say, but probably no more than six or eight. Not to worry, though. We have enough men to handle double that number."

Beckworth agreed. "Even in this part of town, there will be one or two watchmen about who'd notice a large group of men and question it. If Leclair wants to keep his smuggling operations secret, he'll come with a small group, but they'll be the best he has on hand."

A sailor rushed out from the back of the building. "They've just rounded the corner."

Beckworth nodded as Jamie pulled up the scarf before fading into the shadows with Lando and the other sailors.

Stella took a position a couple of feet behind where the thief stirred in his bindings. Michelson stood behind her on her left, and Beckworth behind her on her right.

Nerves tingled across her skin, and with that weird feeling of expectant danger mixed with the comfort of a solid plan, she suppressed the desire to bounce on her toes. Instead, she focused on her persona as the leader of a band of smugglers. She pictured herself standing at the bow of a ship, a pistol strapped to her thigh. One hand rested on her hip while the other gripped the crossbow as they bore down on another smuggler off the English coast. When she realized she'd probably gotten that image from the cover of a bodice-ripper romance novel, she couldn't stop her grin.

And that was most likely the first thing the captain noticed when two men wrenched open the door and rushed in, hands on the pistols strapped to their legs. Behind them, a third man, oozing with confidence, stepped into the light.

He was a decent-looking man, and for a moment, she caught his dark eyes glitter with interest before they shuddered to black holes of coldness. He took in the two men behind her and then his thief, hogtied on the floor.

He strode toward her, stopping ten feet shy of the thief. After they took a moment to size each other up, he glanced down and lifted a brow.

"A crossbow?"

Stella glanced down at it and lifted it up as if seeing it for the first time. It needed a good cleaning. Perhaps some kind of oil to nourish the wood. She wasn't sure, other than knowing it required better care, and she made a mental note to ask Beckworth once the mission was over. While she might never understand why the weapon was so important to her, she would never get rid of it, so she decided to embrace it.

She shrugged and let her crazy-ass grin give emphasis to her words. "It's become my favorite weapon. It was Cheval's as well, or so he said while he tortured one of his sailors." She gave him a quizzical look. "Did you know Cheval, the captain of *The Horseman*?"

When the captain gave her a small nod, her gaze hardened. "He kidnapped me in an attempt to force me to give up my contacts. You can imagine the threats he made to my body as well as my business. Trustworthy contacts, as you must be aware, are invaluable in the cargo trade. I couldn't let his threats go unpunished. So, I imagine either the local magistrate found his body on a beach or the fish took care of him." Her grin returned. "Either way, I have a lovely new crossbow. Well, a new, well-used crossbow."

That had felt good, and for the briefest of moments, she ignored the captain, trusting Beckworth and Michelson would hold him off. She was having a cathartic moment. She'd never spoken about the torture she'd witnessed or the bodily threats Cheval had made in his mad vendetta to take over McDuff's network. She'd never spoken of it to Beckworth, and she understood why he'd never asked. But now he knew. Everyone knew. And a huge weight she hadn't realized had been suffocating her since that day on the beach suddenly lifted.

Cheval had been a bad man. Beckworth was being strangled or drowned—it was just a matter of which happened first. And she'd killed Cheval to save him. Jamie or Lando would have done the same thing. Beckworth wouldn't have hesitated had it been her lying on the sand as the tide washed in with Cheval's hands around her throat. And she hadn't hesitated, either. It had to be done.

Some part of her would never forget the second life she'd taken, but the life she'd saved brought more value into the world. The scales of justice remained in balance.

She gave the captain a long perusal as he stared at her. He wasn't horrified by her admission, though he might wonder a bit about her state of mind. He didn't seem the least bit concerned by her actions. There was a gleam in his eyes. Excitement. The story had enthralled him.

That sliced an edge in her bravado. This man was more dangerous than Cheval. She'd have to tread carefully. When she heard Beckworth shuffle his feet, she knew he was thinking the same thing.

She straightened, and though she didn't lower the crossbow, she relaxed her grip on it. "Perhaps we should start over. I'm Lady Swan. And who might you be?"

28

Beckworth struggled with a myriad of emotions as he watched Stella's exchange with the captain. Why, at this moment, would she share details about her time aboard *The Horseman*? He wanted to know more, but that she'd shared some of it now, while others listened, ignited his protective nature. All he wanted to do was pick her up and rush her back to Waverly, where they could be alone and away from danger.

Yet the other half of him was filled with pride at how she'd taken control of the meeting. He'd almost laughed out loud when she demanded to know who the captain was. She was his hero, something she and AJ always said of the other, though it usually involved wine or marionberry pie. The thought made him want to smile again.

He kept his eyes on the captain's men, but his focus kept returning to Leclair. On the surface, he was doing all the right things in the presence of a lady, but something else rode underneath that suave persona that kept Beckworth's senses on high alert. This was a dangerous man, and Beckworth wondered how long Leclair had been captain of a ship.

Based on what little he knew of McDuff, Leclair would be

the type of man he'd want as a captain in his network. He most likely secured high-value cargo, but depending on how quickly he rose through the ranks, how much did McDuff trust him? After the debacle with Cheval, Beckworth would never want someone that close that he couldn't trust, but when working with smugglers, one didn't have much to choose from.

The captain gave Stella an elegant bow and replied, "I'm Captain Leclair from the *Nighthawk*." When Stella's blank expression didn't change, he continued. "I've heard of a Lady Swan who sails on a mysterious ship up and down the west coast of England. Should I presume you're that same lady?"

Stella's throaty laugh pricked at Beckworth's protective nature again, and he hated to admit it in this situation, his lust. And he caught a glimpse of the same in the captain's gaze.

"Good god, I hope so. I'd hate to think there were two of us sailing around England. But I do love how you make me sound so enigmatic."

Her bold nature caught the captain off guard, but he recovered quickly enough. He peered into the shadows and then down at the thief, who kept looking from one to the other, waiting to learn his own fate. Leclair kicked the thief's midsection, resulting in a muffled groan. "Perhaps we should continue this conversation in a more comfortable setting. I know it's late, but have you eaten?"

Beckworth expected to hear Stella's stomach growl. He'd heard it earlier and assumed she hadn't had much of an appetite before the mission. No growl came, but he wasn't surprised by Stella's response. She understood what they needed.

"I've been so busy with last-minute tasks before our departure tomorrow, I'm afraid I haven't taken the time."

The captain took a step back and held out his arm. "Perhaps you'd be willing to join me at my favorite London pub?" When she hesitated, he glanced at Beckworth and Michelson. "Of course, your two men are welcome to follow. But I must insist the others remain behind." He wasn't a fool to think there were only the three of them.

Stella didn't hesitate as she handed her crossbow to Beckworth and walked around the thief to take the captain's arm. "I assume you'll follow the same rules. Two men and no more."

"But of course." His smile was genuine, though it didn't reach his eyes. Beckworth understood at that moment the captain had no plans to do what she asked. Fortunately, their side didn't play by the rules, either.

Fitz would have a small team watching Leclair's men and would follow them. Once the location where Leclair's men waited was confirmed, a sailor would return to inform Jamie, who would send the rest of the team to secure a border around them.

With Chester's crew still on the streets, no one would take them by surprise.

When Stella had stepped around the thief, she'd brushed against Beckworth. It was barely noticeable, happening within a blink of an eye, so chances were good he was the only one who'd noticed. But he'd understood that she was fine. If she'd been worried, she would have done something more dramatic, most likely in the form of questioning the change of location or the number of men she was allowed to have with her. The fact she was comfortable didn't change Beckworth's diligence with her safety, but a knot loosened in his chest.

If an attack came, it wouldn't be until after Leclair heard what Lady Swan had to offer. French arms, or the rumor of them, would run like wildfire through McDuff's network. Leclair would see this opportunity as another way to rise within the network with a handsome payday. He'd take the time to listen before doing anything rash.

Beckworth left the crossbow by the thief, whom the captain

left behind as he walked out the door with Stella. No doubt there were plenty more where he came from if the captain wanted to pursue collecting the rest of the jewelry.

Leclair led Stella four blocks away as if they were strolling through Hyde Park. Beckworth knew this pub. In fact, it was also one of his favorites. It was suitable for discussing private business, had decent ale and stronger spirits, and the last time he'd been here, which had been some time ago, served excellent food.

Before they reached the door, two drunken sailors entered, each one leaning on the other. Beyond the pub, farther down the street, he caught sight of another man, who wore a top hat. Though his clothes appeared old and ragged, the man walked with a proud and steady gait until he turned a corner. Beckworth grinned. He knew several men who wore top hats, but only one sailor. An odd man that Jamie had found up the coast in Scotland, but one of the best sailors either man had seen.

It was all he needed to know that Fitz had just entered the pub, and Jamie's men would soon be in place.

S tella's anxiety returned during the walk to the pub. She had no problem letting her mouth run wild when Beckworth was beside her and Jamie's men were there as backup. But she remained quiet, not trusting Leclair, whose tense muscles were easy to feel under his jacket. One look at Beckworth when she'd handed him her crossbow was enough to understand he didn't trust him either.

"It's not much farther," Leclair assured her.

She wasn't appeased. For all she knew, his statement could be a signal to the two men who walked behind Beckworth and Michelson.

"As long as the food is as good as you claim. Most of the food in the pubs down here is barely edible."

His laugh seemed an honest one. "You have to be in a different part of town to find anything dependable." He glanced down at her and tugged her close. "I'm surprised you didn't know that, especially with all the time you spend with the aristocrats."

She rolled her eyes, tired of making up stories, so she used the adage to stick as close to the truth as possible. "I don't come to London often, and my foray into noble society has been difficult. I suppose after eating in pubs along the west coast, I expected something better in such a large city."

"Well, you'll be happy with the dining here."

She glanced up in time to see two drunks enter the establishment. She laughed when she recognized one as Fitz. She'd seen too many of his disguises to be fooled, and some of her courage returned. "It appears the ale is good."

When he took note of the drunks, he chuckled again. "In their condition, I wouldn't trust those two with knowing a fine meal nor an excellent ale."

Once inside the pub, which was nicer than she'd expected, and any threat of being attacked in an alley was behind her, her nerves settled. Similar to McDuff, there was a table waiting for Leclair in the back of the pub. Was this captain taking his cues from McDuff, or did he have the same plan as Cheval to someday overthrow him?

Beckworth and Michelson found a place to stand along a wall opposite where the captain's men stood. They were too far away to hear anything but close enough if needed. The captain remained silent until the server came, and before she could say anything, he ordered for her. At least it was roasted pork rather than fish, but her irritation rose over his attempt at control, though she didn't argue when the wine was poured. She did her best not to swallow it down like water after a long walk in the desert.

"Where have you been all this time?" Leclair asked, keeping a watchful eye on her as he took a rather large gulp of wine.

The question surprised her, and she involuntarily took a longer drink. She licked her upper lip. "What do you mean?"

His gaze followed her tongue before he refocused on the conversation. "McDuff has been looking for you. From what I understand, you made a commitment to show him cargo for a possible trade and then up and disappeared."

Thank the gods. This was something she had an answer for. She set her glass on the table, a little too hard, and gave him a puzzled look. "Didn't you listen to a thing I said in the warehouse?" She had danced around McDuff. He'd been suave and flirtatious, and it seemed the right balance for dealing with him. This man was none of that. He played at being as sophisticated as McDuff, but some people couldn't mask their dispassionate side. Her best option would be to play it more assertively and test the waters.

When he seemed perplexed by her response, she sighed—loudly. "The last time I saw McDuff was an hour before Cheval kidnapped me. Are you suggesting he's unaware of that? He must know Cheval is dead."

He gave her a tight smile that didn't last long. This man would never trust her. McDuff hadn't trusted her, either, but at least he was a gentleman with proper manners. Good grief. Proper manners. Maybe she'd spent too much time in this time period.

"He did hear about Cheval and some auburn-haired woman who might have been responsible for his demise, but he had no way to validate who the woman was." He leaned toward her as his tone chilled. "And wasn't there something about a wedding?"

She did everything she could to stop the surprise from

coloring her face, but her intake of breath gave it all away. She blinked and took a long sip of wine. If she didn't slow down, she'd be drunk before the food arrived. She could salvage this if she simply paused and put some pieces together. Now that he'd mentioned the event, it wasn't difficult remembering that moment with McDuff while Thomas yelled about her not escaping the wedding. She'd forgotten that Beckworth had Thomas break up the dinner meeting because Cheval's ship had been seen mooring on the other side of the docks.

She squirmed to appear uncomfortable, which wasn't all that difficult. The hairs on the back of her neck were standing at full attention.

"That's one of the reasons I'm in London." She sipped her wine and let her gaze flit around the room, as if she wasn't prepared to discuss something so personal. Her gaze fell on Fitz, who was in deep conversation with another sailor, but he caught her eye for a brief moment. It gave her the lift she needed. "I've taken care of the problem."

His brow lifted, and he leaned back. He seemed intrigued. "And how did you do that?"

She straightened in her seat. "That's none of your business." She scanned the room again, her glass hiding the lower half of her face. "And it's not safe to discuss here."

If he'd thought her a dainty female before, he didn't anymore. He gave her the first true smile of the evening. "Very good." He pushed his mug and leaned in again. "Let's discuss your proposition. How do you know about the jewelry?"

"I have a connection or two among the aristocracy. You're not the only one raising capital for cargo." She sat back and quieted as the plates were served. She took a bite of the pork, waited a moment, then nodded. Better than she'd expected.

"Go on."

McDuff didn't like to discuss business during dinner, but

Leclair's approach was fine with her. The faster they got through the meal, the faster she could escape back to the coach and Beckworth's arms.

"I was at one of the balls where your thief took a necklace right off a lady, not two feet away from me. I had no idea what was happening, but she immediately knew it was gone and went on and on about the designer. It took a few days of boring garden parties to discover the thefts all had one thing in common—the same French designer."

"And why are they of interest to you?"

Stella barked out a laugh that made several nearby people glance her way. She dabbed a napkin over her lips while she controlled her grin. "Because I'm a woman who appreciates fine jewelry, and I know how much a collection like that could sell for."

"And why would I give them to you?"

She shook her head as if speaking to a child. "Please, Captain Leclair, I'm not new to this game. As I told your thief, I'm not asking you to give them to me. I'll pay a fair price."

He continued to hold her gaze. "I already have a very interested buyer. Someone close to the designer who died a couple of years ago. They hold a sentimental value."

She rubbed her finger around the rim of her wine glass and narrowed her eyes. After a moment of contemplation, she leaned in, and her words were spoken so low, the captain was forced to hunch over the table. "More value than French arms?"

When his eyes lit with a new fire, only one word came to mind.

Gotcha.

Beckworth walked into the study at Templeton's manor to find Barrington already seated in front of the fireplace with a glass of whiskey. The bottle and an empty glass sat on the table next to him.

"You put the coach up rather quickly." Beckworth had made a stop downstairs, where he'd found Libby pressing one of Stella's dresses. He'd told her to go to bed, and while she nodded at his command, he knew she wouldn't listen. Stella had given her the entire next day and night off, and Libby wanted to ensure Stella had everything she would need before her return, even though Maggie had proven capable enough.

Since arguing with Libby rarely worked, he'd squeezed her arm and kissed the top of her head. "Thank you for watching out for her."

She'd screwed up her face in disgust and waved him off. "Enough of that. You forget your place." He didn't miss her grin before she turned away from him to focus on the dress.

"One could say the same of a certain lady's maid." He was still smiling when he slowed his approach to the study to peek in the library.

Though it was late, Bart and Lincoln had their heads down, staring at the chessboard. They played so frequently he doubted they counted their wins and losses anymore. This was how they spent their time discussing philosophy, medicine, and current events. Even living in his old cabin far away from London, Bart couldn't stop his intellectual mind from churning. And though time was taking a toll on his body, his mind remained sharp.

Beckworth was still considering various ideas of how to support Bart once Lincoln moved to London for his medical education. Leaving Bart alone wasn't an option, and removing him from his cabin would be equally detrimental to his mental health. He still had some time, but it was narrowing. With a sigh, he'd moved on to the study where he'd found Barrington.

Barrington poured whiskey into a glass and pushed it toward the empty chair. "Templeton's staff enjoys having something to do. Two stable boys were waiting for the coach when we returned."

"I didn't see them." Beckworth dropped into the chair and sipped his drink.

"Stella seemed tired, but Jamie said the meeting was a success."

"It was, but you know what it's like when on a job. Between the nerves and playing a role, even successful jobs can drain one's energy."

"And she does put a lot of energy into everything she does."

"How do we keep getting sucked into these missions? I worry every time she's on her own with these smugglers."

Barrington didn't respond, which meant he was gathering his thoughts. He finished the whiskey and set down the glass. "You have natural abilities that were encouraged and developed during your time with the crews. Those skills became beneficial to the duke, especially with your likeness to your half-brother. But it wasn't until Hensley discovered your talents that your deeds became vital to the good of England. And while we both grew up in the slums of London, our hearts still beat for our country. It's difficult for a man like Hensley not to use every ounce of his own skill to harness that talent."

"And it's his own love of country that forces him to make those decisions. But why Stella?"

Barrington chuckled. "You still don't see it?"

"She's brave and smart. I do see that."

"The two of you are the same. Oh, you don't have the exact same skills, but what you do possess works well together. Her outspokenness can get her into trouble, but it also gets her out of it. She adapts and thinks fast. And she's not above killing in the defense of others."

Beckworth winced. "To save me. It's not something I would have wanted for her." But he'd witnessed her ability to adapt since the first day they'd been on the run. "Finn always worried that AJ enjoyed the adventure too much. I think it's part of the reason AJ isn't happy with us returning here. Both women have a wild streak."

He drained his glass and rubbed his face before leaning back and stretching his legs. He could use a good, long sleep, but that would have to wait until the mission was over. "I've completely lost track of obligations. We must have missed several committed engagements by now."

"Only one evening event, and it wasn't anything of note. At least not in the circles where you endeavor to stay involved."

He snorted. "Even those people are more interested in Stella."

Barrington grunted in response.

"Have there been any more thefts? We have the thief now, but he could have snatched something else before this evening. And I'm not convinced the second bloke with him this evening was his partner at the parties."

"From what Eleanor tells me, Elizabeth personally contacted the women who owned the remaining known pieces of the Deschanel jewelry. They've all promised to keep the items safely tucked away until they hear the thief has been caught."

They spent another half hour discussing housekeeping notes and plans for after the mission. He left Barrington staring into the fire and made his way up the stairs, wanting nothing more than to spend the next two days locked in their bedroom with Stella. If only.

Stella was in bed as expected. The only light was from a single bedside lamp and the low flames of the fire. He added two logs before removing his boots and clothing. At times, he wondered why he bothered with a valet. The poor man was rarely called into service with Stella around. She enjoyed dressing and undressing him, and he could only shake his head. He wasn't any different when it came to Stella's attire.

He opened the drapes that overlooked the garden. The moon was almost full, casting the gardens into pockets of light and shadow. He stayed there for some time as he let his mind wander.

"Are you going to come to bed anytime soon, or should I grab my robe and come to you?"

He left the window with the drapes open and added a third log to the fire before extinguishing the lamp's flame and crawling into bed. She immediately rolled into him, and he held her tight, kissing her temple, her nose, and then her lips.

She sighed contentedly as she snuggled close. "What a day."

"A successful one."

"Will Hensley be able to get the firearms in time for tomorrow night?"

"Jamie will have the crates picked up before noon, then he'll take them to the warehouse where we've been watching the clubhouse."

"Is that safe?"

"As safe as anywhere. Hensley is supplying his own men in addition to several of Jamie's crew to keep an eye on the wagon and the building. They'll move the wagon into position an hour before the meeting. Now, let's not worry about tomorrow night. We have a whole day to spend before then."

"There's a luncheon at some viscountess's estate. I've already sent a message to Lady Howard with regrets for her evening party."

"You'll have to send your regrets to the viscountess as well. Perhaps you can invite her to a garden tea next week."

"Why? What's up?" She struggled to sit up, but he held her tight in his arms.

"We're going to have a long morning sleep-in, then I'm taking you on another tour of London. We've barely scratched the surface on places I want to show you."

"Are we inviting Eleanor?"

"We're not inviting anyone other than Barrington, who will drive the coach."

"Poor man. He must get tired of splitting his time between butler and coachman."

"He actually enjoys driving the coach. It gives him time to catch up with the other coachmen, and he always brings along something to read."

She nudged him. "I told you men like to gossip more than women."

He laughed and squeezed her. "Are you in the mood for gossiping?"

"When aren't I?"

He ran a hand over her hip and then lower to caress her thigh. "Tell me what Libby's discovered from the kitchen maids while I focus on other things."

He slowly worked his way down her body as she shared the latest gossip from the staff. He planted small kisses and gentle licks in all the right places until her throaty laugh encouraged more naughty things, and all thoughts of gossiping disappeared.

29

———————

Stella rushed down the hall, tugging her wrap around her.

Libby raced after her. "You forgot your dagger."

Stella stopped short and turned around, checking her pockets, though she could clearly see Libby holding the dagger as if she were ready to stab someone.

"I thought I took it out of my other dress." She'd worn a lovely rose-colored day dress for Beckworth's tour of London, and though it seemed silly, she'd refused to leave the dagger behind.

"You did take it out, but it was hidden under one of the other dresses."

Libby meant under one of the multitude of dresses Stella had tossed around the room with her indecisiveness. She needed the right dress that would fit Lady Swan's style but would also allow freedom of movement if something went wrong. Part of the problem was that they'd returned later than they'd planned, with only minutes to spare before dinner. They were to meet Leclair at ten that evening, which was barely an hour away.

She shoved the dagger in her pocket then continued her

march to the stairs. "I don't know what Beckworth did with my crossbow."

"He said it was in the coach."

She stopped again. "I didn't see it in there."

"It's in the boot."

She continued on as she considered that. Now she remembered. They'd tossed several weapons in the boot before they left the docks the previous evening. Beckworth must have decided to leave them since they'd be needed tonight.

She was halfway down the stairs when she noticed the woman standing in the foyer.

"Elizabeth!" Stella lifted her skirt and rushed down the remaining stairs. "What are you doing here?"

The dowager's determined expression was hard to read. "I've come to wait with Eleanor."

"I thought there was a party this evening."

Elizabeth nodded and allowed a footman to remove her cloak. "There is. Mary gave them my regrets."

"The party would take your mind off things. You know Beckworth will keep you updated."

She gave Stella a hard look. "I can't go to a party while you and Beckworth are risking your lives for my necklace."

Stella took Elizabeth's arm and guided her to the library. "I'll do everything I can to retrieve your necklace, but you know there's more at stake."

"Of course, I do."

Stella didn't mind Elizabeth's aggravated tone. "Well, keep up that attitude. You'll need it if you're going to spend the evening with Bart."

Elizabeth choked on a laugh, and they had to stop until she got her breath back. There were tears in the dowager's eyes, and Stella chose to believe it was from the coughing and not desperation over the necklace being returned.

"Stella, we need to leave."

The women turned as Beckworth marched down the hallway, pulling on the jacket he used when visiting the East End.

"Sorry, Elizabeth." He kissed her cheek. "I've arranged for a light repast to keep everyone energized until our return."

Elizabeth took his arm. "I want my necklace back, but don't put yourself in unnecessary risk."

"Don't worry." He gave her a winsome smile that Stella knew he didn't feel. "This will be a simple trade."

"Besides," Stella matched his smile, "we have two crews watching our backs, and Hensley has men keeping an eye on those French firearms."

It sounded good, but at that moment, Stella wasn't sure she believed her own words.

They were saved from comforting the dowager when Eleanor strode down the hall like a soldier on a mission. "Don't worry about them, Elizabeth. They love this type of adventure. Now, Bart is looking for a good game of whist."

The two women moved toward the library while Beckworth pulled Stella back to the foyer.

"Where have you been?" Stella raced to keep up with him.

"Last-minute instructions with Jamie and Lando."

"Aren't they at the docks already? Who's watching the firearms?"

"As you said, Hensley sent men with the wagon. Stop fretting, and worry more about your own role."

She huffed as she hurried down the steps where Barrington waited at the open door to the carriage. He gave her a tight grin as she was loaded in with Beckworth right behind her. They didn't talk on the drive, but held hands, which was words enough.

In order to keep Lady Swan as mysterious as possible, they decided not to venture to the meeting place from the *Daphne*.

Barrington parked the coach several blocks from the warehouse by the docks, where the exchange of cargo was to take place. Chester's crew was familiar with the building. It was primarily used for overnight storage, and the man who owned the building was known to work with smugglers.

Two of Chester's crew would stay with Barrington and the coach in case of unexpected trouble. After the shenanigans with Cheval overtaking their team when Stella had been kidnapped, they weren't taking any chances. She also noted six sailors waiting for them—their security detail for the walk to the docks.

Once out of the coach, Barrington opened the boot and handed out the weapons, including additional daggers and swords for anyone who might need them.

When she was handed her crossbow, she lifted a brow. "Won't it appear strange if I walk in with this?"

"He's already seen you with a crossbow, and exchanging firearms isn't for the faint-hearted." Beckworth tucked his pistol into a thigh holster and attached a scabbard to his belt. "You can be assured Leclair and his men will be heavily armed."

She gulped. She knew this. Why else had she been concerned about where her crossbow was? The reality of watching everyone weapon up brought a hiccup of a giggle. It was like watching a two-hundred-year-old earlier version of a SWAT team preparing for a bust. She ignored the look Beckworth gave her; she couldn't stop her grin. It seemed the manic side of her personality slipped out whenever she stormed into danger. For the briefest moment, she wished AJ and Finn were there with them. AJ would have her quiver of arrows and bow swung over her shoulder, along with her harness of throwing daggers. The giggles returned, and she turned away from the men in an attempt to find her game face. What would the captain think if she burst into hysterical laughter at the theatrics their meeting created?

She calmed when a hand landed on her shoulder, knowing it was Beckworth.

"Let's get closer to the warehouse. A walk in the brisk air should calm your nerves."

She took his proffered arm but only nodded because she was scared to open her mouth. When another giggle erupted, Beckworth squeezed her arm.

"Didn't you take a drink of whiskey before you left?"

"Damn. That explains it. I forgot."

"I can't believe Libby did."

This time she laughed out loud, which released all her pent-up giggles. "She would have asked for both the glass and the bottle, claiming it would calm her nerves while waiting for our safe return."

"She does have a smart mouth, but it makes her good for jobs."

"Well, you can't have it both ways."

He stopped and turned to face her. His smile made her heart skip a beat. He was a beautiful man, even dressed down as a smuggler, and she could only grin when he said, "Don't I know it."

They stopped in an alley a few blocks from the warehouse. Two from the crew waited for them, in addition to a dozen men from the *Daphne*. Michelson was one of them, and he walked over to meet them.

"Jamie, Lando, and Fitz are in place. The wagon and its guards have arrived."

Beckworth nodded. "Any word on the captain?"

"Fitz spotted two dozen men coming out of the clubhouse, including the captain. They stopped at another building and picked up an empty wagon."

"That's good, right?" Stella asked.

Beckworth tugged at his sleeves. "It's good that they're

expecting to leave with crates of firearms. The question is whether they're willing to trade rather than think they can just take."

Beckworth led their growing group to where the wagon and men waited, two blocks from the meeting place. Michelson walked a step behind with Stella following. The eighteen sailors walked three to a row and monitored the buildings, roofs, alleys, and every street they crossed. He wouldn't take any chances, and though he should have asked a handful of sailors to walk in front of him, Chester had watchers on the streets. They would let Beckworth know if there was trouble ahead. The risk was reduced since Hensley had contacted the night watchmen to keep them out of the area until after the exchange.

The first thing he noticed was the three men with rifles standing at the entrance to the alley. They kept close to the walls of the buildings to make themselves harder targets, and Beckworth assumed there were another three at the other end of the alley. These would be Hensley's men. The spymaster expected the firearms to be returned. There was a fifty-fifty chance the handful of crates would be lost to the captain, but they'd do their best not to let that happen.

When the men with rifles heard their approach, all three pointed their flintlocks at the group until one recognized Beckworth and lowered his rifle. The men didn't say anything as they stepped aside to let the group pass before returning to their stations.

Stella had increased her pace to walk next to him. "I know we have a lot of men, but I'm not feeling so good about this."

He glanced down at her, but she wasn't looking at him. She'd caught sight of the wagon; her jaw tightened and her brows wrinkled. He'd thought it was just him who felt something was off. He couldn't put his finger on it because they had the upper hand. Or they should.

"It's just normal jitters." He grabbed her hand. It was ice cold and couldn't be explained away by the light touch of fog that brought a bit of dew.

She gave him that look that confirmed she didn't believe a thing he said, but there wasn't anything he could do to relieve her anxiety.

A driver and a man with a rifle sat on the wagon's bench. No one in their right mind would attempt walking down the alley with the dozen hard-looking men, rifles in hand, huddled around the wagon. They were all Hensley's men.

Jamie, Lando, and Fitz waited nearby.

"You're late, little man." Lando leaned against a building as he sharpened his dagger. The soft sound of blade on whetstone echoed through the alley. For as many men standing around, they were extremely quiet.

"I'd rather not be the first ones to arrive." Beckworth glanced at Stella, whose worried expression had increased. "And you know how long it takes a woman to get ready."

Fitz squeezed Stella's shoulder. "Take a breath. You're more nervous than a virgin on her wedding night."

Stella snorted, and his statement seemed to release her tension because she sagged a bit. "I'll take your word for it. I've never married, and it's been some time since I was a virgin."

A few of the men laughed, and those who didn't know her gave her an appraising look. They wouldn't have expected those words out of a lady, but they'd know soon enough exactly how bold she was.

Fitz grinned at her. "That's better. Now, just handle this bloke like you did McDuff."

"We never got this far with McDuff."

"Maybe not for a trade, but you still led him on a merry chase. Just remember, you're in charge of all these men."

Her return laugh had a bit of a croak to it, but she gave the crossbow a loving stroke before leaning toward him. "I'd believe your Irish blarney if I thought you'd listen to a thing I'd ask of you."

"I've been telling him that for too many years to count." Jamie gave her a wink. "Are you ready, lass?"

She sobered quickly, and when she glanced at Beckworth, he nodded and gave her the one piece of advice she always followed.

"Time for your game face."

"Where's the meeting place from here?" she asked.

"Just another block or so." Beckworth leaned in and touched her cheek. "You've got this."

Beckworth took the lead with their expanded group, including Jamie, Lando, and Fitz. All of Hensley's men would remain with the wagon until it was needed.

They walked without speaking, but their boots made enough noise on the cobblestone streets to announce their arrival. When they were two buildings down from the warehouse, Beckworth stopped.

"Michelson and I will lead you through the entrance, and once we confirm it's safe, we'll step aside for you to take the lead. The rest of the men will have your back."

She listened intently. They'd gone over the plan twice while they'd eaten dinner, though she'd only picked at her food. Nervous energy was to be expected; he just needed her to expel it before going in.

"Do you remember the items of jewelry that were taken?" he asked.

She rolled her eyes. "Of course." Her tone was snappish. "Do you honestly think I can't remember jewelry?" She stormed off but stopped after several steps. One hand landed on her hip, and her grip appeared to tighten on the crossbow, though the dim light made it difficult to confirm. She glanced over her shoulder and demanded, "Are you coming or not? We're late."

He could have sworn he caught a hint of humor in her tone. Either way, she'd found her game face.

30

Beckworth and Michelson caught up to Stella as they approached the warehouse, but when she saw the two men standing next to the doors, she replaced her earlier grin with her all-business smile. If there hadn't been more than a dozen men hovering in the alley, she would have kissed Beckworth for getting her head back in the game.

She checked her pocket for the crossbow bolts she'd been given earlier and released a breath when she counted eight. More than enough if they got into trouble—or so she hoped. When Beckworth and Michelson slowed, she pushed past them. It hadn't been the plan, but she took their action as a sign that this was the time for her to lead.

The two men wore sour expressions and didn't move when she reached them.

"I assume Captain Leclair is already here. Are you going to let me in, or do I require a special invitation?" She lifted her crossbow and cradled it against her chest. Just in case they hadn't seen it.

"You're late," the one on the left said. He was a big bruiser with a crooked nose and scraggly beard, but he carried two pistols, one on each thigh. No doubt he had a dagger or two in his jacket, or maybe a boot.

She sneered at him. "A woman's prerogative." When neither man moved, she shrugged. "I went to a lot of trouble for this meeting, but if the captain's no longer interested, then so be it." She turned and took several steps back the way they'd come, surprising Michelson but not Beckworth.

"Wait."

This time when she turned, she wasn't pleasant. "I'm not in the mood for your hogwash or your games."

"Hollister, let her in." The command was shouted from somewhere in the warehouse, but it didn't sound like the captain's voice.

Hollister spat on the ground before opening one of the doors.

She ignored him as she passed into the building but turned when she heard the unmistakable sound of flesh hitting flesh and the thud of something hitting the ground. The something was a someone—Hollister—and he glowered as he got to his feet. Beckworth stared down at him with a smug expression. The man's partner backed away, hands up.

Beckworth winked at her, and she nodded, doing her best not to grin like a lovestruck ninny. He was her hero.

She marched into the warehouse, quickly scanning the area as she'd been trained to do.

It was larger than the building where she'd first met Leclair, more similar in size and style to the warehouse the team used to monitor the clubhouse. She glanced up to the landing where a couple of men stood by the railing. If there were others, they would be hiding behind the closed doors of the three offices.

More than a dozen men were positioned around three sides of the building, leaving the side she'd come through with just the two men who'd been stationed at the door.

There were two closed doors at the front of the building, but they opened briefly for two men to step inside. They were most likely put in place in case Stella came from the main street rather than the alley. An empty wagon was positioned on the far side of the warehouse, led by two horses that twitched their tails and shuffled their feet. There were stacks of crates and barrels to her right, still leaving the warehouse two-thirds empty.

The captain and his two bodyguards stood next to the crates with their arms folded across their chests.

Leclair frowned as he took in Stella, who still clutched the crossbow. "Sorry about my men. They get cantankerous when they have to wait."

"His impatience has been dealt with."

The captain looked beyond her as if concerned for his man.

"Oh, don't worry. Other than his jaw, only his pride has been injured."

"I don't see a wagon."

Straight to business. That was fine with her. The last thing she wanted was to carry on a loathsome conversation as if she liked this man. And if he wanted to play the annoyed game, then two could play.

"I want to see the jewelry first. Once I've determined it's the merchandise I'm looking for, I'll call for the wagon."

The captain's expression soured, and he started to say something, but instead shook his head as if giving in. He stepped toward a short stack of crates, his two bodyguards just a step behind him. She stopped a few feet shy of the crates and waited. Leclair glanced around the warehouse before pulling out a purse-sized linen pouch. He was surprisingly gentle when he opened it and laid out the four stolen pieces.

When the last piece, the diadem, was added to the others, he waved her closer.

"I'd prefer it if you took a couple of steps back." She gave him a cross look. "We're all friends here, right?"

His lips thinned, but he did as she asked. Beckworth and Michelson remained close as she stepped up to the crate. She kept the crossbow in her right hand and used her left to pick up each piece for inspection, though her gaze immediately landed on the necklace she'd last seen around Elizabeth's neck. All the pieces were accounted for, but she couldn't stop admiring the amazing craftwork and intricate designs, which were even more impressive when the pieces were gathered together.

She turned to Beckworth. "They're all here." To the captain, she said, "I've brought six crates of French firearms to trade for these. If that's acceptable, I'll call for the wagon. It will only take a few minutes."

When the captain nodded, seeming more relaxed, Beckworth waved to the back of the building. She didn't need to look at him to confirm that Leclair planned on double-crossing them. They'd expected it, and when the captain didn't question the number of crates in exchange for the jewelry, it only validated their suspicions.

She remained by the jewelry, unwilling to let it out of her sight while they waited. Beckworth and Michelson stuck close as the men they'd brought quietly repositioned themselves inside the building, a couple of them moving far enough in to keep an eye on the men on the second floor.

"Where did you get the rifles?" Leclair asked.

Stella suspected he didn't expect a truthful answer and was only filling the silence occasionally disturbed by the soft rustling of the horses. "I have a contact on the north shore of France."

"And they're reliable?

She shrugged, trying to remember, to no avail, what, if anything, she'd told McDuff. "They have been for the last several months." The only thing she recalled telling McDuff was her story of how she came to England, which hadn't been that long ago, so her answer seemed reasonable.

The captain's gaze turned unfocused, and she wondered if he was having the same wet dreams Cheval had about stealing her contacts. Fat chance, but she couldn't blame him for considering it.

The sound of approaching hooves made everyone straighten. Game on.

Stella took a step closer to the jewelry but turned to face the back door while keeping an eye on the captain. His focus was fully engaged on the doors, and he licked his lips in anticipation. However, she didn't miss the bodyguard on his left who inched in the direction of the jewelry.

The back doors opened wider to allow the wagon through. The same two men were on the bench—one driving and one gripping his rifle. But the back of the wagon no longer held just the crates of firearms. Six men, all with rifles, were positioned in the back. Two of them trained their weapons on the second-floor landing, while the other four pointed their rifles toward the front of the building at the captain's men.

Leclair nodded to one of his men, who approached the wagon. Lando, who'd walked beside it as it entered, waited at the back of the wagon and lifted the tarp covering the crates. He pried open one of the lids, which Stella could only tell by the creak of wood rubbing against nails.

When all six crates had been checked, the captain's man nodded that the inventory checked out. He helped Lando pull the tarp off the crates before they both stepped back.

The captain waved his wagon forward, and several men walked with it, most likely the muscle to move the crates. Stella leaned her crossbow against one of the crates and took the liberty of picking up the pouch to put the jewelry back in. She tensed when the captain approached but managed to get a brooch tucked inside.

"There's one more thing before we conclude our deal." He barely got the words out when shouting came from the back of the building.

"We've been betrayed. Trouble coming." The voice that came from the back of the building was distinctly Fitz.

Stella glared at the captain, but he appeared as shocked as she did. He might have been faking it, but she didn't think so. He turned his attention to the doors as he stepped back. Hensley's men held their positions inside the wagon, keeping their guns trained on the men upstairs and Leclair's men who'd followed the empty wagon. Everyone else was looking around, wondering what the hell was going on.

The front doors were flung open as men streamed in, firing weapons. She tried to count how many before she was dragged to the ground as return shots echoed through the building. Horses screamed from the chaos as men attempted to find cover.

The captain's bodyguards shielded Leclair.

"Michelson, stay behind the crates with Stella." Beckworth's following words were drowned out by the weapons fire.

Stella was already moving behind the crates but had to backtrack to where she'd left her crossbow. When she felt resistance, she turned to see Michelson handing her the weapon. She took it, glancing back to Beckworth, but he was already on the move, ducking low, his pistol in hand.

It wasn't long before she heard the telltale sound of blades on blades. The building was too small for the number of men with firearms, especially when it took time to reload.

She'd just loaded two bolts in the crossbow when someone crashed into the stack of crates she was hiding behind. They didn't topple, but the force had been enough to knock two pieces of jewelry to the ground. She turned her head in time to see one of the captain's bodyguards rushing in from her right, his eyes locked on the jewelry.

Oh, no, he wasn't. She aimed the crossbow at center mass, but Michelson nudged her at the last minute as he backed up. Her shot went low, though not wide enough to entirely miss. The bodyguard dropped when the bolt hit his upper thigh, and though his mouth opened in a scream of pain, she couldn't hear it through the shouting, sword fights, and firing weapons.

The horses tethered to both wagons were having none of it, and they raced toward opposite doors, wanting nothing more than to get out. Though from her position, it appeared the drivers were just as eager. Reality kicked in when she caught blood on the shirt of both of Hensley's men as the wagon rushed past on their way out the doors.

The first bodyguard crawled toward the crate, not willing to give up. The other one, who'd moved with Leclair to hide behind a row of barrels, made a move toward her—or, more likely, the jewelry.

Stella grabbed the diadem that managed to stay on top of the crate and fussed with fitting it into the pouch. She reloaded the crossbow and lifted it just in time to fire at the bodyguard. He'd just passed his friend, who was still crawling toward her, and a blind man could have hit him; he'd been that close. Yet, instead of hitting him in the chest, the bolt slammed into the man's right side. She probably hadn't killed him, but he still dropped as his left hand grabbed the top of the crate before he slid to the ground. She waited a beat to see if he'd get back up, but he rolled around, clutching his side.

Stella scrambled on her knees, swearing as she stopped to pull up her dress to get it out of the way. Unsure what to do with the pouch that was too big for her pockets, she lifted her dress higher to tuck the bulky item into the waistband of her drawers, not giving a fig about modesty.

She winced each time a knee landed on a pebble, but her eyes were locked on Elizabeth's necklace.

When the crawling man reached it at the same time, she dropped the crossbow, pulled out her dagger, and stabbed him in the hand as it covered the necklace. He screamed as she tugged to release the blade. Once it was freed, she grabbed the necklace, hoping she hadn't gotten any blood on it, and shoved it into a pocket.

She held onto the dagger and all but lay down as she stretched to reach the last stolen piece—the second brooch. Before her fingers touched it, she looked up into Leclair's fiery gaze. He was inches from her.

"What have you done?" he yelled.

"Those aren't my men. I thought they were yours."

The captain nudged closer, his eyes on the brooch. She grabbed it before he had the chance and was just as stunned as he was by her quick reflexes.

"Here's my deal." She had no idea what possessed her to say that, other than the fact she was holding all the stolen jewelry. She glanced over her shoulder to see Michelson focused on the skirmish. It would be pretty simple for Leclair to toss her over his shoulder and escape while everyone was busy.

She checked her first pocket, which was filled with jewelry and crossbow bolts, and after issuing a quiet curse, switched hands with her dagger. She fished around and pulled out a swan, disappointed by its misshapen wings.

"If you're interested in completing this deal, give this to that messenger at the pub where I met the thief. My ship still leaves at first tide, but a couple of my men will be staying for several more days. I'll have one of them visit the pub during that time. He'll also have a swan. They're my calling card. He can negotiate a time and place to deliver the firearms. I want this partnership to work."

"You think these other men are associated with your husband?"

They obviously weren't, but if he was willing to believe it, why not run with that? "If you weren't expecting them, I don't know who else could be that angry with me." Her brows scrunched together, thinking about Cheval. "Not unless one of us has a spy in our midst."

There was no time to hear his response as she was pulled away by two strong hands. The captain didn't look pleased, but he backed away when someone tapped him on the shoulder. It looked like everyone was trying to get the hell out.

Beckworth and Michelson had a hand on each of her arms, and they bent low, covering her like secret service agents as they rushed her toward the back of the building. They'd made it a few feet before Beckworth lost his footing, but he regained it before falling. If he said anything, it was impossible to hear over the continued shouts and weapons fire.

Men sprawled on the ground, trying to stand, crawl away, or simply lying still. Several were being helped out, and though she couldn't be certain, they appeared to be sailors from the *Daphne*. She saw little else as Beckworth held her head down as they continued their crab walk to the door.

The last thing she saw as they moved into the dark of night was someone dragging an unconscious, or possibly dead, Fitz.

Once outside, there was no reprieve from the chaos. The team had managed to stop the horses harnessed to the empty wagon, and she caught a glimpse of two men on the bench. She didn't know what happened to the captain's men, but they were no longer with the wagon. She recognized one of the sailors who held the horses steady with the reins.

When she was allowed to straighten, she noted men loading the injured into the back of the wagon. She didn't see anyone who didn't have bright crimson staining their clothing. Some of the men limped but continued to assist others who were worse off, while others pointed rifles in various directions, watching for anyone attempting to ambush their retreat.

Then she was being dragged away toward the carriage as Beckworth and Michelson kept firm grips on her. Barrington stood near the open door. She glanced behind her, sickened by what she saw.

How many were dead? All of this for a bag of stolen jewelry. Then she reminded herself it was much more than that. It was about stopping a smuggling network.

She tried to wrap her head around what had happened and when it had all gone wrong, but all she could see was an unconscious Fitz being dragged away.

"Beckworth!"

The men turned in unison, dragging Stella around with them to see Jamie racing up. She blanched when she caught sight of Beckworth's face for the first time since scrambling out of the building. His cheeks were blotted with red patches, and there was a raging fire in his eyes. He was angrier than she'd ever remembered seeing him.

"What the hell was that?" Beckworth yelled.

Jamie shook his head. He appeared more devastated than angry, but she imagined that would change once he'd cared for his men. "I don't know. We caught two men who tried to ambush us and take the wagon. We don't know who broke up the exchange; they might have been more of Leclair's men."

"Chester's crew should have seen them."

"That's who told us there was trouble. From what the old

man said, it appeared the men were hiding in a nearby building. But that needs to wait for now. I have three severely injured men, and several others needing medical attention."

Beckworth nodded at Michelson. "Go with Jamie, we've got it from here." Michelson was the *Daphne*'s medic, and the sailor didn't question the order.

Michelson raced off, but Jamie remained, deep concern in his gaze.

"Michelson won't be able to help the gravest of them. We need Bart."

"How many?" Beckworth asked. He rubbed his forehead. "Three, you said?"

Jamie nodded.

"We can make room in the coach," Stella suggested as she handed the crossbow to Beckworth.

He hesitated for only a second before agreeing. "I can ride on the bench with Barrington. Get them in quickly before the watchmen decide to make an appearance."

Stella wasn't prepared when the first injured man the sailors brought over was Fitz. He was still unconscious, but at least he wasn't dead. Not yet.

No. Don't think it. Don't even say it. Focus.

"Let's get him loaded." She was surprised by the command in her tone, but they just needed to get to the manor. Bart would fix this. She recognized the second sailor but couldn't remember his name. The third man, she wasn't as sure about. He had one of those common faces with no scars or anything that made him stand out. Even his hair, as blood streaked as it was, was a common brown.

One of the men who'd carried him over held a bloody shirt over the man's belly, and he carried a second shirt under his arm. Without another thought, she tugged the man out of the coach.

"I'll take care of that." She took the clean shirt he offered and climbed in. Blood seeped from the man's belly, and she applied pressure on the wound. "Let's go."

The door slammed shut, and moments later it lurched forward as Barrington maneuvered their way out of the alley. She hadn't seen Lando and hoped he was alright. That everyone would be alright.

She kept her hands on the shirt for several minutes before gathering enough courage to check the injury. It pulled away with a slight suction sound. There was so much blood. She couldn't tell if he'd been shot or skewered with a blade. She replaced the bloody shirt, packed the clean one over it, and reapplied pressure.

She stared at the crimson puddle forming beneath him.

The memory of her shooting Gaines, Gemini's man, came to mind, but someone had quickly moved her to a sofa, never allowing her to see the results of her actions. Cheval had bled from the crossbow bolt, but he'd been lying on soft sand with the tide washing over him. Whatever blood there'd been had washed away with the waves.

The man behind her mumbled, and she turned to make sure he wasn't moving. The last thing she needed was for him to roll off the bench. His bandage was blood-soaked as well, but they'd been able to tie shirts around him to keep it in place.

"It will be alright." Words of encouragement slipped out without any thought. "You're safe. We're taking you to get medical attention." She shook her head. He wouldn't understand that. "Help. We're getting you help."

She looked down at the man underneath her. Then stared at her sticky hands. So much red.

She continued the pressure. Even though she was on the floor and all but sitting on the man's legs, she forced herself to stay upright each time the carriage made a sharp turn, barely slowing. The only good thing was the late hour. The streets would be empty of traffic.

She glanced at the man on the bench when he moaned again. His head rolled back and forth, and she couldn't imagine how much pain he must be in.

She took a deep breath before finally screwing up the last of her courage to look at the third passenger.

Fitz.

His face was gray. He didn't move.

She found a single spot where, in the dark, she imagined the slight rise and fall of his chest. Her focus remained on that spot all the way to the manor while she maintained pressure on the man beneath her and ignored the growing puddle soaking into her dress.

All she could do, all she was willing to do, was repeat the same mantra over and over.

"You'll be alright. You'll be alright. You'll be alright."

31

———

The ride to the manor seemed to take forever, yet Stella wasn't prepared for the abrupt stop. The door was ripped open, and Beckworth was there. He gently pulled her out, and considering the late hour, she was dazed by the number of people standing around.

Someone must have ridden ahead to alert the manor. Footmen with makeshift stretchers removed the injured men and hustled them up the steps.

"We need a blanket and a towel here." Beckworth grabbed the towel first and cleaned Stella's hands until all that was left were the crimson stains that had seeped and dried into her skin. He was handed two blankets, and he wrapped them both around her.

She hadn't realized she was shaking until she tried to grip them, yet somehow managed. "There was so much blood. I tried to stop it, but it just kept coming."

"Hush. That's alright. We've got them now."

Then Libby was there.

"Is she hurt?"

Beckworth shook his head. "Shock, I think."

At some point on the drive back, a buzzing had begun in her ears, and it muted Beckworth's last words, but it sounded like he needed to get to Hensley. The crowd began moving inside, and she was surprised to see Elizabeth waiting at the bottom of the steps.

"We need to get her out of those clothes." The dowager started up the steps ahead of them. "And have coffee and brandy brought up."

Stella wondered where Eleanor was, but she'd be with Bart and the injured men. That's where she needed to be, but she couldn't stop shaking. Coffee and brandy. That should do the trick.

When they reached the bedroom, Libby quickly removed her dress and washed the last of the blood from her hands and arms. She was settled in front of a blazing fire with a fresh blanket wrapped around her.

Libby stared into her eyes for a moment, then nodded, apparently satisfied with whatever she saw. "Just sit for a minute while I gather another dress."

A glass was shoved into her hands.

"Drink." Elizabeth stood next to her and wasn't going to move until Stella followed her orders.

She didn't hesitate. It was whiskey, not brandy, and she managed to hold off coughing until after the burn reached her belly. "Didn't you say brandy?"

"The maid hasn't brought it yet, but there was whiskey on the stand. It's close enough." Elizabeth was in her Dame Ellingsworth role, and Stella was too exhausted to fight, so she took another sip.

She couldn't afford to be tired or have a breakdown. She hadn't killed anyone this time. Well, that one bodyguard had a bolt in his side, but she doubted it had been a kill shot. Of course, without antibiotics, anything was possible. She blinked away the images of blood, but it wasn't easy.

Her head popped up when Elizabeth stuck a mug of coffee in front of her. The rich aroma stirred her brain cells, and the shaking began to subside. Though the coffee was too hot, she took several long gulps. Elizabeth and Libby paced behind her while she finished the brew. Once done, she held up the mug.

"Libby, another round."

She struggled to her feet, tossing the blanket away and then tripping over it when she tried to put distance from the fire. Between it, the blanket, and the whiskey, the shivering had stopped, and beads of sweat dampened her skin. Once she found her footing, she managed to stumble to the bed and grabbed a bedpost to lean on.

Elizabeth shoved another glass in front of her. "This one is brandy, though I wouldn't bother sipping it."

She didn't argue and slugged it down. The fire in her belly kicked her into motion. "I need one of my East End day dresses."

The words were barely out of her mouth before Libby took the glass from her and handed it to Elizabeth. Then she nudged Stella to step into the dress she'd already had prepared.

"I'd make you change your undergarments, but luckily the blood didn't seep through." Once the dress was on, Libby handed her a refreshed mug of coffee. "Let me do something with your hair."

When Stella fought against being pushed to the dressing table, Libby added, "I know you want to check on the men, but it would be easier if your hair wasn't in your eyes."

She relented, but after a few brush strokes, she shoved Libby's hands out of the way. "Where did they take them?"

"They're downstairs near the kitchen." Libby managed to

sneak in one hair pin. "Bart wanted to be close to hot water and a sink."

Stella was headed for the door when she snapped her fingers and turned. "Can you grab my first aid kit?" While she waited, she refilled her mug.

"Are you sure you're ready?" Elizabeth gave her a stern perusal but appeared satisfied with what she saw.

"I'm well enough." She reached for the first aid kit, but Libby brushed her hand away.

"I'll follow you down. I doubt you're going to let go of that mug."

"I have two hands." She would start babbling soon if she didn't get her head on straight. She'd need one hand for the railing. With her luck, she'd stumble down the stairs and be one more patient for an overburdened Bart.

She gave the woman a small smile and held out her hand. "See. Hardly shaking at all." She ignored the women's shared glance.

She gulped the coffee as she marched down the hall, taking another sip every few feet. Libby and Elizabeth trailed behind her as she made her way through the manor and down the stairs to the kitchen.

The scent of blood hit her halfway down, and though she hesitated for a moment, she refused to let it bother her. She weaved her way through the footmen and housemaids who scurried around. Two footmen carried buckets of water. One disappeared into a room where they handled minor household repairs, while the other entered the staff's dining room. A housemaid scurried out with blood-soaked towels while another went in with fresh ones.

Eleanor bustled from one room to another, calling out orders in a stern and commanding tone.

"We'll be in the way more than we'll be of help." Elizabeth kept her back to the wall with Libby beside her.

Stella nodded and, emptying the last drop of coffee, exchanged the mug for the first aid kit. "I want to check on everyone's condition and see if Bart needs the medication I brought with me."

Instead of moving toward a room, her feet froze in place. If she didn't go in, if she continued to hope, they'd all still be alive. Even if they weren't, they would be in her head. At least for a little while longer.

Then Eleanor was there. "Stella. Stella."

The second mention of her name pulled her out of whatever fugue she'd fallen into, and she wished Beckworth were next to her. Where was he, anyway? Hensley. He was going to Hensley's.

She followed Eleanor's wave before the woman ducked into the room where shoes and other items were repaired. She immediately recognized the man on the table. He'd been the one on the bench who'd been moaning.

His shirt had been ripped open, and the blood had been washed away, leaving only his bare, pale chest. Off to the side was a row of surgical equipment. They looked more like barbaric torture instruments compared to their twenty-first-century counterparts.

When she noticed Lincoln tying a suture, she came fully awake.

Lincoln was performing surgical tasks as he completed another stitch. Bart must have trained him for simpler injuries. Not that what she was witnessing appeared simple. His movements were swift and methodical, but sweat beaded on his forehead. She held back a hysterical giggle when one of the housemaids pressed a towel to his forehead. She didn't know anything about his technique, but he was going to make an excellent surgeon if his calm demeanor was any indication.

He glanced up at that moment, his expression more serious than she'd ever seen it. "Bart said you might have something to deal with an infection. He's lost a lot of blood. They all have, but this man's injury wasn't too bad. I got the ball out and most of the debris. If we can keep the infection away, he should mend quickly once his blood is restored."

Stella laid the kit on a nearby table and pulled out several items before unfolding a piece of paper that she laid next to the kit. She ran her finger down the list of items and matched them to the labeled containers.

"I have antibiotics to help with the infection." She pulled aside a small tin filled with pills.

Adam, AJ's brother and a lawyer with questionable connections to a motorcycle gang to whom he once owed a rather large debt, had supplied her with a large quantity of antibiotics and a few other pharmaceuticals. Each drug had been written down with its intended use and the proper dosage amounts.

Maire, Finn's sister, had a way with herbal medicines that she'd learned as a young woman from the Irish Travellers who visited her town every year. She'd added her knowledge of herbs to the list in addition to the herbs kept in the kit.

Stella looked at the injured man, guessed his body weight, and pulled out several pills and two types of herbs. She waved to a housemaid who waited nearby while Lincoln kept a kitchen maid busy helping with the bandages, his stitch work apparently completed.

When the housemaid came to her side, Stella provided instructions. "It's best to crush the pills and add them to water. Make sure he drinks it all as soon as he's awake. He'll need broth to help restore his blood. Add these herbs to it. They should also help guard against an infection. Bart has something for the pain, but we can reassess that later. Do you understand?"

The housemaid nodded, and Stella felt comfortable that her

instructions would be carried out. "I'll come back later and check in."

She packed up the first aid kit, but before she left to go to the next room, she squeezed Lincoln's arm. "Are you okay?"

He stopped the bandaging long enough to look at her. His face was haggard, but his eyes were clear and focused. He'd be alright. Yet, something tugged at him, and she knew straight away that they'd lost someone.

She closed her eyes as her thoughts flashed to a grinning Fitz as he'd teased her before going into the warehouse. *Hold yourself together.* She shook the image out of her head and turned away.

There was one room where the staff continued to bring clean water in and bloody water out. The towels weren't as red-stained as they'd been earlier.

"You don't need to go in there." Elizabeth stood in the same place, watching but not interfering with Eleanor's commands.

"Yes, I do."

No one stopped her as she sucked in a breath and followed a housemaid into the room. Her gaze immediately fell on the face of the dead man, and a whoosh of breath blew out.

It wasn't Fitz. That didn't mean he was okay, but for now, it wasn't Fitz.

But this was someone she recognized. He was the man she'd been trying to keep alive, and all she could remember was her hands covered in his blood. She laid down the first aid kit and blinked away tears as she stood over him. His body was covered with a sheet, his face a deathly pallor, and his lips tinged blue. There wasn't a drop of blood on him. They'd washed him as well.

Warm hands caressed her arms before she was pulled against a firm body, and strong arms encircled her.

"This wasn't your fault." Beckworth's words soothed her, and she clutched his arms briefly before running a hand over the dead man's forehead and stubbly cheek.

He'd been an older man, though age was difficult to tell with what had once been a tanned face wrinkled by the sea and harsh sun.

"I feel bad that I don't remember his name. I remember how helpful he'd been, how nice he'd been to me."

"Tucker. He was a good man. One of Finn's, who'd stayed on with Jamie."

She turned and laid a cheek on Beckworth's chest, but after a sniff, she pulled her head back. His shirt was bloody, and it wasn't from dried blood. "You're injured."

"It's nothing."

She pushed him back. "Let me see."

He shoved her hands away. "Jamie's already taken a look. It's only a flesh wound. Bart will take a look once he's done working on Fitz."

Her brain shifted gears. "He's still alive?" Her gut wrenched when Beckworth's gaze shifted away.

"For now."

She gave a last look at Tucker, then grabbed the first aid kit and Beckworth's hand, dragging him to where Lincoln was finishing up.

"I have a new patient for you." She kept tugging Beckworth, who had slowed his walk. "He says it's just a flesh wound, but it's still bleeding."

A footman came in with another bucket of water, and she stopped him from leaving.

"I want you to ignore any order coming out of this man's mouth." She pointed to Beckworth. "You only listen to this man." She pointed to Lincoln. "This man—" she pointed back to Beckworth, "—requires medical treatment, and he's not to leave this room without it."

The footman shuffled his feet, looking from Beckworth, who was currently the lord of the manor, and Lincoln, who, until this evening, was a prospective student. She understood the footman's dilemma and turned to Beckworth.

"You're not going to be a problem, are you?" she asked.

Lincoln waved at a chair, and Beckworth glanced at the unconscious man still on the table. When he turned to Stella, a protest coming, he changed his mind.

He looked at the footman. "Tell Eleanor we have an injured man ready for a room." He turned to Lincoln. "Let's get this done. I have to get back to Hensley." He tried to pull his shirt over his head but grimaced in pain.

Stella slapped his hands away and looked at the footman, who hadn't been sure whether to follow her orders, but now looked at her for approval of Beckworth's request. She held back a grin and nodded for him to go.

When she turned back to Beckworth, he grinned. "You've ruined the staff."

She tsked. "All will be back to normal once I'm gone. Can you lift your arm at all?" When he proved he could, she rolled his shirt up and pulled it over his head. She took a quick glance at the wound and agreed it was most likely a flesh wound. Then she remembered him losing his footing on their way out of the warehouse. He must have caught a stray bullet. She shivered but gave him a quick kiss and grabbed her first aid kit.

"I'll be with Bart and Fitz." She rushed from the room, but instead of going directly to the staff's dining room, she leaned against the wall and took several deep breaths.

"Are you alright?" Libby rubbed her arm.

"No. But I will be." She looked toward the door to the dining room to see more towels being taken in. If Fitz wasn't going to make it, wouldn't it be better if he had friends by his side?

"Come on." Libby took her hand, seeming to read her

thoughts. "It's a rather bloody scene, but Bart's doing everything he can."

Libby led her at a slow pace, and with each step they took, Stella's resolve returned. This was Fitz, and he wouldn't appreciate all the handwringing. She released Libby's hand, stood straighter, and marched in to see what she could do to help.

She stumbled a bit at the state of the room. How anyone would be able to eat here again was beyond her. There was blood everywhere. Or there had been. The maids were still scrubbing the floors, trying to stay out of the way. The buckets of water had to be refreshed often, but the stream of footmen had slowed.

The coppery smell of blood and stringent antiseptic was overpowering. An enormous amount of herbs would need to be burned if they ever had hope of clearing out the scent of blood and who knew what else.

She lifted her gaze to the table where Fitz lay. Bart leaned over him, his hands stained red, and carefully stitched the skin closed. He wouldn't be so meticulous if Fitz were dead, right?

Without another thought, she stepped up to the table and stood next to one of the kitchen staff. She thought the woman's name was Helen, and if memory served, Eleanor had mentioned she was also a midwife. It made sense that she would be the best person to assist Bart while Lincoln had been working his own magic.

Not wanting to get in the way, she moved around Helen to be close to Fitz's head. He was still unconscious and was most likely given some type of sedative. His face didn't appear as gray as it had, but that might be the lighting. Even simple lanterns provided more light than the darkness of the coach. She brushed the hair off his forehead.

"If you insist on being here, then move back to the other side of Helen," Bart scowled. "I don't believe in such nonsense, but it couldn't hurt to hold his hand. Give him some encouragement to live. I can't be expected to be his only salvation."

Stella did as he asked, not concerned with his abrupt tone. He might say he didn't believe in the healing comfort of touch, but she remembered him saying something distinctly different when Beckworth had been badly injured.

"Was he shot?" she asked, squeezing Fitz's hand while she stroked his arm.

"Twice." Bart pointed to his legs, which were covered with a sheet. "One in the thigh. Missed his femoral vein by an inch, but it's stitched up now. This one in his belly is more worrisome. I got the ball, and he's not bleeding anymore, but I'm worried about infection." He was still stitching as he spoke, but he lifted his eyes to her. "I was hoping we might have something more than what I have on hand to combat that possibility."

"We do." She continued stroking Fitz's arm and gave his hand a tight squeeze. "Are you listening, my friend. There will be no dying on my watch."

A moment later, a hand rested on her shoulder, and at first, she thought it was Beckworth.

"Thank you, lass, for watching over him." Jamie stayed behind her as they watched Bart finish his work.

"I'm sorry about Tucker." Tears overwhelmed her, but she refused to release Fitz's hands to stop them from overflowing. "There was just too much blood."

Jamie rubbed her shoulders. "There wasn't anything to be done. He died in service to the Crown, and it might not mean a lot to some, but it meant everything to him."

Stella understood. Tucker was an Englishman, serving on the *Daphne* that had an equal number of Irishmen on board. She doubted the Irish would be the first to step up to die in service to the Crown, but an Englishman would. Fitz was an Irishman, as was Jamie. They and everyone onboard the *Daphne* did the Crown's bidding while working for Hensley, but it typically wasn't the Crown they felt beholden to. Not unless it was as good for Ireland as it was England, which she thought rarely coincided.

Jamie, Fitz, and the crew of the *Daphne* fought for what was right. Sometimes, that meant that the Crown. And the Irishmen fought for the same cause.

When Bart stepped away from the table, everyone looked to him, but all he did was shrug. "I've stitched him back together. Now it's up to the medicine and his will to survive."

"Can he be moved?" Stella asked.

"Best to do it now before he wakes. I don't want to have to redo his stitches."

Within seconds, several men stormed the room. Sailors, not footmen.

"I have a room ready on the second floor." Eleanor scurried in and started moving maids, buckets, and chairs out of the way. "Let's use the board to carry him up."

The men picked up the makeshift stretcher and, with the barest of jostling, positioned Fitz on the board, then moved him out of the room. When Stella made to follow, Bart stopped her.

"Let him get settled. We'll start the medication when he wakes."

She planted her hands on her hips, readying for an argument. "Then let's get you cleaned up and find you some food and whiskey."

"Whiskey first."

Libby was there in a heartbeat, handing him a glass that he swallowed in one gulp.

"Where's Lincoln?" Bart asked.

"He's cleaning up." Libby refilled the glass, and Bart swallowed that one too.

"Alright. Let's get this blood off me."

Stella followed Libby as Bart was led to the kitchen. She spotted Beckworth whispering to Jamie by an outer door. He gave her a worried glance, but it disappeared when she gave him a weak smile and a wave. She refocused her attention on Bart. The health of the healers was just as important as that of the injured. Once Bart and Lincoln were settled, then she'd find out what the hell had happened.

32

Stella trudged up the stairs from the kitchen, tempted to search for the rooms where they put Fitz and the other sailor. She'd have to ask Jamie his name. But her energy waned, and her first priority was to find where the men had gone. They were probably in the study, but Beckworth might have returned to Hensley's with Jamie. When she reached the first floor, she noticed the blood on her day dress. She sighed and climbed the stairs to the second floor instead.

Libby was in the bedroom already laying out another dress.

"Always a step ahead of me." She plopped down on the bed, then immediately stood and moved to a chair. If she stayed on the bed, she was sure to tip over and fall asleep.

"I knew you'd be too stubborn to get some rest. You should let the men figure it all out. It will all look better after a few good hours of sleep."

"I could fall asleep just sitting here. But if I go to bed now without having some answers for what happened, I'll be staring at the ceiling in an hour."

"Here, drink this." Libby pushed a mug of coffee into her hands. "That should keep you going for another hour. If you're not back up here ready for your robe by then, I'll come for you myself."

Stella sucked down the coffee, which was the perfect temperature. "This did the trick."

"What did you plan to do with these?" Libby held out the jewelry Stella had stuffed in her pockets and a blood-stained linen pouch. "Beckworth found the pouch in the coach."

"Oh, my god. I can't believe I forgot all about them. It's a miracle I didn't drop the pouch getting in the carriage."

"You had more important things on your mind."

Stella set down her mug and rubbed her hands together. The blood stains were long gone, but at times, she still saw the blood drip from her fingers. She took a deep breath. "Too many things." Her head popped up. "Where's Elizabeth?"

"She should be with the men downstairs. That one is as stubborn as you."

Stella chuckled, picked up her mug, and drained the contents. "Let's lay everything out and make sure nothing was damaged." She was energized again in anticipation of seeing Elizabeth with her necklace.

Libby spread the pieces out on the bed, and they went over each one.

"Do you see anything wrong?" Stella asked.

"Not that I can see. They're beautiful pieces. I can understand why someone would pay a lot of money for them."

"I'm not sure they were worth anyone's life." Stella wiped away a tear and picked up the necklace.

"You know what happened tonight had nothing to do with jewelry and everything to do with French arms."

Libby was right, but it was difficult to accept in light of the fallen and injured. Who were those men who busted up the exchange? Leclair had been as surprised as she had been. She was sure of it.

"Time to get these back to their rightful owners." She carefully placed the necklace and the rest of the items in the pouch and pulled it shut.

She left Libby and strode down the stairs, another burst of energy keeping her on her feet. Images from the evening flashed, but nothing they'd done could have prepared them for what had happened. She was so focused on the replay of events, she almost missed the voices coming from the library. She backed up a few steps, and when she entered the room, she found everyone had gathered around the fireplace.

"There she is." Hensley looked haggard at this late hour.

She wasn't sure what time it was, but it had to be closer to dawn than midnight. "I didn't know you were here."

"I can't sleep when a mission is underway. Even Mary found it difficult."

Beckworth brought a chair to the informal circle the group had created. Jamie and Lando were seated by the fire on either side of Hensley. Bart and Lincoln were still up, though they looked twice as tired as the rest of them, with good cause. Eleanor and Elizabeth rounded out the group.

Stella dropped into the chair and waved off a glass of whiskey. She noted Elizabeth's glance at the linen pouch before her focus returned to Hensley.

"Do we know who those men were?" Stella didn't have to explain who she meant. They all knew.

Lando, who appeared uninjured though there were dark circles under his eyes and dried blood stained his shirt, answered the question. "We managed to take two of them alive. *The Horseman* has a new captain with plans to take Cheval's place in McDuff's network. He thought stealing the French arms would be easier than trading for them."

"Someone has a mole in their operation," Beckworth added.

Stella turned her attention to Hensley. "Do you know who or how?"

"Not yet." Hensley suddenly looked more tired than when she'd first walked in. It had to be difficult doing all the planning and then waiting to see the outcome. "I lost one of my men, and the others are taking turns questioning the two prisoners. We'd originally assumed it was an unexpected move by Captain Leclair."

Stella shook her head. "He accused me of a double cross. And I don't think he's a good enough actor to have faked his shock."

"I'd agree," Jamie said. "He lost a few of his own."

"Did we save the rifles?" Stella asked.

Hensley nodded. "They're back where they belong."

Stella nodded as she stared down at the pouch gripped in her hands. "He wasn't going to let me take these. I had to put a bolt into both of his bodyguards, though I think they'll survive." Her hands began to shake, and she gripped the bag tighter. "I might have mentioned something about another meeting to conclude our deal." She looked up to meet Elizabeth's gaze and gave her a weak smile before she opened the pouch and placed the four pieces of stolen jewelry on the low table in front of her.

Elizabeth's loud gasp came seconds before she rushed over to pick up her necklace. Tears streamed down her face as she held it to her chest.

"A couple of the pieces fell off the crates when the rogue men showed up, and with all the gunfire, I just grabbed them and stuffed them in my pocket. I don't think they were damaged, but I don't know for sure."

Elizabeth took a closer look, slowly running a finger over every inch of the necklace. Her voice was thick with emotion. "It looks perfect. It just needs a little cleaning." She squeezed Stella's arm. "Thank you for this."

Eleanor led Elizabeth back to her seat and stroked the dowager's back. "I'm sure all the ladies will appreciate what you did this evening."

"It came at a great cost." Stella stared down at her hands, still seeing blood stains.

"No!" Hensley's emphatic response was emphasized by his fist slamming into the table next to him, almost dumping his glass of whiskey to the floor. "There will be none of that. This mission was about smugglers and their attempt to use French firearms to stir up rebels against England. The retrieval of the jewelry is a welcome success in a rather dismal night. We were lucky to have only lost two men, though we have many injured. With good fortune, we'll see them healed and back on their feet soon."

"Here, here," Jamie said and lifted his glass in salute. "Slainte." The men lifted their glasses and took a drink. "And as bad as it is, we might have discovered friction in McDuff's network."

Stella lifted her head. "How so?"

"The captain of *The Horseman* basically declared war against Leclair." Lando, unable to sit still for long, stood to lean against a bookcase. "Leclair already appeared tight with McDuff. He was seen moving cargo on the network's behalf. Based on our surveillance, we didn't think he was a captain at the time, but we were either wrong, or he gained a ship in the last three months."

"That in itself wouldn't mean that McDuff had anything to do with his rise to captain," Beckworth added. "But, based on the information André has been gathering, it's pretty clear he's here on behalf of McDuff."

"And the captain of *The Horseman* could argue he didn't know Leclair had set up the exchange. That it was all a terrible mistake, and McDuff might look favorably on his initiative."

Jamie finished his drink and rubbed his eyes, the first sign of his weariness.

"Makes us much sense as anything else," Hensley agreed. "We still have loose ends, but my men might be able to fill those gaps tomorrow. The question before us now is how to get back into the good graces of Leclair."

Stella had been studying the remaining jewelry in her lap, going over each one to confirm they were in good condition, or, as Elizabeth stated, simply required a good cleaning. She wished she could see Inspector Littlefield's face when he was told the jewelry had been recovered and was stolen to finance a smuggling ring. She hoped he choked on the news. That was when Hensley's words caught up to her.

"Oh my god," Stella sat up so quickly, she had to grab the jewelry from slipping to the floor. "I forgot about the deal I made with Leclair."

Hensley's hawk-like stare focused on her, and she squirmed in her seat. "Yes, you mentioned earlier something about another meeting."

"No." Beckworth gripped her hand. "I think Lady Swan needs to step out of this one. We've already told Leclair that she was leaving London in the morning. The surprise raid would only confirm her need to leave."

"I agree." Stella squeezed his hand before releasing it, needing to stand on her own for the next part. "I assure you, I've had enough of Lady Swan for now. There was so much confusion that once I'd snatched the last piece of jewelry from Leclair, I thought he might try to abduct me while everyone was fighting." She paused to consider her next words. In for a pound and all. "If I showed interest in working out a partnership, he might leave me alone. I told him I had men who would be remaining in London for a short time." She played with the strings of the pouch. "I told him I'd send a note to the messenger at the pub to discuss a new arrangement for concluding our deal since I was taking the jewelry."

"You mean André?" Beckworth asked.

She nodded. "I might have mentioned something about future trades."

Hensley and Jamie exchanged glances before Lando said, "Smart. This leaves us a nice opening."

"How will they know it's your man if you didn't give him a name?" Hensley sipped his whiskey, his eyes pinning her over the rim of the glass. "I assume you didn't give him one."

She shook her head and reached into her pocket for the other item she'd grabbed before leaving the bedroom. She laid the origami swan on the coffee table in front of her. "I gave one of these to Leclair and told him these were my calling cards. I said my man would have one when he met with the messenger."

Beckworth grinned, but Jamie laughed out loud. "We're going to need a lot more of those before you leave for home."

***

Ten minutes later, Beckworth guided Stella up the stairs.

She pulled her arm away. "I can manage."

He understood her mood. And as much as he wanted to ignore her, lift her into his arms, and carry her to bed, he wouldn't diminish her need to regain some control. But there was one thing he could say that would give her permission to relax her guard.

"I didn't do enough to protect you this evening." It was mostly true. He'd left Michelson to watch over her so he could find a safe path out of the chaos. He had trusted her to survive when all he wanted to do was drag her behind the crates and cover her until everyone fled the scene. He'd done the right thing. At least he thought that was what Finn would do.

She leaned against him, finally giving him permission to take care of her. "You did everything you were supposed to do. You dealt with saving the firearms and getting our team out while I recovered the jewelry."

He kissed the top of her head and squeezed her waist. "You're right as usual."

Libby met them at their bedroom door, but Beckworth refused to let Stella go.

"It's time for you to go to bed. I told Mrs. Evans that the staff can sleep in an extra three hours."

Libby gave them a weak smile. "I wouldn't mind getting off my feet." She was partway out the door when she turned back. "What happened to the jewelry?"

"Elizabeth wants to return the pieces herself." Stella pushed Beckworth away and dropped into a chair. She bent over to pull off her shoes, and he grabbed her elbow to straighten her when she leaned too far to the left.

"Barrington will drive Elizabeth and Mary to visit the three women." He sat next to Stella and removed his boots. "Two of Jamie's sailors will go along for protection. Elizabeth wants to make sure Stella gets credit for retrieving the jewelry and not the inspector, which I imagine would be the story if we turned the jewelry over to him."

"Good riddance to him, I'd say." Libby made a face that made Stella smile.

"What about the duke?" Stella asked. "I don't remember anyone mentioning him."

"Hensley will send a message in the morning. He'll be informed that Lady Caldway discovered a connection between the items and, being acquainted with Hensley, advised him of who she believed had the jewelry. Hensley sent men to recover the items. Case closed."

"I like that. A happily ever after." Stella leaned against Beckworth's arm with her eyes closed and an odd smile.

"Alright. It's off to bed with you." Beckworth hauled her up and turned her toward the bed.

Libby laughed as she closed the door behind her.

Stella held onto the bedpost while he unbuttoned her dress and pulled it over her head. Her arms got stuck, and she tugged with too much effort. Once she was free of the dress, she tumbled onto the floor. Her laughter filled the room, and Beckworth could only grin.

"How much have you had to drink tonight?"

"Not much at all." She lay flat on her back and giggled helplessly. He'd seen her like this on several occasions, either because she'd drunk too much wine with AJ, or she hadn't gotten enough sleep. This time, it was more likely a combination of lack of sleep, whiskey, and the trauma of the evening's mission.

She was still giggling when she held her arms up so he could pull her upright. It wasn't graceful, but they managed, and before she could get away from him, he pushed her onto the bed. He removed the rest of her clothes, then rolled and tugged until she was under the covers.

Before he could back away, she grabbed his hand and kissed it.

"What was that for?"

"You're so good to me."

He grinned. "Yes, I am. And in the morning, I'll remind you of your loving words."

She giggled again and rolled over toward his spot.

He removed his clothes and crawled in behind her, spooning

her close. They'd just settled down when she snapped her fingers and struggled to get up.

"I almost forgot."

She fought with the bed covers, and he pulled her back down. "It's nothing that can't wait until morning."

"No. It can't. I forgot to check on Fitz and…" She tried to sit a second time, but he hugged her tighter. "I never asked the other sailor's name."

"It's Timothy, and Bart said they'll sleep until morning. You can check on them when you deliver the antibiotics."

She relaxed, and he closed his eyes, thinking she'd fallen asleep.

"I didn't handle myself very well tonight." Her voice was sad. Her laughter was gone.

"I thought you did quite well handling Leclair. Your foresight to promise a future opportunity gives Hensley a great deal of leeway on how to proceed."

"Not that. Although I did good with that, didn't I?"

He sensed a smile on her face, but it disappeared as quickly as it came.

"After that. With the injured men. I didn't do so good then."

"You jumped into the coach without a second of hesitation. You did the best anyone could have done in that situation."

"It wasn't enough."

"Most of the time it never is." When he felt her shudder, he pulled the covers higher. "This time period has many good things, but there are many not-so-good things. After experiencing your time period…" He squeezed her and modified his statement. "Our time period. I can clearly see how much the bad outweighs the good."

She was silent for a moment. "Maybe. There are many good people here, doing their best to survive. When I consider our new timeline, many things have changed, many for the better, but not always in the way that counts."

Another moment passed before she whispered, "It was the blood."

He closed his eyes. He never wanted this for her. None of this would have happened if Hensley hadn't coerced him into a mission during their first trip back. And now, they'd come to London to visit friends, attend fancy parties, and tour the city. Yet, once again, they'd been caught in the web of Hensley's machinations.

"It's never pretty when someone dies—whether they're good or bad—it's always ugly. And it should be. It's nothing to become accustomed to. But we all take the risk when we join a mission. And even the best of plans go awry."

She turned over and wrapped an arm around him. He pulled her close until their skin touched, their legs entwined, and her breasts pressed against his chest. She nestled her cheek against him, and contentment rolled over him.

Lying with her was the only time he felt true peace. And regardless of what time period they were in, he had to do a better job of protecting her.

"He'll be alright," he murmured, aware of her worry over Fitz.

"You're all I need to make things better."

33

───────

Stella stared out at the garden, enjoying the soft, warm breeze on her cheeks, unusual for this early in the day. They would be leaving for Waverly in a few hours, and she would miss London, even after all the madness.

The terrible night at the warehouse was two weeks ago, and Fitz survived the worst of it. She'd spent most of the early days sitting by him, only leaving when his mates came to see him, which was often. There had been a slight complication with a secondary infection, but Bart caught it quickly, and the dosage of antibiotics was increased. It set Fitz's recovery back a few days, but if his spirit were any indication, he'd be walking without a cane soon.

"Are you still out here?" Beckworth strolled out to the balcony with Libby behind him.

"I told you she'd be here. If she isn't with Fitz or Timothy, she likes to sit out here."

"Sorry, I should have known better than to question you, but I've been busy trying to wrap things up."

"Has the *Daphne* left?" Stella asked before taking a sip of her coffee. At dinner the night before, Jamie said he wanted to leave

366

at first tide. She glanced up at the sun. It was still early, but she guessed the tide had come and gone.

"Yes. Jamie and Lando will meet us at Waverly once they reach Bristol."

Bart insisted Fitz needed more bed rest, preferably on land rather than sea. By the time the *Daphne* reached Bristol and the men arrived at the manor, and with too many housemaids doting over him, Fitz should be fully recovered.

"That horrible inspector stopped by again." Libby poured Stella more coffee, and Beckworth took a seat next to her.

"I'll never speak to that rotten little man." Stella had been blindsided by Inspector Littlefield the day before when she was leaving to meet Mary, Elizabeth, and Flora for a farewell lunch. Fortunately, Beckworth had been a few steps behind her and intercepted him, sending him on his way.

"I can't believe he thinks you were the master planner behind the thefts and only returned the jewelry because you felt guilty." Libby glanced through the breakfast items Stella had picked her way through and found a tart that had escaped intact. It took a moment before she smirked. "Not that you couldn't have organized it, and Littlefield would never have been the wiser."

Stella laughed. Libby could always make her smile.

"You won't be seeing him again." Beckworth took her hand, kissed it, then rubbed a thumb over it as he spoke. "His office will be receiving a stern notice from the duke that the incident was classified as national security and to consider the case closed."

"From what Mary's lady's maid told me," Libby added, "Dame Ellingsworth told all the women at the party last night that Lady Stella was a hero for finding the thief."

Beckworth squeezed Stella's hand until she winced. Message received to let him speak first. "Elizabeth is right. The episode with the firearm exchange aside, nothing erases the fact that with your lead, along with Libby, Eleanor, Mary, Elizabeth, and Flora, and let's not forget some very street-smart urchins, the thief was tracked down without any help from the inspector or the constables."

"The only thing the aristocrats are unhappy about is that you're leaving so soon." Libby licked her fingers after finishing off the tart. "They think you're leaving because you were being harassed by the inspector. Doesn't look very good for him. Rumors about the duke's message to his office will be all over the city in a couple of days."

Stella grinned, surprised by the support, and she picked up the other half of a tart she hadn't finished. "When you put it that way, I'm sorry I'll miss the limelight."

"Elizabeth and Mary have been telling others that you're caring for a sick friend who will be traveling back to Waverly for recovery." Libby giggled. "That just makes you more loved."

"Good god, Libby. Enough. She'll be insufferable now."

Stella stifled her giggles. "I'm glad Timothy was able to leave with Jamie."

"If you ask me, Fitz is enjoying the pampering too much," Beckworth said.

Stella squeezed his knee. "You're just jealous."

"You've discovered my weakness."

When silence descended after the laughter, Stella twisted her fingers together as she stared at them in her lap. She'd become melancholy, and she didn't want to leave London that way, but she couldn't help it.

"I wish we had more time to spend with Chester and Katherine." Stella would miss them, and there was no telling when she'd return to London.

Barrington had brought the couple over the day after the fiasco at the warehouse for a leisurely afternoon in the garden, where they played card games and visited with Fitz. They'd stayed for dinner and drinks with Jamie and Lando. Then a few days ago, she and Beckworth had stopped in the East End for lunch during one of Beckworth's multifaceted tours of the city. At least she'd had the chance to say goodbye.

The three of them remained on the balcony, reminiscing about their time in the city until Beckworth stood.

"I need to check on Bart and Lincoln while you finish packing the trunks."

Stella watched him go and sighed. "Might as well get this done." She stood and leaned over the railing to get a long, last look at the garden, then closed her eyes as she took in a deep breath. A moment later, she marched inside, rejuvenated and ready to get back to work.

She was putting her jewelry and hairpins into a box when Libby touched her elbow, making her turn around.

"Don't think so badly of London." Libby's whimsical expression made Stella smile. With everything the young woman had gone through in her life, the fact she could still see humor and wonder in the world said a lot about her spirit. Libby turned her gaze to Stella's. This was the first time she'd noticed the gold ring around Libby's dark-brown eyes. It gave her that look of innocence that had been stolen from her long ago.

"It can be difficult," Libby continued, "when you see it from both sides—the beautiful and the ugly. For most, they live in one or the other. One side trying not to see the other, while the other wishes to one day be on the other side. Though in their hearts, they know that will never be."

Stella grabbed Libby and gave her a tight hug. Libby had given up fighting Stella's need for the occasional hug, and she held on tightly. "You're my rock."

Libby snorted and pulled back. "That never made any sense to me. I'd rather be mysterious and adventurous."

"Well, you're certainly both of those. Let's finish the packing and tell me the best parts of London. I'll start with the flower market in Whitechapel."

They spent the next half hour storing everything away until Libby handed Stella her crossbow. She ran a loving hand over it, glad to have it back. She'd lost track of it when she'd jumped into the carriage to help the injured men. Lando had taken it and given it a good cleaning, freshening the wood with oil. It was a darker color now, and it looked better. It also made it more hers. She placed it on top of the other items and closed the lid.

She gave Libby a wicked grin. "Now that that's done, shall we go see how things are going with Fitz?"

They locked arms as they left the bedroom, Stella giving it one last glance.

"No one would think to fuss with Eleanor, except for Bart," Libby said.

"I have a feeling he's giving it a go anyway."

They giggled as they strode down the hall, already hearing the loud voices coming from Fitz's room.

———

Five minutes after entering Fitz's room, Stella was ready to leave. She couldn't make heads or tails of what Fitz and Bart were yelling about, but when Eleanor gave her the nod to go, she didn't hesitate. If this were any indication of how the journey to Waverly would go, there wouldn't be enough wine in all of England to get her through it.

Fortunately, she and Eleanor had planned ahead. Taking a cue from how AJ and Maire contended traveling with a cantankerous and injured Finn, Bart had been happy to add a strong sedative to Fitz's pain medication. He should be fast asleep before they reached the outskirts of London.

She'd made a last stop in their bedroom. That last-minute review everyone preformed before checking out of a hotel room to ensure nothing was left behind. After stopping to say goodbye to the staff, she finally made it down the stairs to enter the waiting carriage, forgetting there would be two coaches traveling to Waverly. One had been modified to widen one of the benches to accommodate Fitz. Stella and Libby would start the journey with him. Lincoln would drive the second carriage with Bart and Eleanor, while Beckworth rode his horse.

On the second day of their journey, after an overnight stay at an inn, Bart rode with Fitz, while Stella and Libby joined Eleanor in the other carriage. Eleanor and Bart got along most of the time, but they both needed their space. Bart was happy because he could read his journals. The motion would have had Stella puking the entire way home.

Through it all, Fitz slept.

It was a happy homecoming when the carriages stopped in front of Waverly Manor, and Mrs. Walker had dinner waiting after receiving Beckworth's message of their return.

Fitz was settled into a room but, with help from Beckworth, insisted on coming down for dinner. Though he fidgeted in his seat through the entire meal, eating only a portion of his usual large servings, his humor was on full display. When he insisted on staying for drinks afterward, Bart gave him a stern no, and Beckworth took him upstairs. He remained with Fitz for an hour, sneaking him whiskey and his pipe.

Their plan was to spend two weeks at Waverly before returning to Baywood, and they spent every minute enjoying the manor as it was meant to be spent. Most days, they worked in the garden, enjoyed leisurely lunches on the back patio, and took long horseback rides. Stella refused to admit how much she enjoyed time with Smudge, but Beckworth knew, and that was all that mattered.

Fitz spent time outside with them. He sat as they toiled, occasionally puffing on his pipe or sharing various sailing adventures, and sometimes breaking out in song with old sea shanties.

They'd been home ten days, and Beckworth worried they might have to extend their time at Waverly if Jamie didn't arrive before their scheduled return to Baywood. Stella didn't care. They hadn't overstayed their time to the point where it would worry AJ or Finn.

Two days later, Jamie and Lando arrived just before lunch. Between their dust-covered clothing and fatigued expressions, they looked as if they'd ridden for days rather than the few hours it took to ride from Bristol.

Fitz, who'd been in the barn with the colt, must have heard the riders, and he limped out on the cane Lincoln had made for him. The two bullets that Bart had dug out were on his left side, and the injuries continued to be sensitive. However, his labored gait would have been more impressive if Stella hadn't caught him two days earlier walking across the solarium to refresh his glass of whiskey without the cane.

She held her grin as she watched the fleeting sympathy cross Jamie and Lando's faces. Fitz gave the men a huge smile, obviously having missed his friends. But he'd glanced at her with that wide grin, pleased that she kept his secret.

"Is everything alright?" Beckworth waved the stable boys over to take their horses.

"A story to share, to be sure." Jamie gave Fitz an enthusiastic handshake. "It's good to see you up and around. We thought we'd lost you for sure." He glanced at Beckworth and gave him a wink. "I'd heard from Finn that riding in a fancy coach isn't that special when you're injured."

Fitz stuck out his chest and scratched his chin where he'd let his whiskers grow and didn't seem eager to shave them. "I managed to sleep the whole way. Barely remember the inn or eating dinner."

Jamie and Lando glanced at each other, not ready to believe it. When they looked at Stella, she managed to maintain a blank expression, unwilling to give away her and Eleanor's secret.

"Why don't we get you settled, then we'll feed you." Stella waved them toward the stairs. "Hensley and Mary are due to arrive this afternoon. They'll stay until we leave for Baywood." She took Jamie and Lando's arms and walked them up the steps. "Fitz, let Beckworth know if you need to be carried."

Jamie and Lando snickered.

Fitz grumbled. "It was a nice and relaxing stay up until a few minutes ago."

"You might want to work on that limp as well, mate." Beckworth nodded to the footmen who were picking up the saddlebags taken from the horses. "I think I've seen you use a similar one during that mission down in Portsmouth."

"I remember that one," Jamie. "You looked like an old English gentleman in that suit and tie."

Stella glanced over her shoulder in time to see Fitz pull at the collar of his shirt. "That cravat almost strangled me."

They all laughed as they ventured into the manor—even Fitz.

34

Beckworth watched the three women on the patio play a card game called Go Fish that Stella had taught them. It was a child's game, but the simplicity worked in their favor when all they wanted to do was gossip. And regardless of how many times she did it, Mary always got a thrill when she yelled "Go fish!"

"They're waiting for you in the west study." Barrington stepped next to him and stared out the solarium window. "She seems fine."

He nodded. He wasn't sure when it happened; it was never just one thing, but more a collection of everyday life events after something traumatic that seemed to settle her soul. Her role as lady of the manor, playing with the colt, their horseback rides to Bart's and Eleanor's cabins, and playing a simple child's game with good friends seemed to have restored Stella's bold, charitable, and sometimes irritating as hell temperament.

His thoughts made him chuckle.

"What's so funny?"

Beckworth shook his head. "Nothing important, but I agree. Stella's fine." He tugged at his shirtsleeves. "Let's see what Hensley has to share. And while Stella appears demure at the moment, on the inside she's more than curious about why Jamie and Lando were late."

Barrington huffed as his gaze traveled around the landscape. "The gardens are looking well. I hear you have plans for changing some of the beds."

"I'll share the plans tomorrow. I think Stella has finalized her changes." With a last look at her, he turned for the door. "Let's see what tales the men have to share."

He'd expected Stella to manipulate Jamie and Lando into sharing their journey to Bristol, but the two men had expertly maneuvered around her questions with several amusing mishaps. He was certain the incidents had nothing to do with the trouble Jamie likely found. She'd seen through their deflections and had let it go rather than persist in her pursuit.

Sooner or later, he'd know the story, and he'd promised never to hold back the truth from her again. Until then, she seemed content to remain in her happy place. If that was what she needed, that was alright by him.

He let Barrington take the lead as they strolled through the manor from the solarium to the west study. If not occupied, there was a chair by the window with a view of the garden where he could keep an eye on her. He didn't need to. She was fine with the women, but for some reason, it comforted him to know she was close.

When Barrington opened the door, the conversation died as heads turned to greet them. Hensley sat at Beckworth's desk as expected. Jamie was in a chair in front of the desk, while Lando leaned against a bookcase. Fitz, who puffed on an unlit pipe, rested in a chair across the room with his injured leg propped on a stool. Beckworth took the chair by the window, while Barrington took the seat next to Jamie in front of the desk.

"So, what happened on your sail to Bristol that you feel the need to keep secret from Stella, or perhaps the ladies in general?" Beckworth turned to Hensley when he added, "I won't keep secrets from her. Not anymore."

"No one is keeping secrets." Hensley appeared perturbed by Beckworth's statement but relented. "On further reflection, I made a mistake in asking you to do that. Particularly after she ended up in the middle of it anyway." He pulled out a handkerchief and blotted his forehead before taking a sip of something amber colored. Hensley preferred Scotch but seemed to be gaining a taste for Jameson. "Somehow that woman ends up in chaos without lifting a finger," he muttered. Then he chuckled when everyone else did. "Jamie, share your story, and then we can discuss what to do about it."

"It's a simple enough story," Jamie started. "We'd left the Thames and were an hour past the Narrows when Lando noticed a familiar ship following us. It took some time before we decided it must be *The Horseman*."

"*The Horseman* again." Beckworth considered it. "Why would they be following the *Daphne*?"

"That was our question, so we decided to test the theory. It might have been a coincidence, and they were on their way back to the western coast, where McDuff likes to prey. We moored at Southampton for a night and let the men have some time ashore. We weren't an hour out of port before the ship was behind us again."

"They must have found a place to moor and wait for you to pass," Fitz suggested.

"Aye." Jamie glanced at Hensley. "Do you want to tell him?"

Hensley sighed and turned to Beckworth. "Do you remember what Stella told Leclair when she took the jewelry?"

"She suggested finishing the trade, and though she'd be leaving the next morning, she'd have one of her men contact André." It had been a wise decision in the heat of the moment, as long as it didn't depend on her involvement.

Hensley nodded. "She'd also mentioned at her dinner with Leclair that she'd taken care of her troublesome betrothed, and not with a simple farewell note."

The men chuckled at the implication.

Hensley finished his whiskey as he reviewed a parchment while waiting for the men to quiet. When he felt he had their attention again, he continued, "I decided to use Thomas as our go-between."

"Thomas?" Beckworth glanced around. "He was in London?"

When Jamie and Lando didn't meet his eyes, Hensley answered. "It wasn't meant to be a secret. Since he'd been associated with Stella and her supposed fiancé, we wanted to keep him out of the way in case anyone recognized him from Tenby. No telling who might have seen him there after he pulled Stella out of her dinner engagement with McDuff, or in the alley when she was kidnapped. But with Stella's fabrication, this puts Thomas back in play."

"How so?" Beckworth asked.

"The cover story is that she paid Thomas to get rid of her pesky suitor in exchange for a share of her operations."

"I take it Thomas is now onboard the *Daphne*?"

Jamie nodded. "He's making himself seen around Bristol, seeking new cargo for a run to France. He's going to try to make it to Waverly before you and Stella leave."

Something nagged at Beckworth. "I assume Thomas told someone in London that he would be following Lady Swan to France. If they assume Thomas is on the *Daphne*, which is probably why *The Horseman* followed you, shouldn't you appear to be on your way to France? Heading north up the coast is the wrong direction."

"I told you the little man was smarter than he looked." Lando gave Beckworth a huge smile.

Beckworth ignored him. Sooner or later, Lando would give up on the blasted nickname.

Jamie's eyes lit with humor. "We used an old trick of Finn's and rigged the sails to make it look like we took damage. While the Daphne is in port, I decided to replace an old yardarm. It will take long enough to replace that it will seem like a required repair. We'll make a quick trip to Dublin, then head south for France."

"And you think *The Horseman* is out there, waiting somewhere?" Beckworth asked.

"They made port in Bristol the day after we arrived, and we've seen a few sailors keeping an eye on the *Daphne*," Jamie said.

"So what happens after France?" Beckworth saw potential in the operation, but he wasn't sure what Hensley's endgame was.

"I've given Jamie three crates of French rifles," Hensley said.

"From our unsuccessful exchange?" Beckworth asked.

Hensley nodded. "Jamie will go to the monastery. It's been some time since his last trip. I have messages I need to get to France, and I've already given him the letters from Sebastian."

"And you expect *The Horseman* might follow?" Beckworth felt out of touch with all his questions, but he was still trying to put it all together.

Jamie shrugged. "It won't be easy for them, but worth the risk if they want to discover our contact. Though I think we can manage not leading them directly to the monastery."

"Then what?" Beckworth understood Hensley's network had to get more involved in the smuggling to make a difference, but the *Daphne* was only one ship against McDuff's network, whose size was unknown.

Hensley sat back and clasped his hands over his belly, a predatory smile on his face. "On his return, he'll stop in Bristol to check in before sailing up the coast to Scotland and then to Ireland."

"With any luck, we'll find McDuff before we get too far," Jamie added.

"And what will you say when there's no Lady Swan?" Beckworth didn't like where this was going, though he'd be lying if he hadn't seen it coming.

The men glanced at each other, but no one responded. After a minute passed, Fitz laughed out loud.

"I think I'll start the pool as soon as I return to the *Daphne*. I'll give it three and a half months until we're sitting with Hensley in this same room waiting for Beckworth and Stella's return."

Why did hearing that give Beckworth equal measures of both excitement and dread?

The meeting broke up shortly after the revelation of Hensley's plan for their pursuit of McDuff and what might be a larger network of smugglers than previously thought. With Hensley, the mission was never about smuggling. His concern was the rebellion McDuff was stirring up by supplying firearms to rebels in Ireland who could open ports to French naval ships.

The question Beckworth had to answer, and would need to discuss with Stella, was how much they wanted or needed to be involved. He knew the outcome of the war. The problem with knowing how things turned out was that one could never be sure what actually turned the tide. Was it just one large action or a cumulative number of events—smaller battles won or lost, the secret whispers of spies in the right ears, or a destroyed smuggling network—until there was only one possible ending?

Were Hensley's missions critical to winning the war? Or was it just that Napoleon overreached? Would he have won if he'd been able to get his warships closer to England?

He didn't know, and thinking about it only gave him headaches and long nights in the study with Barrington, staring into a fire that never provided an answer. It was best to focus on what was in front of them. Whether it helped win a war or not, they had to consider what impact the smuggling network had on England and Ireland.

He was the last to leave the office, other than Hensley, who remained to write more letters and devise more plans. Jamie waited a few steps down the hall.

"Sorry to have hidden so much from you," Jamie said. "It wasn't intentional. Most of it was decided just before we left port."

"I don't work for Hensley anymore, mate." Beckworth couldn't blame Jamie. It was how Hensley worked, and while Beckworth would never hold back information from Stella again, that requirement didn't apply to those Hensley employed.

When they reached the foyer, Jamie stopped and opened his jacket to reveal the binoculars Beckworth had given him for their sail from London.

"I thought you might want these back before you leave."

Beckworth scratched his chin and glanced around to see if anyone was about. "I assume they helped in identifying *The Horseman*."

"If we didn't have them, I'm not sure when we would have noticed the ship."

Beckworth considered his next action, and while risky, his concern for his friend outweighed the possible discovery. "I shouldn't be leaving them with you, but with this smuggling network..." He let the sentence go, not feeling the need to explain more.

"They're more dangerous than others we've dealt with."

"They're organized and not above pirating."

"With England worried about France, and Napoleon worried about England, you have to be somewhat foolish to be caught by local patrols."

"Or unlucky." Beckworth scanned the doorways and staircase to ensure they were still alone. "Either way, I want to leave the binoculars with you. Their existence needs to remain secure, but you'll need every advantage. It's risky enough traveling the Channel and English seas with French firearms, but if smugglers are watching you, someone's nervous."

"Not McDuff?"

"I don't think so. He can get French firearms one way or another. We aren't the only ones claiming to have access to them. And while Stella intrigued him, she isn't worth chasing."

"So a competitor."

"And who better than the ship Stella made a fool of? The question is whether the captain is in charge or he's getting his orders, and most likely funding, from someone else. The captain has somehow connected the *Daphne* to Lady Swan. We weren't hiding it, but we weren't shining a light on it, either."

"Aye, I'm not sure how that connection happened, but we're looking into it."

They turned silent, both understanding the risk, but also knowing the mission had to continue. Something larger than their initial assessment was being uncovered, and it was too late to walk away from what Hensley had put into motion.

Beckworth slapped Jamie on the back. "Enough of this. Let's check on the colt before the women decide the rest of our day. I want to see this technique Hensley tells me you have for training young horses."

The two strode out of the manor, down the steps, and had turned for the stables when a movement caught Beckworth's attention. It was only for an instant, but the flash of periwinkle happened to match the color of the dress Stella was wearing. He grinned. She was watching him, and it was only fair since he'd been watching her earlier. The question was what she was up to.

He let it go. He'd know soon enough.

Stella watched Beckworth and Jamie meander along the path to the stables in deep discussion. Now that their meeting with Hensley was over, their attention had turned to the colt. Perfect. When those two got involved in anything pertaining to horses, they lost all track of time.

That worked in her favor. Mary and Eleanor were in the kitchen, discussing the next handful of days with Mrs. Walker and Nellie. Elizabeth, tired of the London season, was due to arrive soon, preferring to spend time at Waverly before Beckworth and Stella returned to Baywood. With Jamie and Lando arriving later than planned, the decision was made to stay a couple of days longer since the extension was still within the time frame AJ and Finn expected for their return.

She strolled through the manor, peeking into rooms where Beckworth had started making changes to the decor before he'd left for Baywood. After gaining a sense of what Beckworth was doing, she made notes of further modifications—artwork to be moved or discarded, colors for new paint or wallpaper, and new fabric for drapes. Once she reviewed the changes with Beckworth, she'd leave the list with Barrington to have the work accomplished before their next visit. And regardless of the chaos that always seemed to await them, she couldn't imagine not returning to Waverly. She'd always wanted a second home, but she would never have guessed it would be an English manor rather than a coastal retreat somewhere along the Oregon oceanfront.

The door to the west study was closed, and though she didn't hear any voices, she suspected it wasn't empty. After taking a deep breath in and a slow breath out, she knocked on the door and waited.

"Come."

She opened the door and gave Hensley a friendly smile. "I know you just arrived, but I wanted to make sure we'd have time for a game of chess before I left."

He peered at her over the rim of his glasses and laid down the letter he'd been reading. "Sit down, and let's discuss why you're really here. I doubt you've spoken with Beckworth yet. Jamie's been itching to work with the colt."

"I'm surprised you're not in the stables with them." She took a seat in front of the desk and clasped her hands in her lap.

"I will be shortly. I wanted to write a few letters while my thoughts were fresh."

"Fresh from whatever your discussion was with the men?"

His brows remained lowered, a deep frown on his face as he gave her a long perusal. Then he sat back and chuckled. "I find myself enjoying the subterfuge with you almost as much as I enjoy discussing the strategy of a mission."

It was impossible not to agree with him. She felt the same way—as long as the subterfuge didn't last long. She returned his smile.

"Then to facilitate your time with the colt, why don't we just cut to the chase today?"

"A worthy bargain. Give me one moment to finish this letter." He took his time reviewing it. The ink must have already dried because he didn't wait to fold and address it before placing it on top of a short stack of similar messages.

He closed the inkpot and moved papers out of the way

before leaning his elbows on the desk, giving her his full attention. She listened to the recap of his earlier meeting with the men and would confirm her understanding with Beckworth later. For now, once Hensley finished, she sat back and digested everything she'd heard. It was a lot to unpack, but she was impressed with Hensley's ability to piece together events and find a path forward.

She didn't need to be told that the path was fraught with risk and many unknowns. The idea to bring Thomas back into the mission was golden, but all the risk lay with the crew of the *Daphne*. It wasn't that she didn't think they could handle it. She was concerned by how outnumbered they were, assuming what McDuff told her about the size of his network was true. And it was obvious that the plan still required Lady Swan, something she and Beckworth would need to discuss.

Hensley watched her intently, just as he did when they played chess, though she doubted his mind had quieted. He was probably running through her possible reactions while developing various responses to them. So, she let him sit as she considered the situation. Then she grinned, wondering how he'd respond to her checkmate response.

"I think you're going to need another ship."

He stared at her with what she guessed was incredulity. It was bound to happen more frequently the more he got to know her, but she was surprised, considering their last mission, that this was the first time she'd seen it from him.

But as quickly as it came, his expression slowly changed as he considered her statement. He finally settled on a warm smile and eyes lit with possibilities. "Why don't we take a stroll to the stables and see how the men are doing with the colt?"

35

───────

Stella rolled over, a bit surprised to find Beckworth still asleep next to her. He'd left the bed earlier, but she'd been too exhausted to open an eye. The scent of coffee reached her senses, and she smiled at his persistence in keeping her happy.

Eleanor and Mrs. Walker had prepared a huge farewell party the night before that included their guests and the staff. It had lasted late into the evening, giving all the staff an opportunity to join in. She'd dropped into bed like a boat anchor, and Beckworth had followed some time later, momentarily waking her up with a sweet kiss and then spooning.

She lay on her side and watched him sleep. It was a rare moment since he was such an early bird. His eyelashes were lusher than hers, and fine lines edged the corners of his eyes. Libby had once mentioned that he smiled more than he had in the past, and she hoped she'd been the cause of that change. That she had given him more joy than pain. She held in a snort. God knew she could definitely be a pain.

She lightly ran a finger down the bridge of his nose and over his cupid-bow lips. AJ had been right. He was a handsome man.

Those lips, so kissable, could turn playful, irritated, and even cruel, though she'd only seen the latter a couple of times, either when dealing with Gemini or during a mission.

Early morning light shone from the French doors that led out to the balcony. Beckworth started leaving a bit of the drapes open each evening. He never said why, but she suspected it was so she could tell the approximate time when she woke. Every action he took seemed to have her in mind. How more perfect could he be?

His lashes fluttered, the first stirring of wakefulness. She ran her hand down his chest, over his belly, and then farther until she found just the right spot to force a smile on those fabulous lips. Rather than stop her or take over as he usually did, he stretched, his eyes still closed, then put his hands behind his head, a heavenly smile on his lips.

She followed the trail of her hands with her lips, ducking under the covers. A few minutes later, the covers were thrown back, and he hauled her up before rolling over her.

"I like the way you wake me up, Lady Caldway."

"Always at your service, Lord Beckworth."

His grin turned to something more passionate as he performed his own foreplay rituals. She ran her hands through his hair, loving the feel of it through her fingers as his lips and tender nips moved over her body.

When they joined, the staccato beat of her heart made it difficult to breathe. She didn't care. Afterward, she draped her loose limbs over his body.

"I need coffee." She kissed a spot just below his ribs.

"If you're expecting me to get it for you, you'll need to move."

"Mmm. Maybe it can wait a few more minutes."

He chuckled as he rolled her off him before things became more heated. "We still have some time before our last breakfast with friends, and I could use a cup myself."

He poured two mugs and placed them on the table by the bed, but he didn't join her. Instead, he wandered into the dressing room. A few minutes later, he walked out wearing his robe and holding an envelope-sized package wrapped in brown paper.

He crawled into bed and handed her a mug. They sipped their coffee, and though she tried to ignore it, it was impossible not to be curious about the package. And she sensed a tension in Beckworth that hadn't been there earlier. The only way to speed up events was to finish the coffee, and she chugged it down.

He grinned, though there was something lurking behind his cornflower-blue gaze she couldn't name. Worry was the first thing that came to mind, but that didn't make sense.

"What's this?" She decided to take the direct approach.

"I wondered how long it would take you to ask."

"Well, it didn't seem as if you were going to say anything." She nudged the edge with a finger. "What is it?"

He took her mug and placed both on the table before sitting up and turning to her, the bed covers pooled at his waist. For a moment, she couldn't stop gazing at the small bit of chest revealed by the robe before slowly lifting to meet his eyes.

He picked up the package and fondled it until she blew out a sigh.

"Do you want me to open it?" she asked.

He shook his head. "Just give me a minute."

He was nervous, and it was making her equally anxious. When he finally opened the package and a black satin pouch fell out, she tilted her head, then licked her lips. More jewelry? It had to be.

He opened the strings of the pouch, but instead of taking out whatever was in there, he simply held onto it.

"You made a comment when we argued about you and Libby tracking the thief down that alley." His words were light, and he caught her gaze. "You called yourself an oddity, and it bothered me."

She laid a hand on his knee, and though she couldn't feel anything more than the lump of its form, she felt a slight reflexive jerk. Instead of pulling away, she squeezed his knee, and he gave her a small smile.

"I know I spent a good portion of the fancy balls with the men, leaving you to the ladies, but I'm not naive about the women who attend those parties. It wasn't a surprise that you received more invitations than you could possibly attend, and I understood why, even before you made your comment."

He took her hand. "I hear the rumors and the innuendos. Consort, mistress...the words are all the same, and they never bothered me before because I knew what you were to me. Not what others might see, but what I see. What I know."

She wasn't sure where this came from, though she remembered using the word oddity and the flash of pain in his gaze. "You know I don't care about that."

He smiled. "Maybe."

She squirmed, refusing to admit that it might have bothered her a little bit. Not for her, but how it might make him feel.

If he noticed her growing discomfort, he ignored it. "One day, when I was riding through London on my way to see Hensley, I passed a store where I've done business once or twice before."

He tipped the pouch over, and a silver ring fell into his hand.

She gasped, not prepared for this. Her hands shook, and she clasped them together after pulling the bedcovers around her tighter. "Teddy."

"Shush." He took her hand, and though she tried to pull it away, he held on tight. "I love you, Stella, and I have no intentions of rushing into anything. Not until we're both ready. But I don't want anyone to get the wrong idea about what you mean to me. Perhaps someday you'll tire of me, but until that day comes, I want to show you my commitment to this relationship."

Still holding her hand, he held up the ring. "You don't have to wear this for more than a few seconds, and only if you're just as committed to this strange bond we share. Then you can take it off and hide it in a drawer until you're ready to wear it for all to see."

She curled her fingers around his hand and blinked back tears. "Maybe you should put it on." She gave him a half shrug, though she couldn't stop shaking. "You know. Just so I can see how it looks. It might not even fit."

He grinned and slid the simple silver ring onto her ring finger. She instantly pulled her hand back to get a closer look. It wasn't as plain as it first appeared. Intricate filigree designs encircled the ring, and she ran a finger over the unique patterns.

He cleared his throat. "There's etching inside the band."

She pulled the ring off and squinted as she read the inscription. "Forever your Teddy." A tear slipped as she put the ring back on. She stared at it for some time, and Beckworth said nothing as he waited to hear her response.

"I love you, Teddy. You know that." She pulled back. "I wasn't expecting this."

"I probably didn't do this right. I should have waited and asked Finn."

"No. It's surprising, that's all. Yet somehow perfect for our last day at Waverly." She stared at the ring for some time before giving another shrug. "I don't know how I feel about wearing it." She gave him a quick glance and reached out to grab his hand. "You know that has nothing to do with how I feel about you."

He laughed, and whatever tension was there earlier was long gone. "I'm only grateful that you didn't toss it back in my face. I know we're not ready to make things official."

She squeezed his hand. "You mean I'm not ready."

He ran his knuckles over her cheek. "I don't want others dictating who we are or setting expectations for us. This isn't about you or me. It's about us. I never want you to doubt what you mean to me. I'm all in."

"Me too."

They fell back and cuddled. She held out her hand so they could both look at the ring. "It has the unique attribute of being new here, but it will be considered an antique when AJ sees it."

"You'll show it to her then?"

"Eventually. For now, it's just between us. When we're ready, we'll make a splash."

He chuckled. "That sounds more like us."

She ran a hand over his cheek. "I'm a lucky woman, Lord Beckworth."

"And I'm a lucky man, Lady Caldway."

When a knock sounded moments before the door burst open, Stella hid her hand under the covers while Beckworth shoved the pouch behind him. Libby barely gave them a glance when she waltzed in.

"Sorry to disturb you, but you're both running late. The group is already waiting in the dining room." When she rushed past them into the dressing room, Stella pulled off the ring, and Beckworth stuffed it back in the pouch, both of them laughing like children caught doing something naughty.

He pulled his robe closed and got out of bed, slipping the pouch into a drawer before heading to the dressing room as Libby raced out with a sage-green day dress.

By the time Beckworth appeared in his riding apparel, Stella was sitting at the dressing table while Libby worked on her hair.

He gave her a peck on the cheek and whispered in her ear, "You are my world, Lady Caldway." His next words made her blush. Then he kissed her temple and walked to the door. "I'll keep the masses busy until you join us."

"And what were those whispers about?" Libby asked. "They must have been naughty to make your cheeks so rosy."

"Nothing for you to be so nosy about." But Stella couldn't stop her grin, and through the mirror, her gaze locked on the drawer that held her ring. And she could still feel it on her finger, as if she'd never taken it off.

***

After a long and rowdy breakfast, Beckworth led Stella to his study, where Barrington, Mrs. Walker, and Libby waited. They reviewed plans for Waverly until their next return trip, which was planned for early August. Afterward, Mrs. Walker took Stella down to the kitchen, where Nellie and Eleanor wanted to discuss more detailed issues.

"Barrington," Beckworth spoke once Stella and the housekeeper had left, "do you mind giving Libby and me a few minutes?"

"Not at all, sir." Barrington stood and gave Libby a quick glance, who merely shrugged, neither of them knowing what was up.

Once the door closed behind him, Libby squirmed in her seat.

"Have I done something wrong?" she asked.

Beckworth rose and poured two whiskeys, sliding one to her when he returned to his seat behind the desk.

"I could provide a list, but it would be a wasted effort." He leaned back in his chair and watched as several emotions ran over his favorite spy—curiosity, worry, and that stubborn boldness that was so much like Stella. "I wanted to thank you for taking care of Stella."

She blushed, which was a rare sight, and then her eyes

squinted as she stared back at him. "You know it's nothing. She's a fine lady of the manor."

"Enough of playing the proper lady's maid. Stella is bold and tends to create chaos wherever she goes. She can be the perfect lady when she wants to be, but she also has the mouth of a sailor."

Libby snorted, then took a sip of the whiskey. "She's not your normal lady of the manor."

"Which is why you make the perfect lady's maid." When she smiled, he added, "But it worries me at times when the two of you put your heads together. Mostly, it's nothing to worry about, but the rest of the time, the two of you terrify me with your antics."

Libby straightened at that. No doubt expecting a reprimand.

"That said." He drank half the whiskey before pulling a sheathed dagger out of a drawer. He placed it on the desk and pushed it toward her.

"I know you still carry that tiny blade I gave you years ago, but if you're going to continue to follow Stella into dangerous scenarios—" he held up his hands when Libby opened her mouth, "—and you can say what you want, but we both know we haven't seen the end of those days."

Libby relaxed and shrugged, knowing it to be true. She reached out and touched the sheath, running her fingers over the leather before pulling it to her. The blade shimmered as she pulled it out, then she gave the hilt a closer look. "Is this bone?"

"Stag horn."

Libby wiped an eye then twirled the blade. "It has a good balance."

"How's the grip?"

"Perfect. But this is too much."

"Nonsense. You've become Stella's protector when I'm not

around, and you need to know how irreplaceable you've become. If you're going to continue in that function, then you need a proper weapon. And you're more than deserving of it."

She wiped at an eye again, and Beckworth knew she was embarrassed.

"Finish your whiskey and get back to your duties. I'm sure Stella's wondering where you are."

She downed the drink, slid the dagger back in its sheath, and stuck it in her pocket as she hurried to the door. Before leaving, she turned around.

"We're going to miss you, sir." Then she was out the door.

He was going to miss her and all the staff as well. He wasn't sure what he would do if the day ever came when they couldn't time jump.

Stella, dressed in her pants, shirt, and boots, took a last look around the bedroom. She touched the pocket where she'd stuffed the pouch with her ring in it. At first, the sight of it had terrified her. Now, only a few hours later, she never wanted to be parted from it.

She opened the cabinet where she stored her dagger and touched the warm wood of her crossbow. A tingle of excitement went through her, and she quickly stepped back and shut the door.

The last thing she should be thinking about is what Hensley had in store for them on their next trip. When she raced down the steps to the foyer, Fitz stood up from a bench where he'd been sitting. There was no cane in sight.

He strode over and held out an arm for her. "I thought I'd walk with you."

She placed her arm through his, and they strolled through the manor toward the solarium and then out the back door on their way to the woods.

"I don't see a limp," she said.

He rubbed his side and then his leg. "I still get a twinge every now and then. Otherwise, I'm good as new." He leaned down to whisper. "With many thanks to you and your medicine."

She chuckled. "I doubt you needed it. You're too ornery to die."

"Truer words," Lando said as he met them on the path where the gardener had already started the planned renovations.

"It's true I have unending stamina." He winked at Stella. "Or so the ladies say."

They laughed when they reached the woods where Jamie and Beckworth waited.

"Will you be heading back to the *Daphne* soon?" Beckworth asked.

Jamie shook his head. "Thomas is on his way, and we decided it might be best not to be seen in Bristol while the ship is under refitting. Fitz could use a few more days, regardless of what he says."

Stella knew it was more than that. Mary said they decided to stay another couple of days before heading to their home in Bristol. Elizabeth would go with them to attend Mary's pre-planned garden party the following week. That would give Hensley time to work out mission details with the *Daphne* crew and Thomas. No one had spoken of their next mission, but that didn't mean the men weren't thinking about it.

They continued on to a small gap in the trees where the others waited to see them off. Beckworth shook hands, while Stella gave hugs and a few kisses on the cheek. She punched Barrington in the arm, which made him grin. Then she hugged Libby until her lady's maid slipped out of her grasp, both of them laughing, though Stella saw the tears Libby was holding back.

Beckworth led Stella some distance away, and she hefted the duffel over her right shoulder. She stared down at the silver ring she wore, the small Mórdha stone mounted in the middle of a Celtic circle. Sebastian said the Celtic knots were a protective symbol, and so far, it was working well.

She took Beckworth's hand as he recited the Celtic verse from memory, and she waved at their friends. Their images blurred like a fading black and white photo as the fog rolled in and the bright light blinded her. Her stomach tightened painfully, and she blew out air, attempting to release the tension before the ground slipped out from under her.

Beckworth's hand squeezed harder, refusing to let her go. Then she was on her own as she landed on her feet. She took a few steps until her duffel hit her in the back of the head, and she fell face first onto a wooden floor. She heard an "umph" next to her, which she assumed was Beckworth—or some poor bystander who was in the wrong place at the wrong time.

The bright light dissipated into rain. Not a pouring rain, but also not a drizzle. She crawled a few paces then turned around to sit on her backside. Beckworth was already standing, and he reached out a hand to help her up. She breathed a sigh when she realized she'd been sitting on the dock next to Finn's new sailboat.

They hurried up the hill and were soaked by the time they reached the inn.

"Their car and truck are gone." Beckworth pulled her toward the front of the inn rather than the back deck.

"They could be anywhere." Stella didn't argue when Beckworth ran for their car. He checked under the back fender, grabbed the spare key, and popped the trunk. They tossed in their duffels, then he handed her the key.

Once inside the car, both drenched, they stared at each other and laughed.

"We live the craziest lives." Stella leaned toward him.

Beckworth gave her a long kiss and said, "Let's go home."

***

Stella stared up through the canopy of trees to the sapphire sky and puffy clouds beyond. It hadn't taken the rain long to disappear, leaving a beautiful spring day behind. She was wrapped in a light blanket to ward off the slight chill of their back patio.

Beckworth strolled out and hung a hummingbird feeder on the branch of a tree.

"I suppose we should get ready before AJ comes knocking." She sat up from the chaise lounge but didn't stand. Her short nap had dulled her brain, but she became fully awake when a cup of coffee appeared. "I don't pay you enough."

Beckworth chuckled. "We also have to stop at Donna's for pies." He waited for her to take a couple gulps, then he took the cup away. "Come on. The group will want to hear everything twice over."

She'd called AJ as soon as they'd gotten home. Finn had already called her to tell her Stella's car was missing. He must have arrived minutes after they'd left. AJ then called Maire and Adam, her brother, and Helen, her mother, for an impromptu dinner. That meant everyone would be there, including Ethan and Sebastian, of course. Then there was Helen's beau, Professor Emory, and Madelyn, Adam's wife, and their three kids.

After starting their day at Waverly, it would make for a long day, but they had two hours to relax before everyone could gather. They stopped at Donna's, and Beckworth took twenty minutes selecting pies for dessert and one for everyone to take home. Now, Stella had a fantastic memory, but she still didn't know how Beckworth remembered everyone's favorite pie.

When they reached the inn, she counted the cars. Beckworth had been right. They were the last to arrive.

Neither moved to get out. They stared at the front of the inn.

"You're sure about this?" Beckworth asked.

She nodded. "It's time. We're in too deep. I don't think we have any other choice."

He squeezed her hand. "I agree."

They got out of the car just as the front door opened and Finn and Ethan exited the house.

"Welcome home, travelers." Finn shook Beckworth's hand and gave Stella a long hug and kiss on the cheek.

Ethan helped Beckworth with the pies, and the next few hours were filled with stories about fancy balls, elegant dresses, and updates on old friends. Beckworth handed out letters to Finn, AJ, Ethan, Maire, and Sebastian that they tucked away to read later.

Once dinner was cleared and the kids were in front of a movie, a second bottle of wine was opened, and Finn brought over a new bottle of Jameson. While he poured the whiskey and Ethan poured the wine, Beckworth cleared his throat to silence the multiple conversations. When he had their full attention, he lifted his glass of whiskey.

"To a safe journey!"

Across the table from him, Maire shouted, "Slainte."

When the glasses were set down, Beckworth took Stella's hand, and after a solemn nod, they turned to the group. They'd discussed it on the drive to the inn, and though Stella initially believed she should be the one to do it, she'd finally agreed that Beckworth would set a better tone.

Beckworth took a long look around the table, his gaze landing on AJ and then Finn.

"Everyone, settle in. We have quite a story to share."

Thank You for Reading!

Stella and Beckworth's adventures will continue!
The question is whether their love story can handle the stress of constant peril that seems to follow them—or more accurately, tends to follow Stella. But then, what can one expect when they take a chance on traveling through the fog?

If you've read more than one or two of my books, you know I always like to leave a bit of an appetizer for the next book in the series. At the time of this writing, my thoughts are a jumble with all the possibilities for Stella and Beckworth's next adventure. However, I do have one scene I feel confident will be in the next book. I'll warn you—it's a bit of a cliff hanger, so buckle up.

The Swan Syndicate - Book 3
(title still pending)

Stella and Beckworth, unable to leave their friends behind in the past, have decided to make a habit of returning to Waverly Manor. The only problem—Hensley, unwilling to let go of his best spy, is always ready to dangle a mission in front of Beckworth.

The difference this time is that they know exactly what's waiting for them, and it's more than a simple search mission. But nothing is ever simple. While trying to build evidence against a notorious smuggler who's stoking a rebellion against

England, a new competitor has joined the playing field with eyes on taking over the entire smuggling network.

———

Keep reading for a preview from the next edition of *The Swan Syndicate.*

Enjoy!

<h1>BOOK 3 OF THE SWAN SYNDICATE</h1>

Beckworth followed behind Stella, frustrated by the townspeople who were obviously hiding firearms but were stubbornly tight-lipped. He understood, not as well as Jamie and Fitz did, but well enough, having grown up in London's East End.

This seaside Irish village had no love of the English. What they didn't understand was that the French wouldn't treat them any better. As much as they might believe France would be a more generous overlord, it was doubtful they'd see their independence under Napoleon.

"This has been frustrating." Stella ran a hand through her auburn hair. Its wavy nature had taken over, giving her an appearance of a beautiful lass who'd just woken for the day. Her uncontrollable hair drove her mad, but he found it alluring.

He scanned the area. Something didn't feel right, but he couldn't put his finger on what bothered him. "The townspeople are vexed with England and see salvation in the lies McDuff has been spreading. You've spent time with the man. You know how charismatic he can be."

"And just as deadly."

"Stella! Lady Stella!" A young girl's voice came from behind them, and they both turned to see a young pixie with freckles that matched the color of her strawberry-blonde locks. She raced toward them, tripping over something but able to remain on her feet.

Stella grinned and squatted down to meet the girl on her level. "Hello, Sadie. I wasn't sure we'd see you today."

Sadie pushed back her long, windswept hair and gave Stella a huge grin. Her smile was missing two top teeth, which only made her adorable. "Sean said you were leaving today. Can't you stay until the fair?"

Stella glanced up at Beckworth, and he shook his head, sorry that he couldn't make that happen. They were too close to finding McDuff to waste three days waiting for the fair.

Stella tucked a strand of gold-streaked hair behind the girl's ear. "I wish we could, but we've overstayed our time here."

The girl frowned. "People haven't been very nice to you."

"They just don't know us as well as you do. We're strangers. We understand."

Sadie stepped back and kicked a rock. "Well, I don't."

Stella held out her hand. "We're on our way to the fish market. Why don't you walk with us? I bet we can find something sweet to eat."

Sadie looked at Beckworth as if she were sizing him up again. He smiled and nodded his encouragement. She must have approved because she shrugged and gripped Stella's hand. "Okay. It will have to do."

Stella grinned at Beckworth and held out her other hand to him. He took it and they strolled down the street toward the fish vendors. They'd only walked a block when Beckworth noticed a man hurrying down the other side of the street. His head was down, his shoulders hunched, making it impossible for Beckworth to see the man's face. There was something familiar about him; he just couldn't pin down what it was.

The man sprinted across the town's park, heading in the direction of the church.

Interesting.

He squeezed Stella's hand, and when she turned to him, he nodded toward the park. Stella glanced over, a frown marring her beautiful face. He glanced down at the girl, then said, "I forgot something back at the mercantile. I'll catch up."

Stella's frown deepened. "I'll let Jamie know." Something in her eyes made him pause, but the man was up to something. He was sure of it. "Be careful."

Sadie looked up to Stella. "Why does he have to be careful? No one will hurt him."

She ran a hand over the girl's hair. "I know. It's just something we say to each other when we go off on our own."

Sadie gave it some thought. "I guess that's a nice thing to say."

Stella smiled. "That it is. Come on, I'll race you."

Beckworth watched them run off. Fortunately for Stella, Sadie didn't run that fast, but Stella wanted to get to Jamie without scaring the girl. It was probably nothing, but he hurried across the street to the park, scanning the area for any other suspicious-looking men. He didn't see anything that drew his attention.

He quickened his pace. The man was already out of sight, and he moved into a light jog. Then he saw the man climbing the steps into the church.

No one thought to check the church, but what a perfect place to hide firearms. He could be wrong, but the man racing into the building didn't look like he'd been in a rush to confess his sins.

Beckworth raced up the steps, slowing before he went through the front door. He kept a hand on his flintlock and slowly entered. It was deathly silent. He moved through the lobby to the open double doors that led into the nave. Ten long, wooden pews lined both sides of the aisle, which ended at the dais.

A sound of a door closing came from the right, and he ran that way. The first door he came to opened to a supply closet. The next one, just a few paces down the short hallway, opened to a set of stairs. Muffled voices floated up to him.

He pulled out his pistol and cocked it before slowly taking one step at a time. He was almost to the basement when the voices became louder, and he heard the low whimpering of children. What the bloody hell?

The stairs ended at a small landing that turned to the left. He peeked around the corner, but whoever the men were, they were still out of sight. However, a good portion of the room was within view. There was a bookcase that held handmade toys, a few books, a flute, and a ball. He only saw one wall, which was painted white and covered with children's artwork.

The men's voices began to rise, and he took the last three steps quickly, lifting his gun as he surveyed the room. Two men faced each other, neither looking in his direction. The man he'd seen on the street was older than Beckworth, of average height and weight, and had the weathered face of a sailor. The other was a priest. He was slight of build, but he faced the sailor with anger rather than fear.

Six children huddled in a corner, their faces filled with terror, and Beckworth understood why. The sailor held a pistol that he waved around, first at the priest and then at the children.

"I need the key," the man said. "I'm not going to ask again."

"For the last time, I don't have it." For all his apparent fierceness, the priest's voice was shaky. "They don't trust me with it."

"I'll shoot the kids. I don't care. I need what's in those crates."

The priest shook his head and lifted his hands in supplication, as if that alone could defend him from a lead ball piercing his body.

"I suggest you put that gun away." Beckworth took several steps, his pistol firm in his grip as he leveled it at the sailor. "You don't want to do this." He moved toward the children, who appeared to be a wide mix of ages, while keeping his gun trained on the man.

The sailor turned his gun toward Beckworth, but his hand shook. If he fired, there was no telling where the ball would go. "Who are you?" He glanced at the priest then back at Beckworth. "You don't sound Irish. You can't be from here."

"Let's just calm down and talk this through. We can do it without the weapons." Beckworth glanced at the priest. Though his expression remained stoic, beads of sweat glistened off his forehead.

"You need to stay out of our business." The man forgot all about the priest as he turned toward Beckworth.

"Alright. As long as you let me take the children out of here. They're not part of this." By then, he'd managed to get in front of the huddled group, and he forced himself to ignore the tear-streaked faces of the youngest children. Two older boys had moved in front of the younger kids, and though they didn't shed any tears, they were as frightened as they were bold. Protectors.

The sailor sneered. "I think maybe I should just take you out and then finish off the rest of them."

Beckworth was ready to take the shot when an explosion rocked the church.

Stella released Sadie's hand so she could run ahead of her. She could run in the boots when she had to, but this wasn't one of those times. Sadie slowed so Stella could keep up, but the girl didn't stop until she reached the vendor where Stella had bought sweet tarts the day before. The woman who ran the stall wasn't fond of Stella. Most of the townspeople weren't happy with anyone from the *Daphne Marie*, but that didn't deter her from spending money at the local businesses.

"Stella!"

She turned to see Jamie jogging up to her. Everyone seemed to be running today.

"Where's Beckworth?" He opened his mouth to say something when he spotted Sadie by her side.

Stella held up a finger, then turned to order a sweet tart from the woman who was giving her the stink-eye. She felt a tug on her dress and looked down.

"Molly is over by the dock." Sadie pointed in that direction, and Stella noticed the tall blonde girl, who was about Sadie's age. The girl waved at them.

"Do you think Molly would like a sweet tart?" When Sadie nodded, Stella ordered a second tart from the mulish woman, who gave her a reluctant smile as they exchanged coin for tarts.

"Thank you, Lady Stella." Sadie hugged Stella's legs, then ran toward Molly. The two girls chattered as they wandered off down the dock, nibbling the tarts.

"I think I just got swindled," Stella quipped and winked at the woman.

The woman had to grin, most likely at Stella being a chump. "Those two are nothing but trouble."

Stella returned the smile. "Just my kind of girls."

"Stella, we have to go." Jamie tugged at her arm.

She sensed his urgency and waved at the woman before he

pulled her away, rushing them toward the dock where they'd left the jolly boat.

"Where's Beckworth?" This time, Jamie's tone was filled with a combination of anger and concern.

"What's wrong?"

Jamie stopped as Fitz, who also looked worried, ran up to them. Then he refocused on Stella. "Just tell me."

"He saw a man who looked suspicious and wanted to check it out." Now worry plagued her as well as she glanced back the way she'd come. "I think he was headed toward the church. What's going on?"

"A ship just arrived with open gun ports. They're a threat to the village. The *Daphne* is bringing her broadside to bear."

"I don't know what that means." That was a partial lie. She had a pretty good idea what he meant, and it was confirmed when Fitz answered.

"It means the *Daphne* is turning with gun ports open to engage the ship."

"They're going to battle? This close to port?" Her voice rose an octave. "What ship is it?"

"It's *The Horseman*." Jamie gripped her arm. "You need to get to the jolly boat."

She yanked her arm away. "Not without Beckworth."

Jamie blew out a breath. He was thinking of fighting her on this but must have decided it would only be wasting time. "Let's go."

She broke into a run behind Jamie and Fitz, thankful she'd saved her energy from earlier. They were almost to the park when the men stopped and yanked Stella to the ground. She heard a swooshing sound mere seconds before a huge explosion rocked the ground. Seconds later, another explosion could be heard from the cove.

Then she was being hauled up as they continued their run to

the church. Townspeople were also running toward it, while some were running away.

Dust filled the air, blocking her view of the building. Her heart beat like a drum solo, and her stomach lurched. A second loud boom came from the cove, and she turned in time to see a large sail fall into the smoke and orange flames that she assumed were on *The Horseman* based on its position in the bay.

When she turned back to the church, she gasped in horror. Dust still filled the air, but it had cleared enough for her to see that the entire building appeared to have collapsed upon itself. They stopped twenty yards from it.

Several men were trying to move the rubble as others ran up to assist. She would have questioned why the men were so frantic to remove the splintered wood and crumbled stone, but only one thing kept pounding in her head.

Beckworth had been in that building.

She hadn't seen him go in, but she knew it. She knew it deep down in her heart that clenched with a horrific pain.

"*The Horseman* is sailing off," Fitz said.

"They accomplished what they came for." Jamie had taken a step back toward the dock but stopped. "They won't get far with a broken mast."

"And they know the *Daphne* won't follow. Not now." Fitz kicked the dirt, then turned back to the church. "Are you sure he was in there, lass?"

The townsmen continued to pull wooden boards and rocks away. One of the men fell away from the rubble and turned to the people who clustered around, obviously in shock as they stared and mumbled to each other.

He yelled at them. "There were children in the church."

That triggered some of the onlookers to jump in, but there was so much debris, it would take hours to make a dent.

Children and Beckworth.

Stella dropped to the ground. Tears blurred her vision. She should be helping, but every ounce of energy had drained away.

It wasn't supposed to end like this. Not now. He couldn't be in there. He couldn't be lost to her. When she looked up at Jamie, searching for any sign of hope, he was still staring at the building, and she was sorry when she glanced at Fitz.

Their expressions told her everything she didn't want to know. She burst into a full-on crying jag as she leaned over, one hand fisted against her chest. The other clawed at the grass as if she could tear up the ground to find him.

Oh, god, Teddy. Don't you dare leave me. You promised me forever.

The tears stopped as quickly as they came. Anger flared. Anger at *The Horseman* for firing on innocent people. Anger at McDuff and his entire goddamned network. Anger at Beckworth for being in the wrong place at the wrong time.

She huffed out a long sob, then got to her feet. Jamie and Fitz stood next to her like sentinels. She began walking but was soon running toward the broken building. He was in there. Dead or alive, she wouldn't leave until she found him.

THANK YOU FOR READING!

I sincerely hope you enjoyed a glimpse of a somewhat dark
scene from *The Swan Syndicate - Book 3.*

If you haven't already read the original series, here's your chance
to catch up on how it all began!

A Stone in Time
The Mórdha Stone Chronicles - Book 1

AJ Moore stands on a precipice. Her ambitions stalled after an
unexpected loss.
A two-hundred-year-old sailing vessel appears through the fog.
This could be the story she's been waiting for. The story to
salvage her sluggish career.

When she meets Finn Murphy, the enigmatic captain, he's
nothing but arrogant, annoying, and tight-lipped. But she's not
one to give up easily. He's just not aware that he's met his match.

Finn Murphy has only one thing on his mind. Find an ancient stone necklace and return home. But he wasn't expecting to be hounded by a reporter. The more she comes around, the more he wants her to stay.

But the stakes are too high, the mission too important to be tempted. The longer it takes to find the necklace, the weaker his resolve becomes.

Join AJ on an adventure where honor and friendship can beat the odds—and love transcends time.

"Time travel with unique twists and many layers..."
"This is a captivating story! The atmosphere is richly evocative and well-rendered, and the characters are brought to life beautifully!" InD'tale Magazine.

A Stone in Time is the first book in a time travel romance adventure series, and it comes with cliffhangers...just so you know. THIS IS A COMPLETED SERIES

Buy Now!

If you're interested in other stories written by me, I have two series you might be interested in.

The first is a Time Travel SciFi and Fantasy Adventure with a slow-burn romance.

Time Renegades - Book 1
Earth has a new world order after the Climate Wars.
As close to utopia as a human population can achieve.
For Sergeant Rowan Lockwood, the future isn't as bright after
a single mistake shatters her world.

Yet, she is the only one who can save the future from those who wish to remake the past.

Sergeant Rowan Lockwood isn't anyone's first pick to save the world. She can barely save herself. After one horrific mistake, her world is shattered by a tragic loss. Another mistake forces a transfer out of the unit that's been like family.

Rowan is thrown into a mysterious murder case she's not trained for and saddled with a partner she doesn't want.

Her new partner, Keene MacGregor, isn't any happier to find himself tied to a partner. One he hopes to shake loose.

Too soon, they're running for their lives. And Rowan finds herself working with a mysterious group of anthropologists with more secrets than her new mission.

But Rowan has her own secrets. Her childhood visions have returned. And they might hold the key to saving Earth.

Join Rowan on an adventure through time as she races to save her future.

This is Book One of the Time Renegades series. Beware of cliffhangers.

Buy Now!

You might like my urban fantasy series, *Of Blood & Dreams*. A touch of mystery...with just a pinch of spice.

Seduction in Blood, Of Blood and Dreams - Book 1
A thief. A vamp. A walk on the wild side.

Cressa Langtry is the best cat burglar on the West Coast. But she owes a large debt to the wrong kind of people. Her only way clear is to steal something for the city's notorious and ancient vampire – Devon Trelane.

Devon Trelane can't forgive the one man who cost him a seat on the Council. Luckily, a thief has fallen into his lap. A woman with the skills he requires to take down his greatest enemy. There's only one hitch—a simple business arrangement becomes complicated when their dreams collide.

<u>**Pick up your FREE copy today!**</u>

Want to know when my next book will be available?
Sign up for my newsletter!
You can also follow me on Amazon, Goodreads, Bookbub,
Facebook, or Instagram

ABOUT THE AUTHOR

Kim Allred grew up in Southern California but now enjoys the quiet life in an old timber town in the Pacific Northwest where she raises alpacas, llamas, and an undetermined number of free-range chickens. Just like her characters, Kim loves sharing stories while sipping a glass of wine or slurping a strong cup of brew.

Her spirit of adventure has taken her on many journeys, including a ten-day dogsledding trip in northern Alaska and sleeping under the stars on the savannas of eastern Africa.

Kim is currently creating worlds while shooing cats and dogs away from her lap, and the mighty parrot, Willow, from her keyboard. Willow can peel the keys from the board in fifteen seconds flat.

Kim's current works include her time travel romance series, the Mórdha Stone Chronicles and The Swan Syndicate, and the urban fantasy romance series, Of Blood & Dreams, and the time travel scifi and fantasy adventure series: Time Renegades.